A Secret Strength

The Oberlin Faith Series ~ Book 2

By
Katrina Lyman Jones

Printed in the United States of America.

ISBN 9798990671911

Edited by Sarah Lamb

Formatting by Nancy Fraser

Cover design by Jeana Atkison

DEDICATION

This book is dedicated to my husband, Kirk, one of the best men I know.

I'm glad he's all mine.

And to all good men everywhere.

In all his trials he was sustained and at times even exalted by a secret strength in himself. The soul aids the body and at moments uplifts it. It is the only bird that can endure a cage.

- Victor Hugo

LEWIS FAMILY TREE

Joseph (b. 1829) + Julia (b. 1834)

|

Eleanor (b. 1854)

Irene (b. 1856)

Lovenia (b. 1858, d. 1885)

Samuel (b. 1860)

Eleanor (m. 1874) + Andrew

|

Elizabeth (b. 1875)

Josiah (b. 1877)

Seth (b. 1879)

Delcena and Daniel (b. 1881)

Julia (b. 1885)

Henry (b. 1888)

Samuel (m. 1886) + Phoebe

|

Benjamin (b. 1888)

Mary (b. 1889)

Cyrus (b. 1891)

Lucy (b. 1894)

Rose (b. 1896)

TABLE OF CONTENTS

PROLOGUE

Samantha sat, holding tightly to the chair, trembling and willing herself to breathe. She told herself to be calm, to look at things rationally, to remember what was most important, what was *truth*. But her mind felt muddled and her thoughts were slow to process what had just happened and what must now be done.

Finally, she stood on unsteady legs and clumsily gathered the book, pen, and paper from the table. Holding them to her chest, she walked woodenly out of the richly decorated library. She stole a glance down both sides of the plushly carpeted hall, then quickly made her way up the long, elegant staircase. Somehow, as if through a haze, she found her room, stumbled through the door, and pushed it closed behind her. She leaned back against its solidness, feeling drained of all strength, and tried not to think or feel. But the unfair accusations Cordelia had made, the harsh tone of her voice, the steely determination in her face, and the vows she had made still rang in Samantha's head.

She slid slowly down the door and sank to the floor, dropping what she held and hugging her knees up against her chest.

It was at times like these that she cursed her imagination, for she clearly saw in her mind's eye the person Cordelia must see in her: conniving and controlling, selfish and unworthy. It was an ugly, bitter picture and she wanted to turn it off, to erase it somehow. She wouldn't want such a young woman for her son, either! She felt sick to her stomach.

I am not any of those things, her soul cried out. *They are all untrue!* She took a shaky breath while hot tears coursed down her cheeks.

That's right, she thought, allowing the part of her nature that insisted on honesty in all things to rise above the mess of the ugly picture. *I don't need to take ownership of Cordelia's accusations because she has it all wrong—hasn't she?*

Unfortunately, the truth didn't change the fact that the woman did not want her in her house and, in fact, did not want her in her son's life at all. That was quite a hurdle to overcome, and Samantha felt no hope anymore of winning the woman over. She had tried that for days and made no progress whatsoever—and she would never be able to, as long as Cordelia remained fixed on the idea that Samantha was such a horrible combination of lacks and failings. *Which I am not!* her brain insisted. But then it betrayed her by wondering if she and Sterling really had put on an "embarrassing display." Her cheeks flamed to imagine it, but as she remembered the reactions of other people around them, she couldn't remember anyone looking at them as if they were offensive. Quite to the contrary, she had caught glimpses of respect and understanding.

Her head throbbed with all these agonizing thoughts, the headache back now with a vengeance. Oh, she was so tired!

Her gaze fell upon the paper on the floor, where she had so happily written Wordsworth's beautiful quotes only a short time ago. How had that been this same week, let alone this same day?! Now she wondered if the words actually held any veracity after all: "There is a comfort in the strength of love." She had felt that before, but what if one person proved to be an insurmountable obstacle to love? Now that Cordelia knew how closely tied Sterling and Samantha were, would she continue to allow her son peace and space, the freedom to live his own life as he had the past few years, free of her meddling and controlling ways? Or would she repent of her "permissiveness" and reel him back into this world she controlled? What if she followed them to Ohio and somehow prevented them from seeing each other? What if she created wedges and thrust up ultimatums that sucked the life and joy out of Samantha's relationships with those she loved? The "what ifs" began to build in her mind and pile up, one on top of the other, making her feel desperate.

Her heart throbbed with pain.

Samantha curled up into herself even more, feeling the need to protect herself from any more hurt. Arms tightened around her knees, she pressed her head into them, her dress soon splotched with wetness from her tears.

She wished she were home—oh, how she wished she were home in quaint, unassuming Oberlin, a place she understood and could navigate with ease and confidence. She craved to be back in her friendly, somewhat disheveled home, devoid of the sumptuous beauty of this house, but not pretending to be anything other than it was: honest, true, and sound. How had she gotten herself into this mess? It had started out so perfectly, too...

Chapter 1

REUNITED

Samantha smiled to herself as she bustled around the kitchen. She and Sterling had so much to discuss! After nine months of separation and a myriad of changes for both of them, they needed to become reacquainted.

She could not believe Sterling was finally back in Oberlin again, that he had actually come here to see her! The incredible realization that not only had he *not* forgotten her but had, in fact, not been able to *forget* her filled her with wonder. It was all so amazing she thought her heart would burst with the joy of it. After their reunion in the woods yesterday, their confessions to each other, and an electrifying kiss, they had ridden back to Samantha's house to get out of the rain—this time with Samantha holding Champion's reins and Sterling seated behind her. Such a different scenario from their last ride together! This time, Samantha was the one in control. They both knew where they were going and that they wanted time together, and they were headed to a chaperoned location.

It was a jubilant, albeit wet, ride for all three of them. Sterling praised Samantha's care of the large, black stallion and expressed his gratitude that she had bought Champion when he left, as he had grown fond of the horse in the three months he lived in Oberlin. "This old boy definitely lucked out," he said, patting the horse with one hand while his other arm encircled Samantha's slim waist. "He couldn't have a better owner, I'm certain."

Samantha laughed and admitted that Martin cared for Champion at least as often as she did. "But I have learned a great deal," she said. "I can do many things now that I never thought of doing before."

Sterling raised his other arm to her waist, steadying himself in the saddle, appreciating the feel of her in his arms, as he had dreamed for so many months. "I look forward to hearing all about all you have learned," he said. "I have missed our talks."

Samantha blinked, pulling out of her involuntary reverie of yesterday's exciting turn of events, and began setting the table. Today they would begin their conversation anew and try to make up for lost time. It was another drizzly day, so Sterling would join her here at the Jennings mansion for the midday meal, chaperoned by Mrs. Dolittle in the dining room.

Samantha carefully balanced a bowl of fresh spring salad in one hand and a plate of apple pie slices and a wedge of cheese in the other. In both hands, Mrs. Dolittle carried a large pitcher of chilled apple cider from the cellar. They also added a plate of sliced beef and a warm loaf of brown bread with a little crock of butter on the side. When the table was nearly set, a knock sounded at the front door. Samantha's heart jumped and Mrs. Dolittle turned to her, a twinkle in her dark eyes. "Would you like to answer that, my dear, or shall I?"

Samantha untied her apron with trembling fingers and smoothed a strand of golden hair back into the pins that held it up. "I'll answer it," she replied, her voice barely quavering, but her heart hammering in her chest. She handed the apron to Mrs. Dolittle, who smiled and returned to the kitchen, and Samantha took a deep breath. She walked slowly to the front door, grasped the handle, and heaved the heavy door open.

There stood Sterling, clean and well-groomed as usual, neat brown suit coat protecting his broad shoulders against the rain. He removed his hat, one wave of dark hair falling across his forehead as he nodded at her. "Good afternoon, Samantha," he smiled warmly. "Might a hungry man have a bite to eat?"

Beaming, Samantha took his hand to pull him inside. "Only if you promise to eat everything Mrs. Dolittle prepared for us." She closed the door firmly behind them and they stood there, very close, in the entryway. Neither was quite sure what to say, feeling the newness of their relationship, yet each wanting to drink in the presence of the other. Being together at last was a beautiful miracle.

Sterling looked down at her slender form clad in a becoming, muted blue gown with two layers of ruffles that flared out along the hem. He had never seen her in blue and he liked how it brought a different shade into her gray eyes, deepening them somehow. He searched her face for a moment, so glad to see her, even though it had only been several hours. Grasping both her slim hands in his, he was unsure whether his heart could contain such happiness. "The wait to see you this morning was interminably long." His brown eyes drank her in even as her gaze lingered on his face.

She smiled at him, her head tilted up, aware of how small she felt next to him, even though she was taller than most women she knew. "I am so glad you're here, Sterling. In Oberlin. In my home. This is a dream come true for me."

"For me, as well." Sterling's deep voice resonated through the entryway's high-ceilinged space, and she tightened her grip on his hands.

Suddenly, he knew he didn't want to waste any more time in not saying what he really felt. After all their time apart and the hundreds of hours he had spent wishing to speak his heart to her, now he could finally start telling her all the things he had stored up for so many months. "Did I tell you yet that you are the secret dream I've kept in my heart all these months?"

Samantha's eyes widened. "Am I?" The question was simultaneously an expression of disbelief and wistfulness.

Sterling pulled her into his arms and she relaxed into him as he rested his chin in her hair. She noticed the pleasant scent of him, as she had the evening before when they sat astride Champion. It was a delightful combination of clean leather and some kind of spice, like nutmeg or cinnamon. She breathed it in and wondered at how very at home she felt in his arms.

"You are," he affirmed. "I didn't sleep well last night; I was too happy and excited. I still can't believe you felt the same way about me this whole time, while I was convinced I had either ruined your life or meant nothing to you." He gave an ironic chuckle, but she heard the pain behind his words.

She swallowed and took a steadying breath before pulling away from him to look more fully into his face. "I thought about you constantly, but was afraid I was not very memorable." She gave a pained smile. "I always held out hope, though."

"You, not memorable?" Sterling smiled wryly and shook his head. "Where I am concerned, you have always been very memorable." He paused, then offered, "I am glad you

3

kept hoping. There were times I despaired of things ever working out. I am just beginning to learn the truth found in Matthew: 'With God all things are possible.'"[1]

Samantha smiled up at him, "I am learning that too, but in Mark."

Sterling chuckled and noted, "It seems we have both turned to the ultimate Literary Work recently. And it appears my verbal sparring partner is as quick and ready as ever. I've missed this."

Just then, Mrs. Dolittle poked her head into the hallway leading from the dining room. "Lunch is ready, you two. Anyone hungry?"

"Famished!" Sterling returned. "Thank you kindly, Mrs. Dolittle."

Samantha took his offered arm and together they walked down the hall.

As they ate, Mrs. Dolittle bustling in and out at intervals, they discussed what they had each done during their long separation.

"I obtained a traditional teaching position at a boys' school in Worthington," Sterling told Samantha after a bite of tender beef. "It was not what I thought I wanted to do, but it ended up being the right thing for me. I learned so much from those boys and hope I am a much better, more well-rounded teacher than before."

"Not just a teacher of 'modern writing' now, then?" Samantha asked, taking a small bite of buttered bread.

"No." Sterling shook his head. "Certainly not what I had planned for my life, but now, in hindsight, I think it needed to happen." He bit into his own bread and closed his eyes in enjoyment. "I could get used to eating Mrs. Dolittle's food all the time! How can bread be so delectable?"

Samantha laughed. "It is very good, isn't it? She takes good care of us. But, Sterling," she paused and looked at him seriously. "May I ask you a question?"

"Of course." He swallowed the mouthful and looked at her expectantly.

"I know you were afraid you ruined my reputation in the woods that day before you left last year, but I still don't understand why you felt it necessary to leave Oberlin altogether. And so suddenly! It pained me that you didn't even bid me farewell. I was confused for a long time."

---

1. All scripture references throughout this book are from the KJV Bible.

"Oh." Sterling looked at her in concern and blinked. Her bare honesty was a bit disarming, but he was glad for it. He wanted to know what she had felt in his absence, and she didn't appear to harbor a grudge against him: her expression held only confusion and openness. "Yes, I can see that now." He dabbed at his mouth with a napkin while he thought about how to answer. "I am deeply sorry for handling that situation so poorly. I was…" He shifted uncomfortably in his seat and looked away in embarrassment. "Well, the truth of the matter is that I was a coward, Samantha." His gaze returned to hers, gauging her reaction. *It's true, I was!* he thought. *Even though I didn't realize it at the time.*

Her perplexed expression propelled him to further explain himself. "You were a young woman without a mother or other female relative to chaperone you and I was afraid others would decide I had taken advantage of that situation."

"But no one saw us in the woods," Samantha pointed out, still trying to piece things together. "And I, who did not yet understand the conventions of society nor have any connections, did not even have anyone to tell such things…" She trailed off as she saw Sterling's continued embarrassment. "Oh," she concluded. "That was precisely the problem. I was completely unprotected and you…"

"…Didn't want anyone to find out the circumstances and make assumptions that would sully your reputation," he finished her sentence, nodding.

She looked at him contemplatively, the questioning in her eyes now replaced with understanding. She thought for a moment. "I did tell my dear friend Katherine much later, in my attempt to figure out how to feel."

Sterling shifted again, feeling only slightly less uncomfortable than before. "Did that help?"

A slow smile spread across her face. "Actually, yes. She told me your…kiss…did mean something and that I had every reason to believe you had feelings for me. That was a comfort."

He looked relieved. "I am glad. She was right, of course. But truly, I respected you too much to do anything that would damage your good name in any way. I only hoped when I left that I hadn't already done so!"

"Why did you care so much what other people thought, when you had done nothing wrong?" Samantha queried, fair brows pushed together.

Sterling's eyes widened in surprise. "I… Well, I was raised to be aware of that at all times. How others perceive our family is very important to my mother. Our standing in society is of paramount importance and in our formative years she constantly reminded my brother and I of the necessity of keeping ourselves above sullying influences—or more particularly, of what others would *perceive* as sullying influences. I guess I've never thought about *not* following convention..." he trailed off, mystified.

Suddenly it dawned on him what her perspective on the whole situation must have felt like. He looked at her in a new light and his expression cleared. He ran a hand over his face. "So let me get this straight: I essentially professed my love to you in the woods that day—which you hadn't yet considered a possibility. You didn't know much about the rules of courtship or what is proper, so you were not thinking about how your reputation could be harmed by that kiss. Instead, you were wondering what it meant and how I felt about you."

Samantha nodded.

So Mrs. Tomlinson was right all along! he realized with a pang. He needed to remember to heed her advice more completely in future! Aloud, he continued his musings: "And then I suddenly departed Oberlin without even saying a word to you, and without sending word."

"Yes," she said softly.

"It was more than that, though. Yes, I was trying to help you save face, to remove myself—the offense—from your reputation. But also..." he hesitated, looking away again. "I didn't know what to do with the feelings I was having—feelings I'd never had before. I really struggled to know what to do—but I never intended to make you feel abandoned." His gaze shifted back to hers, his expression pained.

Samantha considered this, her head tilted to one side. "Abandon is perhaps too strong a word... But it was as if you had vanished from off the face of the earth. And yet I knew you had to be out there somewhere. It did seem like you felt something for me, but because you left I wasn't certain. I have no experience in these matters." She laughed softly at herself. "My mind vacillated back and forth like that little ritual young women do with flower petals—'He loves me, he loves me not'—over and over again."

He clasped her hand across the table, the meal temporarily forgotten. "I am sorry I left the way I did. And I'm sorry my belated letter never arrived! I know I took much too long to write it," he shook his head regretfully, "but perhaps it would have helped. Of course, it was rather dry," he admitted, one side of his mouth turning up as he considered how businesslike the words had been, how flat and devoid of emotion.

"It would have helped," she agreed, "but it isn't your fault it never arrived." She squeezed his hand and let go to pick up her fork and resume her meal, turning the topic. "But I am so intrigued: how did you end up in Worthington, of all places?"

Sterling bit off another piece of bread and butter as he considered the question, chewing for a moment. "I don't honestly know. Now that I think about it, I don't understand it myself. I essentially ran from Oberlin," he shrugged, looking sheepish, "and kept riding the train until it felt right to get off. Then the job fell into my lap so quickly and easily that I just stayed on. It was not easy work, though, especially there at the beginning." He gave a dry chuckle. "My students had to be so patient with me for those first few weeks because I really struggled."

"But you didn't give up," Samantha pointed out. "That's the important thing."

"Never. I determined not to quit without giving it an earnest effort—especially if quitting meant returning home, like a dog with his tail between his legs. Mother would have reacted pretty smugly to that, and I could not give her that satisfaction. Or allow myself the failure."

"You haven't told me much about your mother," Samantha observed, cutting off a small piece of beef and spearing it with her fork.

Sterling's smile looked more like a grimace. "There is not a great deal to tell. She lives the pampered and privileged life of the wife of a prosperous equine breeder and hemp farmer. She adores parties and social events—and making her oldest son feel uncomfortable for his decision to earn his own living." Sterling took a sip of his apple cider. "That said, she and my father did donate a sizable sum to the Franklin County writing contest fund. And that indirectly led to me finding my way back to you. So," he mused, "I suppose I have her to thank for that."

"It sounds that way," Samantha agreed. After a pause she added, "I am not sure she would approve of me." There was no self-recrimination in the statement, it was merely an observation.

Sterling sat still, considering. "I wondered the same thing when I went home for a visit last Christmas. I used to share her social lifestyle and cared, to a point, about some of that. But now I have found things that are so much more meaningful and real to me that it is even more difficult to find common ground between her and I. I don't know if she feels the disparity or simply won't acknowledge it, but it is there. And you," he looked at her pointedly, "are so much more real than the society girls she wishes me to meet that there is really no comparison."

Samantha warmed at his sincerity. "Thank you," she said simply. "You know, I have learned a great deal about my own mother over the past few months. Of everything that transpired in your absence, that was one of the most significant."

"Really?" Sterling was instantly interested and gave her his full attention. She loved how alive his brown eyes were, and how attuned they were to her own.

Samantha told him about that all-important day when she discovered her mother's journal in her father's library. "Learning about her, coming to know her through her writing, making that connection with her for the first time, changed my life," Samantha told him honestly. "Somehow, I feel that knowing her better has helped me know myself better. It's a bit of a strange concept, perhaps, but a powerful one. I have a sense of belonging now that I've never had before."

Sterling looked impressed. "That's not something I have much considered. But it makes sense. Have you reconnected with your father, as well?"

Samantha offered Sterling the serving plate and he accepted another piece of the warm bread. "Not exactly. I want to, and plan to soon. I have not yet told him about my trip to Worthington. I think he may want to know how it went, but even if he does not, I plan to tell him anyway. It is past time for him to move on with his life and this may help." Her determined tone of voice warmed him. This young woman was no shrinking violet in the face of difficulty.

He nodded thoughtfully. "When I came upon you in the cemetery, it looked as if you had just found your mother's headstone. And there were two people with you."

"Yes. After days of searching, that was quite the day of discovery. I was so grateful my two dear friends could be there with me. I really needed their support."

"I wished *I* could be that support when I saw the young man holding and comforting you." Now he was the one being completely honest and open, and his vulnerable expression showed how the sight had pained him. "But it did not seem the time to intrude, so I slunk away and retreated to my room to brood and become even more despondent." He gave a self-deprecating chuckle.

She looked at him with compassion. "I am sorry that scene was so difficult for you," she replied. After a brief moment of contemplation, she added, "But you were right not to make yourself known at that time. I think your appearance would have been too much for me in that highly emotional moment. Although, I am sorry you thought Rupert and I were romantically involved. I never felt that way about him."

Sterling waved a hand as if to brush away the apology. "It was probably good for me to feel a sense of competition, to recognize I needed to fight for you." He shook his head in a dazed sort of way. "My, so much has changed in twenty-four hours, has it not?" He reached for her hand again and Samantha placed her hand in his.

"Yes," she whispered. Tears sprang to her eyes as she thought about all the hardships of the past several months and all the times she had felt lonely for lack of him, and how completely everything had reversed in a day She laughed and blinked, wiping at her eyes. "I think I have cried more over the past few weeks than I ever did during the whole rest of my eighteen years combined!"

Sterling squeezed her hand and looked at her tenderly. "I, too, have been through quite the emotional wringer. And I have learned so much through the process. Mrs. Tomlinson helped me through some of that."

"Who is she?"

"Her son, Jerome, was a student in my class: a freckled, red-haired lad who has an amazing gift for fixing things around the school and making beautiful woodwork. Mrs. Tomlinson is a widow with a small farm and orchard that she maintains with the help of Jerome and one hired hand." By the increased warmth and enthusiasm in his voice, Samantha could tell he had a special fondness for these people. "She is a wealth of wisdom and motherly advice and care. From her, I have learned what a good mother is and does. She encouraged me in regard to you, and urged me to hold to my decision to come back and speak with you."

Samantha smiled. "I like her already."

"She would love you. I look forward to the two of you meeting each other. And," he added, pointing at the pie, "I look forward to trying that and seeing if it is as delectable as Mrs. Tomlinson's. Growing up, I always thought our cook, Nancy, made the best apple pie in the world, but Mrs. Tomlinson's is somehow even better."

Samantha moved to cut it and lifted out a slice for Sterling. "I don't know how it could be any better than Mrs. Dolittle's, but try it and tell me what you think."

Sterling's fork bit down into the perfectly flaky crust and soft, spiced apple, then up to his mouth. Eyes closed, he savored his first bite. "It really doesn't get any better than this, does it?"

Samantha laughed. She watched the exquisite pleasure on his face as he thoroughly savored the mouthful. "So? What is the verdict?"

He opened his eyes and she caught a mischievous glint. "I think they may be tied, but I'll have to eat a few more bites to know for sure."

***

After their meal, they carried everything back to the kitchen where Mrs. Dolittle insisted on finishing the cleanup herself and shooed them out the back door for a walk in the watery sunshine, where she could see them from the window. They set out on the path beneath the trees, Samantha holding the hem of her long gown in one hand to keep it from touching the soggy ground. She began giving Sterling a tour of the land behind the mansion, pointing out her favorite things here and there—particularly the massive maple tree she could see from the library window. Its new green leaves spread out in a luxuriant canopy. Sterling took her hand in his and she breathed deeply of the moist, fresh air, reveling in the beauty all around them, marveling at her complete and utter happiness.

"We took so many walks last summer," he mused as they strolled along.

"Was it only last year?!" she exclaimed.

"Seems incredible, doesn't it?" he replied seriously. "It has been an exceptionally long year. His hand tightened slightly around hers. "But not a one of our walks last year was like this." He gestured at their hands. "I wanted to…"

"But it was not the right time," Samantha finished. "I know. I feel that way too. I think you would have scared me away, so it is good you didn't." She gave him a smile. "Don't you feel like everything worked out right after all, even though neither of us would want to relive those months?"

Sterling nodded slowly. "I do now. If your reception of me yesterday had been different, however, I am not sure I could say the same."

Samantha's glance was soft as she gazed up at him a moment, her smile sweet. "I wanted to see you long before yesterday." Turning her gaze back to the path, she told him, "You know, I had a peculiar feeling all day yesterday, even before I received the telegram of your pending arrival, that something wonderful was about to happen. So I was not surprised when you found me in the clearing when you did."

"Really? How curious. About that telegram... What did it say?"

"That you left Worthington at one o'clock and were headed here. You didn't send it? It was addressed to me as if it were you."

Sterling shook his head. "No, I didn't. But I have an idea who might have." One side of his mouth turned up in a smile as he thought about this. "I realize now that I should have done it myself."

"Yes, you should have," she agreed, a slight scold in her voice. "I would have appreciated even that small word from you."

Sterling felt the ache in her words and it twisted his heart in return. He pondered how best to respond. "That letter I wrote... I sent it to you in December, and by March, when I still had not heard back from you, I was afraid there was no hope. But Mrs. Tomlinson encouraged me to continue believing. She thought it might have gotten lost in the mail, and it appears that it did."

Samantha nodded slowly. "I suppose so. My friend Katherine says, 'God is in the details' and I think she is right! Like your Mrs. Tomlinson did for you, Katherine helped me keep hoping. My writing helped me continue moving forward, as well, and to process all I was going through. Thank you for that gift." The remembered pain of the silence between them during their separation faded away as she remembered what he had given her and the fact that she could now thank him for it in person.

"It was my pleasure," he told her. "Truly. You always had the potential inside you. I just helped bring it out."

"Yes. But who knows how long it would have taken if you had not come along!"

"God is definitely in the details," Sterling affirmed. "And I still think I learned far more from the process than I ever taught you. That's the funny thing about teaching..."

Samantha nodded thoughtfully. "I have recently begun wondering what it would be like to be a teacher. Will you be staying on at the boys' school?"

"Yes," Sterling replied. "I signed my contract for next year and look forward to the challenge. But..." He sighed, his expression thoughtful and pained. "I don't like the idea of us being so far away from each other again."

"Neither do I," Samantha agreed sadly. "How long can you stay in Oberlin?"

"School is out for the summer,[2] so I could potentially stay a long while. I will have to figure things out. I left in such a hurry, I didn't really think it all through."

Samantha's eyes sparkled as she thought about other times when he had reacted spontaneously. She knew that over the past year he had regretted his spontaneity in whisking her off into the woods, unchaperoned, in kissing her without asking, and in leaving Oberlin suddenly for an unknown destination. But his spontaneity was something she appreciated because of her lack of it. There was something childlike and open about that tendency of his. How like him to return the same way he had left! And yet, as she thought about it, there were also times when he had *not* reacted as he had felt compelled to: for example, when he had seen her in the cemetery. Maybe now his spontaneity was more mature, a little better directed.

"Well, for now, let us just enjoy these next few days," she told him, wanting them both to focus on the present. "I am certain we will be able to work things out in time."

"Wise words, spoken like the wise woman you are," Sterling smiled. "I like that idea of enjoying the moment. I have done precious little of that over the past several months. In fact, right now I feel truly relaxed for the first time in ages." He stopped walking and turned to her. "You are good for me, Samantha. Being with you feels like coming home."

Samantha's smile shone up at him. "I feel the same way about you." She took a deep breath, held it in silent contemplation, and then let it out slowly. "But I also feel this strange conflict inside. I know that I love you, Sterling, but there is still so much I don't know about you. About us. I feel impatient to make up for all the lost time together, yet I also feel that we need to take time to become truly acquainted." Her fair brows puckered together in an expression of sudden frustration. "My thoughts are all confused and conflicting!"

Sterling laughed and pulled her into his arms. "That's all right. I don't have anything figured out either." Then, after a beat, he whispered mischievously, "Do you think Mrs. Dolittle can see us from the back porch?"

"I don't know," she whispered back, forehead smooth again, eyes bright. "But I don't think I care."

Sterling's laugh rumbled through them both and he bent his head to kiss her.

---

2. https://files.eric.ed.gov/fulltext/EJ1134242.pdf

***

After their tour of the grounds, Samantha led Sterling to the large barn where Champion was housed during inclement weather. The black horse whickered when they arrived at his stall. "He definitely remembers you," Samantha noted, rubbing a hand down his velvet nose. The big horse snorted at her. "I take him out for a run as often as I can when the weather is fine—and sometimes when it isn't. He has been cooped up too much lately, due to all the rain. He is always itching to stretch his legs."

"Yes, I remember that about him." Sterling patted his former horse and scratched him under the forelock. "He looks very content here, and well cared for."

"He was my only connection with you for a long time," Samantha reflected. "But if you would like him back now, you can have him."

"Oh no," Sterling shook his head. "He has the best of homes here and I have nowhere to keep a horse at the moment. But I may ask to borrow him now and then, if you aren't opposed."

"He would love that," Samantha smiled.

Chapter 2

REACQUAINTING

Over the next several days, Samantha and Sterling spent as much time together as they could. They exchanged writings that each had worked on over their months apart and delighted in reading what the other had written about life, things learned, trials, and love. As the rain dissipated and the weather warmed, they took many walks together and discussed anything and everything, including history, family, current events, literature, and their growing faith. It reminded them both of their animated discussions the previous summer, only even more enjoyable now.

On June 5th, they joined the town in paying their respects at the funeral of John Henry Barrows[1], President of Oberlin College. He had died prematurely of pneumonia, which shocked everyone and saddened Sterling, who had known him briefly during his short time at the college.

As they attended community events, several people Samantha knew congratulated her on her winning poem, which they had recently seen in the newspaper. The attention and praise surprised her each time, making her a little embarrassed but also pleased. On Sundays, Samantha and Sterling attended church, and twice they took Champion and

---

1. https://en.wikipedia.org/wiki/John_Henry_Barrows

14

another horse for a run in the fields. These were days to savor and bask in, and they both did so freely. Samantha wrote in her journal:

I feel so light and free having Sterling near me again that it seems as if I have wings and my feet do not touch the ground. It is incredibly gratifying and heart-warming to know that he truly feels about me the way I feel about him. I am still not quite sure how that is possible, but the realization delights me over and over again.

I have never had much in the way of physical contact with others before this past year and never knew I needed it. But with Rupert and Katherine's kind contact and now Sterling's affectionate touch, I find it such a comfort and a wonderful connection. The only drawback about this addition to my life is remembering my childhood and seeing it with new eyes as a stark and loveless experience—except for the care Mrs. Dolittle always showed me. I cannot recall any embrace from Father or hearing him express love to me. I keep finding myself having feelings of...perhaps anger...? toward him. How he could show such little love or regard for me—his own blood, the offspring of his beloved wife—baffles me. I do not understand him, and it is beginning to frustrate me more and more. It must be time to confront him again, to talk through some of this. With any luck, he has finished reading Mother's journal and will allow me to take it back.

***

For his part, after another afternoon with Samantha, Sterling wrote:

When I consider where I was in both mind and heart over a week ago, I can scarcely comprehend where I am now! I have long considered Samantha a light in my life, a small sun that blazes brightly and warms me with mere proximity. But now I feel she has some particular transformative power over me as well, for just by being near her, she has made me the happiest of men. Not only that, but simply thinking of her, picturing her warm smile and gentle touch brings comfort to my soul. Every time I am with her it is reaffirmed to me that there is so much more to her than any other young woman of my acquaintance. She is deeper, truer, and more lovely than any woman I have ever known. I think it may take a lifetime to find all the hidden facets of her wonderful luster. I consider myself blessed, indeed.

***

On another afternoon, Sterling wrote a letter addressed to a particular farm in Worthington:

Dear Mrs. Tomlinson,

I am writing to apologize for my belated absence at the supper you invited me to several days ago. But I have the feeling you know exactly where I am and why I left as hastily as I did. Am I also correct in assuming you were the one who sent that mysterious telegram, which Samantha thought she received from me? It should have been me, as you knew. And I thank you. Because of that message, she was looking for me and, while we did not meet up at the train station as you undoubtedly intended, I did see her there and was heartened by the sight.

Now I am sure you wish to know what happened when we did at last find each other, though I am confident you have guessed that too, as wise and insightful as you are. I was surprised and elated to find that, not only did she harbor no ill will toward me, she had—incredible as it seems—pined for me as I pined for her. My feelings toward her are reciprocated in the sweetest and most genuine manner and I have never been happier. I thank you for all your accurate advice and encouragement, and for insisting it was best for me to return to Oberlin. You could not have been more correct!

I expect to stay here for a while longer, possibly most of the summer. Samantha and I have so much reacquainting to do, and we need to figure out where things go from here. Of course, I will also need to prepare my curriculum for the next school year, so I must leave myself time for that as well. And I know you could certainly use help on the farm, especially when the harvest nears. I dearly want Samantha to meet you and hope at some point to bring her to Worthington. I will keep you apprised. In the meantime,

Hoping this letter finds you and Jerome well,

Sterling

***

That same evening, Samantha met Sterling at a cafe in town. He had spent a couple of hours settling some affairs, shopping for a few items, and writing the letter to Mrs. Tomlinson, but he wished to treat Samantha to an early supper. He had picked up a large cinnamon roll at the bakery for Mrs. Dolittle as a small token of his appreciation for all the delicious meals she had fed him. The bakery had kindly placed the treat in a small box, which he kept near him at the table.

Knowing what errands Sterling had, Samantha insisted he needn't come by for her, that she could just as easily meet him in town, and as the day had been full of sunshine and the roads passably dry, she enjoyed the walk. She had chosen a simple walking dress of deep green with a hem that ended a few inches above the road, and sturdy brown boots. On her head she wore a small-brimmed straw hat with a matching swath of green ribbon that wrapped around the crown. She did not much care for the ostentatious fashions of the day, preferring styles that were simple and sensible, as was the norm for Oberlin. But she had learned from Katherine what styles flattered her and had adjusted her wardrobe accordingly. The combination, to Sterling's eyes, was just right, and he smiled appreciatively, rising from his seat as Samantha walked toward the table he had reserved for them in the small cafe. She took the chair he offered, and he sat across from her, taking her hand in his.

Numerous small round tables stood about the room, covered in blue and white gingham tablecloths, wooden chairs pulled up to them neatly, shining with lacquer. Never having been inside before today, Samantha observed the scene, warmed by the obvious care the owner took to keep his establishment clean and attractive. Theirs was a private and cozy spot in one corner near a window, away from the bustle.

"How are you?" She knew he asked because he really wanted to know.

"Very well, thank you!" she smiled back. "Were you successful in your errands?"

"I was," Sterling affirmed, handing her a menu. "I accomplished everything I hoped to, including writing to Mrs. Tomlinson."

"Good," Samantha said. "No doubt she will be relieved and glad to hear from you. How about your room in Worthington? Will the landlord allow you to keep it while you are away?"

"I believe so. As long as he continues to receive his monthly payment, I can't imagine he will protest. I wired him the money and sent a telegram, so I should think that will settle everything."

Samantha nodded. "It seems like everything is coming together."

"Yes," Sterling agreed. "It does, doesn't it." It was a grateful statement, not a question.

The two ordered their meal and proceeded to talk about the headlines they had been most impacted by during their months apart.

"I was so busy with planning, teaching, and correcting homework that I didn't purchase a newspaper as often as I normally do," Sterling told her. "But I did try to stay abreast of things as much as I could. I remember there was an explosion in the New York subway, which killed a few workers." He shook his head. "A tragedy, no doubt about it. Yet I can't help but be amazed that more people haven't been killed in that underground construction."

"I don't know if I would like traveling underground," Samantha admitted, "much less consider working in its construction! I, too, am amazed there has not been a greater loss of life."

They spoke of Cuba's recent independence from the United States, of how China's empress had forever banned footbinding, and of the coal mine strike that had just begun in Pennsylvania. They remembered bits and pieces of news about the Boer War in South Africa that had just ended, and how much conflict there was in Belgium as demonstrations occurred as citizens demanding better living conditions, education, and the right to strike, among other things.

"It seems there is always a group of people somewhere in the world who lack basic rights and finally gather enough strength to mobilize and demand them," Sterling noted. "I hope their leaders eventually listen to them and improve their situation, before more people are killed."

Their meal arrived and they enjoyed eating it while continuing their conversation. The little cafe was only sparsely occupied at this relatively early hour, but as time passed, more patrons arrived and the noise of happy chatter and the smell of delicious food began to fill the place.

Sterling took another bite and held up a newspaper. "Have you seen this yet?" he asked. "The headline contains awful news. I almost don't want to mention it."

Samantha's fork stopped midway between the plate and her mouth. "No. What is it?!"

"There was an absolutely horrific volcanic eruption on the island of Martinique only a few days ago."[2]

Samantha's eyes widened. "That's in the Caribbean, correct?"

---

2. https://bit.ly/4c0RoVC

"It is," Sterling affirmed. "You know your geography well." His tone was light but his expression grave as he handed her the paper.

Samantha took it from him, her food forgotten as she read quickly through the article. "Almost thirty thousand people dead?" she asked, looking up at him, shocked. "The entire city wiped out in a moment!"

Sterling's look of disbelief matched her own. "Unthinkable. The saddest thing to me is that Mt. Pelée gave the people of St. Pierre warnings for days before the explosion, but they had seen the volcano smoke that way before, with nothing worse occurring, so they assumed this was the same. And then when a cloud of ash descended over the city, the newspapers still assured everyone there was no danger."

Samantha scanned the article once more, her expression sad, then folded the paper and handed it back to Sterling. "Such a senseless tragedy. Those poor people! The ones who died instantly were lucky. I cannot wrap my mind around a temperature of two thousand degrees. No wonder everyone was dead in sixty seconds and the city burst into flames! It is hard to fathom that many people dying at once."

"Yes, it is. They're calling it potentially the worst volcanic disaster of the 20th century."

"And we're only into the second year of this century," Samantha grieved. "May there be nothing worse the rest of the 1900s!"

"Amen."

They were quiet for a moment and then Sterling gestured to their meal. "Sorry, I didn't mean to ruin our supper."

Samantha inhaled slowly and gave Sterling an ironic smile. "Here we sit in comfort when on the other side of the world an entire city has disappeared. And yet, we can do nothing about it and must go on, so we may as well eat." That was the realistic way of looking at it, but Samantha hated how cold and dismissive it sounded.

Sterling took a bite to show his agreement, even though he, too, was shaken by the news and wished he could change the tragedy. Samantha reached again for her fork. The food really was very good, she just needed her former appetite back. She was glad when Sterling changed the subject by asking her what books she was currently reading.

Her face brightened. "I am virtually eating up *Jane Eyre*—by Charlotte Bronte, of course. And at the same time, I am thoroughly captivated by *Up from Slavery*."

"By Booker T. Washington!" Sterling exclaimed. "Wasn't that published last year?"

"It was," Samantha acknowledged. "And I have always wanted to read *Jane Eyre*. But my father's library doesn't contain any fiction, so I mail-ordered it."

"I have wanted to read Washington's book, too. And *Jane Eyre* is such a classic!" His brows suddenly furrowed as he contemplated his recent reading experience—or lack thereof. "I think I completed the past school year without reading even one book for pleasure," he said regretfully.

Samantha was not surprised. "You were exceptionally busy, just trying to stay ahead of your students, I imagine." Then she offered, "When I am finished, would you like to borrow my copy of *Up from Slavery*?"

"I would!" Sterling returned. "I am sure it will provide us with many topics for discussion."

Samantha nodded in agreement as she cleaned the last of the meal from her plate. "*Jane Eyre* has much to discuss as well."

"Indeed," Sterling rejoined. "What an incredible, strong, and courageous woman protagonist. Bronte paints such a vivid and detailed description of Jane's persona and character that one would know her on the street!"

"I agree. I am not quite finished with the novel, but I keep being amazed at her resilience in the face of all her difficult circumstances. Even more incredible is that through it all, she is true to who she is deep inside and will not let herself be cowed or overpowered by others, regardless of their supposed superiority to herself."

Sterling paused at her words, looking at her for a long moment in thought. "I see similarities between the two of you, truth be told," he told her, his brown eyes soft.

Samantha wasn't sure about the accuracy of such a comparison, but she offered, "Reading about her life has made me grateful for my own little trials. And I do identify with Jane quite a bit as I consider her constant longing for family and belonging. I, too, have felt and do feel that yearning."

"Have you figured out where your mother's side of the family lives, if they are still living? Could there be any remaining in Worthington?" Sterling looked at her with eyes wide, as if this thought had just occurred to him.

"Yes!" Samantha's gray eyes were alight with a particular fire that Sterling had only ever seen as she spoke of her mother. "I mean, I think so. I have not made any contact with them yet, but I believe I do have living relatives there. That is another big project I need to undertake."

"Please let me be of service in that endeavor, if I may," Sterling said. "Worthington is a small town and I know several people there who could probably steer us in the right direction."

Samantha beamed. "Thank you. It seems I will have more than one reason to visit Worthington once you return."

A teasing glint came into Sterling's eyes and he cocked one dark eyebrow as he asked, "But which of those reasons will draw you there the most?"

Samantha acknowledged the quip with a quick smile, but considered his question seriously for a moment. "Of course I will ache again, being so far from you, Sterling. I do not look forward to that time."

Sterling nodded, his expression sober once more.

Her face was earnest as she continued. "But I have to admit that you *and* my relatives will be quite the draw. You must remember, I have had neither brother nor sister, uncle nor aunt, nor any other family to call my own. Other than my father, of course."

"I understand. And I will do all I can to help restore you to them."

"Thank you." She squeezed her hands together as if giving herself a little hug, her smile like sunshine. "I feel so blessed, as if I were on the cusp of discovering even more wonderful things and making other coveted connections. I felt such joy as I read about Jane Eyre literally stumbling upon her relatives and how much it healed her heart to find connection with them. She endured so much before that time! As I said before, reading about her trials made me grateful for my own in a way I never have been before."

Sterling nodded. "It is an empowering thing to be grateful for one's own difficulties and not covet others' lives."

"Truly," Samantha agreed, then asked with raised eyebrows, "so what are you grateful for about *your* life and difficulties? I know your family life is not what you wish it would be, either."

"No," Sterling answered thoughtfully. "Though I do not see eye-to-eye with my mother, my parents provided my brother and me all the necessities of life and had no vices that disrupted the stability of our home. Those are certainly blessings to acknowledge." He continued his verbal list, counting them off on his fingers: "I am also thankful my parents never beat me, that I never went hungry, that they provided me a college education, though that was not their vision for my future. And now, as a grown man myself, I can look back and identify particulars that I want to change for my own future family, and things I do not wish to perpetuate." He placed his hand on the table, palm up, and she slid her hand into his. He slowly rubbed his thumb over her fingers as he considered the topic, looking into her face. "I imagine you have had similar thoughts."

"Yes, I have. I wish to emulate my mother without repeating the mistakes of my father and of my own upbringing. Such isolation and neglect made me self-reliant and independent, but at such cost!" Her eyes filled with sorrow for a moment, but lightened with her next words. "I am grateful you showed up in my life when you did, Sterling. I thank God for you every day."

Sterling wanted to kiss her, but of course now was not the time or place. And it was just as well, for two people unexpectedly approached their table. One was a beautiful young woman about Samantha's age, petite, with dark brown hair and long-lashed blue eyes. The other was a sturdy-looking young man of average height and straight, light brown hair.

Samantha looked up and brightened. "Katherine! Rupert! How good to see you." She hurriedly removed the napkin from her lap and stood to greet them, Katherine with a hug, Rupert with clasped hands.

"Samantha, is this...?" Katherine's gaze shifted to Sterling and then back to Samantha, an expression of amazement on her face.

"Yes," Samantha answered softly, her color heightened in a way that delighted Sterling. She gestured to him as he stood, head and shoulders taller than they. "This is Lee Sterling, lately from Worthington."

Sterling shook hands with Katherine and Rupert as they were introduced, and drew close to Samantha as he said, "I understand you are Samantha's dear friends who recently accompanied her to Worthington. Thank you for aiding her in finding her mother's grave. I know that meant a great deal to her."

"Oh, she is our dear friend," Katherine replied. "And it was our pleasure to accompany her. It was quite an adventure for me! Now I feel like a seasoned traveler," she laughed.

Rupert nodded. He seemed a little bashful, perhaps a bit intimidated by Sterling's presence, but he looked up at the taller man and said with conviction, "It was an honor to be asked to go. I was glad to do it."

Sterling noticed that Samantha's eyes shone with unshed tears as she looked at her two friends. Then she swallowed and smiled, indicating the small table behind them, empty plates stacked neatly to one side. "Do you two need a table?"

"Yes." Sterling gestured, following her lead. "Please. We were about ready to leave and it looks like this place is filling up now."

"Thank you," Rupert nodded. "We appreciate that."

"It's so wonderful to see you," Samantha repeated, hugging Katherine once more.

Her friend's eyes held a myriad of questions, but she merely smiled and hugged Samantha back. "We need to talk soon," she whispered in Samantha's ear.

"Yes, we do," Samantha whispered back. "Enjoy your meal. I love seeing you two together."

Rupert held the back of one chair while Katherine sat, pushing it in for her, then took the opposite chair and lifted a hand to Samantha and Sterling as they made their way out of the cafe.

***

Mrs. Dolittle looked up from her seat at the small kitchen table as Samantha's slight frame darkened the doorway. "You're back!" she smiled. "How was your supper at the cafe?"

Samantha sighed happily and smiled as she sat across from her. "It was lovely. Not quite as delicious as your cooking, of course, but still good. Oh, and this is for you." She held out the pastry box and Mrs. Dolittle took it in surprise.

"For me?"

"A little token of Sterling's appreciation for all your delicious meals."

Mrs. Dolittle chuckled. "That may be more bachelorhood talking than tastebuds, but he is very kind." She opened the lid and smelled the cinnamon roll with obvious pleasure. "I shall enjoy this. Tell him thank you." She set the box next to her on the table and took a sip of tea from the small cup before her. "I imagine the company was of more interest to you than the food."

"Yes." Samantha reached to remove her hat and set it in her lap. "Any time with Sterling is time well spent. Since he returned, we have spent hours and hours together, and yet it never seems enough. We have not run out of things to talk about yet! This all still amazes me."

Mrs. Dolittle nodded approvingly. "I'd say it's true love," she offered.

Samantha cocked her head and looked at her older friend. "How did I get so lucky? Little, plain, inconsequential Samantha...?" she shook her head in bewilderment.

Mrs. Dolittle looked at her fondly. "You are a good girl, Samantha, and always have been. You're strong, genuine, and talented. You care deeply about people and want the best for them, and help where you can fill a need. There is much for Mr. Sterling to see in you!"

Samantha's face lit at Mrs. Dolittle's words, but she didn't dwell on them. "That is very kind of you. But what do you think of *him*?" Her gray eyes watched the housekeeper with intensity and interest. "You have spent enough time with him now to know what kind of person he is, and I value your opinion."

Mrs. Dolittle returned her gaze thoughtfully. "I see great goodness in him, as well. He aims to help and lift others, to find truth and follow it, and he strives to better himself. In short, I don't think you could do better, my dear."

Samantha searched her face, then slowly nodded. "I see all those things in him too. But Rupert also possesses those qualities, don't you think?"

"Oh, to be sure," Mrs. Dolittle affirmed. "But the attraction isn't quite the same now, is it?"

"No," Samantha laughed. "Rupert is a wonderful friend, but I never felt interested in him in any other way."

"And Sterling's looks don't hurt either, do they?" Mrs. Dolittle quipped under her breath. "The Good Lord certainly blessed that man with beauty, didn't He?"

"Mrs. Dolittle!" Samantha cried in surprise, one hand flying up to cover a laugh.

"Well," Mrs. Dolittle chuckled, "I may be an old woman, but I am still a woman."

Samantha's cheeks colored, but her eyes sparkled. "I must confess, I do like to look at him." She paused in thought, then continued. "I am not sure what he sees when he looks at me, though. I have never been beautiful, and it has never mattered before."

Mrs. Dolittle placed a gentle, rough-worn hand on Samantha's hand and told her firmly, "I have observed him when he looks at you, and what he sees in you is obvious to anyone with eyes. You are the girl he loves, my dear, who is everything he has ever wanted. You are the one with whom he shares all his thoughts and his heart. I think he loves everything he sees in you!"

Tears sprang to Samantha's eyes at her friend's sincere insights. "Thank you, Mrs. Dolittle. I hope you're right."

"It is the gospel truth, my dear. So don't you forget it." Mrs. Dolittle gave Samantha one more pat, then stood to wash her cup at the sink, leaving Samantha to ponder her words.

Chapter 3

MEETING PROFESSOR JENNINGS

June 1902

A couple mornings later, Sterling donned his hat as he left his room, closing the door tightly behind him. The hotel was fast becoming his comfortable and familiar home away from home, and he had already made friends with the manager, arranging to pay a discounted monthly rent on the condition that he do all his own cleaning and take his laundry down to the laundress himself. This arrangement allowed him more privacy, reduced the workload on the housekeepers, and still provided guaranteed income to the hotel for the next few months, so it was mutually agreeable. Sterling would have preferred to live closer to Samantha, of course, but the daily walk to the Jennings mansion kept him active and gave him time to contemplate as he walked both ways each day. It replaced his usual routine of walking through his favorite Worthington cemetery—but with an even happier result at the end.

Walking quickly across the hotel's carpeted landing, he descended the stairs two at a time, tipping his hat to an elderly man and woman making their slow way up. Adjusting the satchel on his shoulder, he mentally ticked off the items he needed and confirmed that he had packed them. He was ready for a day of lesson planning at Samantha's. He felt he had taken a long enough break from school, and now it was time to direct his thoughts back to his responsibilities in the next academic year. He wanted to take note of all the things he desired to do differently this time, as well as record the lessons, discussions, and activities that worked last year before he forgot them.

His thoughts full of such memories, he began making a mental list as he strode through the streets, absently lifting a hand as he passed regulars who waved at him in return. The early morning air was cool and pleasant, and he filled his lungs with a long draught of it, feeling the joy of youth and purpose. His long legs kept up a steady gait, muscles flexing and stretching at the pace he had set for himself, his body warming under his suit coat. He felt more alive than he ever had, all thanks to an incredible young woman who meant everything to him.

After a few more moments of walking, he realized he had lost his original train of thought. Samantha was so much more fun to think about than school. He laughed aloud to himself. So much for that list! He considered how her love infused him with a power and direction he had never felt before. A few years ago, his focus and drive had been to get his college degree and become a renowned writing teacher. He had succeeded in obtaining the degree, but smiled now as he thought about how poorly his lofty career goal had turned out. Or had it? For it was through teaching writing that he had come to know Samantha.

After leaving Oberlin last year, his goal was to survive his first year of teaching the best he could. But a weight had hung over him of all that he felt for Samantha and left unsaid. His dream, once he recognized his love for Samantha, was that she would someday return that love. And now he knew she did! The wonder of it still hit him at odd moments.

Some dreams must be more important to God than others, he mused, *and from where I stand now, it is obvious that having a relationship with Samantha is more important than being a famous writing teacher. I should really consult God more often.* He chuckled to himself. *Things turn out so much better when I let Him be in charge.* At the same time, he felt that all he had learned and felt over the past year had strengthened and improved him, and that perhaps the joy he experienced now would not be so sweet without all the bitterness he had passed through. He felt immensely grateful in that moment that God could and did turn hard things into good.

So now what was his dream? What goals did he have for the future, and where did he want to end up? He and Samantha had both independently done a great deal of thinking about their dreams and their individual goals, but now it was time to consider how their separate dreams could fuse into one—for he knew that a future without Samantha would not be much of a future at all. He was eternally grateful he no longer had to worry about that possibility, as he had daily over the past nine months. Instead, his heart could rest and rejoice in the knowledge that his beloved returned his feelings wholly and completely. What a wonder that such a woman saw all his flaws and weaknesses and loved him still!

He arrived at the Jennings mansion and forced himself to slow his pace as he walked up the path. He removed his hat and ran a hand through his hair, trying to tidy it. Despite his efforts, he knew his hair was usually disheveled and that a strand would inevitably flop down over his forehead, but he could at least start out looking presentable. He ran a hand down the front of his suit coat, checking quickly for lint or dust, and then used the large brass door knocker. After tapping it to announce his presence, he waited for the sound of Samantha's light footsteps in the entryway a few moments later.

She pulled the heavy door open and smiled a welcome that warmed him through. "Come in!" she exclaimed, stepping back to allow him entrance. She smoothed a stray lock of strawberry gold hair back into her bun and looked down at herself. "Oh, I forgot to take this off!" She laughed and began to untie an apron spotted here and there with some kind of red substance.

"Here, let me help you," Sterling offered, knowing full well she needed no help. But she let him.

As he untied the bow at her back and lifted the large apron up and over her head, she explained, "Mrs. Dolittle and I have been making strawberry rhubarb preserves all morning. Everything ripened all at once and I couldn't let her do all that canning alone." She looked up into the brown eyes that never failed to pull her in and wondered what he was thinking as he looked at her. "Besides," she added, "she is teaching me valuable lessons in the home arts, and I have much time and learning to make up for."

They stood very close as he handed her the apron. "You are an excellent pupil, Samantha. I am certain you have learned much in a short time." His smile made her heart squeeze.

She reached up to touch the dark wave of hair that fell across his forehead and let her fingers trail down to his strong jaw. How was it this good and handsome man loved her?

Without a word, Sterling gathered her up in his arms and kissed her soundly for a long moment. Breathless, she clung to him until she regained her balance and then stepped back to look up at him, his arms still around her. "How am I so blessed?" she asked softly.

"I ask myself that same question hourly," he told her seriously. He pulled her toward him again, resting his chin on her hair. "And I love you more every day."

"Thank you for loving me," she said against his chest. "I don't know why you do, but I am ever so glad."

After a moment, Sterling eased her away from him, his large hands on her shoulders. "I think Elizabeth Barrett Browning said it best:

'How do I love thee? Let me count the ways.
I love thee to the depth and breadth and height
My soul can reach, when feeling out of sight.'"

Samantha smiled in remembrance and joined him in the recitation:

"'For the ends of being and ideal grace.
I love thee to the level of every day's
Most quiet need, by sun and candle-light.
I love thee freely, as men strive for right.
I love thee purely, as they turn from praise.
I love thee with the passion put to use
In my old griefs, and with my childhood's faith.
I love thee with a love I seemed to lose
With my lost saints. I love thee with the breath,
Smiles, tears, of all my life; and, if God choose,
I shall but love thee better after death.'"

As they finished the famous words, they stood there in the mansion's large entryway, ceiling high above them, smooth, polished floor beneath them, thinking how aptly the poet described what they each felt.

Sterling lowered his hands from her shoulders and Samantha spoke. "I don't like thinking about that last part of the poem, but I believe that is exactly what my father has done."

"He has loved your mother more after death?" Sterling questioned.

Samantha nodded. "Yes. Although he loved her so completely in life, that seems an impossibility."

"What a beautiful legacy," Sterling said thoughtfully. "For all his faults, it sounds as if he truly knew how to love what was most dear to him."

"Yes, he did," Samantha agreed. "I must remember that." She smiled again. "Now, I must return this to the kitchen," she held up the soiled apron, "and inform Mrs. Dolittle that we will be in the library. She has some knitting to do and will join us there."

Soon Sterling followed Samantha into the large library that had long been both a refuge and a schoolhouse for her. On the end of one bookshelf was posted a child's recreation of the new Ohio state flag, which had just recently been adopted, though Ohio had become a state nearly one hundred years ago, back in 1803. As the 17th state accepted to the union, it was the only state flag that was not rectangular in design, but was instead a swallow-tail burgee.[1] When he asked Samantha about the banner, she explained that Katherine's little sister had made it at school and offered it to her in a fit of generosity after Samantha helped her with an end-of-year writing assignment. She thought it made a nice addition to the wood panel and he agreed.

Every wall of the library held floor-to-ceiling shelves and every shelf was filled with books of all sizes, types, and descriptions. Sterling had spent time inside many libraries, but never one this extensive inside a personal residence. And he had spent countless hours inside the finest mansions of the affluent horse country of Lexington, Kentucky, including his family's own.

"Oh my," he breathed. "No wonder you felt no need to attend the college! No wonder you spent hours reading every day for years! What a fount of learning these must be." He craned his neck and walked in a slow circle, trying to take it all in.

Samantha thrilled at his appreciation of the room that had been such a friend to her throughout her lonely growing up years. She let him look a moment more and then took his hand and led him to the small table near the large window. "Here is where I wrote that poem," she told him, "as well as many other things."

"It's your special spot," he noted, taking in the scene. "With that view of the gorgeous maple and the grounds beyond, one could not help but be inspired here!"

"No," she agreed. "Though I have experienced many moments of frustration as well."

"Undoubtedly," Sterling nodded. "All great writers do. It makes the moments of flow all the more poignant."

Mrs. Dolittle entered then, gave them a cheery wave, and settled herself in a cushioned chair on the opposite side of the room. She pulled out a couple pairs of men's socks to darn, as well as her knitting, and set to. It looked as if she would be busy for a while.

---

1. https://en.wikipedia.org/wiki/Flag_of_Ohio

Following her example, Sterling and Samantha sat at the small table and began their own work. Sterling spread a few books in front of him: science, mathematics, English grammar and vocabulary. Toward the end of the last school year, he had discovered that when the different subjects overlapped each other, corresponded and connected, the boys tended to learn the concepts of all of them better. Now, in planning his curriculum for next year, he wanted to facilitate that connection between the subjects as best he could. He set to work and was soon engrossed in his lesson planning, trying not to be distracted by Samantha's presence.

Samantha dived into what had become her daily Bible study, loving the language and wisdom of Proverbs. After reading a few chapters and writing down the thoughts or questions that came to her mind, or things she learned, she paused and flipped back to the pages just inside the front cover. This Bible she held in her hands was the well-worn but well-kept Bible her mother had lovingly used throughout her life. Samantha had recently located it here in the library and clasped it to her bosom literally and figuratively. She loved finding her mother's notes written in the margins in her neat hand, or certain words underlined that must have had particular meaning for her mother. It felt like another window into her mother's soul, another connection to the woman she had never known.

Previously she was overjoyed to discover a couple pages of family information written neatly inside the front cover. Ever since her trip to Worthington, she had wanted to start the process of locating other relatives, and thought this Bible might be the right place to start. Now, as she looked at the names that possibly represented living family members, the image of her mother's gravestone came into her mind:

Lovenia Lewis Jennings

1858-1885

Beloved wife, mother, daughter, sister...

This simple statement meant Samantha might have living grandparents, aunts, and uncles! She traced the names on the Bible pages until she reached her mother's. Right above Lovenia were listed her parents, Joseph and Julia Lewis. And alongside Lovenia's name were three siblings: Eleanor, Samuel, and Irene. *Aunt Eleanor, Aunt Irene, and Uncle Samuel!* Samantha thought with a thrill. Surely some of them were still alive!

Then she had a sudden thought that squeezed her heart. Samuel... Samantha... Their root was the same. Was she named after her uncle, her mother's beloved brother? Lovenia would have fit right in between Samuel and Irene, as written here in the pages of the

Bible. Samantha's desire to meet more family suddenly grew in a great leap and she inhaled sharply as she thought of the possibilities.

Sterling raised his head and looked at her questioningly. "What is it?" he asked.

Samantha smiled apologetically. "Sorry, I didn't mean to disturb you. I was just think-ing about who these family members are and how I might find them."

Sterling moved his chair close to hers and read where she pointed. "What a marvelous find! Do you think they live in Worthington?"

"That is where I will start," Samantha affirmed. "This is really all the information I have to go on, so it isn't much."

Sterling nodded. "We will have to be detectives," he said, with a theatrical raise of one dark eyebrow. "I, Dr. Watson, will assist you, Sherlock, in any way I can."

Samantha laughed. "I appreciate that, Dr. Watson. I will let you know when your services are needed. Until then, please return to your side of the table. I did not mean to distract you from your work."

They both glanced at Mrs. Dolittle across the room and saw her head slumped in sleep and the knitting needles dropped into her lap.

"Your very presence is a distraction," Sterling whispered, winking and kissing her cheek, then moving his chair back to its original position.

They worked at their separate tasks for another hour or so, Sterling making adequate progress with his record-making and lesson planning. Samantha, her thick spectacles resting against her upturned nose, drafted a letter to her eldest aunt, Eleanor. She did not have an address for her, of course, but she was determined to find one somehow.

She knew that some counties had directory books, so she started searching for one among the shelves, even though she knew it might be a long shot. It was true that, though she had never seen one in here before and was very familiar with these books, she still came upon things unexpectedly, at times, as in the case of finding her mother's journal months ago. But as she continued her search, her frustration only mounted until, about half an hour later, she decided to give up and think of another method. She returned to the table, removed her spectacles, and stared off into the distance deep in thought. What documentation might be available in this house that would provide an address for even one of her relatives?

Sterling looked up from his study and watched her for a moment. "You didn't find what you were looking for," he stated simply.

Samantha shook her head. "I need more information in order to contact my aunts and uncle, maybe even my grandparents." The thought of relatives struck her again, as if for the first time, as it often had over the last few weeks. "Grandparents!" she said in wonder. "That may be too much to hope for, but at least one of these people must still be alive." She gestured at the old Bible in front of her, still open to the front pages. "Even with you actually living in Worthington, you cannot go traipsing about the whole town looking for Lewises. We must have *something* else to go on."

Sterling admitted that would be helpful, then mused, "What about a letter sent here to your mother after she moved to Oberlin? Do you think your father would have kept any correspondence?"

Samantha's eyes brightened. "You are right! He might have."

Sterling's gaze intensified. "Do you want to ask him?" He knew that talking to her father was something of an event.

She thought a long moment, eyes focused elsewhere, then nodded and took a deep breath. Reaching across the small table, she took Sterling's strong hand in hers. "Will you come with me?"

He squeezed it gently. "I will."

"Things might get a little…uncomfortable," she cautioned. "I have saved up so much to tell him and to ask him, and he never responds the way I expect. Last time, my frustration and emotion took over more than I intended…" She gave him a pained expression.

"I am here for you," he told her firmly. "I'm not afraid of frustration or emotion. If you need to lean on me, I will be right there beside you."

"Thank you." Samantha exhaled slowly and then stood up, releasing his hand. Sterling came to stand by her, putting an arm around her and pulling her close for a moment. Then together they stepped quietly out of the library, leaving behind a still sleeping Mrs. Dolittle.

***

Many of the doors they passed were closed, but whenever he saw one open, Sterling noted furniture inside covered with drapes to keep off the dust. They reached a staircase and Samantha, holding up her skirts with one hand, led him up to the landing on the second floor. Another long hallway stretched in both directions, with doors indicating another several rooms. But Samantha led him up another flight of stairs to the third floor, where the ceiling was lower and there were fewer rooms. The air here smelled musty and unused. "Father is the only one who spends any time up here," she explained. "Mrs. Dolittle comes up to give him his meals three times a day, but otherwise he's left alone."

Sterling nodded, his mouth suddenly dry. He was about to meet the father of the woman he loved and he did not quite know what to expect, though he knew it might be awkward. No matter; he was here to support Samantha however he could.

They stepped to a door at the far end of the hall and Samantha paused, letting go of Sterling's hand and smoothing her skirts for a moment. Then she knocked once, twice, three times. After a pause, they heard a rustle on the other side of the door and Samantha called, "Father? It's Samantha. May I come in?"

After another long pause, they heard a tired male voice say, "Enter."

Samantha took hold of the doorknob and turned it slowly, then pushed the door open. Her father sat in front of the window at his desk, much as he had the last time she spoke to him. But this time, he turned in his chair when she entered and looked up at her. His gray hair and beard were slightly disheveled and his blue eyes looked weary.

"Hello, Father," Samantha offered softly. "How are you?"

Basil Jennings waved a hand vaguely in the air without answering, and then asked, "How have you been, daughter?" He caught sight of Sterling behind her and slowly stood, but said nothing.

"I am well. I came to tell you that I was successful in Worthington a few weeks ago."

Professor Jennings looked at her questioningly, and she nodded. "I found Mother's grave and my brother's grave too."

Her father closed his eyes and seemed to struggle within himself for a minute or two. Samantha looked back at Sterling and he grasped her hand with a firm grip, stepping forward to stand beside her.

"Good," Basil said at last. "It is good you found what you sought."

"Yes," Samantha affirmed. "It was a singular moment for me. I was so glad to have dear friends with me to help in my search and to give me the support I needed. Thank you for providing the means to make the trip possible."

Professor Jennings waved a hand again, as if to dismiss his part in it.

"I wish you had come too, Father," Samantha said suddenly, surprising herself. "It might have helped you as well."

Her father shook his head. "No. Not yet."

Samantha let that stand, deciding that the word "yet" brimmed with potential hope. No one said anything for a long moment before she remembered she had not made introductions. "Father, this is Lee Sterling. Sterling, this is my father, Basil Jennings."

Sterling reached forward, hand outstretched, and Basil slowly leaned forward to let him clasp his hand. "So good to meet you, sir," Sterling offered in his deep, strong voice. "I did a short stint at Oberlin College last year and your name was mentioned more than once with great respect. Apparently, you made quite the impact while you were there."

Professor Jennings blinked, then looked closer at Sterling, his eyes seeming to clear briefly. "They still remember me?" he asked, sounding baffled.

Sterling nodded and smiled. "They do indeed, sir."

The old man seemed too stunned to say anything more on the matter, but gestured questioningly at the two young people in his doorway, his bushy eyebrows raised.

Samantha guessed what the look meant and continued the introduction. "Sterling is the young writing teacher I mentioned last summer, the one I studied with. He taught me how to write, how to verbalize what I have learned throughout all my years of reading. It was just what I needed," she ended quietly.

Professor Jennings nodded slowly. "I see. And now?" In an unexpectedly observative way, he indicated their clasped hands.

Samantha colored slightly, taken off guard that he would notice, when he never seemed to notice anything. But Sterling smiled and offered an explanation that was so open and honest it surprised all of them. "We fell in love, sir, quite unexpectedly and quite completely. But in the meantime, I moved to Worthington and we did not reconnect until a couple of weeks ago when I came back to see her."

"Ah." Her father's expression was absolutely unreadable and Samantha could not tell if he approved or not.

"At any rate, I wanted to ask you something," she hurried on. "It would mean so much to me to connect with Mother's family in Worthington. I found their names in her Bible, but I have no addresses for any of them. Are there letters from any of the Lewises that you have kept, with addresses included?" Her heart pounded and she unconsciously held her breath.

Her father sat back down in thought, and then nodded slowly. "There may be letters saved among her things in the attic. I...I could not bear to go through her effects when she...passed. I believe her friends gathered them up and placed them there, but I cannot say for certain what was retained." He passed a hand wearily over his grizzled face and looked away.

Samantha felt a pang of sadness. Her father still mourned. She did not want to distress him further, but she was glad she had asked. "Oh, that is helpful! I never realized... Do you mind if I look through them?"

Basil shook his head. "No. Consider it all yours. She would have wanted you to have it."

"Thank you, Father." She stepped forward and clasped one of his knobby, veined hands in hers. "Thank you."

He raised his other hand and awkwardly patted her cheek. "They should have been yours long ago," he admitted, regretfully. "I am sorry you did not know about them until now." He lowered his hand and Samantha stepped back.

"That's all right. Better late than never!"

He gestured to a book on the desk behind him. "I think you want this back, but I am not yet ready to part with it."

Samantha knew it was her mother's journal and her heart dropped. She had so wanted it in her possession again, to hold it in her hands and re-read her mother's words. But she could wait. Her father probably needed it more than she did right now. She nodded in acknowledgement. "I understand."

He looked at her with something like relief, and Samantha felt her heart soften toward him a little more. "Thank you for the information, Father." She looked at Sterling, unsure of what more to say, and he stepped in again.

"A pleasure to meet you, sir. You have a wonderful daughter who teaches me many things daily. I hope we meet again soon." He turned toward the door and held out a hand to Samantha. She took it, smiling gratefully. Together they stepped out of the room and Sterling closed it quietly behind them.

***

Up in the attic, Samantha knelt in front of an old wooden trunk with a creaky lid and stale smell of dust and aged wood. Sterling joined her and they sorted through the items together. "This was definitely my mother's," Samantha said quietly, lifting out a few items of women's clothing from a bygone era. She placed them on a crate nearby and reached in again. She admired a small stack of handkerchiefs bordered with fine tatted lace, initialed with "LLJ" in exquisite embroidery. And when she found a small framed photograph of her parents' wedding day, she lifted it out in amazement, inhaling sharply. "A real photograph!" she exclaimed. "This is even better than the picture Mrs. Ridgewood gave me. Look how young they were!" Her eyes shimmered with emotion as she held it up to show Sterling.

He examined the photograph with interest, noting the resemblance between mother and daughter. While Lovenia's hair was dark, a contrast to Samantha's fair locks, the oval shape of Lovenia's face, the high cheekbones, delicate chin, and pert nose were the same. Standing next to a much younger-looking Basil Jennings, she stood a few inches shorter than Samantha did to him now, and was very thin. He remembered Samantha saying something about her mother having frail health much of her life, so no doubt that was why she looked fragile. Basil was clean-shaven, his light-colored hair neatly combed back and unfaded. They wore wedding attire and both beamed with happiness, Lovenia holding to Basil's arm with one hand, her other hand in his large one. Sterling found he could not take his eyes off the photograph. Happy, Basil looked vastly different!

Samantha rubbed Sterling's arm. "Now you are the one getting misty-eyed!" she observed gently.

Sterling blinked and ran a hand over his eyes, chuckling. "I guess I am. They just look so...joyful!"

Samantha nodded. "They certainly do. I will be taking this back to my room. It should be on display, not hidden in this trunk." She placed the photograph gently on top of her mother's clothing, then carefully lifted out a small cream-colored bundle and traced the beautiful stitching with one finger. "This must have been the tiny baby clothing she made for my brother." Her expression was sad and Sterling squeezed her arm comfortingly.

"Maybe you wore them, too," he said. "Look, they have a few stains, so they were used at some point."

She peered closer to see what he meant. "You are right!" Gently rubbing the cloth, she imagined herself as a baby, motherless, with a grieving father. "It's hard to believe I was ever this small, isn't it?"

Sterling smiled. "I am sure you were the light of your father's life."

Samantha looked at him thoughtfully. "Do you really think so?"

"You are for me," he said, his brown eyes soft.

Samantha smiled at him gratefully. "You know, it was not as difficult talking to my father this time as I expected. Thank you for being there with me."

"I was glad to be of some small service, and happy to meet him." He paused a moment, his head cocked a little to one side. "You know, I don't think he is trying to be difficult or neglectful. He simply seems weary and...and very sad, like he is still grieving. Maybe he is in a slump he can't get out of by himself."

"Hmm." Samantha nodded slowly. "Maybe he is tired of being sad and is ready for a change and a new direction."

Sterling looked at her questioningly. "It sounds as if you have something in mind."

"I think I may. I'm still mulling it over..." She trailed off. "For now, let us see if we can find any letters in here." She rummaged around some more, and while everything was of interest to her, she did not find any correspondence. Disappointed, she stood and stretched her back. "I guess this search will take longer than I hoped. But," she gestured around the attic, "at least now I know where to look." She carefully placed the items back in the trunk with Sterling's assistance and they closed the heavy lid. Then she picked up the wedding photograph and they made their way to the rectangular hole in the floor with its dropdown ladder. Sterling held the framed picture while Samantha carefully descended, skirts in hand, then reached down to hand her the picture and followed her down the ladder.

When they reached the main floor, Mrs. Dolittle was just closing the library door behind her. She looked refreshed, but a little sheepish. "You two should have awakened me!" she told them. "I'm afraid all that bottling this morning tired me out a bit. I am not turning out to be the best chaperone, am I?" She chuckled and rubbed her face with one hand. "I am sorry. This old body is wearing down."

"It's all right, Mrs. Dolittle," Samantha laughed, patting her shoulder. "We went up to talk to Father."

Surprise registered in Mrs. Dolittle's dark eyes. "Did you now?" she intoned. "I'm glad. The sight of you two, a happy couple, might just lift his spirits."

"Oh, I hope so." Samantha held up the framed photograph for Mrs. Dolittle to see. "And look what we found in a trunk in the attic!"

The old housekeeper clasped her hands together in delight. "Oh, Samantha! For years, I have wondered where that ended up. Lovenia used to keep it on her vanity in her room where she could see it every day." Mrs. Dolittle smiled fondly at the picture. "Seeing that brings back so many memories." She laughed and blinked a couple times, then waved a hand at them. "You had better take it away before I turn into a puddle right here in the hallway."

Samantha understood completely, of course. "I shall put it up in my room. But for now, I was thinking of having our luncheon under the big maple out back. Do we have any picnic items?"

"Oh, my, yes." Mrs. Dolittle wiped her eyes again and sprang into action, seeming glad to have something immediate to do. She led the way to the kitchen, Samantha and Sterling following behind.

Chapter 4

INSPIRATION and FIREFLIES

June 1902

The weather had dried out significantly and the ground was no longer a soggy mess but instead a brilliant green carpet of grass, perfect for a picnic lunch. The air was warm and pleasant and Samantha lifted her face to the sunshine, eyes blissfully closed. Her dusky lavender skirt spread around her on the blanket and she drew her knees up to her chest, her arms around them.

Sterling lay stretched out nearby on the soft turf, hat tilted halfway over his eyes to shade them, watching Samantha with pleasure. The sunshine lit up the red in her braided and pinned golden hair, and it seemed to glow like a halo.

"You've missed the sun," he observed.

"Yes," she agreed, eyes still closed. "Something about it just makes me happy."

"It seems many things make you happy."

She smiled and turned to look at him. "That is true. I have found joy in many new things over this past year."

Sterling waited, expectant, and she felt him listening, so she elaborated. "Things like writing, flowers, good conversation, friends, discovering family and God, seeing the sun after what seems like weeks of rain..." She trailed off. There were so many more!

"That sounds like the beginnings of a poem," Sterling observed. Then he cocked an eyebrow, "Do I factor in there anywhere?"

She laughed delightedly and pretended to think long and hard before saying, "You're somewhere between good conversation and friends."

He nodded sagely. "Friends. I'm glad we're that."

"Me too, Sterling." She nudged his leg with her foot. "That's important," she said seriously. "I believe trust and friendship belong in a relationship like ours."

"Indeed," he agreed, sitting up. He leaned forward and smiled. "Especially if friends are allowed to do this," he said, and kissed her.

She laughed and playfully pushed him away. "Lie back down," she said scoldingly. "I want to tell you what I have been thinking about."

Sterling obediently complied and looked at her expectantly, propped up on one elbow and readjusting his hat. "I'm all ears."

Samantha straightened her legs out in front of her and leaned back against the maple tree, smoothing her skirts. "Ever since I read in my mother's journal about her desire to turn this into a school," she gestured at the large house behind them, "I have been thinking about doing that very thing. But," she added hurriedly, "I am not a teacher. I have never run anything, nor do I feel qualified to do so. All of this is in the thinking stages."

She began talking faster as she verbalized her thoughts for the first time. "I have wondered what our focus could be here, which people in our community are most in need and who we could serve best. I have thought about simple logistics: Would students and faculty be housed here? How many students could we take? How would we feed them? And how would we find good teachers who would have the same vision for the school that we do? Oh, sometimes the questions are enough to make my head explode!" She sighed and curled her legs under her as she leaned forward in her excitement. "Sterling, I'm not trained for such a venture, but the ideas keep coming to me and the thoughts will not leave me alone!"

He sat up and watched her intently, feeling the depth of her earnestness. "Are you writing these ideas down? Maybe the inspiration comes from a Higher Source."

"I thought of that, and I am. I have a notebook just for that purpose, in the house. And then," she continued in a rush, gesturing to a little book by her side, "for no apparent reason other than interest, I started reading this book." She held it up.

"*Up from Slavery* by Booker T. Washington," he supplied. "Yes, you mentioned it. What are you finding?"

"Well, I had no idea that it would speak to me so strongly! It is as if Mr. Washington is talking directly to me—just at the exact time when I am already thinking about the possibilities of starting a school." She looked hard at Sterling and he was struck by her strength and determination. "Again, I have to believe that God is in the details," she continued. "It cannot be just a coincidence."

"Tell me more," he said, dark brows drawn together in concentration. "What does Mr. Washington say?"

"Well," she leaned against the tree again and opened the book, flipping through the pages. "Here, for example." She placed a finger under the words to mark her place while she explained. "He relates his experience at Hampton Institute, a school for colored[1] people—and the only one in the South at the time. Before he went there, he had had very little education, but when he found out about Hampton, it became his all-consuming goal to somehow make his way there and learn all he could. Sterling," she said, shaking her head in disbelief, "he had to walk five hundred miles! And then he had to convince administrators to hire him to do custodial work to earn his keep[2], as he had no money." Her eyes were still wide with amazement. "That kind of determination inspires me."

She looked down at the book again. "He says here:

'...At Hampton, for the first time, I learned what education was expected to do for an individual. Before going there I had a good deal of the then rather prevalent idea among our people that to secure an education meant to have a good, easy time, free from all necessity for manual labour. At Hampton I not only learned that it was not a disgrace to labour, but learned to love labour, not alone for its financial value, but for labour's own sake and for the independence and self-reliance which the ability to do something which the world wants done brings. At that institution I got my first taste of what it meant to live a life of unselfishness, my first knowledge of the fact that the happiest individuals are those who do the most to make others useful and happy.'"[3]

---

1. The correct term in 1902.

2. https://bit.ly/3Ol4Iu9, https://www.hilbert.edu/social-justice-activists/booker-t washington

3. (*Up From Slavery* by Booker T. Washington, p. 84 of Libby version on phone)

"Hmm. He makes a good point," Sterling interjected thoughtfully. "Oberlin College had a similar policy at the beginning, thus their motto: Labor and Learning. Deserving students lacking the means to pay for their education could work for it instead."[4]

Samantha nodded. "Now that you mention it, I remember learning about that in school." She flipped ahead several pages in the book, scanned over the words, and looked back up at him. "Washington talks here about another school he attended later in Washington, D.C., in 1878.[5] He explains how he learned many wonderful things there but also noticed that the students were better dressed and gave more attention to outward appearances. Because most of those students had their expenses paid for them, they seemed to him to be less self-independent. At Hampton he had to work so hard to earn his tuition and board that he gained a great sense of independence and the respect of others in the process. His education therefore meant everything to him in a way that those other students could never understand. As he considered the contrast between that school and Hampton, he says that at the latter, 'The student was constantly making the effort through the industries to help himself, and that very effort was of immense value in character-building.'"[6]

Sterling nodded thoughtfully, his mind whirling.

"So, he felt like the students at the school in D.C. did not have as solid a foundation as the students at Hampton, for they had no industrial training and, when they graduated, knew less about life and the real world. Besides this, since they were more used to comfortable living, they were less likely to want to go into poor places and help people there, which Mr. Washington feels is one especially important reason for obtaining an education in the first place."[7]

---

4. https://www.oberlin.edu/about-oberlin/oberlin-history

5. https://www.history.com/topics/black-history/booker-t-washington, https://www.history.com/topics/black-history/booker-t-washington

6. *Up From Slavery* by Booker T. Washington, p. 97 of Libby version on phone

7. *Up From Slavery* by Booker T. Washington, pp. 96-97 of Libby version on phone

"Helping people," Sterling echoed. "Industry. Yes. That makes sense to me. That makes perfect sense! It was that independence that I sought in breaking away from my mother's entitlement mentality and going to college myself. And I wanted to do something to help others, to really work." Now he was the one leaning forward. "So you want to start a school that will educate but also teach real life skills and give opportunity to help others. And you want students to work for their keep, to gain self-respect and self-reliance."

Samantha, flushed from excitement, nodded and beamed at him. "That is it exactly!" She gave a laugh of delight. "I knew you would understand." Then she paused and wrinkled her brow in mild consternation. "And yet...this is not really my house to use how I want, so I am putting the cart before the horse, I am afraid."

"You mean, your father owns the house and makes all decisions for its use..."

"Yes, and I have not spoken to him about any of this. I am not sure if he would approve or not." She looked deflated.

"Well, first things first," he said, upbeat. "Great results stem from great ideas."

Her eyes brightened again. "Then you *do* think it a good idea?"

"A great one," he agreed. "And were you hoping to involve your father in running the school or teaching?"

"Yes," she said slowly. "I know he found so much fulfillment as a professor, and I wonder if he might be ready to have that in his life again. It would be different teaching children, of course, but it may be just what he needs."

Sterling looked thoughtful for a moment. "It just may be," he agreed. "Children can be so accepting, and forgiving of faults. And they are inquisitive and ask great questions. Such an environment might be a wonderful thing for your father and give him a new sense of purpose."

"Yes! And did I tell you that Mrs. Dolittle attended Oberlin as a young woman?"

"Did she now..." Sterling seemed only mildly surprised, but intrigued.

"She could be a teacher for the school, as well! I mean, if she wanted to. Of course, if she agrees to help with the school we would also need her expertise in handling the kitchen, or at least overseeing it."

"Indeed. The children would be the most well fed of any in Ohio, I would warrant," Sterling laughed. "Would your school be for colored[8] children?"

She laid the book down beside her again and considered. "I don't really want to dictate a particular race. I think need is what is important here, and there are children of various races who are in difficult circumstances but wanting to learn and gain opportunities. I would like it to be open to any and all who fit that description."

"I think that is a wonderful and noble objective."

Samantha's gray eyes were as full of light as her hair was lit by the sun, and for a moment, Sterling felt as if he were in the presence of an angel from heaven. He moved to sit beside her against the tree and pulled one of her hands into his lap. He traced the long, tapered fingers for a moment and then looked into her questioning face. "You are so lovely," he told her honestly. "You don't realize how enchanting you are, do you?"

Her stunned expression momentarily gave way to a softening, teasing one. "I think that fairy ring last summer really did work, after all. Its spell has distorted your eyesight."

"No," he said, seriously. "It's you. You enchanted me before we ever found those toadstools in the woods. It was no magic that caught my heart; your goodness and light did that. I love your strong moral sense and your quick mind, how you are always thinking of others, yet are innately confident in yourself. You are lovely in every way," he reiterated, still tracing her fingers with his own.

Samantha's heart somersaulted and her eyes glistened with unshed tears. "Thank you," she said simply. "I think that is the nicest thing anyone has ever said to me."

"It's true, every word of it," Sterling said, lifting her hand to his lips and kissing it softly.

***

Katherine sat across from Samantha on the horsehair sofa in the parlor where Mrs. Dolittle had served them a light late morning meal. "You have read a great number of books," she said. "What do you think our book club should read this month?"

---

8. "Colored" was the correct term at that time.

Samantha smiled wryly. Referring to Katherine's first statement, she said, "That is an understatement. But there is so much I have not yet read! It depends on what type of book the club wishes to read. It is only recently that I have branched into fiction."

"That is my preference," Katherine admitted. "I am not as interested in biographies, history, and scientific works as you are, and I think many of the other ladies may be of the same mind. My mother is hosting this month's meeting and I have a couple of books to recommend, but I wanted to see what you might suggest."

"Well, if it is fiction you want, then I don't even have to think twice. I am learning, much to my surprise, that fiction teaches through imagination in a way quite as effective as teaching through facts."

Katherine's blue eyes smiled back at Samantha as brightly as her mouth. "What are you reading that so impresses you?"

"Have you read *Jane Eyre* by Charlotte Bronte?" Samantha asked.

"No, but I believe my mother owns a copy of it," Katherine replied. "So, you think it worth my time, I take it? Even though it is fiction?" she teased.

"I do," Samantha nodded. "I think I appreciate it more now than I would have, had I read it even a year ago. From a writer's perspective, I am in awe of Bronte's ability to describe characters and convey emotions, to understand and portray different personalities, complex life situations, and burdening trials. And," she added, hesitantly, "to describe the varied emotional states of romance, now that I know what it is to be in love…"

Katherine laughed delightedly and clapped her hands.

But Samantha wasn't finished. "It is really quite a remarkable love story, with heartbreak and sacrifice and joy unspeakable. And Jane's moral convictions in the face of the greatest temptation imaginable is astounding. I am not to the end yet, but I really hope there is eventual redemption and reunification."

"It sounds wonderful! You have me intrigued; I will certainly recommend it. But…" she looked coyly at her friend, "it is your own love story I am most interested in right now. I can see that Sterling makes you very happy."

"Can you?" Samantha felt herself flushing a bit and looked down at her lap momentarily. "Yes, he really does make me happy. And I think I make him happy too." She looked up at her friend again, smiling back at her. "He really is wonderful. He understands me and we have so much to talk about. We want the same things in life and find the same things important."

Katherine nodded. "I am not surprised at all. You had that connection before, from what you told me months ago, and now it has only deepened."

"Yes," Samantha said simply. "I am happier than I have ever been."

"I'm so glad," Katherine said. "You deserve such happiness."

"As do you," Samantha replied. "How are things with Rupert?"

"They are going well! When you saw us at the cafe, that was our third outing together. We have been courting regularly since our return from Worthington and..." she trailed off. Now it was Katherine's turn to color a becoming shade of pink.

"And you like it," Samantha supplied. "You like him."

Katherine nodded. "I do. Several young men have courted me, most of them much more debonair than our humble Rupert, but... There is just something about him. He is so unassuming and selfless and good and kind."

"Yes," Samantha agreed. "I recognized all those attributes in him as well. You really cannot find anyone more genuine than Rupert."

"No, and I appreciate it all the more because of the other young men I have met. They were mostly good and interesting people," she hastened to add. "They just were not the diamond in the rough that Rupert is. I feel like I needed that experience before meeting him, to appreciate his goodness."

Samantha nodded in complete understanding. "Life has been working that way for me as well. I keep finding that as I seek God's direction and then strive to follow it, He allows things to fall into place in the right order, to build upon each other."

Katherine looked at her fondly. "My wise friend, who sees things so clearly."

"Oh, not always," Samantha laughed. "Remember when I was in the midst of missing Sterling so much and had no idea if he had feelings for me or if he would ever return?"

"And then he did return!" Katherine exclaimed. "More in love with you than you imagined!"

"I know," Samantha murmured, looking into the distance and rubbing one finger against her lips. "Skinny, plain Samantha—and he finds me lovely!" she said in wonder.

"He sees you as you are," Katherine said decidedly. "I daresay you are more honest and authentic than any young woman he has known before—at least, I am guessing that is the case, knowing his background."

Samantha nodded thoughtfully and refocused her gaze on her friend. "And yet, even with his affluent and privileged background, he is well grounded and practical, while at the same time a visionary. And so kind. And so romantic…"

Katherine giggled and Samantha laughed too.

"Would you like to come to a recital I am singing in next week?" Katherine asked suddenly. "You could bring Sterling and mingle a bit with our other friends and towns-people."

"I think he would like that!" Samantha exclaimed. "And I know I would love to come. I always enjoy listening to you sing."

"Thank you," Katherine said modestly. "It is people like you who deeply appreciate the artistic efforts of others that make it all worthwhile. It is a pleasure to bring music to life when you are there enjoying it."

***

The following week, when Samantha attended the recital with Sterling, Claire, and Mrs. Dolittle, she was swept away in the ethereal beauty of the music, but in particular the song sung so expertly by her dear friend. She had heard Katherine sing several times before, but never a song such as this! It was a piece from an opera by Mozart called *The Magic Flute*, and the notes soared and dipped, reminding her of a bird. She marveled that Katherine's voice, with immense control and precision, could make such superb sounds. And she made it look so easy! What would it be like to bless others' lives in such a way?

Sterling was familiar with the song, as he had seen that particular opera performed in Lexington. He had attended operas often with his family, ever since he was old enough to behave and pay attention. But he confided in a whisper to Samantha that he was not very familiar with the German the piece was sung in. Though she wasn't either, Samantha realized she didn't need to understand the words to experience the emotion in them. She felt honored to be in attendance and to be the personal friend of such a talented singer. And when she glanced across the aisle at Rupert, sitting with a few of his family members, she knew he felt exactly the same. From the way he gazed at Katherine, Samantha could tell that not only was he in awe of her talent, beauty, and grace, but of the fact that such a person returned his love. Katherine sang only to him—and for him she was the only person in the room. Beside him, his little brothers saw his expression, elbowed one another, and clapped their hands over their mouths to keep from laughing out loud. But Samantha thought it was sweet. She was so happy for her two friends' newfound happiness in each other. And doubly happy to partake of beautiful music with her own love by her side.

***

"They're back!" Samantha exclaimed in delight. The shadows of evening were deepening as she and Sterling walked hand in hand near Plum Creek. It was a beautiful Ohio night and flashes of light filled the air around them. An insect brushed near her face and she heard the familiar short thrum, followed by a momentary burst of brightness, and then it was gone.

She stopped mid step and Sterling stopped with her, watching as the beetles took turns glowing, their upward motion making a "J" in flight before going out, then other insects taking their places. "What a lovely ending to a wonderful day," she sighed appreciatively, and Sterling squeezed her hand.

"Another incredible sunset," he observed, looking up as the sky above them blushed a brilliant pink and the sun sank lower behind the trees.

"It is," Samantha agreed, breathing in the humid air that was beginning to cool now that the sun had descended below the horizon.

She felt a deep peace settle over her. Ever since Sterling had returned, about three weeks ago now, she had felt a wonderful contentment and rightness that was difficult to describe. It was as if something in her soul had been missing and, now that he was here again, that piece had fallen into place, and she felt whole for the first time. Knowing their time together was limited, that summer sped swiftly on, she cherished each day as much as she could.

"Did you call them lightning bugs as a child, too?" he asked.

She tilted her head in thought. "I think so. Many people here do. But I was not very old before I found a book on insects in my father's library and learned that they are actually beetles and that their scientific name is *Lampyridae*."

He laughed his low, deep rumble. "Of course you did. And what else did you learn about the fascinating creatures?" He was teasing her, she knew, but he also wanted to know.

"Well, once I learned they lit up to attract mates, I quit catching them in jars. I thought they should be free to find love and I didn't want to interfere with that." Now it was her turn to laugh, as she remembered her young, impressionable self.

"That was very kind of you," he observed, the corner of his mouth still curved up on one side. "Did you know that the females are the ones that make the decision about which mate to accept?"

"I did." She looked at him in the twilight, his chiseled features appearing blunted in the near darkness. She couldn't help adding, "I think it very wise of nature to arrange things that way, don't you? Females can be very discerning, you know."

He chuckled and pulled her close. "I have noticed that lately, in a particular young woman. You would make an exceptionally good firefly."

She pushed him away playfully and darted quickly ahead of him. "And you would make a very good ant," she returned.

He caught up to her in one long stride and recaptured her hand. "Why an ant?" he asked. "Because I am so strong?" He was teasing her again.

"Yes, and so intelligent. Did you know ants are considered one of the smartest insects on earth?"

Sterling began to laugh. "I did *not* know that, but now I shall never forget it."

"See that you don't," she said in mock severity, as if she were a scolding schoolteacher.

"And thank you for the compliment."

Her seriousness evaporated and she laughed too.

"I love our conversations," Sterling said, squeezing her hand once more. "I have never met anyone else I can speak to about such a variety of topics."

Samantha squeezed back and thought about how, while that was true for her as well, saying so carried perhaps less weight than it did for Sterling, since she had been a recluse until the past year. But really, she could not have been more blessed to find such a friend and confidant in him as she had.

As darkness descended, fireflies winking around them, they turned back to the Jennings mansion and walked on in silence for a while.

"I loved watching and catching fireflies as a boy," Sterling mused, returning to their original topic. "I didn't have any tenderness for their love interests, as you did, but I would watch them for hours, winking in jars around my room at night. Mother didn't know I had them in there, or she would have had them carted out in a hurry!"

"Because of the old superstition?" Samantha wanted to know, remembering that some of the older generation believed if fireflies were found in the house it meant that someone would soon die.

"Yes, that—combined with her distaste for insects in the house—would have been more than she could handle. But they fascinated me! I wondered what made them glow and how they turned their light on and off, and I wished I understood their secret messages. They even inspired me to learn Morse code," he admitted with amusement.

"Me too!" Samantha laughed, gratified to find yet another connection with him. "So, if you needed to, you could change careers and operate a telegraph."

"No thank you," he said firmly, shaking his head. "But it did give me something to practice when I was bored or needed to keep my mind busy."

"It served a good purpose, then," she agreed. "And if we ever find ourselves turned into fireflies, needing to relay a message across a field from one another, we will be able to understand what the other is saying."

"Ah," he said, mock seriously. "That will be very useful. But I can tell you already what my message will say."

"What is that?" she asked, with a grin she knew he couldn't see in the near darkness.

"It will be: 'I love you and you are too far away.'"

"Mine will say the same," she replied, feeling her heart drop as she recognized the correlation between that scenario and the reality they would face at the end of the summer.

Sensing the change in mood between them, Sterling's voice turned sober. "I am glad we can write long letters to each other and not have to rely on dots and dashes."

"Exceedingly long letters," she agreed.

"This time with you has been wonderful," he told her. "It goes too quickly, but when I think back to that rainy day when I arrived on the train and saw you in town for the first time in several months..." He trailed off as the memory filled his mind.

"Yes," Samantha replied, knowing how he felt. "It hardly seems the same lifetime, does it?"

"Precisely. Sometimes I still pinch myself when I realize—again—where I am and whom I am with."

"I feel the same," Samantha said, meaning it.

Chapter 5

KNOCKS

June 1902

A loud knock sounded at the door the next morning. Samantha and Mrs. Dolittle looked at each other questioningly. They were tidying up in the kitchen after breakfast.

"That sounded like Sterling's knock," Samantha remarked, "but he does not usually come this early."

"My thoughts exactly," the older woman said, a concerned furrow in her brow. She wiped her wet hands on her apron and headed to the door. "I'll open it."

A minute later, she returned with Sterling in tow, Bible in hand. She was beaming while he looked determined. Samantha looked from one to the other, wondering what would cause such a contrast of expressions.

When Sterling saw her his face cleared, a smile transforming the soberness from a moment before.

"Good morning," Samantha said, smiling back. "What brings you here so early? We have only just had breakfast!"

"I know, and I didn't plan to arrive like this. In fact, I haven't even had breakfast myself." He put a hand to his head, as if to remove his hat, then realized he had forgotten to wear it. He grimaced with good humor and shrugged.

Mrs. Dolittle made a move as if to prepare food for him, but he stopped her with a gentle touch on the shoulder. "Thank you, but first I need my questions answered." He held up the Bible in response to Samantha's raised eyebrows. "In my study of the New Testament, I have started comparing the accounts in the four gospels and I just feel like I'm missing something." He lowered the tome and looked back and forth between the two women. "I want to better understand the culture of Jesus' time, but I don't have any reference books. As I asked Mrs. Dolittle at the door, I wonder if your father's library might contain any scholarly commentary on the New Testament."

"And as I told him," Mrs. Dolittle continued, "I am quite sure Lovenia had books like that filed away. She loved studying her Bible and learning all she could about the places where Jesus walked and the culture of his time."

Samantha tipped her head slightly to the side in thought, her brows now furrowed in contemplation. Sterling waited expectantly, watching her blonde lashes flit from one side to the other as she visualized the library in her mind. After a moment, her face brightened and her gaze shifted back to his. "Yes, I think I might know where to look. Are you sure you don't want to eat something first?"

Sterling shook his head quickly, the wavy lock over his forehead bouncing. "I feel compelled to at least find the right commentary first. I had a hard time falling asleep last night with all these questions swirling in my brain, and when I awoke this morning, they were still there!"

Samantha felt a warmth enter her heart at his words, thrilling at the realization that he sincerely shared her desire to know Jesus. She looked at Mrs. Dolittle and suddenly knew the reason for her happy expression a few moments before. "Well then," she said, tucking her hand into the crook of his arm, "let us go find these books! Would you mind helping us, Mrs. Dolittle?"

The housekeeper shook her head and smiled again. "I don't mind at all."

It took the three of them about half an hour to locate a few commentaries, which were located in different places in the library, rather than all together. Samantha was unsure why her mother had not placed them all in one place, but decided it was another indication that she personally needed to reorganize the books. The prospect seemed daunting!

Samantha and Sterling carried the books over to the round table near the window and settled themselves across from each other, each taking a small stack. When Mrs. Dolittle heard Sterling's stomach growl, she headed back to the kitchen, leaving the library door wide open.

"Thank you for helping me in this crazy, spontaneous search," Sterling said. "I don't really know why it is so important to me, but it is."

Samantha placed a hand on his arm across the table. "I understand! And I agree, it is important. Recently, I came to realize that getting to know my mother was a crucial step for me for many reasons, but especially because it led me to know Jesus better. He is the one I should focus on, as my mother did. And so, I, too, have been wishing I had something or someone to help me better understand His time and place. This will help us both!"

They dived into the books and were already deeply entrenched in their studies when Mrs. Dolittle returned a few minutes later with a loaded plate for Sterling.

After reading for a while, Samantha sat back to think about what she was learning. She lifted her spectacles and rubbed at the bridge of her nose. "Jesus truly was a revolutionary, wasn't he?" she mused.

Sterling looked up from the book in front of him. "What have you found?" he asked.

"I'm reading about women's place in the society of His time. If I think women don't have rights here and now, it was leagues worse for the women then! For Jesus to praise a woman, to give her time and care, was not something that was expected of a rabbi. He blessed and healed women, gave His mother special attention on more than one occasion, and even raised a young girl from the dead!"

Sterling watched her obvious delight as she articulated this information and felt a rush of gratitude. He loved that they were discovering faith together and making religious connections even in an academic setting.

"To me it feels like He was repeatedly showing not only that He values everyone, regardless of gender," she continued, "but also that He sees even the people society has made invisible. He doesn't view us the way everyone else might, but as we really are, and knows how to help us in our particular individual needs."

Sterling nodded, appreciating her insights. "He would have stayed with the status quo if He wanted to blend in and remain safe, but that wasn't His mission at all. He wanted to teach a new and better way of living, a kinder and more merciful way, a way that did not exclude anyone."

"Exactly! He did not even leave out the outcasts of society: the chronically ill, the mentally disturbed. That was incredibly revolutionary too! And after He died, His teachings continued to guide the apostles to understand that Christ's gospel needed to go forth to the Gentiles, not just to the Jews."

Sterling smiled. "Just as His love and healing are for every person on the earth, His gospel and sacrifice are for each of us. Not one of us is too sick, too dirty, or too ostracized to be outside His reach."

"Yes!" Samantha exclaimed. "And yet He won't force it on us. He is always there waiting and reaching, but it is up to each of us to reach back. I am so glad I found and know Him now." Her eyes were misty as she considered how much richer her life was, with this new lens through which to see everything. She felt that she could see better than she had before, and it had nothing to do with her spectacles.

They continued reading and sharing things with each other and Samantha opened her notebook to record impressions as she had them. Sterling noticed that the pad was about halfway full. As she flipped through it for a moment, it fell open to a page with what looked like a poem written on it. He was instantly interested and asked her about it.

"Oh, this is what I wrote after we saw the fireflies last night. I was so filled with thoughts and impressions that I just had to write them down."

Sterling grinned. "Sounds like me! What impressions did you have?" He leaned forward expectantly.

"Well," she said thoughtfully, "I kept thinking about how Jesus brought true light to the world because He is Light. And how many other things in the world with light can remind us of Him. Like fireflies."

Sterling looked at her, intrigued. "The firefly as a symbol," he returned. "Tell me more."

"Here," she said, pushing the notebook across the table. "See what you think."

Sterling took the page in eager fingers and read:

FIREFLIES

Glowing beads, like
Flashes of inspiration
Moving forward,
Pondering, zipping upward,
Trying again.
A spark in time reflects
A life's trajectory,
A mission most important,
Searching, moving forward and upward,
Forward and upward,
Illuminating the world for half a moment.
Luminance from the small, inconsequential
Giving light to darkness

For all the rest and
Inspiring thought where none was.
Gifting a morsel of beauty
To a mundane world,
Pointing to One who is light and love
And life.

He read it over again, slowly. He loved its visual nature, its joy and insight, and he told her as much. "You have so surpassed me in the art of writing poetry that I truly cannot claim any credit for being your teacher. You didn't learn that from me, and more's the pity!" He laughed and she smiled at him, glad he appreciated her writing efforts, even if no one else ever saw them.

"You know," she said, looking down at her hands as she thought about what she wanted to say. "I have thanked you, but I don't know if I ever fully expressed my gratitude for the path you set me on, Sterling." She looked up at him, her expression earnest. "Not just writing, either. You somehow saw a great potential in me when most people did not even see me at all. And you have always listened to my ideas and perspective. Truly listened. I don't think most men of our day typically do that with women."

He thought about that. She was probably right. But what caught him off guard was her open sincerity in thanking him for this thing he had unknowingly done. It touched him that she would express such deep gratitude for his simply being aware of her as a unique individual. And the depth of that sincerity made him suddenly realize that what she was really thanking him for was just *seeing* her. That was something each human being deserved, but obviously the world was an imperfect place filled with imperfect people.

She indicated the book in front of her. "In some ways, the status of women in Jesus' time is not that different from our time. We are the 'weaker sex,' we depend upon men for our support[1], we still have no voting rights, and not until 1887 with the passing of

---

1. http://ap.gilderlehrman.org/history-by-era/womens-history/essays/women-amer
ican-politics-twentieth-century

the Married Women's Property Act did we gain property rights.[2] As a country—as a world—we still have a long way to go."

Sterling looked regretful, as if he were the one responsible for such inequality.

Samantha continued. "Women are still second-class citizens in the eyes of many men of the world, and yet you see me as an intelligent person like yourself, worth listening to like another man—even of value as an advisor at times! I have the feeling Jesus did the same. He even had *disciples* who were women! It didn't matter what the accepted norms of His society were, He showed mutual respect and consideration to all. In your Bible studies, you now know that, but you didn't grow up religious." Her fair brows drew together in contemplation. "So why, Sterling? How did you learn to treat women like equals? Was it your parents?"

"I..." Sterling floundered, not having ever considered the question before. He thought back to his opulent life in Lexington, wondering what had made the difference. "I don't know," he admitted. "I have always tried to see everyone around me as equals, regardless of their gender, color, or station—sometimes with more success than others. Sometimes keeping that perspective was difficult to do when Mother insisted so often that the servants must stay in their place and we in ours."

He thought silently for a moment, a cloud passing over his expression that told Samantha he was remembering former times of conflict. "It is also true that Mother's very nature demands respect from those she associates with, and I can't remember her cowing to anyone. And when it comes to my father," he mused, "he never treated my mother as inferior. So perhaps I unconsciously picked up on some of that." His gaze returned to hers and he lifted his shoulders in a shrug.

Samantha nodded. "It is unfortunate her regard for herself does not extend to those of the supposed lower classes," she said tentatively, not wishing to say anything out of turn when she had never even met the woman.

---

2. https://scalar.case.edu/19th-at-100/womens-property-rights

"I completely agree," he nodded. "She only respects people in their particular station as long as they stay there. And, I am sorry to tell you, she refuses to employ Blacks.[3] As skilled as she is, Mrs. Dolittle would never find employment there."

Samantha looked at him, perplexed.

"It has never sat well with me either." His lips were a grim line. "As a young boy I realized one day that while all our servants and hired hands were white, my friend's properties were run by a variety of whites and Blacks. When I asked Father about it, he said it was to comply with my mother's wishes. Her parents were in favor of slavery and never could forgive Lincoln for freeing the slaves. They were part of the old South that held to those ways with determination. In fact, they blamed Blacks for causing the Civil War, saying they were 'uppity' and asked for more than they deserved."

Samantha blinked in astonishment. "Basic personal freedoms were more than they deserved?!" Growing up in abolitionist Oberlin she had never heard of such preposterous ideas.

Sterling's expression was pained. "I know. I am ashamed to belong to that legacy, though it is only on one side of the family. Jim Crow laws, strengthened by the Supreme Court's decision in *Plessy v. Ferguson*[4] a mere six years ago only gave supposed validity to this viewpoint and bias. At any rate, this is something Mother will never budge on." He shook his head and sighed. "Fortunately, Father's side of the family had no such willful blindness, so he has no quarrel with any race. But in a desire to maintain matrimonial harmony, he defers to Mother's desires." He pulled a face. "I think it does them both a disservice, quite honestly, but I am only a son and can do nothing about it. Especially as I am no longer eligible to take over the place and will not be making any future decisions about its upkeep." A sudden thought brought light back into his eyes. "Perhaps Lucas can bring about change one day..." he mused.

"I hope so," Samantha agreed. They were both quiet for a moment, and then she returned them to the topic at hand. "I am still lacking in my own experience, but I have

---

3. In 2024, the Chicago Manual of Style considers it correct to capitalize this term. In 1902, other terms would have been used instead.

4. https://education.nationalgeographic.org/resource/black-codes-and-jim-crow-laws /

observed enough couple's interactions and heard enough women's talk to know that it is common for women to be condescended to, demeaned—subtly or not—or treated like pets or ornaments."

"I have commonly observed that as well," Sterling admitted. "Yet I don't recall my father ever treating Mother that way. I suppose his deference to her strong personality gave me a different perspective than other men have." He shrugged again, unsure, and a smile tugged at one corner of his mouth. "But when it came to you, it was easy. Your potential was more obvious to me than anything had ever been, and your intelligence too. Our ensuing conversations only proved that as you began to open up." He grinned, remembering his initial astonishment at all her fine mind could remember and how clearly and forcefully she could express her opinions when pressed.

Memories flooded back to Samantha at his words and she couldn't help smiling back. Those had been good times: the beginning of a friendship moving toward love.

"Well," she said gratefully, "thank you for seeing me and for treating me as an equal. I think in that area I have been very blessed. Rupert did the same, and even Father, though our interactions are limited, never treats me the way I know many men treat their daughters."

Sterling smiled. "May this new century improve the perception and treatment of women all over the world. Of all races."

"Amen," Samantha agreed.

***

It was nearing lunchtime when they heard a frantic pounding at the door and looked at each other in concern.

"Are you expecting someone?" Sterling asked.

"No." Samantha's brows drew together in worry as the pounding continued. She stood quickly and he followed her lead as they ran out of the library and into the hallway. Mrs. Dolittle, rushing from the kitchen, reached the hall a little ahead of them, anxiety obvious in her expression. When she heaved open the front door, a woman stood there, weeping, and fell into her arms the moment she saw her. She was about the same height as Mrs. Dolittle, but younger and slimmer, with the same round face and large, dark eyes. Her glossy black hair was in contrast to her mother's gray, but Samantha could see the family resemblance immediately. She also noticed a large red welt on her cheek.

"Mother!" the woman sobbed. "I didn't know what to do! I'm sorry to just show up like this. But he threatened me so violently this time, and I didn't know where else to go!"

Mrs. Dolittle tsked at the mark on her daughter's cheek, touching it gingerly, then rocked her in her arms and murmured something, trying to offer comfort. Samantha's heart clenched at the sight and sound of such grief as the younger woman sobbed for a long moment.

Sterling's heart went out to her and he wondered what he could do to ease her obvious suffering.

"He swears he wants nothing to do with me anymore and I don't know how I shall support myself!" the woman wailed. "I'm so afraid! Oh, why is this happening, Mother?"

Mrs. Dolittle eased her daughter inside the house and Samantha moved forward to quietly close the door. Then she hovered, unsure if she should offer comfort and welcome, or retreat to allow them privacy.

Mrs. Dolittle noticed her hesitation and offered, "Lunch is just about ready and I think we could all do with some refreshment. Here, sweetheart." She offered her daughter a handkerchief from her apron pocket and tenderly began wiping her face.

The woman was probably about ten years older than Samantha, but in this moment her mother treated her as if she were a very young girl. The tenderness touched Samantha.

"You did right in coming here," Mrs. Dolittle soothed. "The Jennings are good people and we will do all we can to help you."

Her daughter nodded gratefully, taking the handkerchief and applying it to her nose.

"As for Phil, I don't know the right course of action either," Mrs. Dolittle said, "but we will figure it out together."

The woman nodded again and sniffled. Her eyes were red and swollen, having obviously cried for a long time before arriving on the doorstep.

Mrs. Dolittle moved to stand beside her daughter, one arm around her waist as she introduced her to them. "Samantha, Sterling, this is my youngest daughter, Claire. Claire, this is Basil's daughter, Samantha, and her gentleman friend, Sterling."

Claire wiped her eyes one more time and acknowledged them both, making an effort to compose herself. "I'm sorry to arrive so unexpectedly. And at the front door, too!" She lifted a hand to her mouth in sudden horror. "I know I have no right to..." She cleared her throat, visibly making an effort to compose herself. "I'm sorry, I am not normally like this."

Samantha heard embarrassment and grief and apology all mixed up in her voice and wanted to set her at ease. She moved forward and placed a hand on her arm. "Claire, it's good to meet you and we are glad to have you. Please, come to any door anytime. I hope you will feel comfortable here." She spread a hand to indicate the house and smiled ironically. "We have plenty of room."

Claire returned the smile with a small watery one of her own. "Thank you."

They followed Mrs. Dolittle to the kitchen where she directed her daughter out back to wash up at the pump and Sterling and Samantha helped set the table. The few moments Claire was outside, Mrs. Dolittle offered a brief explanation of her daughter's background. She told them Claire's husband had always had a tendency for drunkenness that often gave her cause to worry. "I confess I am not too surprised by this turn of events, but it still grieves me to see Claire hurting so. However, considering all the pain and disappointment she has experienced over the past ten years, I have to say, I hope we have seen the last of that man."

"Poor Claire!" Samantha murmured. Then, thinking of the welt, asked, "Does he often abuse her?"

Mrs. Dolittle sighed, placing a platter of baked potatoes on the table. "Drunkenness makes him violent, so yes, he takes it out on her much too often. How many times I have wished she had never married the man! But," she hastened to add, seeing the alarm on Samantha's face, "I feel certain he would never come here after her, so I believe she is safe now. However, I am not sure that, were she to live in my tiny home without male protection, her safety would be as guaranteed."

Samantha nodded, feeling relieved they could provide a safe haven. "I am sure Father will agree with me that she is welcome to stay as long as she needs to. No doubt she will require more than just a physical recovery."

"Yes," Mrs. Dolittle agreed. "Thank you. I will talk to your father. My Claire is a hard worker. I am sure there is much she can do here to earn her keep."

"Does she have children?" Samantha asked suddenly, eyes widening as she thought of the possible ramifications in such a situation.

"No, God never blessed her with children, which has long been another source of pain to her. But considering the circumstances, perhaps it is for the best." She indicated a small platter of sliced ham, which Sterling obligingly took to the table, while she carried a pitcher of milk from the morning's milking. "God moves in mysterious ways."

"Well, we'll just have to see what wonders He will do next to help Claire move forward," Samantha offered. "And we'll do all we can to help her."

Chapter 6

FAMILY LETTERS

JULY 1902

A few days later, Samantha awoke and decided today she would search until she found correspondence from her mother's family. She had not yet made it back up to the attic, and she remembered there were other boxes up there and a cedar chest. Surely, if there were any letters, they would be in the attic somewhere!

Directly after breakfast, she told Mrs. Dolittle where she would be, in case she was needed, and then headed up the stairs to the top floor. As soon as she poked her head into the attic from the pull-down ladder, she felt the stuffiness of the room. Though the attic was cooler in the morning, it never really cooled off during the night, so she opened the windows on either side of the big room. As fresh air suddenly spilled inside, she looked around for a moment, then spotted the large cedar chest she remembered. It was covered with many years' accumulation of dust, but as she found a rag and dusted it off, the polished wooden chest gleamed and she found her pulse quickening with anticipation. Carefully, she opened the lid, the lovely cedar scent filling her nose, and began to slowly lift items out. Each new thing brought a wave of questions to her mind and she filed them away to ask Father someday.

When she finally reached the bottom of the trunk, she saw a bundle of envelopes tied together with a long blue satin ribbon. The ribbon and envelopes were all in perfect condition from their almost two decades inside the cedar chest, and Samantha lifted them out, heart pounding. She had the feeling these were what she was looking for!

Rummaging through the rest of the chest to verify there was not another bundle, she began carefully setting everything else back in. Then she pulled an old rocking chair over to the big window that overlooked the front yard, dusted it off, and sat, the precious bundle in her hands. With trembling fingers, she pulled the ribbon loose and looked at the pile of letters in her lap. Each one was addressed to Lovenia Jennings in a variety of different handwritings. To her delight, these included letters from Joseph and Julia Lewis. She traced their names with one finger and pondered the thought of grandparents. Oh, to meet a dear grandfather and grandmother and to have them love her back! To feel that family connection through the generations, to know they belonged to each other! She pulled the letter out of the first envelope and began to read:

August 10, 1883

Dear daughter,

It was with relief that your father and I received your recent letter, assuring us that you have arrived in Oberlin safely. Thank the good Lord that you survived the journey, and that Basil has found a home and is providing well for you. How is it that you, our child with poor health, should be the one to fly farthest from the nest? I always thought you would stay close to home, that I would be able to watch over you myself and nurse you back to health when you were ailing. Now, I must rely on my faith and prayers that God and Basil will do for you what I no longer can. I hope for you the adventures you have long wanted, along with the stability you need. Basil is a good man, as we have seen firsthand these past four years, and there is no doubt in our minds of his love for you. But your father and I still worry for your well being. Please write often to help ease our worry. We love you with a love unending.

Love,
Mother

Samantha held the letter in her hands for a few moments, smelling the pleasant mix of cedar, paper, and ink. Her grandmother Julia sounded like a loving and capable woman. Samantha imagined what it would be like to send a daughter off to an unfamiliar town over one hundred miles away, knowing she would have to live on the trail for a week or more. Julia Lewis, more than anyone, knew the toll that such a journey could take on her daughter's health. No wonder she had worried! Yet she had not held her daughter back. She had not insisted they take the train, though it would have been an option, even then. She had allowed her daughter to make her own decisions with her own husband and trusted she was making the right choices, even though letting her go must have torn at her very being. Had Julia known she would never see Lovenia again? Samantha's heart ached at the thought.

Why <u>did</u> Mother and Father decide to travel by wagon? Surely that would not have been in the best interest of Mother's health! But then she thought of her mother's giving and unselfish nature and she remembered that many books in her father's library had come from Columbus. They wouldn't have been able to ship that many boxes of books and their belongings on a train. And she also knew her mother had always had an adventurous spirit. She must have felt that this was her one chance to experience something exciting and completely new, and she wanted to undertake it, regardless of the possible repercussions to her health.

Samantha refolded the letter and carefully slipped it back inside the envelope, then pulled out the next one. It was written in a cramped style that indicated either impatience or eagerness, she was not sure which:

August 14, 1883

Dear Lovenia,

What is Oberlin like??? I am sorry to begin my letter with a question, but I have waited so long to ask it! Please tell me everything: the layout of the town, how you like your house, what the people are like, etc, etc. It really is not fair that you, our family's best homebody, should be the first to venture to a new place—a very populated town compared to our small one—when I am two years your senior and have always wished to see somewhere new! But I will forgive you your adventure without me, as long as you write me all about it.

As far as news from home, not much has changed, though your absence is a constant lack in our family's life. You asked if Edward and I are stepping out together now, and the answer is yes—which is exciting and perplexing all at once. I am uncertain what I think of him, but am determined to find out as we spend more time together. He does have a lovely family, and Mother and Father seem to like him. So we shall see. As an "old maid" I know this may be my best chance, so I hope things do work out.

Eleanor asks that I write something for her because she scarcely has a free moment to herself these days. You know how high-spirited her four children are, and the twins, especially, have been so full of mischief lately that she is often beside herself. Of course, she only confides that to those closest to her. To everyone else, she always appears poised and in control. And

66

really, she is a very organized and capable mother, as you know. But I imagine it would be difficult for any mother to return to the kitchen two minutes after she left it and find that the twins had gotten into the flour, spilling it all over themselves and tracking it throughout the room, then letting the puppy in to join in the romp! (God, please save me from the blessing of twins; I do not believe I am of the proper temperament. And please, do bless Eleanor, the dear, stoic soul!) So, you see, by the time bedtime arrives each night, Eleanor is undoubtedly too exhausted to engage in any correspondence. But she does want you to know that she thinks of you daily and prays for your welfare.

Samuel promised to write his own letter to you, and I trust that he shall, as I know you two have always been close.

Please do not forget me, and know that I miss you very much and expect to hear all about your new home, just as soon as you can possibly write.

Your favorite sister,

Irene

Samantha laughed out loud and pressed the letter to her heart. How she hoped this delightful aunt was still alive and that she could get to know her for herself! If she could have a sister, she would want someone just like Aunt Irene sounded.

She pulled out the next letter, noting the masculine script that, though readable, was a bit messy and took a little more time to read:

August 17, 1883

Dearest sister,

I hope you and Basil are doing well and settling into your new life. I confess I have been thinking about what it must be like for you to live in such a big house, but the important thing is that you have a solid roof over your head and a comfortable home to call your own. I continue to work at the post office and enjoy it well enough. As you know, I like to keep busy, so if I am not working there, I am at home reading or helping our parents. Father has felt more of his rheumatism coming on lately and seems to appreciate me stepping in to assist with the more physical chores. I still seek God's direction to know what more to do with my life, but for now, I have plenty to keep me occupied.

I miss you and the frequent talks we used to have. The absence of your gentle, guiding presence has left me feeling empty, I must admit. I did not realize how much I relied on that until you left. Just as you always comforted me when I was a little boy and helped me feel that things would really be all right, you strengthened me and eased my spirits just by talking with me now in my post-adolescent years. I know God can provide me direction, I just hope I can receive and follow it as well as you do.

Thank you, sister, for your example of faith and love, and know that you have a brother who loves you always,

Samuel

The next letter in the stack was written in a flowing and graceful script, and Samantha could see what Irene's previous letter had meant about Eleanor's calm and measured personality. But she sensed a feeling of loss from this sister too, who, even in the throes of young motherhood, keenly missed Lovenia as well:

September 2, 1883

Dear Lovenia,

I hope this letter finds you well and that you feel stronger now that you have had some time to recover from your long journey. I apologize for how long it has taken me to write to you. Irene said she wrote on my behalf, but I know that is not enough, so, having a few moments now before the children wake up, I want to write a little something. Andrew also sends his love, as you are his favorite sister-in-law (he knows you will appreciate the jest). Life for me is full and too busy much of the time, and most of my wishful thoughts are focused on sleep and how to obtain more of it! But even though my little ones get into mischief, make messes, and create a great deal of work for me, I love them dearly and am grateful they are mine. You always helped me see that side of things, the precious nature of life and the treasure that children are, and I thank you for it. Your perspective influences me still. When I have a spare moment, I think to myself that I must walk down the street and visit you, that it has been too long, and then I remember you are no longer there. Even though you are my youngest sister, I have always appreciated your wisdom, and realize now how much I came to rely on that. We are all carrying on here without you, but hope someday to be able to come see you in Oberlin. What a joy it would be to see you, then! Until such time, I am,

Your loving sister,
Eleanor

Samantha found it interesting that each of her mother's siblings had written her a separate letter in a separate envelope, rather than waiting until they had all written and then sending the letters together. It would have saved on postage and was the usual way of doing things. But as she mused on this, her heart lifted to realize what great joy her mother would have had with each and every letter arriving within days of each other. Surely that was why they had sent them separately. They had known Lovenia would want and need that connection with each of them, spread out and arriving unexpectedly, but at delightfully close intervals. It touched Samantha to see this evidence of her mother's family's love for their far-away daughter.

Samantha reached the last few letters in the stack, excited to see her grandfather's name in neat, rounded script on the envelope. She opened the envelope and read a letter sent the following year:

August 22, 1884

My dear Lovenia,

Your mother informs me that congratulations are in order. How happy I am that you and Basil can be parents, and that you can add to our passel of grandchildren. It is my greatest joy to see my daughters happily married and raising families of their own, and I pray that my son will soon find himself in such a situation and continue in his sisters' footsteps. It was a privilege to participate in rearing such wonderful children, but being a grandfather now brings a great sweetness to my life that adds such joy to these later years.

Please take care of yourself. This little one needs a well-rested and healthy mother to bring it into the world. I know you know that, but my father's heart cannot help but remind you. So forgive this old man his unnecessary admonitions.

I send many congratulations and prayers your way, and am always,

Your affectionate father

Samantha blinked. What a pleasant image his words gave: "Our passel of grandchildren"! Suddenly it occurred to her that those children would be her cousins! And surely some of those cousins were out there somewhere, waiting to be found! How many children had each of her aunts had? And did Samuel find a woman to share his life and have a family with as well?

How about Grandfather Joseph, himself? She thought she could picture him writing the letter: joy, concern, and love all mixed together. *Is he still alive?* She sighed. These letters were a wonderful and tender connection to the past, but they inspired more questions than answers. She opened the next one and noticed a small yellow envelope tucked inside with the letter. Her heart dropped as she guessed the nature of the telegram.

Received telegram and await arrival of coffin STOP Wish to meet new baby STOP All grieve with you and hope for your return STOP

It was a strange sensation to read about oneself, even in something as cryptic as a telegram! Her mind flooded with images of a heartbroken father holding his new baby and reading this very message, eyes red with anguish and exhaustion. What an impossible decision he had made, to send the body of his beloved wife back to her family. If he had buried her in Oberlin, would regular visits to her grave have helped him better work through his loss? And why had he never returned to the bosom of his wife's family, who obviously loved him and wanted to meet their new granddaughter? Her heart hurt, just thinking about it all, but she pulled the letter out of the envelope and read it.

March 16, 1884

Dear Basil,

My wife is beside herself, as you can well imagine, so I have taken up this difficult task of writing to you myself. I thank you for sending us the news so quickly. Earlier today you will have received my telegram response to your telegram. As such cryptic missives do not allow for longer, heartfelt messages, I feel compelled to write more now, though I know you may not receive this for at least a few days. My son, I wish you to know of our gratitude for your love and care of our dear Lovenia. Though your time together was devastatingly brief, you made her the happiest she ever was. At times like these it is difficult to know why God allows such things as Lovenia's death to happen, but I pray that we can remember the many good times, and take comfort in knowing she is now free of the constraints of her mortal body and safe in the arms of the God she loves so much. However, I am not so idealistic as to believe that such thoughts will lessen the grief that claims you now. I am certain your feelings are beyond the words of human tongue, and I pray for your strength. You will need it in the caring of your new little daughter. Only God knows how we will get through this, Basil, but we will.

I do not know how to adequately thank you for what you are giving us. It will mean so much to Julia and our surviving children to have dear Lovenia laid to rest in Worthington where we can visit her grave often. Please know you and your daughter are always welcome here, and we long for your return. We look forward to meeting dear little Samantha; her presence will provide a measure of comfort for all of us in our grief. I know you will be holding a memorial service in Oberlin, but we would like to have a funeral here as well, after the private interment. So many in this town knew Lovenia throughout her life and loved her, and we desire to give her this last tribute.

Basil, never doubt that our daughter loved you with the complete fullness of her very large heart, and that she desired the best for you. She wanted you to be happy, and nothing gave her greater joy than envisioning her future with you and becoming your wife. We hope you will always feel a part of our family and will visit us when you are able, along with our precious granddaughter, Lovenia's last great gift to us all.

Sincerely yours,

Joseph Lewis

Samantha blinked back tears, feeling her heart swell with love for this unknown grandparent. Through this one simple letter, she felt so much love from him for both her parents and herself, though he had never met her. What would it be like to meet such a grandfather now? She hoped she would find out, though as she calculated the dates, she realized that if he were still alive he would be over seventy years old.

She returned the letter to its envelope and picked up the next one, surprised to find it still sealed. She looked at the next one and the next, and found them all firmly closed. Her heart dropped. Apparently, her father had shut himself off to his wife's family, as well as to the rest of the world. Had they ever visited him? Had he written to them at all? Why had he stopped his heart to their obvious love and welcome? Surely, a correspondence with them, at the very least, would have helped ease his pain a fraction.

A knot in the pit of her stomach, she began to open and read the sealed letters, one by one. She found that throughout the two years after Lovenia's death, each of her siblings and both of her parents had written to Basil, some of them multiple times, to ask him—to plead with him—to return to Worthington. Their great desire to see him again and meet little Samantha was obvious. After a few months, their asking changed and, since he seemed unable to make the trip, asked if they might visit him instead. By the next year, Lovenia's father's rheumatism had worsened enough that he and Julia stopped asking to come, as it became apparent that he was no longer fit to travel. Eleanor, Irene, and Samuel eventually stopped asking as well, pleading only for a letter from Basil in return, for news of him, for word of Samantha's growth and development—for the smallest contact. And finally, in Joseph's last letter—the last of the lot—he encouraged Basil to turn to God and allow Him to lift the burden of his grief. "Turn to the Father of us all," he urged, "to buoy you up and comfort you. He is there with arms wide, ready when you are. And if we know Lovenia at all, she is by His side, and wants you to be happy and find peace. So please, Basil, don't lose heart."

But he had.

It saddened her that she was the first to read these letters, over a decade after they were written.

Sliding the paper back into its envelope, she felt bereaved. There were no more letters. This was all the contact she could currently have with her mother's family. It had felt delicious to hold these papers in her hands, trace the words with her fingers, taste them in her mind, and imagine each person as she read their words. It was an unfulfilling ending to the letters, to say the least. Samantha's heart was heavy and the familiar grief weighed upon her of relationships never reconnected. If only her father had not closed himself off to everyone and everything! Here was a family who loved him like their own, and he had cut off all contact with them by his silence. How that must have torn at them, devastated them in the end, as much as Lovenia's passing. They had lost not only their daughter, but also their son-in-law and granddaughter. No doubt they must have wished the couple had never set out on that fateful journey to Oberlin!

Samantha closed her eyes tightly and pressed a fist to her forehead. She took a deep breath and let it out slowly. *And yet...*she thought. And yet, Oberlin was so much a part of who she was, as was the Jennings mansion, and the maple tree out back. She couldn't imagine her life—or her person—without them! Would she still be the same woman if she had grown up in Worthington, surrounded by relatives who loved her? That was a lovely picture, but she had to acknowledge to herself that her hardships, her stark and lonely childhood, her voracious book learning, had all contributed to who she now was. She felt a deep conviction that it had all happened for a reason. Not that it excused her father from the poor decisions he had made, or herself for her own mistakes, but it did seem that God could turn bad things for good. Maybe that was the miracle she needed to see in this whole tragedy.

Into her mind came the words she had recently read in the Old Testament, words from the poetic prophet Isaiah: "To appoint unto them that mourn...to give unto them beauty for ashes, the oil of joy for mourning, the garment of praise for the spirit of heaviness; that they might be called trees of righteousness, the planting of the Lord, that he might be glorified."

Her heart took hope and she opened her eyes. Good could yet come from this situation, could it not? She wanted to experience that beauty for ashes, that oil of joy, to be a tree of righteousness. She loved the way the words and images soothed her troubled soul and lifted her heart. There was still time to forge new connections and heal severed ties, and God could guide her in this pursuit, as He had orchestrated her journey to Worthington the past spring.

She restacked the envelopes and re-tied the ribbon carefully around them all, then held them in her lap and slowly rocked in the old rocking chair, back and forth, back and forth, losing herself in her thoughts. Maybe her father needed to see these letters. Maybe he would be ready for them now, after reading Lovenia's journal—not that it would be a pleasant undertaking for him, but she suddenly felt a weight of responsibility about the idea. Perhaps reading them would remind him of what he might still have, when he was ready to make amends.

She pondered this thought for several moments, wondering what the future might hold for her family, hoping this was just the beginning of something better. A shaft of bright morning sunlight poured through the near window, dust motes dancing, rising as if attracted to the light.

Chapter 7

"AIN'T NOBODY A NOBODY"

July 1902

Samantha spent the rest of the day mentally composing letters to her relatives as she went about household tasks, then sat down to write them the next morning. From the little table near the library window, she looked out at the towering maple and thought about her mother's family. Indeed, she had not been able to *stop* thinking about them since she learned their names. She would write to Irene, Samuel, and her grandparents first, since they were all listed at the same address. Then she would write to Eleanor. Samantha hoped that in sending letters to both addresses, at least one would find a living relative. Supposing that all of them still lived at those addresses might be too much to hope for after all these years, but it was all she had at the moment.

After an hour, letters written and envelopes addressed, she stood and stretched, feeling she had accomplished something important. She changed into her riding habit, then headed to the barn to saddle Champion for a ride to the post office and was surprised when Sterling walked in a few minutes later, morning sunlight outlining his tall, wide-shouldered frame as he stood in the doorway.

"Good morning!" she smiled, looking at him over the stall wall. "What impeccable timing you have, and it's not even meal time!" she teased.

Sterling responded with a chuckle and strode toward her. "Ah, but *you* are good enough to eat," he quipped, one dark eyebrow raised as he entered the stall.

"Rogue." She swatted at him playfully with the tack she was about to attach to Champion.

In one swift move, Sterling grabbed the reins and pulled her toward him, kissing her before she could even blink. "Yep," he nodded, speaking like a farm hand. "Sweet as honey and temptin' as apple pie."

Champion snorted and shifted his weight restlessly.

Samantha laughed again, shaking her head at Sterling's antics, but coloring a bit in spite of herself, which delighted him. "You are very cheerful this morning," she observed, slipping the bit into Champion's mouth and drawing the crown piece over his ears and the throatlatch against his neck.

Sterling grinned. "I am, aren't I? You are the reason, you know. Every morning I awake happy, amazed all over again that I am still in Oberlin—because you want me here."

As he spoke, Samantha checked to see that the saddle blanket was in place, but something in his tone made her look up at him. His expression was now serious and she suddenly sensed that same raw vulnerability that she had seen in him so clearly the day they were reunited. Feeling moved to reassure him, she said softly, "I do want you here. I always did. I think it is a good sign that we are happier together than we ever were apart."

Her smiling, sincere gray eyes reassured him and his heart hitched.

She bent to heft the heavy saddle, and he immediately reached to grasp the other side of it. Together they settled the saddle atop the blanket, and Sterling cinched it tight, waiting for Champion to blow out a long-held breath, then cinched it again.

He looked at her from the opposite side of the horse and laid an arm across the saddle. The morning was already growing very warm, so his sleeves were rolled up above the elbows, showing well-defined biceps. "I think that too. But sometimes it still seems unreal. Do you ever feel that?"

She nodded thoughtfully, her mind flashing back to all the heartaches over the past year, the longing, the wishing, the praying and wanting, the wrenching questions and uncertainty about the future. And now, everything seemed so bright and full of hope. There were still many questions, but she felt like they could figure things out together.

Sterling moved around Champion to her side and stood near. "What are you thinking?" he asked, his brown eyes searching hers.

She looked up at him, still lost in thought for a moment. "I am thinking how whole I feel when you are with me—and yet I didn't know I was not complete before. It is hard to explain, but I feel like there was a part of me that was missing without me even knowing it, and when you returned, that piece clicked into place."

He reached for her hands and pressed his palms to hers. Their fingers aligned, his longer ones curling over the tops of hers. "This just feels right, doesn't it?"

"Yes." They stood there, facing each other in the stall, palms together, looking at each other. He touched a kiss to her forehead and she closed her eyes.

"I don't want to go, and yet the summer passes so quickly."

Her eyes flew open and she searched his face, her heart dropping. "When do you have to leave?"

"I think another three weeks or so and I should return, so I have enough time to prepare my classroom and get everything in order for the new school year."

She nodded and stepped back, already feeling a sense of loss.

He kept hold of one of her hands. "What would you think of coming with me—just for a week or so, to meet the Tomlinsons and see the school. You could meet Mr. Grover as well. Maybe he could give you ideas for your own school, or answer some of your questions. But most of all, we need to look for your mother's family!" She could tell he was warming to the subject and his enthusiasm lifted her heart back to its proper place.

"Oh, you're right, Sterling. There is so much to do there!" Her eyes flitted around the stall as she thought about it all. "I wonder if Father would be ready to see the Lewises again...? Maybe he could come with us. We will need a chaperone, after all."

"Ask him!"

Samantha gazed up at this handsome man who made her so happy and wondered to herself for the umpteenth time how she was so blessed. Some would call it luck, but the way all the little details had lined up when they could so easily not have, made her stick to the word "blessed." She reached up to finger the curl over his forehead and traced her fingers down his cheek.

He smiled at her softly, his thoughts along the very same vein.

"Would you like to come with me this morning?" she asked.

"I would," he said. "Where are you headed?"

Samantha turned and bent to pick up the letters she had placed on a pile of straw in the corner of the stall and held them up. "To the post office. Yesterday in the attic I found letters with addresses in my mother's cedar chest, and today I wrote my own letters."

Sterling held up crossed fingers. "May they arrive in the hands of those they are intended for," he said sincerely.

She couldn't help teasing him. "You mean, unlike the letter you sent me last year, which never arrived?"

He gave her a pained expression.

"I will pray them there," she answered simply. "I have a good feeling about this." Lifting one shoulder slightly she said, "Surely at least one address is still current."

"I will pray too," he smiled. "And if the letters don't find the right people, we will simply have to investigate when we get to Worthington. We won't give up on this." His tone was determined.

"Thank you," she said gratefully.

"I borrowed a horse to get here, and it's hitched at the front of the house."

"Perfect! Afterwards, we can go on a pleasure ride." She ran a hand over Champion's flanks and the horse stamped in impatience, making her laugh. "I think Champion feels a little neglected and would appreciate a good run."

Sterling stroked the horse's nose and chuckled. "He always tends to feel neglected. I don't think he could ever get enough running to suit him." They exited the barn together, Champion's hooves clomping between them, out into the bright sunshine.

***

One afternoon a couple days later, Samantha sat at the kitchen table preparing pears for canning. She cut one of the peeled fruits in half and then cut out the core with swift, precise motions, moving quickly to the next pear. She was becoming more and more efficient in the kitchen and today hardly thought of her task as she listened to Mrs. Dolittle and her daughter, who stood talking at the stove as they canned. She enjoyed tuning into their conversations as they reminisced about earlier times and laughed about humorous events in their family. Listening to these exchanges gave her a clear glimpse into Mrs. Dolittle's family life that she had never seen before. And witnessing the relationship between mother and daughter warmed her through. She hoped that one day she could have such a bond with a child of her own, a bond she had long missed with her own mother.

Claire's bubbling laugh tickled Samantha. She was so glad to hear the woman laugh after all she had been through. The first few days at the Jennings', Claire had trailed after her mother in a depressed fog, her eyes red, a handkerchief often pressed to her nose. Mrs. Dolittle had kept her busy and often expressed to Samantha how grateful she was to have Claire in the house: one, for the additional help—for now she could accomplish tasks she hadn't been able to do for much too long—and two, the concentrated time with her youngest daughter allowed Mrs. Dolittle to watch over and support her during this difficult time. Together, they cleaned unused rooms and carefully took drape cloths outside to shake them free of years of dust, leaving them pinned to the clothesline to air out in the sunshine. They polished silver and oiled furniture until it all gleamed in a way Samantha didn't remember it ever doing before. She offered to help them on numerous occasions, and sometimes they let her, but more often than not Mrs. Dolittle would wave her away to spend time with Sterling or her charity groups and other projects.

As she continued coring pears, Samantha thought about the slow transformation that had recently occurred throughout the large house. Only yesterday, the mother and daughter team had rolled up several rugs and hefted them outside one by one to beat them "as they should have been beaten long ago." It seemed as if somehow this mundane chore lifted an emotional burden from Claire, for as she sat on the back porch fanning herself after the last rug was clean, she confessed that she had thought about her husband, Phil, during the rug beatings.

"I'm sorry, Mama," she said, glancing at Mrs. Dolittle, "I know you would say it is unchristian of me, but beating those rugs while I thought about all the times Phil beat me was very therapeutic. I listed in my mind all the unkind things he said and did to me and beat those rugs as if to beat them out of him." She grinned and seemed more relaxed than Samantha had seen her before.

Samantha handed her a glass of cool water drawn from the well and couldn't help laughing a little. "I can see how that would be a therapeutic exercise," she said, handing another glass to Mrs. Dolittle, who shook her head in mock consternation at her daughter's words. But she couldn't hide the smile that touched the corners of her mouth.

Claire stopped the fan in her hand long enough to point it at her mother. "I probably shouldn't say such a thing out loud, but it's only us here, so I am going to anyway: that action was something I needed, Mama. I put up with way too much, married to that man. More than I should have allowed. Only I didn't recognize it until I removed myself from the situation." She began waving the fan again, wiping away perspiration from her shining forehead with the sleeve of her other arm. "I didn't actually know there was so much anger in me until I began beating that poor rug."

Mrs. Dolittle clucked in sympathy. "You have every reason to be angry," she acknowledged.

"And just think, I could beat out all those grievances without touching a hair of his head!"

Samantha nodded. Phil would never know what Claire had symbolically done and it wouldn't affect him in the least, but Claire was changed. "I am sorry for all you've been through, Claire. We should have invited you to live with us long ago!"

Claire sighed. "Thank you. You didn't know—I didn't let most people in my neighborhood know, let alone people here in Oberlin. Mother gave me a great deal of good suggestions and sound advice over the years, but I always thought I could fix things myself—fix him. After all, I knew Phil better than anyone and knew what he needed." She made a derisive, dismissive sound. "So much for that. I tried everything I knew to help him quit drinking, but nothing stuck. I didn't realize until a few days ago that he never really wanted to stop drinking in the first place."

Mrs. Dolittle nodded, reflectively. "The desire for change has to come from within. Not one of us is strong enough to change another person who has no desire to do so."

"Did you learn that in your experience with my father?" Samantha asked, sitting down on the porch step across from them. "Surely you sensed that he needed to do things differently so he could pull out of his melancholia."

Mrs. Dolittle thought about this for a moment. "Well now, I suppose I did," she replied slowly. "He was a good and steady employer and he helped in your care while you were a tiny thing, but once that period of time was over, he pulled away from society and withdrew inside himself completely. Of course, when you were a baby, Claire was only twelve and still in need of a mother's guiding hand, and my next older child was only fourteen. So I was glad Basil could take over with you when I needed to head back home each night."

"There was so much need in both houses," Samantha observed, picturing it more fully: a younger Mrs. Dolittle working all day at the Jennings' and then hurrying home after preparing supper to care for her own children, who also needed a meal. "However did you manage everything?"

"Only the good Lord knows," Mrs. Dolittle said thoughtfully, remembering back to that long ago time. "He is the One who held me up and gave me strength. But it was truly difficult watching Basil struggle on his own, not willing to accept help from the neighbors, nor even reach out to Lovenia's family. I hated seeing him close himself up like that, but there was little I could do."

"And yet you kept up your spirits and continued as faithful and devoted a housekeeper as ever."

Mrs. Dolittle smiled at Samantha. "Those were hard years in many ways, but I had plenty to be grateful for, to be sure, so I tried to focus on that. Mine has always been a full life: the means to provide for my five children and myself after Ambrose passed, and now a way to put away money for my later years and to help my children here and there, should they fall upon hard times." She patted Claire on the shoulder. "I am a simple woman, but a happy one."

"I don't know about simple," Samantha returned with a laugh. "I used to think so, before I knew you as I do now. But that faulty perspective sheds more light on my own ignorance than anything." She turned to Claire. "I suppose you know well the story of how your grandmother came to Oberlin from Virginia, a runaway slave?"

Claire nodded. "That was one of Mama's favorite stories to share with us, growing up. She always told me I took after my grandmother's strong personality." She said this without embarrassment or apology and Samantha loved her for it.

"All that your grandmother endured and all that she made happen by sheer willpower is quite the legacy."

Claire nodded and grew thoughtful. "Yes, I suppose it is."

"Samantha and I have talked about this before," Mrs. Dolittle added, "but you both have strong and wonderful legacies to look to as you move forward in life." She handed Samantha a spare fan and began fanning herself as well. "This heat!" she commented. "It has sapped the energy right out of me."

Claire agreed.

"Let's just sit right here for a while," Samantha urged, "and you can tell us a story."

"A story!" Mrs. Dolittle laughed. "What are you thinking about now, child?"

"Your perspective of the Oberlin-Wellington Rescue. I just realized I've never asked you! You were a young woman by then, weren't you?"

"Oh yes." Mrs. Dolittle's dark eyes grew distant as she gathered the memories around her. "It was the year 1858, which means..." she calculated briefly, "I would have been seventeen years of age. We lived on the east side of the college campus in what was known as 'Little Africa.' We had many good friends and neighbors there whom Mother knew would take me under their wings while she was away at work. She had made a good life for us there and we usually felt safe, but the rumor of slave catchers passing through was always a source of anxiety and alarm for us. I can't tell you how many times it helped calm me to remember that no fugitive slave in Oberlin had ever been returned to slavery, that the town actively supported the freedom of people like Mother who had escaped that life."

Samantha shook her head slowly. She could only imagine what it must have been like.

"Yet that summer had been filled with more tension over slave catchers than usual. That day of The Rescue was certainly exciting: drama and intense worry with some terror thrown in for good measure. I shall never forget it. John Price was only a year older than I, you know. So I knew of him, though we had never been formally introduced. He had a limp, I remember that." She clucked her tongue. "Now, to think about what that young man went through pains me. He had only ever known hard labor and separation from family, and then when he ran away from his owner in Kentucky, he suddenly became a wanted man.

"We felt tense all summer because of three attempts by slave hunters to capture Black families, so I guess we were poised and ready that day when it happened. And the recent news of a captured illegal slave ship bound for Cuba[1] heightened our sense of vigilance. Added to that, we were on edge because a tall, gray-bearded man was in town whom no one had a good feeling about. He carried a couple revolvers and spoke in a thick Kentucky accent, and he stayed in the shadows at the tavern. We knew he was looking for an escaped slave. His name—" she paused, seeming to hesitate.

Samantha waited, giving Mrs. Dolittle a quizzical look.

"Well, I highly doubt he was a relation, dear, but...I still hate to tell you."

Samantha blinked. "What was it?"

---

1. https://www.neh.gov/humanities/2011/septemberoctober/ feature/ when-the-slave-catcher-came-town

"Anderson Jennings," Mrs. Dolittle replied reluctantly.

Samantha tensed and felt a little sick to her stomach.

"After that day, I didn't think about his name for more than twenty years—until I came here to inquire about the housekeeping position and learned that this house belonged to a Professor Jennings. For a moment, I was awash with fear, but as soon as I met your parents, I knew they were not of the same breed as that horrible man."

Samantha relaxed and Mrs. Dolittle returned to her story.

"I remember vividly how Mother and I were washing clothes for her employer, Mrs. Wheaton, outside in the yard that afternoon. It was a cool autumn day and we were up to our elbows in soapy water in two large tin tubs when a white man with bushy brown whiskers ran past us on the street, yelling that John Price had been captured by men in a wagon and taken to Wellington. Since that was the first train stop south of Oberlin, we knew that meant the slave catchers were intent on getting John out of Ohio as quickly as possible and back to his owner in Kentucky. My, the look on Mother's face at that news! Her shock and alarm made her suddenly weak for a moment so that she had to hold on to the tub for support. Then she was suffused with anger and determination. She ran inside the house to relate the news to Mrs. Wheaton, and quickly ran back outside, grabbing my hand before I could process what had just happened. Off we went, running after the man, dripping water and soap suds!"

Mrs. Doolittle gave a long chuckle and Claire laughed with her, saying, "I think I would have done the exact same thing as Nana."

"You would have, too," Mrs. Dolittle agreed.

Samantha sat spellbound, imagining the scene. "Mrs. Wheaton wasn't upset about your sudden departure, was she?"

"Heavens no," Mrs. Dolittle rejoined. "In fact, she followed us. Before long, it seemed the whole town of Oberlin, Black and white, were all hurrying to Wellington in whatever manner they could: horseback, wagon, or on foot. We gathered more information as we ran along—including the fact that there was a $500 reward for each slave he was looking for."

"So much?!" Samanth exclaimed.

"Eventually, a white farmer picked us up in his wagon, which was already nearly full of other pedestrians. We found out from the wagon conversation that a young college student, Ansel Lyman[2], had actually seen John Price being carried off in a wagon. John cried out to him for help, but Lyman knew he couldn't overpower the three white men with John, so he did nothing in that moment. However, he was already headed back to town and hurried fast to sound the alarm. He was a fearless abolitionist and had no intention of staying quiet, unlike the man with him, surnamed Bartholomew, suggested. Soon Oberlin was mobilized, including us.

"When we arrived in Wellington, we followed the crowd to the Public Square, where hundreds of people, both men and women, Black and white, were gathered in front of the Wadsworth Hotel.[3] John and his captors were upstairs. I remember some people voicing their concern about the

Fugitive Slave Law[4], but the general consensus was that we

believed in a higher law and feared God more than man's unjust laws, so regardless of the law we would do what was right.

Mrs. Dolittle was silent for a moment, trying to remember all that had transpired. "Well now, I don't recall everything from that afternoon. But I do remember it was loud and chaotic and no one seemed to know quite what was going on. At one point, the slave hunter, Jennings, came out onto the balcony above the front entrance. He said something about not wanting any quarrel with the people of Ohio and that the 'boy' was his by the laws of Kentucky and the United States. I remember that statement because it made Mother so angry, as it did us all. Someone in the crowd voiced our feelings when he said, 'You dry up! There are no slaves in Ohio and never will be north of the Ohio River.'"

Claire grinned. "I love that part."

Mrs. Dolittle chuckled.

---

2. Distant ancestor of the author.

3. https://19thcenturywellington.wordpress.com/2013/10/17

4. Passed on September 18, 1850, The Fugitive Slave Act of 1850 was part of the Compromise of 1850. The act required that slaves be returned to their owners, even if they were in a free state, and made the federal government responsible for finding, returning, and trying escaped slaves. See https://www.battlefields.org/learn/primary-sources/fugitive-slave-act

"So, then what happened?" Samantha asked.

"He brought out John Price, who was questioned before the crowd about whether he wanted to go back to Kentucky."

Claire scoffed.

"Held by such a man as that slave hunter, what could John say? He was cowed and submissive—no doubt he had learned to be that way to survive. But then one man asked John if he wouldn't rather go to Canada, and another man drew his gun and offered to shoot Jennings while John jumped."

Samantha's eyes widened. "Oh my."

"Yes," Mrs. Dolittle said, nodding emphatically. "Chaos. I remember seeing Charles Langston, who, along with his brother, was the first Black student to attend Oberlin College. He moved from group to group, trying to placate everyone and prevent a mob uprising. He had experienced the devastating effects of such violence and was determined it not happen again.

"As the time for the train's arrival from Cleveland drew closer, we grew more anxious. The rumor was that federal troops would arrive on that train and everyone said that if we were going to get John Price out of the hotel, it would have to be soon. But there was no clear leader and we didn't quite know what to do. Of course, us women were mere bystanders anyway, and we felt the helplessness of our situation."

"Did troops arrive then?" Samantha asked.

"Fortunately, no. So then a new rumor circulated that they would arrive on the *next* train, a few hours later. Finally, when it felt like things were at the breaking point, a small group of men of both races organized themselves and rushed up the hotel stairs. While that was happening, a group of Black men broke through the back door. There was yelling and shots were fired. My heart was in my throat!

"I learned later that both groups met in the hallway outside the door where John, Jennings, and several other men were holed up. A young white man named Richard Winsor[5] was in the room near the door. He was an Oberlin student and John's Sunday School teacher, and had rushed to Wellington to try and save him. When he quietly asked

---

5. https://www2.oberlin.edu/external/EOG/Oberlin-Wellington_Rescue/the_resc uers.htm

John whether or not he wanted to return to Oberlin, John responded that he did. I think by then he realized that a great many of us were on his side and that he might have a chance at freedom after all. Through distraction and force, the men in the hallway were able to push open the door and, the room now being quite dark, Winsor sneaked John past Jennings and then the men passed John down over their shoulders and carried him into a waiting buggy at the hotel entrance. I saw when John was tossed into that buggy and Winsor jumped in behind him, and I cheered my relief that he had gotten out alive—and by the right men."

Samantha exhaled her own relief, not realizing until that moment that she had been holding her breath. "How exciting!" she exclaimed. "Where did they take John Price from there?"

"The James Fitch home. But he was a known conductor on the Underground Railroad, so they couldn't keep him there long, knowing their house would be one of the first searched by authorities. For a short time, though, John stayed in a secret room."

"After that, didn't he go to Professor Fairchild's house?" Claire asked.

"He did. The Fairchilds lived only a couple blocks away and had never harbored a slave before, but the professor didn't even hesitate to accept John Price into his house. John stayed with them several days before being spirited away to Canada on the Underground Railroad."

"And no one knows for sure what became of him after that," finished Samantha, remembering the story from her school days.

"Correct. I always wished we knew how he fared in Canada," mused Mrs. Dolittle, "but I held out hope that he recovered his health, found a good occupation, and made a good life for himself."

"Yes," said Samantha thoughtfully. "I hope he never forgot how two entire towns came to his aid and stood up for his freedom, even though he always felt like a nobody."

"Ain't nobody a nobody," Claire said heatedly, "and I know what it is to feel that way."

"Well, you're somebody important in this house," Samantha replied with feeling.

"And in this heart," Mrs. Dolittle added, placing a hand to her bosom.

Chapter 8

MEETING THORA

AUGUST 1902

A couple weeks later, in her preparations to leave for Worthington, Samantha knew she needed to speak with her father again. She did not expect him to agree to go with them, but she found herself hoping anyway. She felt it might be an important step for him to move through his grief. But he had shaken his grizzled head slowly and declined.

"I am not ready for that," he said. "It is probably something I should do, but not yet. I'm... I'm sorry." And as he looked at her, the stark regret in his sad, blue eyes touched her.

She noted the stack of letters on the desk behind him that she had dropped off at his door weeks before. They rested beside Lovenia's open journal, the blue ribbon untied and the envelopes in a different order. She was pleased to see evidence that her father had at least looked at them. Maybe they would spark something in him eventually. One slow step at a time, she decided.

"It's all right, Father," she said, touching his arm tentatively. "Another time." She paused. "But you have no objection to me going with Sterling? He will accompany me back, as well, and we will be sure to arrange a chaperone[1] both there and back."

---

1. https://en.wikipedia.org/wiki/Chaperone_(social) , https://www.thefrickpittsbu rgh.org/Story-My-Dearest-Love-and-Courtship-in-the-Gilded-Age

Basil waved a dismissive hand. "No objections. I can see you need to do this, and Sterling is a fine young man. I have no concerns."

Samantha felt relieved, but also a little disappointed that he didn't ask more questions or try to become better acquainted with Sterling. She wished he were a little more invested in this experience of searching out her family—his family through marriage. But she supposed she could not ask too much, too soon. After all, he was making improvements, a little at a time.

"All right, Father," she said at last. "Thank you for allowing me to go. When I return, may I tell you about my discoveries and experience?"

He looked a little taken aback. "Of course," he replied. "I would like that."

It was a short response, but it warmed her heart, so she clung to the feeling as she quietly left and closed the door behind her. Maybe by the time she returned from Worthington, he would have memorized enough of her mother's journal to allow her to have it back. Or maybe by then he would at least be ready to allow her to talk about it with him.

***

Samantha bounced a baby on her lap as the train sped along, the trees a vibrant green blur out her window. Actually, she wasn't sure if she was bouncing the baby, or if he was bouncing her! Facing her, the bald, dimple-cheeked little fellow pushed to stand up again, and she lifted him to his feet, where he bounced joyfully and made babbling sounds. Then suddenly he relaxed and plummeted back down to sit in her lap, a moment later pushing to stand again. Over and over. It took a surprising effort to support the little chap like this while he exercised his legs! He was strong and active and Samantha looked across from her at the baby's mother who sat facing them, entertaining a little dark-haired girl of about three years of age, who peered into the book on her mother's lap, asking question after question.

"No wonder Mrs. Hanley needed help traveling!" Sterling said to her under his breath. "This tyke alone is enough to wear me out, just watching him!"

Samantha laughed. "Well, it worked out well for us, providing an easy chaperone headed in the same direction, so I'm happy to help her. And he is such a handsome fellow, don't you think?" she asked, smiling at the boy who was now blowing a long string of bubbles which traveled down his chin, down the front of his clothing, and then the length of Samantha's hands, before dripping a small puddle into her lap.

"Handsome, yes, but a little uncouth," Sterling offered, eyebrows drawn together in mock consternation.

"I would wager that once long ago you were as uncouth as this little one," Samantha teased him. "Surely you weren't *born* a gentleman."

Sterling adopted a theatrical look of horror. "You wound me, miss," he said.

She laughed at him, shaking her head at his antics, but also loving his playfulness. "Pass me his bib, won't you?" she asked, gesturing at the other seat, where his mother kept the supplies in a small bag.

Sterling obliged and Mrs. Hanley looked up for a moment, smiling her gratitude at them both. "He seems to like you," she told Samantha.

"And I like him," Samantha returned. "But he is such an energetic fellow. My arms are beginning to ache!"

Mrs. Hanley nodded in sympathy. "I know that feeling well. Would you like me to take him?" She held out a hand but Samantha quickly declined, knowing the woman likely needed a break as long as possible.

"No, that's all right. I'm certain Sterling can take a turn." She turned a half-teasing, half-serious look at him and he shrugged as if to say, *Why not?*

Between the two of them, they managed to keep the baby occupied and happy for the majority of the trip, except for a couple feedings, which his mother managed to do discreetly under a shawl. Finally, when they were almost at their destination, the little fellow fell asleep.

"At last," Sterling whispered. "He fought it long enough!"

"Life is just too exciting, I suppose. He doesn't want to miss a thing." But Samantha was relieved too. Motherhood was apparently not for the faint of heart—or the weak of arms. Still, she looked across the seat at the baby lying peacefully in his mother's embrace, quiet and still at last, and was glad for her time with him. She had precious little experience with babies and was glad to know she could manage, though there was undoubtedly a great deal to learn!

The train pulled into the Worthington station with a slow squeal and a long hiss and then passengers started reaching for luggage and standing up. Samantha and Sterling exchanged farewells with Mrs. Hanley, who thanked them profusely and assured them she could manage without them from here, as relatives were there to meet them. Sterling gathered Samantha's and his own suitcases and held out his hand to her. "Are you ready?"

Samantha felt a flutter of nervousness in her stomach, but smiled and nodded, taking his hand to rise. "Ready or not," she said.

He tucked her hand in the crook of his arm, then grasped both suitcase handles. "It's alright to feel nervous," he reassured her. "But Mrs. Tomlinson is eager to meet you and I am sure she will make you feel right at home." They began to move down the aisle and toward the exit with the rest of the disembarking passengers. "I am surprisingly happy to be back, myself," he added. "Worthington is starting to feel more like home. I suppose when one puts a lot of time and effort into helping people, a portion of one's heart becomes forever part of that place. But I don't know what I will do when you aren't here also." He gave her a meaningful glance and worry lines puckered his forehead.

"I don't know how I will cope either," she said, pained. "We will just have to figure it out for the next several months. I have the feeling I will be doing a lot of praying."

She could feel Sterling's rueful chuckle through the side pressed into him. "You and me both!"

They reached the exit door and the porter helped Samantha descend the steps, Sterling following behind. Then, one hand tucked in again at Sterling's elbow, they made their way through the crowd of people milling about. Sterling craned his neck and looked around, his height putting him at an advantage for seeing over others' heads. It didn't take long for him to spot them and lead Samantha forward, trying not to quicken his pace too much in his excitement.

As they drew closer to a particular wagon, Samantha saw that on the driver's seat sat a pleasant looking, middle-aged woman holding the horse's reins. She was of medium build, with auburn hair pulled up in a loose bun, the hair at the temples beginning to silver. Next to her sat a gangly boy with somewhat unruly red hair and a healthy smattering of freckles.

When the young man caught sight of them, he jumped off the wagon and began running toward them. "Mr. Sterling!" he called, grinning.

Sterling set down the luggage and clasped the boy in an enthusiastic handshake, which turned into a quick but firm embrace. "How are you, Jerome?" Sterling asked, with obvious happiness.

"Doing well, sir," he replied. "You've been gone a long time!" Then, noticing Samantha as if for the first time, his head dropped shyly and he scratched the back of one leg with the other booted foot.

"Jerome, this is Samantha, the young woman I've been spending time with in Oberlin. Samantha, this is my favorite student, Jerome." In a stage whisper he added, "But don't tell any of my other students, or they might get jealous."

Jerome grinned again, lopsided, and nodded in acknowledgement at Samantha. "Nice to meet you, miss."

During this interchange, Mrs. Tomlinson climbed down from the wagon and secured the horse so she could greet them as well. Her face fairly beamed as she gave Sterling a long, affectionate embrace. "We've missed you, dear boy," she said, pulling back but still grasping his arms as she looked fondly up into his face. "My, have we missed you."

Then turning to Samantha, she enfolded her in an embrace as well. "I don't know if you like hugs from strangers," she said quietly, "but I consider myself your strongest supporter, so I feel like I know you already." She stood a couple inches shorter than Samantha and smelled of clean earth and fresh baking. Her arms were soft, her brown eyes infinitely kind, and Samantha immediately liked the woman, somehow already feeling comfortable with her. No longer nervous, she hugged Mrs. Tomlinson back.

"Thank you for sending that telegram," she said softly, for the woman's ears alone, before they pulled apart.

Mrs. Tomlinson winked at her, as if to say, *we have things to discuss*, then turned to the others and quickly took charge. "Jerome, will you put the luggage in the back of the wagon, please? And Sterling, would you mind driving us home? I would love to get acquainted with Samantha in the back while you and Jerome catch up."

"It would be my honor," he said, bowing in mock formality. Then he handed the women up to the seat in the back and climbed up to the front, ruffling Jerome's hair fondly and clucking to the horse. The wagon jolted forward and they headed away from the town and onto a wide country road at a clip.

Samantha smiled to herself at Sterling's obvious relaxed and comfortable way with this family.

Mrs. Tomlinson caught Samantha's expression and smiled too. "He's quite a catch, that young man."

"Yes," Samantha agreed. "Sometimes I still feel like I'm dreaming that he chose me." Her eyes were wide with honest amazement and Mrs. Tomlinson laughed.

"Oh, it goes both ways," she said. "No doubt about that. He thinks the world of you and did not feel he measured up to you when he left here. I'm just glad something I said helped him keep hoping."

"Oh, so am I!" Samantha said with feeling. She placed a hand on the older woman's arm. "Thank you for giving him the love and support he needed all those months, for being his family. You and Jerome mean so much to him. He talks about you all the time. And thank you for encouraging him to return to Oberlin, to me. I shall never forget that day." Samantha glanced away a moment as the tender memory returned to her.

Mrs. Tomlinson clasped Samantha's hands in her own and squeezed gently. "I knew you were good for him in so many ways, even though I had never met you. The way he spoke of you, the things you made him think about, how you helped him change and improve, I just knew that was something worth hanging onto, and if I could do anything to help, I had to do it."

Samantha gave a tentative smile.

As they jostled on the wagon seat, passing widely spaced farms, the two women soon found themselves talking about many things: their different towns, the Tomlinson's farm, Jerome's latest woodworking projects, their church communities. And in the background she could hear Sterling's enthusiastic comments to Jerome as the boy told him what he had missed during the summer. She liked this feeling of acceptance and friendship and added it to her list of blessings for the day. Staying with these folks would be no hardship at all!

***

Later that evening, they all sat around the sturdy kitchen table, eating a simple but delicious meal of baked potatoes cooked in butter and herbs, collards simmered with bacon, and bowls of pears and blueberries topped with sweetened cream for dessert. Samantha couldn't decide whether she enjoyed the food or the conversation more, they were both so pleasant. Mrs. Tomlinson asked about their plans for the week. They spoke of the school and the cemetery, and other possible places Sterling wanted to show her, and then he said, "But what she most needs to do while she's here is find her family."

Mrs. Tomlinson's spoon stopped halfway to her mouth, her eyes wide. "Family?" she asked. "I didn't know you had relatives here! What are their names?" She set her spoon back in the bowl and looked at Samantha intently. "I never imagined you had a personal connection to this village!"

Samantha patted her mouth with a napkin before answering. "Joseph and Julia Lewis are my grandparents. I didn't even know that myself until recently."

Mrs. Tomlinson looked thoughtful. "I've heard of them, but I don't know them personally—"

"Isn't Lewis the last name of the postmaster?[2]" Jerome interrupted. He already seemed to feel comfortable enough around Samantha that his shyness had mostly melted away.

Mrs. Tomlinson brightened. "You're right, son! I think it is. Why, Samantha, are you all right?"

Alarmed, Sterling turned to look at Samantha beside him and saw that she had grown distressingly pale. "What is it?" he demanded, wondering if she were about to faint. That would be a first.

Mind racing, Samantha saw Uncle Samuel's letter in her mind's eye, which had said, "*I continue to work at the post office and enjoy it well enough.*" Could it be that he still worked there and was now the postmaster? "Is his first name Samuel?" she asked, heart pounding.

"Samuel Lewis," Mrs. Tomlinson mused slowly. "I can't say for sure, but that does sound familiar."

"It *must* be him," Samantha said quietly, grasping the table with both hands. "I expected to search for days before finding anyone. Yet, it *is* a very small town..." She let out an incredulous laugh. "Perhaps we have already almost found my uncle!" Color flooded back into her face that was now lit with hope.

Jerome grinned at her and Mrs. Tomlinson clasped her hands together in excitement, beaming across the table. "Oh my! The post office is closed now, of course, but we could head into town first thing tomorrow morning, if you like."

---

2. Not the real postmaster of Worthington at that time.

Samantha nodded. "Thank you." She turned to look at Sterling and another astonished laugh bubbled out of her. "I might have found my uncle!"

He laughed at her reaction, and with his arm about her shoulders, pulled her into a sideways embrace, their heads touching briefly. He loved seeing her excited like this.

"I don't know if I will be able to sleep tonight!" she exclaimed. Suddenly she was too excited to eat, and her mind whirled with questions, possibilities, doubts, and hopes.

***

That night, after the foursome had spent hours talking, cleaning up, and talking some more, Samantha followed Mrs. Tomlinson down the hall to the bedroom where she would stay. Sterling had agreed to remain the night, since it was already well past dark, but had insisted he sleep on the sofa in the parlor so Mrs. Tomlinson wouldn't have to make up another bed. The older woman held a lamp aloft to light their way, telling Samantha again, "I am so glad you could come to Worthington. And it makes it all that much more poignant that you are returning to your roots!"

"You're right, I suppose I am," Samantha mused. "Funny, how things are coming full circle. I would never have imagined this a few months ago."

"God works in surprising ways," Mrs. Tomlinson affirmed, opening the door. "He must have wanted you here for a purpose, and with any luck, you may discover some of that tomorrow."

Samantha sucked in a breath, then let it out slowly. "Yes. It's all a bit too exciting."

Mrs. Tomlinson set the lamp on the bedside table and chuckled. "You will need your strength to face it all, so I hope you can sleep in spite of the excitement." She gestured at the room. "It's nothing fancy, but it should be comfortable."

"Yes, I am sure it will be. Thank you so much." In the dimness, Samantha couldn't make out all the details of the bedroom, but she could see that the bedspread was a colorful patchwork and the rag rug in front of the bed was equally colorful, and expertly braided into a tight weave. "It's perfect."

Mrs. Tomlinson opened the window to allow a night breeze to waft in. "It's a bit stuffy in here; I hope that helps. Please let me know if you need anything." She turned back to Samantha. "I never like feeling like a guest in someone else's home, so when I have guests

93

I don't wait on ceremony. I want you to feel at ease, as if this is your own home. If you need anything, please don't hesitate to ask."

Samantha nodded. "I appreciate your hospitality. You know," she added slowly, "I just realized I have never stayed in *anyone's* home before, so this is a new experience for me." Under her breath, she added, "There seem to be many of those lately."

Instead of expressing amazement at her words, Mrs. Tomlinson said simply, "Well, I am honored to be your first hostess." She laid a hand on Samantha's shoulder and said warmly, "And I'm glad you chose Sterling. I love that boy like a son, and seeing him so happy now just fills my heart to the brim with joy. I have never seen him this way before. He fairly glows!" Her large smile seemed to brighten the dim room and it warmed Samantha's heart to hear the observation.

She smiled back at the woman and said honestly, "He makes me the happiest I have ever been."

"Good. That is as it should be." Mrs. Tomlinson patted her shoulder a final time and stepped back. "I will leave you to your sleep, then." She headed to the door and then paused and turned back. "Oh, and please call me Thora. Last year I could never convince Sterling to use my first name, but now that he will not be Jerome's teacher at school anymore, I am hoping he will relax his rules of etiquette."

"All right," Samantha nodded. "I would be pleased to call you Thora."

"Good," Thora sounded gratified. "Sweet dreams!" She passed into the hall, closing the door behind her, and Samantha was left with her thoughts in the dimness, suddenly feeling very tired after all.

Chapter 9

LONG LOST LETTER

August 1902

The next morning, Sterling and Samantha borrowed a horse and wagon at Thora's insistence, because in addition to Sterling's two small suitcases, she had loaded him up with foodstuffs that he could store in his room at the boarding house over the next week or two. As it turned out, Thora was involved in a time-sensitive canning project that she needed to attend to and offered Jerome as a stand-in chaperone. He accepted the role dutifully, but brought along a woodcarving project to work on while they did their investigating. He liked to keep his hands busy and "didn't much fancy meeting new people," as he frankly stated. Samantha smiled inwardly at that last admission and thought how well he would fit in with her father and her old self.

In her lap, she held a small reticule that contained a slip of paper with the Lewis addresses on it, and the small framed picture of her mother and father that she had found in the attic. Just before leaving home, she had thought to pack it as a sort of proof of who she was, should she need it. As Sterling maneuvered the wagon into place between two other wagons parked in front of the post office, her heart began to pound again with anticipation. Was she moments away from meeting her uncle?

Sterling secured the reins and gave her a sympathetic smile, putting an arm around her shoulders in a brief, comforting gesture. "It will soon be over, dearest, one way or another. And I have the feeling it will be good."

"Oh, I really hope so," she said, exhaling. "Thank you for coming with me."

"I wouldn't miss it!" He jumped down and held out a hand to help her descend. Turning to Jerome he teased with a wink, "Thanks for holding down the wagon until we get back," as if the boy's weight alone were enough to keep the wagon from budging. Tucking Samantha's arm into his elbow, he walked with her up the front steps and inside the dim, musty-smelling building.

There were a few patrons ahead of them, and while they waited, Samantha studied the man behind the counter. He wore spectacles, much like the wire-rimmed ones she always kept on hand for reading. His straight brown hair was oiled and slicked back neatly in the style of the day, his mustache trim and neat. He was of above-average height and slim build, and something about his cheekbones and facial structure seemed familiar. But was that because she wanted him to be Uncle Samuel, or because he actually was her mother's brother?

Last night, the Tomlinsons' description of him had not been very detailed and Sterling could tell that Samantha had craved a clearer mental picture of the postmaster. Sterling wished he'd been able to supply her with a better description from his brief meeting of the man when he mailed his letter last year, but now, as he looked at him again, he barely looked familiar.

When it was their turn, Samantha was glad no one else had come into the small building behind them because she didn't want an audience for such a private meeting. When the man looked up at them expectantly, her mouth suddenly went dry, her mind grappling for the right words to say.

"Good morning, miss. Sir," the man nodded to them both. "How may I help you today?"

"Um, yes, sir, thank you." She placed a stabilizing hand on the counter between them. "Excuse me, are...are you Samuel Lewis?" She hadn't figured out how to phrase the question politely and vaguely, and hoped the direct approach would work just as well.

"I am." He looked at her quizzically.

Samantha's heart raced and of its own volition, her mouth blurted, "I think you may be my uncle!"

The man's eyes blinked behind his spectacles and she realized how much they looked like her own. "Pardon me?" he asked, his brows puckering together.

She stood straighter, trying to regain her composure, and Sterling placed a fortifying hand on her back. Clearing her throat, she began again. "I'm...I'm sorry, that was abrupt.

My name is Samantha Jennings and I am here visiting from Oberlin. I sent a letter a few weeks ago, looking for my mother's family, the Lewises. I know my mother's brother's name was Samuel..." She trailed off as the man's face paled and he looked at her as if she were an apparition. He clutched the counter much as she had clutched the table the night before, and she looked on in concern.

Sterling reached across the counter and grasped the man's arm. "Sir?" he asked. "Are you all right?"

The man nodded, then took a deep breath and the color slowly returned to his face. He looked behind them through the window, and seeing no other patrons entering, hurried around to their side of the counter and hung a "return soon" sign from a nail on the door before locking it. Then he turned back to face them and stood studying Samantha intently. He looked at her for so long that she began to grow uncomfortable, until she realized that his eyes were glistening with emotion.

"Are you really Lovenia's girl?" he asked at last, his voice hoarse.

She nodded, a lump rising in her throat. "Uncle Samuel?" she asked.

In answer, he held out his arms to her, and she stepped forward into his embrace. With her arms around him, she felt a shudder pass through him, as if with a silent sob, and she tightened her grip. *Uncle Samuel!* she told herself incredulously, joyously. *I have a real uncle, in the flesh!* She thought back to the tender letters he had written her mother and the loving and supportive relationship they had obviously shared. When he pulled back, holding her firmly by the elbows, she looked up at him and smiled, trying to blink away the mist that had gathered in her own eyes.

"You look just like her," he whispered. "Taller, but so like my beloved sister."

Samantha's laugh hiccupped. "That's what my father recently told me, too."

His grip on her elbows tightened. "Basil?! How is he?" Then realizing he still had hold of her, Samuel apologetically relaxed his grip and lowered his hands.

"He is...fine. He has never really recovered from the loss of my mother. But lately he has begun to improve."

Uncle Samuel nodded in sad understanding, his expression full of empathy. "Theirs was true love, and Basil felt things deeply. I have long prayed for my brother-in-law. When he stopped returning our letters, praying was all any of us could do."

"I found those letters in the attic a few weeks ago, in my mother's things. I am so glad you wrote them, even though Father never wrote back. They gave me a peek into each of your hearts and lives. And with the addresses written on the envelopes, they also gave me hope that I might be able to find you. But I didn't expect to discover you at the post office the day after I arrived!"

Uncle Samuel's mustache twitched up in a smile and then his eyes suddenly widened, obviously remembering something. At once, he looked stricken and focused back on her. "I'm sorry. I just remembered something dreadful I did months ago by accident. It was completely unintentional, but I've worked here most of my adult life and I know better!"

"Why, whatever do you mean?" she asked, sure that this gentle man could not have done anything so terrible.

"Oh, I am so sorry," he repeated. "I never meant for this to happen." He seemed to be mentally cursing himself. He held up an index finger. "One moment." With that, he hurried out of the room and Samantha and Sterling looked at each other in bewilderment.

When he returned a few moments later, he held an envelope in one hand and presented it to Samantha.

She looked at it and immediately noted that it was addressed to her in Sterling's hand. "What is—?" she asked at the same time as Sterling asked, "Is that—?!"

Uncle Samuel nodded regretfully. "It came through here months ago, and when I saw the name and address, my heart stopped beating. I always remembered your name, Samantha, of course, and thought so often of you and your father in Oberlin. So when I saw this envelope, I couldn't believe it!" His eyes widened at the remembrance. "It was a busy day with all the Christmas mail passing through, and I only meant to keep the letter in my desk until I could copy down the address, which is a more detailed now than it was nearly twenty years ago. With it, I thought I might try again to contact Basil—or you. But things were so busy here I didn't get around to it, and then a couple days later, I fell ill and didn't return to the post office for over a week. When I did make it back, there was so much extra work piled up, and the Christmas season was fully upon us, and what with one thing and another," he lifted his shoulders in a gesture of acute apology, "I completely forgot it was still in my desk. I know I should never have put it in there," he said penitently. "I've *never* done that before. It's a violation of my duties! I don't know what came over me, but I really just wanted to make contact again."

"It's quite all right, Uncle Samuel," Samantha said, touching his hand to stop the apologies. "No harm done. It all worked out in the end, so you needn't worry. But thank you!" She held up the envelope. "We have wondered for a long time what happened to this letter." She eyed Sterling teasingly. "Now I can finally read it!"

Sterling gave an embarrassed chuckle. "I am not sure you want to. It's pretty awful." But by the look she gave him, he didn't think she believed him. She simply smiled and placed it inside her reticule.

He turned back to Samuel and explained briefly, "I'm Sterling, the one who sent the letter." He stuck out his hand and they exchanged a handshake. "It was my feeble attempt to tell Samantha I cared about her and would return to Oberlin but was not expecting too much."

"Ah." The remorse in Samuel's face melted away and his eyes twinkled as he immediately grasped how things had been between them.

"Yes, one of *those* letters," Sterling chuckled wryly, remembering his anguish and heartache, how he had wanted to say so much more, but did not want to be presumptuous.

Uncle Samuel's brown mustache tilted up on both sides and his eyes crinkled at the corners as he smiled, looking from one of them to the other. "It seems things worked out well, despite my lapse in judgment."

Sterling took Samantha's hand. "They certainly did."

Samantha looked up at Sterling appreciatively, then back at her uncle. "I am so glad we found you! Are there others of the Lewis[1] family living here still?"

"Yes, yes," Samuel said animatedly. "Most of us are still here, actually, just more spread out than we used to be, as there are so many more of us."

"Oh, I want to learn about everyone!" Samantha exclaimed. "I would love to meet them all!"

---

1. There really was a Lewis family who lived in Worthington at this time. Perhaps most prominent among them was Worthington Columbus "W.C." Lewis, who was the mayor from 1902-1905, and owned the W.C. Lewis Department Store. See http://www.worthingtonmemory.org/scrapbook/pictures/worthington-columbus-lewis and http://www.worthingtonmemory.org/scrapbook/pictures/photograph-wc-lewis-department-store-interior.

A tapping sounded at the door and they turned to see a patron looking expectantly through the window.

"We can come back later," Sterling said immediately. "It looks like duty calls."

"Unfortunately, yes," Uncle Samuel reluctantly agreed. "But I will have an hour or so for lunch. Might you return at noon? I could take you over to my home, introduce you to my wife and children, and see about inviting the rest of the family to gather soon."

"That would be wonderful," Samantha said, her heart swelling at the thought of a large family gathering, of belonging to such a group.

"Noon it is, then." Samuel embraced her again. Then he strode to the door, unlocked it, and invited the patron inside, apologizing for the wait.

She and Sterling excused themselves and returned to the waiting wagon where Jerome sat in the back, feet dangling, a small pile of shavings on the ground below. When Sterling had settled himself beside her once again, he said, "Well, how about that?!"

Samantha's head whirled with so many questions and possibilities that she couldn't voice any of them, but only sighed in a rush.

Sterling laughed and took up the reins. "I understand," he said. "It's a great deal to take in all at once. But just wait till this afternoon!"

"I feel overwhelmed already," she said, as he directed the horses back to the main road. "But also very excited."

"You'll be brilliant," Sterling assured, eyes shining.

***

Sterling took them to the boys' school next and let Jerome show Samantha around the building, eventually ending up at Sterling's classroom—which she immediately fell in love with. It showed obvious evidence of a thoughtful, invested, and very capable teacher.

The school wasn't large, but it was certainly no one-room schoolhouse. Each classroom housed a different grade of boys, which begged a question. "How does a town of under five hundred people[2] support a school this size?" she asked Sterling.

---

2. https://en.wikipedia.org/wiki/Worthington,_Ohio

"Students attend from neighboring small towns, but also from Columbus, which boasts a population of over one-hundred twenty-five thousand. Some of them live in town with extended family, going home on the weekends, and others commute back and forth on the train every day."

Samantha was surprised. "That seems so far for children to travel!"

Sterling nodded. "Perhaps, but the trip isn't so long by train. After all, citizens of this town have commuted by train since 1894, so it's a common enough practice by now. And it's the older children who travel alone anyway. They do their homework on the train and don't seem to lose any time that way. But it is definitely a commitment."

"Surely Columbus has many good schools..."

"It does," Sterling confirmed. "But The Worthington Boys' School[3] has developed a strong reputation for innovation and a well-rounded education, and Mr. Grover is always visiting other areas, making connections, and telling everyone about this school he loves so well."

"And that, in turn, brings in enough students to continue supporting the school here in little old Worthington."

"Precisely. It's a good place to be."

"I can see that!" Everything was clean and in order, though after the summer months, a light film of dust covered the desks. There was a bulletin board for student work, which featured poems, essays, and artwork. Apparently, Sterling had chosen to keep them up for the new students to see before he replaced them with their own work. Some of Sterling's favorite quotes were tacked around the room, and one side wall was made up entirely of filled bookshelves, though one shelf contained a variety of rocks, shells, and fossils, instead of books. Jerome wandered over to peruse a bookshelf, something he would not have done last year. Gratified, Sterling observed this without comment.

"I would have *loved* this classroom as a child," Samantha told Sterling, clasping her hands together in delight. "I can tell that you make learning interesting and exciting, and I love seeing evidence of such a variety of subjects, and different ways of learning."

"Thank you," he said, humbled by her sincere compliment. "I learned so much last year and am certain I will learn much more this year, as well. Teaching this age group was not

---

3. This school is fictional.

the profession I thought I wanted, but now I feel like it is the one God had in mind for me all along. It's a pity it took me so long to realize that, but now I can make up for lost time. One thing I appreciate about learning is that there is always more of it to do! I can never learn it all."

"I couldn't agree more. And I love your quote there at the front." She pointed to a paper tacked above the blackboard that read, *Tell me and I forget, teach me and I may remember, involve me and I learn.*

Sterling nodded. "Benjamin Franklin's advice was invaluable to me last year and will continue to be a focus for me this year. I have seen how true that is—for me, as well as for my students."

Samantha pondered this for a moment. "I can see the wisdom in that concept. Franklin was so full of wisdom. When you were gone last year and I was learning so much, trying out things for the first time, and experiencing so much change, I often thought of his counsel that 'When you are finished changing, you're finished.'"

"Indeed," Sterling chuckled. "I think learning and changing should continue on to the end of life."

"And hopefully beyond!" Samantha quipped.

"Now there is a concept to contemplate," Sterling said thoughtfully.

Next, he and Jerome showed her the school's assembly room and the schoolyard, where the boys played during recess or enjoyed outdoor class time and activities when the weather was good. They walked back to the wagon, where the horse grazed on grass that had grown long over the summer. Jerome gave the animal a pat and looked at Sterling and Samantha to see where they would go next.

"This really seems like a lovely situation for you, Sterling," Samantha observed. "I can see why you enjoy teaching here so much."

"And you haven't even met the superintendent yet," Sterling noted as he led her to a separate building nearby, Jerome following along behind. "The success of this school, the teachers' high morale, and the students' respect of the administration all tie back to Mr. Grover. He is a wonder: allowing me enough freedom in my curriculum that I feel like I can truly become invested in it and personalize it to my class, but creating enough structure and accountability that I don't veer off track."

"I can see how that could be a difficult balance."

"But he handles it so well and sincerely seems to care about everyone. I have really appreciated all I've learned from him."

Samantha squeezed his hand.

"Here is his door. Let's see if he's in; I would like you to meet him." Sterling rapped lightly and after a moment, they heard footsteps and the door opened.

A slight man of average height poked his head out and, seeing Sterling, broke into a delighted smile. His face was mostly unlined and looked surprisingly youthful for the shiny crown and graying fringe of hair that accompanied it. "Sterling!" he exclaimed with pleasure, shaking his hand. "You're back! And Jerome Tomlinson! How are you, my friend?" He shook Jerome's hand next and Jerome grinned at him.

Sterling grinned, too, as he exchanged an energetic handshake with the man. "It's good to be back, sir! And I would like to introduce you to Miss Samantha Jennings. Samantha, this is Mr. Grover, the school's superintendent."

Mr. Grover eyed her with curiosity, pushing his spectacles up his nose a bit with one finger. "So this is the girl you spent most of last year pining over," he teased lightly.

Sterling smiled lopsidedly.

Hearing this outside perspective of that difficult time so succinctly distilled into one sentence gave Samantha the desire to both giggle and comfort Sterling. But she just smiled at him.

"I can see why." Mr. Grover took her hand and shook it in both of his. "Samantha, it is a pleasure to make your acquaintance." She appreciated his open, friendly manner, and was further gratified by his upfront demeanor when he said, "By all appearances, you accepted Sterling and the two of you have reconciled. That is a wonderful thing and I am glad to see it. We surely appreciate Sterling around here."

Samantha nodded in acknowledgement. "Thank you for all your support of him last year. He speaks very highly of you, as does Thora Tomlinson, whom I met yesterday."

She was surprised to see Mr. Grover's cheeks color faintly at the mention of Thora's name, but he said only, "We would love to have Sterling stay on for many more years to come, but I have the feeling that may not be in the cards for him." He winked.

"Perhaps not," she replied, glancing at Sterling who, for once, seemed at a loss for words, his lips slightly parted in surprise. "We still have much to decide," she told Mr. Grover vaguely. "But he has been telling me all about his commitment to making this his best year yet."

"I don't doubt that in the least," Mr. Grover returned, clapping Sterling on the shoulder.

Sterling closed his mouth and cleared his throat. "Thank you, sir. We won't take up any more of your time, but I am glad we could say hello. I want to show Samantha around town some more."

They made their goodbyes and, with the remaining time before lunch, Sterling drove them to the cemetery. Once again, Jerome stayed in the wagon, looking on and whittling as they walked across the brilliant green lawns, past rows of headstones of all shapes and sizes. Sterling took her hand again and allowed the peace of the place to distill into his soul as it had so often before. "It still amazes me to consider how important this place is for us," he said. "And that it happened independently for each of us. It became my haven from a busy workload and a relief from anxious thoughts about you." He looked down with a thoughtful and reminiscent smile.

Her left hand clasped in his, Samantha grasped his arm with her right and drew a little closer, her skirts brushing against his legs as they continued their leisurely walk. "It really is the dearest little coincidence that this is the cemetery we were both drawn to."

"Perhaps it was no coincidence," Sterling offered.

She glanced up at him, one fair eyebrow raised, as if to ask if this was really the first time the thought had occurred to him.

He chuckled. "Of course, you reached that conclusion long ago, didn't you?"

"Of course," she smiled up at him.

He shook his head in amusement. "You are always one step ahead of me."

She shrugged. "Maybe sometimes, but not in everything."

"That's kind of you to say, but I'm not sure I believe it," he returned, still laughing. "I feel that, mentally and intellectually, I am always running to keep up with you. And spiritually, too."

Now Samantha was laughing as well. "If you are behind at all, it is only by a split second—and then you rebound and give me much to think about. Besides, you are so good with people: you are leagues ahead of me, socially."

"That's not your fault," Sterling pointed out. "Making up for seventeen years of isolation in one year was a monumental task! But you learn so much, so quickly, whatever you're striving for."

Samantha considered this. "Thank you. I'm trying. Here, I think my mother's headstone is close now." They slowed to look more carefully at the inscriptions and she added, "For me, this place became a connection to my mother and brother, a place where I found beginnings and closure all at once—a curious combination, to be sure."

"I believe it," he said, remembering that day months ago when, quite by chance, he had come upon the tender scene of Samantha and her friends at her mother's headstone.

She let go of him as she focused on the graves around them, searching for the one forever imprinted in her mind's eye. A couple of minutes later, she let out a small cry and motioned for Sterling to join her as she made her way to a modest white marble stone with *Lovenia Lewis Jennings* engraved across the front. She stood gazing at it, noticing it looked more defined in the bright summer sunshine than it had in the watery light of wet spring. She trailed a finger under the letters, then the years 1858-1885, and thought about how short a life Lovenia's had been.

Sterling came up quietly behind her and placed gentle hands on her shoulders. "Does it sadden you to think about how young she died?" he asked.

"Yes." Samantha swallowed down a lump in her throat and reached up to touch Sterling's fingers and draw them down to intertwine with her own. He pulled closer and she leaned back into him, needing to feel his strength and constancy in this moment. "Many things about her passing make me sad, but I keep reminding myself of her life and legacy. She did so much good in the short time she had, and was a light to all around her, even in her limited capacity."

"When it comes down to it, no one can ask any more of another than that," Sterling mused, pressing a kiss to her hair.

"I suppose you are right," Samantha agreed. "I think she was so filled with Jesus' love, she couldn't help radiating it."

"Hmm," Sterling said thoughtfully. "Like a hot coal taken out of the stove radiates its warmth. Or the moon at night reflects the light of the sun."

"I like that. You're waxing poetic, Sterling." He heard the humor in her voice and then she said seriously. "I have much to live up to, but it's a worthy life goal."

"Indeed," he said, resting his chin on her hair. He felt so complete here under the trees, Samantha in his arms, a new school year ahead of him and the old insecurities, worries, and inexperience behind him. Having the woman he loved here with him, in the town he had grown to love, felt like everything had come full circle. He closed his eyes and just breathed in the peace for a minute.

He felt Samantha sigh and then she asked, "What are you thinking about?"

"About how you are already so much like your mother."

"How so?" Samantha asked, letting go of his hands and turning to look up at him, her blonde brows raised with hope. Hearing this never grew old and she always craved to know more.

"Being around you always makes me want to be better. And I am sure all your friends would say the same," he said with conviction. "From what I have learned about your mother, she was that way too. You *are* a light, Samantha, and a very bright one." He placed his hands around her slim waist and bent to kiss her slowly. Then he pulled back, their noses still touching, and admitted, "Of course, in my case the light you shine is even more compelling than perhaps it is to others, for I am as a moth attracted to the flame."

She smiled and he noted that her gray eyes held a twinkle of mischief. "There are two things wrong with that simile."

"Oh? Do tell," he said, kissing her nose and straightening up.

"One: you will never be as unintelligent and foolish as a moth. And two: my flame isn't fatal."

Sterling whistled in mock relief. "Thank goodness on both points, or I wouldn't have a chance with you!"

"True," she laughed.

Chapter 10

UNCLE SAMUEL'S FAMILY

AUGUST 1902

Near noon, they arrived back at the post office, where they greeted Uncle Samuel, just locking up. He took the seat in the back of the wagon and directed them to his house, where Jerome offered to unhitch the horse and lead it out to pasture. "I want to keep working on my carving," he told them. "Mother packed me a lunch, so I'll be fine outside while you have a nice visit."

"Are you sure?" Samantha asked him, brows knitted together. She had been ready to introduce him, along with herself and Sterling.

But Jerome nodded confidently, smiled, and led the horse away.

So Uncle Samuel led Sterling and Samantha to the pump out back, where they washed up before wiping off their feet on the way up the back steps of the covered porch. Samantha noted that the white clapboard house with dark green shutters was modest in size and style, but obviously well kept, if a little worn.

"Phoebe," he called as he opened the door, "I brought guests!"

In only a moment, they heard footsteps hurrying toward them and then a woman with dark blonde hair in a loose bun entered the other end of the hallway. She looked to be in her early forties, like Uncle Samuel, and she smiled expectantly as she stopped in front of them and asked, "Who have we here?"

Samuel put an arm around her and said, "You are not going to believe this, my dear, but my long-lost niece, Samantha, has found her way to us at last!"

Phoebe's pretty, pink-cheeked face looked at him in surprise. "Lovenia's daughter?"

"Yes, and her gentleman friend, Sterling." He motioned to them. "All the way from Oberlin."

"So far?!" Phoebe exclaimed. "Welcome to our home!" She stepped forward and grasped Samantha's hands in her own. "We are so happy to have you." And she looked it, with her cheeks beaming and her eyes shining.

"Thank you," Samantha said. "I am very happy to meet you, Aunt Phoebe." She loved the taste of the title in her mouth. Her first aunt!

The woman shook Sterling's hand and beamed up at him, as well. "Please, come into the dining room. Lunch is ready and I made plenty."

They followed her to the middle of the hall and entered an average-size dining room with a large table and heavy oak chairs. A cheery, red and white gingham tablecloth covered the table and an open door led from the dining room into the kitchen.

Aunt Phoebe disappeared back into the hall for a moment and they heard the loud, repeated clang of a large dinner bell. She re-entered the room and took her seat as the sounds of childish feet pounded across the floor above them and down the nearby stairs.

As children tumbled in, one after the other, Samantha looked at them closely, not trying to hide her great curiosity and delight. They hurried to their seats, talking loudly among themselves, until they noticed, almost simultaneously, that they had visitors.

"Papa, who's that?" the youngest one asked, poking a little pink finger at them with one hand and pulling bashfully on her lip with the other.

Uncle Samuel looked fondly around at the full table, making certain everyone was listening. "Children, I'd like you to meet your cousin, Samantha Jennings. And this is her friend, Sterling."

"Are you my cousin, too?" the little girl asked Sterling.

Sterling smiled and, without missing a beat, said, "I would like to be."

The girl nodded, satisfied.

The oldest boy, who looked to be around fourteen, asked, a little defensively, "Jennings? I don't remember an aunt and uncle Jennings."

Aunt Phoebe supplied the explanation: "Papa's sister Lovenia, who died, was married to Basil Jennings. Samantha is their daughter."

"Oh." The boy was placated, but his expression remained guarded.

"Before things get too chaotic," Uncle Samuel said, turning to Samantha and Sterling, "let me introduce you to the crowd."

One by one, the children were introduced, and Samantha rehearsed the names to herself over and over again, so she wouldn't forget. Benjamin was the oldest, and she was right in guessing the blond lad was fourteen. At thirteen, Mary was the oldest girl, and though reserved, Samantha could tell by her bright eyes that she was brimming with questions. Serious Cyrus was eleven, and whether it was his wire-rimmed spectacles or the way his intelligent eyes closely examined her, he seemed the studious type. Eight-year-old Lucy swung her legs in her seat, unable to contain all her energy, and beamed at Samantha, much as her mother had a few minutes before. Little Rose was six, and though a bit bashful, watched her new cousin openly and didn't look away when Samantha met her gaze. They all seemed like such intelligent, well-grounded children that Samantha couldn't wait to become better acquainted.

Uncle Samuel offered grace and they began to eat. The food was good and the conversation lively. In fact, as it turned out, there was not much opportunity to speak because at times the children's conversation was so noisy that Sterling couldn't even hear Samantha's voice when she tried to talk—and she sat right next to him. But as he watched her soaking in the scene, learning about each person in her newfound extended family, smiling and laughing, appreciating the varied personalities and topics, he knew she didn't mind at all.

And she didn't. In fact, she appreciated that Uncle Samuel and Aunt Phoebe were not the type to follow the common rule that "children should be seen and not heard." This chaotic display of love and sharing—with the occasional argument—before her was more natural. She could tell that this daily experience fostered communication and social growth within the family unit. It was not something she had ever thought about before, because she had never experienced it, but she loved being in the thick of it for this fleeting moment. It couldn't have been more opposite from her silent, solitary upbringing, and she respected her aunt and uncle for allowing their children the freedom to be themselves and to openly converse, learning and working out conflicts together.

The children ate surprisingly quickly, for all their vocal outbursts, and in about twenty minutes they had all finished and asked to be excused. All except Mary, who shyly asked if she could stay. Samuel excused the other four with a wave of his hand, and Phoebe reminded them to take their dishes to the kitchen sink on their way. When they had all traipsed out to return to their previous activities or run outside, Samuel and Phoebe looked at Samantha and Sterling and let out an almost simultaneous sigh. Then they all laughed and finished eating, chatting as they did so. Mary listened with interest, and Samantha could tell she was soaking in everything and trying to formulate an opinion about her.

Samantha and Sterling learned that Samuel and Phoebe married the year after Lovenia died, and it had taken two years before Benjamin came along. The delay had concerned Phoebe a bit, but then Mary arrived the very next year, and their lives had quickly become very busy. "With two children so close in age, it was almost like having twins," Phoebe remarked, glancing fondly at Mary. "There were days I was so exhausted just trying to maintain the house and keep us all fed, in between caring for the two little ones, that I would melt into a puddle of tears when Samuel walked through the door after work." She laughed and patted Samuel's hand. He nodded as he remembered, respect for what she had experienced evident in his expression.

"I laugh now," she continued, "because I have time and perspective on my side. But it was very difficult then. I knew it would be. I come from a large family and saw the exhaustion of my mother on many occasions. But, like so many things in life, I didn't really *know* how hard it would be until I went through it myself. However," she added, "I also didn't truly understand how fulfilling motherhood could be, and how much love I would feel for my family—even when the little tykes were getting into things and making more work for me."

Samantha nodded thoughtfully. "Aunt Eleanor mentioned that very thing in a letter she wrote to my mother. She commented about her twins getting into mischief and how tired she was."

Uncle Samuel chuckled. "I remember those days. That was before Phoebe joined the family, but I can recall dropping by to visit Eleanor and to play with the children, and noticing dark smudges under her eyes. But she was always patient with the little ones, and very good at redirecting their attention and energy when needed."

"Yes," Phoebe agreed. "In my early years of motherhood, when I was harried and needed advice, I appreciated Eleanor's gentle suggestions. She never imposed her ways on me, but I recognized the value of her perspective, since she had so much more experience than I did. She wanted to help me more, but as she had her last baby the same year I had Benjamin, and cared for five other children besides, she would send her two oldest children over instead, at least once a week after school, to help me however they could. They did that for several months. They were a godsend; such responsible children."

"I can see how helpful that would be," Samantha acknowledged. "How is Aunt Eleanor's family now? Uncle Samuel mentioned that everyone still lives nearby."

"Everyone but them, actually. Though they aren't too far by train. Benjamin wasn't a year old before they moved to Columbus, when your uncle Andrew was offered a partnership in a law firm there. He had already been commuting to Columbus daily for a couple of years, but when that offer came through, they realized his position would be permanent. They decided they needed to live closer to his work so he could spend less time commuting and more time with them."

Samantha nodded, taking in all the information.

"Now Eleanor and Andrew are already grandparents many times over!"

"Cousin Elizabeth has three children of her own," Mary offered softly, then blushed as if she had said too much.

Aunt Phoebe nodded and ticked off Aunt Eleanor's children on her fingers. "Josiah also has three, and Seth, who married last year, has a new baby too. Our numbers just keep growing!"

Samantha's eyes widened and she did the math, realizing her oldest cousin would be in her late twenties by now. "So many new people to meet," she said under her breath. "More than I realized!"

Her aunt and uncle smiled at her kindly across the table. "One person at a time," Samuel reminded her. "Already, you have met seven of us, which was probably overwhelming, given the energy level around this table. I apologize if that was a bit too much."

They joined in his laughter, but Samantha insisted, "I loved it. You have a wonderful family and I appreciate you bringing me into your home like this, with no notice."

Aunt Phoebe gave Uncle Samuel a knowing glance and then looked back at Samantha. "Actually, Samuel received your letter last week, addressed to his mother's house, and then I had a dream only two nights ago that you showed up at our back door."

Samantha looked at her, speechless.

"Really?" Sterling asked. "It sounds as if you were pretty well prepared, then, after all."

Uncle Samuel reached across the table and folded his larger hands around Samantha's. "As a family, we never lost hope of being reunited with you again someday. And over the past—eighteen years, is it?—I have never stopped thinking about or praying for you. I knew you might be up against some hard things, given how difficult your mother's passing was on your father, and I prayed that your strength might be equal to your trials."

Samantha's eyes filled with tears at the thought of someone she hadn't known praying for her all these years.

Sterling put a gentle arm around her shoulders and told them, "She *has* been incredibly strong."

"Thank you so much for remembering me," Samantha finally managed, blinking the tears away. "I needed those prayers. And my father needs them still." Suddenly remembering the old photo in her reticule, she pulled it out and showed it to them. "I did not find this until recently, but I brought it to show you, in case you needed proof of my identity." She laughed, a little embarrassed now that she had thought that might be necessary.

"Ah, yes." Uncle Samuel let go of her hands to reach for the picture and showed it to Aunt Phoebe and Mary. "I remember this! They were such a happy couple. Basil just doted on her, and Lovenia took such good care of him."

"It seems she did that for many people, in different ways," Samantha observed. "Even in a letter you sent her, you thanked her for her 'gentle, guiding presence,' and mentioned that you had frequent talks."

"Yes," Samuel said, nodding a bit sadly. "She was the sister I always felt closest to. Even though she was only two years older than I, it seemed she was always caring for me, helping me, teaching me, comforting me. All my sisters are wonderful in their own ways, but Lovenia was the best of sisters for me."

Samantha's heart constricted at the thought of him as a young man receiving word that Lovenia had died in a far-away town and he would never see her again. She could only imagine the hard blow that must have been for him. The question resurfaced in her mind that she had wondered for a while and suddenly this moment seemed the right time to ask it. "Uncle Samuel... Do you know if my mother named me after you?"

"Well..." Samuel pondered this for a moment. "Perhaps we will never know for sure, but there was one time, as children, when we imagined our future families and told each other we would each name a child after the other. When she had the baby boy who died, she never did name him. Somehow, with her near death and Basil nursing her back to health, it just never happened. I don't think Basil felt he could name the baby without your mother's input, and she was weak and unaware for so long... But when we received word from Oberlin that Lovenia had died, and that she wanted you to be named

Samantha, I had the feeling she was making good on her promise, especially considering its meaning."

"Meaning?" Samantha asked, looking at him blankly. "In all my studies, I never thought to study the meaning of my own name!"

Uncle Samuel's gaze was direct and compelling. "Samuel and Samantha both mean 'God has heard.'"

Samantha drew in a breath of surprise, her eyes instantly flooding with tears again. She thought of her mother's journal entries that expressed how very much she wanted a child and how happy she was while carrying Samantha, certain she was a girl. Lovenia had definitely felt that God had heard her and granted the desire of her heart at last.

"My middle name is Lovenia," Mary offered shyly.

So Uncle Samuel fulfilled his promise, too! Through her tears, Samantha looked at the sweet girl and saw in her face the honor she felt at the privilege and burden of this legacy.

Noticing that Samantha's handkerchief was almost wet through, Aunt Phoebe handed her another, and Samantha took it, wiping her nose and laughing through her tears.

"In my case," Uncle Samuel offered, his mustache twitching up on one side, "I think my naming was an expression of gratitude and relief to finally have a boy, after three girls."

Phoebe swatted at him playfully. "You know those girls were always good and didn't cause your parents any trouble." She paused and then giggled. "Or at least, two of them didn't."

"Yes, Irene always somehow gave them a run for their money, though I don't think she meant to."

"How is Aunt Irene?" Samantha asked, holding the two handkerchiefs in her lap and hoping she wouldn't need to use them again. "I confess I liked her letter best. She seemed so full of energy and good humor."

"That describes her well," Uncle Samuel confirmed. "You are an astute observer. She can be opinionated and forceful, but also full of fun and affection—and she is the favorite aunt, without question."

"Did she end up marrying Edward?" Samantha asked, remembering Aunt Irene's mention of him in her letter.

Aunt Phoebe shook her head. "No. She would have liked it to work, but when it came down to it, they simply were not compatible enough. Irene very much wanted a family of her own, but she has always been so spirited and independent that I don't think the young men knew quite what to do with her. She told me once that every time she was in a romantic relationship, she felt stifled and as if the young man expected her to be different than she was to fit the mold of the housewife he envisioned. She liked who she was and craved the freedom to be herself, and she never found a man who was her equal."

"Very true," Uncle Samuel confirmed. "But she remains a happy person, integral to this family, and the best entomologist I've ever met. Well," he admitted with a laugh, "the *only* entomologist I've ever met, but she has all the credentials to prove it. She is highly valued by colleagues and students alike."

"Fascinating!"

"You should see her insect collection!" Mary piped in. "She knows so many facts about each one."

"I hope to see it!" Samantha told the girl, impressed. That would be interesting, indeed. Suddenly, she felt the urge to ask what had been weighing on her heart the most. "I have another question—and I hope I am not asking too many—but," she hesitated, "are your parents—my grandparents—still alive?" She braced herself for the answer, afraid that it might not be what she so fervently wished.

"Your grandmother Julia is still alive and well, but…" Samuel trailed off and looked at Mary, who seemed to be gaining more confidence and had opened her mouth to answer the question.

"Grandpa Joseph died the year I was born," she offered.

"1889," Aunt Phoebe confirmed.

Uncle Samuel continued the flow of information. "His rheumatism flared up pretty badly after Lovenia left and he never really got control of it again. He and Mother wanted to go visit Lovenia and Basil after they moved away, but with Father's health declining, they were never able to do that. I think his concern for her wore him down, and after a few years he just didn't have the strength to keep fighting." Samuel sighed, remembering. "That was tough for all of us, to see the head of our family failing and becoming more enfeebled each year. He died at home of apoplexy,[1] which was quite a blow to Mother, as you can imagine. But it was bittersweet. We missed him dreadfully, but we were grateful

---

1. The term used at the time for cerebral hemorrhage or stroke.

his suffering wasn't prolonged any further." After a thoughtful silence he added, "He always yearned to meet you, Samantha."

Samantha lifted the driest of the two handkerchiefs to her face again and said, trying to laugh, "Don't make me cry again, Uncle Samuel!"

Sterling gently rubbed her back in a comforting gesture and addressed her aunt and uncle. "Thank you for answering Samantha's questions. I know she's had them for a long time, and it means so much to her to find you, make connections, and receive some answers."

Samantha quickly composed herself again and smiled at them gratefully. "May I come back and visit again before I go back to Oberlin?" she asked. "I would very much love to get to know the children better, and spend more time with you."

"Of course!" Aunt Phoebe exclaimed, standing up and moving toward her, Uncle Samuel and Mary following suit. "We wouldn't have it any other way."

Samantha stood to meet them and was engulfed in an embrace of many arms on all sides, her heart swelling with joy for this good family.

"We expect you to come back as often as you like, dear girl!" Phoebe told her, her own eyes wet with tears.

"You're one of us," Uncle Samuel confirmed, his voice tight with emotion. "We have a great deal of time to make up for."

Mary piped up, "Let's have a big family gathering, Papa, so everyone can meet her!"

"Yes," Samuel agreed, stepping back to look at Samantha. "Would tomorrow evening be amenable?"

Sterling stood close by, smilingly watching the touching scene, and Samantha glanced at him.

Uncle Samuel clapped Sterling on the shoulder. "We would be pleased to have you join us, as well, young man."

"Thank you," Sterling replied. "I appreciate your hospitality. We would be honored to join you."

"Wonderful!" Phoebe beamed, clasping her hands together. She turned to her husband, "Do you think Eleanor would agree to host it?" She turned back to Samantha and Sterling to explain, "She has the largest house."

"I am certain she will," Samuel responded. "She is undoubtedly as eager to meet you as I was. Where might I send you word, once all the details are arranged?" he asked Samantha.

"I'm staying with the Tomlinsons," she answered, "but they live a couple of miles out of town, so it might be best to send word to Sterling at the boarding house near the boys' school."

"Then it's all settled," Uncle Samuel said, smiling broadly.

They made their goodbyes and Uncle Samuel helped Jerome lead the horse back to the wagon and hitch it up, then he climbed in the back and they returned to the post office. There he dismounted and tipped his hat in farewell. "Until tomorrow," he said, his mustache twitching upward and his eyes shining.

***

That afternoon they stopped by Sterling's boarding house room to take his things from the wagon bed, carry them up the rickety flight of stairs, and deposit them in his room. Then Sterling turned over the reins to an eager Jerome, who drove them back to the Tomlinson farm. Sterling and Samantha sat together on the seat in the back and considered all that had occurred. What a whirlwind day! As Samantha thought about the remarkable moment when she saw Uncle Samuel for the first time, she suddenly remembered the letter in her reticule and pulled it out. Sterling watched with trepidation as she opened it, remembering his emotional conflict during that time. He was so glad not to be in that difficult place anymore, but as he re-read the long-lost letter Samantha held, all those feelings came rushing back to him:

December 14, 1901

Dear Miss Jennings,

I write to you with a heavy heart for any dishonor I have brought upon you by my conduct, this July last. It is with strong feelings of regret that I offer you my sincerest apologies and profoundest wish that I can in some way atone for my imprudent actions. I am presently employed as a teacher at the Worthington Boy's School and can therefore do no traveling until the end of the term, at which point I hope to meet you to express my heartfelt apologies in person.

Wishing you the best of a beautiful life and the blessings of your bounteous talents,

I am yours sincerely,
Lee Sterling

They finished reading it at nearly the same time and Samantha looked up at him, her eyes liquid gray pools of empathy, with no hint of teasing. "Oh, Sterling," she said. "You were really suffering when you wrote this, weren't you?"

He swallowed, feeling the old vulnerability again, the uncertainty of what had happened to her, and the agony of their silence.

She put a hand to his face and said softly, under the clatter of the wagon wheels and the clop of horse hooves, "I'm glad the letter was found, so I could finally read it. And I'm glad you came back to find me. I will keep this always, as a reminder of what we went through. We've come a long way, haven't we?"

He smiled and felt the old anxieties melt away as he held her gaze.

Chapter 11

A HOUSE FULL OF RELATIVES

AUGUST 1902

When they arrived at Aunt Eleanor and Uncle Andrew's large house in Columbus the following evening, Samantha was struck by how beautiful and homey it looked. The large house stood two stories high and was painted a lovely cream color, with red shutters around the largest windows, and a black asphalt roof. The long and wide front porch was roofed and symmetrically set in the center. On the porch's left side was a large, shuttered window on the ground floor and a smaller window above it, all under a pitched roof. On the right side were two smaller windows, one above the other, and a pitched roof at the top. Above the porch, the second story had three small windows side by side, with a flat roof over them. The overall effect was cheery and inviting, and Samantha's heart suddenly leapt with excitement at the anticipation of who she might meet. Sterling offered his hand to help her down from the horse-drawn cab they had hired from the train station. He didn't let go as they walked up the path to the house and she squeezed his hand, grateful to have him by her side.

Mary met them at the door before they could even knock, and they heard someone farther inside the house shout, "She's here, everyone! Samantha is here!" Mary smiled wide and welcomed them, stepping aside to let them in. Samantha hugged her cousin and told her how glad she was to see her again. Mary beamed and accepted a hug from Sterling as well, looking up at him a little starry-eyed.

A beautiful, dark-haired young woman who appeared to be near Samantha's own age entered just as Sterling and Mary pulled away from each other and she gaped at him for a second before clamping her mouth shut.

"I'm Sterling," he said, bowing respectfully.

The young beauty reverently offered her hand, which he took and gently squeezed, then released. Finding her voice, she replied, "My name is Julia. After my grandmother." Her rosy lips pursed and her elegant dark eyebrows arched in a way that made it obvious this was important information. Her hair, done up in very becoming ringlets, shook slightly when she moved.

"Her mother is Aunt Eleanor," Mary explained helpfully.

"It is so good to meet you, Julia. I'm Samantha."

Julia seemed to see her for the first time and appraised her with a calculating eye and a serious expression. "I know," she said. There was a weight to the words and a distinct coldness emanated from her. But then other people began spilling into the front hallway and Samantha was caught up in a whirlwind of introductions and embraces from strangers who somehow looked a bit familiar. Many had the high cheekbones and small upturned nose that Samantha had inherited from her mother. Many were tall and thin like her as well. It was a strange feeling to look around and recognize shared physical characteristics in people she had never seen before. But it was a wonderful feeling too.

Aunt Eleanor, a woman of average height and medium build, had light brown hair that was decidedly fading to gray. But the only detectable wrinkles were those at the corners of her eyes, and as she spoke and laughed quietly, Samantha could tell they were the laugh lines indicative of a happy person. Her tender embrace warmed Samantha and when she pulled back to look at her niece, her blue eyes were moist. Uncle Andrew stood behind his wife and gave Samantha a friendly smile and a nod. His gray hair and close-cropped gray beard gave him a distinguished air.

Suddenly Aunt Irene pushed her way to the front of the crowd by the door, as if she could not wait another moment. Samantha noticed that her hair was darker than her sister's and only slightly silvered, her build tall and strong. With a gaze that was direct and yet friendly and open, she embraced Samantha so tightly Samantha thought her breath would fail her. Finally, her aunt released her and said, "Welcome to the Lewis family, child! We have waited far too long for this moment. Forgive us if we are overeager."

Samantha did not know what to say or do as the children crowded around and everyone seemed to talk at once. She tried to learn everyone's names and connect each child with the correct parents, but quickly realized she would just have to be all right with asking names repeatedly as she sorted them out over time. Finally, once some of the children had satisfied their curiosity about her and wandered off, Aunt Phoebe and Uncle Samuel were suddenly there beside her and motioned to an older woman who had been watching the interchange off to one side. Samantha stared at her, willing herself to always remember this moment. She knew the woman must be her grandmother. The realization was sweet but also painful as she thought about how many years they had missed in knowing each other. The older woman's gray hair was done up in a large, pretty bun at the nape of her neck. She stood small and a little stooped, but her brown eyes shone bright and alert, and her smile was one of the most beautiful things Samantha had ever seen.

"Mother," Uncle Samuel said quietly, "I would like to officially introduce you to your long-lost granddaughter, Samantha Jennings. She has eagerly awaited the chance to meet you."

Samantha wanted to say so many things, but suddenly her mouth went dry and all her carefully prepared thoughts flew. As it turned out, the moment was too big to contain in words anyway, so both women simply reached for each other and quietly wept. Neither noticed anyone else, the hushed whispers and shuffles, or the muffled sniffs of multiple empathetic relatives.

Finally, Samantha composed herself enough to say, "I am so very glad you are alive and well, Grandmother Julia. I feared I might never be able to meet you!"

Her grandmother gave a choked laugh and wiped her face with the handkerchief Uncle Samuel handed her. "I am still here, thank the good Lord. I only wish Joseph could have lived to see this day. He always pined to know you, right from when he first heard of your birth. He loved all his grandchildren very much and it weighed on him that all he could do for you was pray."

Samantha nodded. "I think his prayers must have worked, even though I was unaware of them. I have found God and now I have found all of you!" She motioned with one hand as she looked around at the many people who smiled and wiped tears of their own. "And even my father is starting to come around, so I am hopeful that one day he will be reunited with you, as well."

The awkward silence that met that statement jolted Samantha back to the reality of all her individual relatives. She saw a few people look at each other with meaningful glances and then lower their eyes noncommittally. Samantha was unsure what this reaction meant, but she had no opportunity to ask because Aunt Eleanor announced brightly that the food was ready and the children were anxious to eat.

They all piled into the dining room and everyone began taking their places—apparently so used to this arrangement that they all knew where to sit. Eleanor gestured to Samantha and Sterling, offering them seats by herself and Uncle Andrew at the head. As not everyone could fit at the large table, children old enough to eat on their own sat at a smaller table off to the side. Sterling held the chair for her and scooted it in as she sat, then took the seat beside her.

"Large crowd," he commented, just loud enough for her to hear.

"Yes," she said, almost breathless. Trying to adjust to the unfamiliar situation with all its noise and organized chaos left them feeling a little off balance. It was like being at Uncle Samuel's table, only multiplied a few times!

Uncle Andrew offered grace, thanking the Lord for the miracle of being reunited with Samantha and the opportunity to share this family time, and then the chatter started back up immediately as people passed the food around. Samantha looked around the busy room, noting its bright and cheery ambiance. Late golden sunlight streamed in from windows that made up two sides of the large dining room. Every window's sash had been pulled up to allow in fresh air (but not flies, thanks to the screens[1]), in the hope that a breeze might blow through and offer a bit of relief from the heat. She loved the effect of the natural light and told Aunt Eleanor so.

Her aunt laughed as she spooned mashed potatoes onto her plate. "Thank you. I love the windows now too, but when we had so many little grimy hands around, it was the bane of my existence. For several years there, it seemed that the lower half of all my windows were always smudged."

Samantha nodded, smiling. She hadn't thought about that. Sterling passed her the steamed vegetables, then the roast beef, and the dishes kept coming. Before long, her plate was filled to overflowing.

It was a delicious meal and, like at Uncle Samuel's, it was difficult to make her voice heard over the din, so she just listened while she ate. Occasionally, the adults would smile at each other as they overheard parts of the children's conversations, and other times they ribbed each other about an anecdote that had happened some time in the past. Samantha realized with a twinge of regret that it would take quite a while to truly feel a part of all

---

1. https://bit.ly/4b2g26f

this. She was not familiar with any of their histories, personalities, or shared memories, and they had time and familiarity on their side. *But*, she told herself, *this is not a race or a competition and I need to focus on just getting to know everyone.* That might take quite a while, but she looked forward to the journey.

Several times as she looked down the long table, trying to memorize each face and remember their names, she caught young Julia watching her with a cold, reproachful eye. At first, Samantha thought she was mistaken, but the impression only grew as the meal progressed.

When supper was over, everyone old enough to help carried dishes to the kitchen, swept the dining room floor, or put leftovers away, in a practiced way. As Samantha stood by Sterling, wondering how she could help, Aunt Eleanor touched her shoulder and said, "The family rule is that whoever cooked the meal is off cleanup duty, and guests are not required to help."

Aunt Irene stepped up to join them. Samantha was about to protest when Aunt Irene continued where her sister left off. "We cooked the meal, and as you can see," she indicated the busy room, "there are plenty of hands to help. So," she clapped her hands together, "let us reconvene to the parlor." She walked out of the room, fully expecting them to follow her, and Samantha smiled inside. Apparently, Aunt Irene had no qualms about taking charge and taking care of people.

Aunt Eleanor motioned to her mother, who stood beside them now as well. "Mother, come and join us for a visit."

Grandmother Julia took her daughter's arm and smiled. "I think I will."

They followed Irene out the door and Samantha looked up at Sterling questioningly. He grinned and hooked a thumb in the direction of the kitchen. "I think I will find some men to wash dishes with...or something."

Samantha nodded, smiling, and hurried to catch up to her aunts and grandmother.

The parlor was another large and attractive room with a few stiff couches, a low table placed between them, and small end tables with lamps. A piano stood against one wall and a grandfather clock on the other. A fireplace graced the wall in between.

"You have a lovely home, Aunt Eleanor," Samantha told her, sitting on the couch across from the other women.

"Thank you. Andrew has always worked hard and been blessed to provide well for us. I appreciate that he was able to build us a fine house, comfortable for our large family."

"Uncle Samuel told me he is a lawyer." Samantha offered, realizing she knew precious little about any of her relatives.

"Yes, and a very good one, if I may say so," Aunt Eleanor replied. "People have come to respect his clear-headed perspective and professional way of representing them, and his services are much sought after."

Samantha nodded, impressed.

"But enough about us," Aunt Eleanor said. Beside her, Grandmother Julia's brown eyes were focused intently on Samantha, obviously filled to the brim with questions. "Mother, I know you want to talk to Samantha."

"I do." Grandmother nodded slowly and seemed to be trying to order her thoughts. Then she clasped her hands together tightly and exclaimed, "Oh, I never thought I would see this day!" Her voice was not as clear or as strong as it must once have been, but Samantha could hear the emotion in it from years of anguish.

In her longing to soften that pain and help heal the sorrow if she could, Samantha suddenly found herself moving across the room and kneeling at her grandmother's feet. She looked up at her dear face with the crinkles at the corners of her eyes, and asked, "What would you like to know, Grandmother? There is much I do not know, but I will share with you anything I can. Did you know my mother kept a journal up until she died?"

Sudden tears sprang to Grandmother Julia's eyes.

"That sounds like Lovenia," Aunt Irene said.

"Yes, it does," Aunt Eleanor said softly. "She enjoyed recording feelings and events. It was a quiet activity requiring little energy and she became quite good at it, with all the practice."

Samantha thought about that. She had been so focused on hearing her mother's voice through her journal that she had failed to recognize what a good writer she was! But it was true. "I knew nothing about her journal until the beginning of this year, when I found it in my father's library."

Grandmother grasped Samantha's hand and pulled it into her lap. "You truly knew nothing?" she asked in surprise.

Samantha shook her head in confirmation. "But reading it changed me."

Grandmother nodded in wise understanding.

"Where is the journal now?" Aunt Irene inquired.

"My father has it," Samantha explained. "When I finished it, he asked if he might borrow it to read it again. I did not want to let him at first," she admitted, "but I realized that I almost had it memorized and he had likely forgotten much of it."

Grandmother patted her hand. "You are a good daughter," she said simply.

"I also realized that Mother was his before she was mine, and he deserved to have it for a while. He promised I can have it back when he is finished."

The room was very quiet for a minute and when Samantha glanced up to see what the women might be thinking, she noticed that Aunt Eleanor looked thoughtful, Aunt Irene's lips were compressed into a hard line, and Grandmother Julia's gray brows puckered together in either concern or frustration, Samantha wasn't sure which. She pushed herself up from the rug and sat on the low table behind her, so as to be on a level with the other women. "I am sorry if I said something wrong," she offered. "I sense that the topic of my father is a heavy one, and somehow fraught with controversy."

Aunt Irene's expression instantly cleared and her lips turned upward. "My, you are perceptive, child," she said, with a self-deprecating laugh.

Aunt Eleanor placed a hand on her sister's knee and hurried to explain. "The loss of your parents affected each of us differently and we have dealt with it in our own ways, some more effectively than others."

Aunt Irene looked as if she wanted to say something more, but clamped her mouth shut and refrained.

"She is hardly a child anymore, is she, Irene?" Grandmother observed with a decided look of respect. "Samantha, I would say you have dealt with your losses and hardships admirably. You have grown into quite a remarkable young woman."

She reached a hand out for Samantha again, and Samantha leaned forward and clasped it, recognizing her grandmother's need for physical contact with her long-lost granddaughter.

"We hope you will feel part of the family and visit us any time." Grandmother's small hand tightened around hers.

"Yes," Aunt Eleanor agreed, nodding. "And letters! We hope you will keep in touch through the post when you are back in Oberlin."

Samantha couldn't help herself: she laughed in delight at the thrill of being so quickly accepted as one of them and suddenly having such women to turn to. "Thank you. It is hard to express how happy I am at finally having aunts and a grandmother! I have the feeling I will get very good at writing letters over the next several months, as I will also be writing Sterling."

Aunt Irene looked at her with raised eyebrows. "I have the feeling you already are good at writing letters, based on the ones you sent us. And based on your award-winning poem…" She trailed off expectantly.

Samantha sat back in surprise and Grandmother released her hand. "You read my poem?" she asked them. "I didn't imagine you would have seen that!"

Aunt Eleanor nodded. "Irene has been a regular newspaper subscriber for years and she was the one who saw it first. She could not help wondering if the author was the same Samantha Jennings we lost long ago, so she showed it to us. It is a lovely poem," she added.

"Thank you," Samantha said humbly. "I was not sure how it would be received, so I felt very vulnerable sending it off. I couldn't believe they wanted to publish it!"

"Do you have any more where that came from?" Grandmother asked. "I would love to read them, if you do. I tried my hand at poetry long ago, and have always had a soft spot for it."

"Oh, yes!" Samantha said, surprised and delighted. "I am not much for rhyming, but as long as I can write free verse, I have much to say in poetry. I have filled one notebook so far."

"Wonderful! Next time you come to Worthington, bring it with you," Grandmother suggested.

Samantha's heart squeezed, realizing there would be a next time—hopefully many return visits.

"Now you have grown up into this wonderful, strong young woman with a bright future ahead of you," Aunt Eleanor commented in her characteristically optimistic way, "and we hope you will include us in it. I know there are so many of us to get to know and it may take a while, but we love you."

Samantha became misty-eyed again. "I already love you all too! The connection happens quickly, doesn't it? Thank you for accepting Sterling and I, and for opening your hearts and your homes to us."

"The whole family is delighted with your return," Grandmother assured her.

Samantha remembered a certain unhappy face down the length of the dinner table and laughed softly. "Perhaps not everyone."

Grandmother looked at her in confusion, then over at her daughters for clarification.

Aunt Eleanor looked as stymied as her mother, but Aunt Irene nodded slowly. "I did sense some friction between you and a certain high-strung seventeen-year-old cousin."

"My Julia?" Aunt Eleanor asked in surprise. "Did she say something to you, Samantha?"

"She...didn't really have to," Samantha admitted reluctantly. "I am not sure why, but she very clearly doesn't care for me."

"Ah." Now it was Grandmother who looked as if she knew exactly what was going on. "I think I know the problem. I love my namesake dearly, but that girl has always been a little too proud of her status, I am afraid." She looked at Aunt Eleanor apologetically.

Aunt Irene immediately continued the train of thought. "And now it appears she feels threatened by your sudden arrival and celebrity status, Samantha. That silly girl should know her place in this family won't change. She should be happy for a new cousin, and one who is so close to her own age!" Then glancing at her sister's face she said, "I'm sorry, Eleanor. I love young Julia as much as anyone, but you know how strong-willed she can be. I have wondered many times how it was that *you* received a daughter so like *me*!"

Samantha watched them all laugh together and felt a rush of love for these three women who had lived in the same household with Lovenia and knew each other so well. They were all very different from one another, yet their strong tie to each other was obvious.

"I will talk to her," Aunt Eleanor said decidedly to her sister. "She must be feeling insecure and needs to be reassured of her standing." She turned to Samantha. "And I am sorry she has given you such a reception."

"Oh, it is not your fault, Aunt Eleanor. I understand. I have only ever been a sad story in this family's history and she has grown up knowing her important place. And then I come waltzing in and all the attention is on me. But I hope she can one day come to accept me and see that I have no intention of changing anything for her." She paused for a moment, remembering something that made her giggle. "At least, she seems to have accepted Sterling just fine," she mused with good humor.

Aunt Irene rolled her eyes. "Julia has quite the interest in young men, so I am not surprised. Plus," she gave Samantha a pointed look, "he is very good on the eyes, is he not?"

Aunt Eleanor choked on a laugh and Grandmother Julia chuckled even as she scolded, "He is too young for you, Irene."

"Oh, of course he is," Irene told her mother, matter-of-factly. "But I still know a good-looking man when I see one." She turned back to Samantha. "How did you two meet? Are you engaged yet?"

Samantha felt her face flush, but she laughed at her aunt's direct and rapid-fire questions, happy to share their story. Partway through the telling, Aunt Phoebe poked her head around the door and smiled at them. "Sorry to interrupt," she said, "but may I join you? The men are finishing the dishes and everything else is tidied up."

The women motioned her in and they all resituated themselves as Samantha continued an abbreviated version of what had happened to her and Sterling over the past year. When she concluded with her account of that amazing day when Sterling unexpectedly returned to Oberlin to declare his feelings for her, her aunts and grandmother were spellbound.

"And no, Aunt Irene, we are not engaged at this point. Although," she felt her face warm at the admission, "I think we are headed in that direction."

The women all nodded in agreement and Aunt Irene winked at her. "I think so too."

"We have seen each other every day since his return until now, as he was able to stay in Oberlin all summer. But now I am here with him because he will be teaching another year at the Worthington Boys' School and needs to make preparations before it starts. I wanted to see more of the town he has come to love, meet some of his friends, and see if I could find any of you. I just never imagined I would find so many!" She laughed, still amazed, and they smiled fondly at her wonder. "When I found my mother's grave last spring and saw the words carved into her headstone, I suddenly realized that she left behind many others—not just Father and I—that I might have aunts and uncles and grandparents!" She paused a moment and looked over them all; such dear faces to her already. "It has been quite the journey," she finished quietly.

The women nodded thoughtfully, imagining all she had been through.

"How much longer are you here for?" Aunt Eleanor asked. "How can we help you?"

"Only through the end of the week," Samantha replied with a sigh. "I will leave on Monday. That seems so soon now! I am certain I'll be back sometime, but I don't know when." She spread her hands in a gesture of emptiness, feeling sad with the prospect of leaving so soon.

"Hmm," Aunt Irene said, obviously deep in thought. "Do you *have* to return then, or might you stay another week?"

"I—Well, no," Samantha responded in surprise. "I suppose I don't have anything pressing at home. I could telegram Father and let him know I'll be here a little longer..." She trailed off, thinking about it, the wrinkle between her brows smoothing as she realized that the idea of staying another week eased her sadness and felt like the right thing to do.

Chapter 12

AN EXTRA WEEK

August 1902

A couple of afternoons later, Samantha walked from the school to a quaint little cottage fronted by a white picket fence. Sterling needed to work in his classroom for a few more hours and Samantha wanted to spend time with her aunt Irene. She opened the gate and passed through, latching it behind her, then followed the large, flat stones up to the small front porch. A double-width wicker chair piled with colorful pillows sat off to one side. Lifting the knocker with a slender hand, she tapped three times on the door. She didn't have long to wait before her aunt opened the door and invited her in.

She followed her inside, down the hall, and into a cozy kitchen. They chatted over cookies and herbal tea, Aunt Irene winding down after a busy day at the university, and Samantha telling her about her time with the Tomlinsons and how much she loved and respected Thora, whom Irene was not acquainted with.

Samantha reflected on this aunt whom she had come to love so quickly through her letters. She had only truly met her recently, but her love for the woman grew with each visit. She was bright and perceptive, seeming to miss nothing, and didn't hesitate to ask and answer questions openly.

"How did you first become interested in entomology?" Samantha asked her after a while. "Did you always love insects?"

Aunt Irene nodded. "I did." She smiled in recollection. "While my sisters were squeamish about even watching insects crawl near them, I always wanted to touch and learn about the creatures. Eleanor and Lovenia thought me quite strange and understood nothing of my fascination, but Mother and Father never tried to dissuade me from my unique interest. I think they recognized what a precocious and inquisitive child I was and that I had to see this thing through to the end." She smiled wryly as she added, "Though, I am sure neither of them expected it to take this long!"

"Because there will never be an end?" Samantha guessed, smiling.

"Exactly," Irene confirmed. "As to your other question, I think my interest must have stemmed from the first night I experienced fireflies."

"Really?! Sterling and I have discussed our first remembered fireflies during childhood, too. I even wrote a poem about them. Your experience must have left quite the impression as well!"

"It certainly did. I remember lying in bed afterward, my mind exploding with questions about them."

Samantha nodded. "I had many questions about them at an early age, too."

"And what did you do about it?"

"I searched my father's library for answers."

"Ah." Aunt Irene's lips turned up at the corners. "And did you find them?"

"Enough to satisfy me. I found a book about insects and basically memorized it. But then I moved on to other topics."

"In my case, I begged my parents for another book—and then another. For me, the answers always bred more questions." Aunt Irene laughed at herself and lifted her shoulders as if to say, *that's just how it is with me*!

"So you started your training during childhood for your life's calling," Samantha observed.

Aunt Irene tipped her head slightly in thought. "Yes," she mused, "I suppose I did, though it didn't seem like anything more than a thrilling hobby at the time. Over the years, some have referred to it as an obsession." She spoke matter-of-factly, but there was a tinge of regret in her words, that others would perceive her as some kind of fanatic.

"Your sisters?" Samantha asked.

"No, not them. They never understood my fascination, to be sure, but they took it in stride and didn't hold it against me. However, most of my schoolteachers tried to dissuade me. It wasn't ladylike, you see. Butterflies and ladybugs were one thing, but beetles and earwigs and centipedes were decidedly not fit topics for a girl to show such interest in."

"But you ignored them," Samantha guessed, with a smile.

Aunt Irene let out a sudden belly laugh, tickled at her niece's perception. "You know me so well already! I certainly did ignore them, and I stubbornly persisted in finding ways to make enough money to order a new book on insects every few months. The way I scoured those books...!" She shook her head at the memory, smiling. "I am sure Father wished I would study the Bible as diligently and deeply. Eventually I did, but it took me a long while to feel that spiritual need. In my early years, everything was focused on learning about, finding, collecting, and cataloging insects in all their stages of development. I learned Latin well enough to understand the scientific names. I studied the functions of human internal organs in order to understand their purposes and compare them to insect physiology. I studied life cycles, reproductive systems, and mating behaviors. And I learned that none of these things were fit conversation for polite company, particularly conversations with potential suitors." She laughed sadly.

Samantha felt the resignation in her words, even after all these years. "You couldn't speak about your interests and discoveries with any of your friends or suitors?" she asked.

Aunt Irene shrugged. "Nothing of any depth. Until I met Edward. He seemed more interested than anyone had and as our relationship developed, I felt able to share some of those things with him. I was very hopeful."

"What happened?" Samantha asked.

"Well," Aunt Irene mused, "it turned out that he was more tolerant than interested—which, in and of itself, may have worked out. The problem was what he expected of me, and it was just too high a price. Perhaps if he had been willing to make concessions and sacrifices also, to want to work together and find a way to help us both realize our dreams while raising a family, it could have happened. But he had his standards and expectations, and he wasn't willing to budge to include mine. And I couldn't bear to sacrifice all my career dreams to fit his mold. In the end, I had to tell him we were too different. For a time I thought he truly loved me: He seemed truly devastated when I turned down his proposal. But shortly thereafter, he found a woman better suited to him and that was the end of it."

"And you never found anyone else?"

"I was shattered for a while," she admitted, "and determined not to keep looking. I felt that I had failed my parents and myself, that I must be broken. But after a while I recognized that I really had done the right thing and that had I moved forward in that relationship with all our different ideas about everything, I would have regretted it the rest of my life." She looked at Samantha and declared firmly, "I would rather be alone than married to the wrong kind of person."

She was silent for a moment in serious contemplation, then gave a slight smile and continued. "I have never given up hope of still finding someone, but I have a full and enjoyable life. I find great fulfillment in my position at the university and truly enjoy working with students who are as interested in entomology as I am. And I appreciate being able to collaborate with colleagues in my field—people who actually feel the way about insects that I do."

"You waited a long time for that experience, didn't you?" Samantha noted.

"Indeed, I did," Aunt Irene agreed. "But now, after eleven years, the entomology department at The Ohio State University is fully developed. I have a place there, and our chairman, Herbert Osborn[1], is a wealth of knowledge and expertise. He continues to inspire students and faculty alike and his contributions to the department are prolific. So, in the end, I feel that I am right where I am meant to be. And that is the best feeling in the world."

Samantha looked at her aunt soberly, thinking about all the disappointments she had been through and what a strong woman she'd become, as a result of her struggle against societal norms and expectations, and her determination to contribute in her chosen field. "I think you are wonderful," she said at last. "And if no men are smart enough to see that, it's their loss. The world needs more women like you—not afraid to be themselves or to pursue education in areas that have previously been pursued only by men."[2]

Aunt Irene patted her hand and smiled in the open and direct way that Samantha had grown to expect. "Thank you, child. I sense much of that in you as well—but with much of your mother mixed in, which is a much more palatable combination, to be sure. I always

---

1. https://bit.ly/4aohoZP

2. Aunt Irene would have been delighted to know that just the year before, Clara Southmayd Ludlow received her Master of Arts degree in Botany from Mississippi A&M, "reportedly 31 years before a graduate program was formally offered by that institution" (https://en.wikipedia.org/wiki/Clara_Southmayd_Ludlow), and that she eventually became known as the Mother of Medical Entomology.

rubbed too many people the wrong way." She laughed and shook her head. "But I am beyond all that now and the pain is a distant memory. I really am happy with my life, especially now that my long-lost niece is found."

"I am so glad to be found," Samantha responded simply.

The two women spent an hour or so in Irene's insect display room and Irene became increasingly impressed, though not surprised, at Samantha's interest, knowledge, and natural intelligence. If she wanted to, Irene thought, Samantha could have joined the advanced students she taught and compete with the best of them. Yet Irene recognized that entomology was not Samantha's passion and that her life had a different trajectory and focus. She had worthwhile interests and talents of her own that she would continue to pursue. She and Sterling were so young, but Irene suspected that they would accomplish their individual purposes together far better than they could alone.

For her part, Samantha was fascinated with both the insect displays and the extent of her aunt's knowledge. Irene could answer any and all questions Samantha asked—and she asked many. To accompany her answers, Aunt Irene opened tidy logbooks filled with her cramped but neat script which included dates, descriptions of the insect's environment, and artistic renderings of the insects themselves. While Samantha did not care for the smell of the chemicals that preserved the specimens, she was impressed with the neatness of the room and the organization of all the frames and boxes filled with tidy rows of pinned insects. The butterflies were her favorites, of course, with their bright colors and intricate designs. Even the moths that were drab in comparison, were beautiful in their own ways. But it was also interesting to peruse the displays of beetles of all colors, sizes, and shapes, and to learn about their characteristics. She admitted to her aunt, who laughed good-naturedly at her distaste, that she didn't like the ugly maggots or fleshy, bloated caterpillars floating in liquid in jars (though she didn't mind the fuzzy pinned ones), but she could find redeeming qualities in most of the other creatures.

Thinking of her conversation with Sterling months ago about fireflies, she asked further questions about them and examined the different species with interest. Then the mighty mantis in its predatory pose intrigued her and she enjoyed learning about its life and behavior, Irene obviously relishing the opportunity to teach a willing student.

Noting the vials of chemicals, small boxes of pins of all sizes, and empty display boxes, Samantha asked if Aunt Irene still actively collected.

"Always," the older woman affirmed. "Every walk in the woods, I am prepared. And every time I am in my garden, I am on the lookout for insects I have not yet identified or studied. Although," she added as an aside, "that is becoming more and more rare as the years pass, since my collection is so extensive. But that just makes the occasional discovery all the more thrilling." She chuckled. "I am sure what I do seems odd to most people, but this has become my life's work and I have learned not to mind others thinking me eccentric. I suppose that image is consistent with my spinsterhood, anyway."

"Well, I think it's wonderful, all that you know about this tiny animal kingdom." Samantha made a gesture with her hands to take in the whole room. "And you have an obvious passion for it that I am certain your students feel and appreciate. In fact, that same sort of passion was what set Sterling apart from other teachers in my eyes," she smiled unconsciously as she remembered those early days with him. "I hadn't experienced that very often from other teachers in my life. So, when I sensed how much this new kind of writing meant to him—writing that was honest, open, and brave—and how deeply he desired for me to catch his vision, it intrigued me. I wanted to write with that same passion, to inspire others the way he had inspired me."

Aunt Irene's eyes turned soft as she looked at her brilliant and talented niece. "And it would appear that you mastered it quickly and completely."

Samantha blushed a little under her gaze. "Thank you. I hope I have. There is still much to learn, but I truly feel changed, improved, and...set free somehow. So many wonderful things have come into my life as a result. In fact, at times it has been rather too much," she admitted.

Aunt Irene nodded knowingly. "I can imagine!" She clasped Samantha's hands in hers and looked at her with sincerity. "I hope you will allow me to continue to be involved in your life, all along the way."

Samantha squeezed back, her response equally sincere. "I wouldn't have it any other way."

***

During that extra week in Worthington, Samantha spent a delightful afternoon at her grandmother's, walking around the bedroom that Lovenia had shared with her sisters and going through memorabilia from her mother's childhood. Grandmother Julia was eager and willing to talk about her youngest daughter, and Samantha received ready answers to her many questions. It was a renewing time for Julia Lewis and a revelatory time for Samantha, and they both basked in their newfound relationship. Samantha even left with a small sampler her mother had sewn as a child. As an eight or nine-year-old girl, Lovenia had sewn remarkably straight, even stitches, which showed her early attention to detail and her impressive ability to focus on the task at that young age. Samantha knew very little about sewing, but she appreciated the simple beauty in the colorful flowers and the pattern of the leaves, and she was grateful to have in her possession an item her mother had created with her own hands.

Visiting Lovenia's grave together provided another special time for both women. Then Samantha followed her grandmother to a different section of the cemetery where Grand-father Joseph had been laid to rest. There, Grandmother told Samantha of her husband's hard work throughout his life to provide for his family, and that, though they had never had extra money, they had always had enough. She told of his unwavering commitment to them and to God, his unfailing patience and good humor, and the great love he showed for each of his children. Then she expressed the joy he felt with each grandchild who arrived. Her description of Grandfather matched the impression Samantha had received while reading his letters. How she wished she could have met him!

Samantha accepted two more invitations to Uncle Samuel's house (lunch one day and supper another), and two to Aunt Eleanor's (for supper with just her own family, and another with the whole extended family once again). Sterling accompanied her to each gathering and they both became more familiar and comfortable with the extended Lewis families and their homes. They enjoyed getting to know the cousins and cousins' children through conversations and games, and soon they could remember who belonged to whom.

She was not sure what to expect when they arrived that second time at Aunt Eleanor's, knowing that young Julia would not be thrilled to see her. But fortunately, while the young woman was unnaturally subdued with Samantha, her eyes no longer shot daggers at her. And by the end of the week, with Sterling there to act as a buffer and inspire conversation, Samantha sensed a thaw starting to take place—although part of this was undoubtedly due to Julia's continued admiration of Sterling and her desire to impress him. When Samantha mentioned this observation to him, he merely rolled his eyes good-naturedly, as if to say how little Julia's admiration meant to him, and bent to kiss her.

***

When she wasn't with family, Samantha worked hard with Thora in the gardens and kitchen, hoping to help her get ahead and, however inadequately, thank her for her generous hospitality. Samantha greatly enjoyed spending time with the older woman who had become such an integral part of Sterling's life. She felt drawn to her and wanted to understand what made her keep pushing through hard things with such a cheerful, down-to-earth attitude.

One morning they discussed what it might have been like to attend the recent coronation in England of King Edward VII and his wife, Alexandra—which had been postponed because of the king's emergency abdominal surgery.[3] And they exclaimed over the deaths of ten thousand people in the wake of a 7.7 earthquake on the border of China and Kyrgyzstan a week before. Such news made it hard to feel safe in this world, when one realized how helpless humankind was against the powers of Mother Nature.

But then, returning to the present, and thinking about the issues at hand here on the farm, Samantha asked, "How do you manage all this with only one hired hand?" She looked around at the vast garden and orchard that surrounded the house and felt troubled just thinking about all that was required. She bent again, helping Thora fill baskets with late cucumbers, squashes, peppers, and tomatoes. Next, they would move on to check the corn. "I love gardens, but this seems so daunting to me!"

Thora looked up and pushed a strand of fading auburn hair behind one ear. "Oh," she laughed, soft lines radiating from the corners of her brown eyes. "It often *is* daunting! I actually can't say as I really know *how* it all works out. Yet each year, all the planting, cultivating, harvesting, and food preservation is somehow finished in time. I spend half of every winter marveling that we did it again!" She laughed good naturedly. "But I give God the credit."

Samantha smiled. "I would wager that is your secret."

---

3. https://en.wikipedia.org/wiki/Coronation_of_Edward_VII_ and Alexandra

"Agreed. We couldn't do it without Him, that is certain." Thora placed a few more cucumbers in her basket and moved on to a large tomato plant. "And yet..."

Samantha looked up from the pepper she was snipping off, but Thora was silent for a few moments. "And yet?" Samantha prompted at last.

Thora straightened and looked at her thoughtfully from under a large straw hat. It reminded Samantha of the hat she used to wear regularly. "I don't know how long I can maintain this pace," Thora admitted. "I am not getting any younger, obviously, and the work is unrelenting. I can't afford to hire another hand. Alfred is getting on in years, himself, but I don't wish to replace him as he has been so hard-working and reliable, and he needs the money. And while Jerome is now to the point he could take care of most things around here in adulthood, his heart isn't in it. I see him wanting to do other things with his life."

"Wood-working?" Samantha guessed. "Repair work and construction?"

Thora nodded. "Yes, and anything else he chooses. He can't do the things he has the natural aptitude for *and* maintain a large farm simultaneously. There simply are not enough hours in the day."

"And you don't want to tie him here."

"No. I want him to be free to choose his future and make his own life."

"You are such a good mother," Samantha mused. "Sterling has reminded me often that having the freedom to choose and to make something of himself was very important to him before he left home—and was an important step in becoming who he is now."

Thora looked at her thoughtfully, one hand poised to pick another tomato. "It really was," she acknowledged. "And I want Jerome to become all he is meant to be, too. I have always taught him to work hard, to be kind and honest and God-fearing, but someday in the next few years he will fly the nest, taking all those attributes with him to strengthen him and help him succeed. Still, I doubt life will be easy for him. It isn't for most of us."

"Perhaps not, but he will be well-equipped to handle it," Samantha assured.

"That is my hope," Thora agreed. But she still seemed concerned about something.

Samantha hazarded a guess. "But...then you will be short one person to help around here, and you can't do it without him. Is that it?"

Thora carefully placed another large tomato into her basket and chuckled. "Not much gets past you, I can see. And you are right. I know God will show me the answers at the proper time, but sometimes I wish I knew them a little earlier, just for my peace of mind."

Samantha's eyebrows raised in memory. "I can relate," she said empathetically. "Sometimes that waiting is the hardest thing of all."

***

On Friday morning, Samantha knocked on Mr. Grover's office door and he graciously ushered her in. They had an appointment to discuss school administration and Samantha was ready with all her questions. The superintendent pulled his chair around to the front of the desk and gestured for her to take the seat opposite him. She sat and opened her notebook, thanking him for taking the time to talk with her. She explained about her mother's dream for a children's school and briefly outlined some of the ideas she and Sterling had talked about.

"Unlike Sterling, I do not have a teaching degree. In fact, I feel very inadequate to even be thinking along these lines, since I have so little background. I only know what I experienced in primary school. My further education is based solely on my own studies, though I admit they have been extensive."

Mr. Grover nodded thoughtfully. "And your father was a professor at the college there, correct?"

"Yes," Samantha said in surprise.

"Sterling mentioned it to me once," Mr. Grover explained. "And you have quite an incredible library, from what I understand."

"We do."

"And you are gleaning information and ideas from all and sundry, wherever you go."

"Yes," Samantha confirmed, wondering where this was leading. "The concept continues to grow and blossom and is constantly on my mind."

"Every powerful dream is like that," Mr. Grover mused, quiet for a moment. Then he smiled at her and gave a decisive nod. "Well, I would say you are on the right path, headed in the right direction. Not everyone can be a teacher or run a school, but I think you and Sterling and your father, together, might just have what it takes. Plus, you have the humility to seek help and direction from different experts in the field, and that in itself will take you far."

"Thank you," Samantha said, surprised at his insights. "I appreciate that vote of confidence very much. Might I ask you a few questions about effectively overseeing and running a school, and hiring teachers?"

"I have reserved the next hour for you, Miss Jennings," he said, pushing up his spectacles with one finger, his eyes twinkling. "I don't claim to know everything about this job, but I am happy to share with you what I have learned in my many years in such a capacity."

***

That evening, unable to put it off any longer, Samantha and Sterling reluctantly discussed their departure plans. They sat on Aunt Irene's porch swing behind her little house, swinging gently back and forth as they talked. Irene called the swing her "one extravagance," which she put up at the beginning of every spring and took down at the end of every fall. It allowed her a comfortable place to oversee her backyard and garden area, and she insisted that it had single-handedly helped her solve several different issues that had come up at the university—everything from misunderstandings with the administration, to difficulties with students or research, to needing inspiration for teaching. This evening, she had urged Samantha and Sterling to sit there while she tended to the bees at the far end of her property.

She returned to them a while later, holding up a large jar of golden honey triumphantly in one hand, the still-steaming smoker in the other. She set down both items on the small table near the swing and removed the veiled white hat. Her eyes were bright with the victory of another plentiful harvest, and she looked at them with interest. "What did I miss?" she asked, sitting at the table. "I mean, if you were discussing something for my ears," she teased. "I don't need to hear any of the overly sentimental stuff."

Sterling chuckled. "We were just discussing how I will get Samantha back to Oberlin. We need a chaperone, of course, but haven't figured that out yet. And I still have more to plan and prepare than I expected, so I need to make certain I return in time to do that before school begins."

Aunt Irene nodded, then said nothing for a moment, obviously in thought. "What if I were Samantha's chaperone and you stayed here to finish your preparations? Would that arrangement be helpful to you both?"

"Oh!" Samantha said in surprise. "You want to come all the way to Oberlin with me?"

"I admit I am curious to see the town my sister was so happy to desert me for," Irene said ironically. "But mostly I want more time with my niece."

Sterling looked at Samantha and then back at Irene. "I am happy to make the trip again, but I'm sure Samantha would love to have more time with you, as well. What do you think?" he asked, turning to Samantha.

"It's a great idea!" she responded without hesitation. Turning back to her aunt she asked, "Do you want to stay the night at our home? We have plenty of room."

Aunt Irene cleared her throat. "Actually, no." Her voice was regretful, yet firm. "I am not yet ready to face your father. I wish I could say I was, after all this time." She held up her hands in an unnecessary gesture of apology. "I will get there, but not yet."

Samantha swallowed down the disappointment and reminded herself that these things could take a while. "All right. What day shall we leave?"

They agreed to depart on Monday morning and, arrangements concluded, Samantha and Sterling sat in glum silence, forgetting to set the swing back into motion.

Suddenly Aunt Irene burst into laughter. "You two!" she exclaimed. "You both look as if you're ready to attend a funeral."

They looked at her in surprise, then laughed at themselves.

"We have had such a wonderful time being together this summer," Samantha explained. "We've known since June that this time of farewell was coming, but I kept hoping it never..." she trailed off, not trusting her voice.

Sterling untangled his fingers from hers to put an arm around her shoulders and draw her closer. "I hate this too," he said, honestly. "At least we will see each other again during the Christmas holidays."

"Ah, young love," Aunt Irene mused. "Christmas seems a very long way off, doesn't it? But you'll manage. Somehow, the time will pass, and you will exchange lots of letters in the meantime. And Samantha, if you get too lonely rattling around in that big, empty house of yours, just come on back to Worthington. You can stay with me anytime you wish."

"Thank you," Samantha said in a soft voice. "I appreciate that. Having that option may just make the waiting seem bearable."

Aunt Irene stood. "Now, why don't you come in for cookies before you go? I'll make some mint tea and we can sweeten it with this delectable honey made by my glorious, wondrous bees." Her grin was contagious and Samantha felt her heart lift.

***

Saying goodbye to Sterling at the train station hurt Samantha's heart. Leaving him standing there, hat in hand, watching her as she tearfully boarded and walked to her seat, she knew she was leaving part of herself behind. And judging from the expression on his face, as she looked back at him through the window, he felt the pain of their separation just as acutely. She dashed at a tear on her cheek and tried to smile at him.

He smiled back at her, swallowing down the lump in his throat. They had known for months that this day was coming, and they had had so much time together, so why was this inevitable separation still so difficult? He realized his shoulders were a little stooped in dejection, so he tried to stand straighter, to keep smiling and not make this more difficult for her than it had to be. They would see each other again in about three months, after all, he reminded himself. And surely, though that felt like an eternity, as they developed their routines again and stayed busy, the time would pass quickly enough. At any rate, it wouldn't be the nine interminable months they had been separated before. And this time they would write to each other often. This time, they knew they loved each other. For him now, there would be no anguished questions of whether she remembered or thought of him. Now they had a strong foundation for their relationship and their bond was strong, their desires and dreams for the future aligned. As these thoughts flooded Sterling's mind, he raised a hand in farewell. The train began to move and he mouthed the words, "I love you," as it slowly pulled away and gradually picked up speed.

Samantha blew him a tearful kiss and waved goodbye as the train began to move, then forced herself to face forward in her seat as she dried her eyes on her handkerchief. She took a deep breath and let it out slowly. Now, time to focus on her aunt and be cheerful, for there really was much to be happy about.

Beside her, Aunt Irene patted her hand comfortingly. "I know this must be very difficult for you, but remember, you can come back anytime! You have a very large family now who loves you. And that handsome young man would love nothing more than to have you here again too."

Samantha nodded. "Thank you. I know that's true. I wouldn't leave at all, but I feel the pull to home—for my father's sake." She paused a moment, then admitted, "Not only for him, of course; Oberlin is where I belong, where I feel grounded and most like myself. But I also think Father may be on the brink of recovery and I am his link to the outside world. He needs me, Aunt Irene."

Her aunt's eyes clouded over, but only for an instant. "You are probably right," she agreed. Then she added with an ironic chuckle, "Although, I have to say, I think you are more than he deserves."

"He has been through a great deal," Samantha said, feeling the need to defend her father, realizing with sudden surprise that she no longer felt anger toward him anymore, only compassion. "I know he did not handle things the way we wished he would have, but I sense a time of healing beginning, and I want to see it through. He really loved her, you know—my mother."

Aunt Irene nodded slowly. "He really did. And I loved him for it at the time, for Lovenia deserved that kind of devoted love. I must remember that, whatever else he has or has not done since then." After a moment's reflection, she added, "I am glad he has you, and I'm sure he needs what you have to give."

The two women talked, then, about everything they could think of throughout the train journey. In Samantha, Irene found an eager listener who made keen observations and asked insightful questions. In her aunt Irene, Samantha also found a listening ear and an understanding heart, one who gave inspired suggestions and didn't sugarcoat the truth. It was a pleasant time of making further connections and cementing their new bond.

That night, Irene treated Samantha to dinner at the cafe before retiring for the night at the hotel. They parted affectionately and both promised to write.

Chapter 13

HOME AGAIN

September 1902

After two weeks away from home, it was good to be back to familiarity and routine. Samantha visited with her father, who asked a surprising number of questions about the extended Lewis family. And Mrs. Dolittle and Claire wanted to hear all about everything that had transpired, as well. It was good to reconnect with them all and to recount her experiences in Worthington.

While speaking with her father in his sparse bedroom, sitting across from each other on plain wooden chairs, Samantha asked him again if he had finished reading her mother's journal.

He nodded slowly. "I have; some places over and over again." He inhaled deeply, then exhaled as if letting go of something heavy. "It has...helped somehow."

Samantha reached across the space between them and placed a hand over his, squeezing gently. She felt the ropy veins of his large, knuckled hands and noticed the coldness of his fingers, despite the heat of the day. "I'm glad, Father. It helped me too. I didn't know who my mother was before I read it."

"And I am sorry about that," he said gravely, startling her with the immediacy and strength of the statement. He studied her from under his bushy gray brows. "You should never have had to learn about your own mother that way, when I was here all along. And you should not have had to wait so long to know about her journal." The admission pained him, that was clear, but something in his visage lightened almost imperceptibly at the heartfelt apology.

Samantha settled back in her chair and nodded, accepting his expression of regret. "May I ask you a question about her?"

Basil inclined his head once, but his eyes squinted slightly, as if bracing himself.

"In real life, was she the way she appears in her writing?"

Her father relaxed as he thought about that. "Yes. To know her in person was to know her in writing, and vice-versa."

Samantha nodded, unsurprised but still glad. "Did she have any flaws? Did she make mistakes or have any weaknesses besides physical ones?"

Basil looked at her for a long moment and his bearded mouth slowly turned up at the corners. "She was not perfect, if that is what you mean. But she was the perfect companion for me. And when she did grow frustrated with me or responded angrily to something a family member said or did, she apologized quickly."

Samantha pondered that. With a trace of humor in her voice she said, "So she really was human."

Her father gazed into the distance as he remembered. "Yes, fortunately for me." His eyes drifted back to her face as he added, "As you well know, I am no saint. But sometimes I teased her that she was. She never liked that and would quickly correct me."

Samantha nodded. "Her family speaks of her as if she were an angel. They all looked up to her so much and none of them remembers anything uncomplimentary. So I wondered if you two ever quarreled or if she ever did anything that bothered you—that sort of thing. Right now, in my mind, she seems so perfect that I despair of ever really becoming like her."

"You are already more like her than you may ever know," Basil answered, surprising Samantha with his sincerity. Moisture glinted in his eyes.

"Thank you," she said softly. She wanted to ask for specifics, but she sensed her father wasn't finished speaking of her mother, and she wanted to hear more. She couldn't believe he was saying so much!

"There was one time when she..." He trailed off, then tried again. "I was not quite certain how to respond to..." He faltered.

"Yes?" she pressed. "What happened?"

"It was after I accepted the position at Oberlin College and we were preparing to sell our house in Worthington and make the journey here."

Samantha nodded, feeling her pulse quicken at the realization that not only was her father telling her a story about her mother, but he was willingly recalling something painful—for her benefit. It felt like a giant step forward.

"Your mother was always honest and never could keep secrets from me for long. So it was very unlike her to keep this secret as long as she did. After I accepted the position and she saw how thrilled I was to have the opportunity, she told me she had been the one to initiate it."

He paused, getting that distant look in his eyes again as the memory flowed through his mind. "I remember her words tumbling over each other as she hurried to explain why she had written to the college on my behalf. And why she had not told me about it for so many weeks. She simply could not bear the omission any longer."

His gaze shifted back to Samantha and he said abruptly, "I was upset."

"You were?" she asked in a small voice, shrinking inside herself at the thought. "She wrote that she was afraid of what you might say if you found out."

"She knew me well," Basil said ruefully. "Not that I ever touched her in anger," he quickly added. "I have never been prone to violence. But she knew I was upset with the idea that the job offer had not come about naturally. However, I calmed down once my pride was softened by the realization that she wrote as if she were me, not as the wife inquiring on her poor husband's behalf. I realized it had taken a great deal of courage for her to do such a thing and that she did it out of love. She apologized for inadvertently deceiving me. And when she explained how much she wanted me to be able to fulfill the desire I had long held, I loved her all the more for orchestrating such a bold move. If not for her concern for me, she would never have done such a thing. She was not often thought of as a bold person, but she was always ready to do whatever she could on behalf of someone she loved."

"Even if it was unconventional or frightening?"

"Even then."

Samantha thought of Aunt Irene and how much boldness was woven into her personality. It seemed Lovenia was made of at least some of the same cloth as her sister, after all.

"But I did ask her not to do such a thing on my behalf again." One side of his mouth eased upward in an ironic smile.

Samantha grinned. "She only did it because she knew you never would on your own, due to your concern for her health."

"I know. And after that, I listened to her with a more open mind when she made suggestions or offered advice that she thought I needed. That letter she wrote to the college caused a drastic change in our lives. And teaching there was exactly what I needed at the time. So that helped me realize that she was my champion and really had my best interests at heart, and that I needed to listen to her, even when it was hard to hear."

"Thank you for telling me that story, Father," Samantha said quietly. Then added with a twinge of humor, "But I don't see how that shows her at a disadvantage. Not really. Her motives were pure."

"Yes," her father agreed. "I suppose I did not really answer your question after all."

"But," Samantha quickly supplied, "you did give me a clearer picture of the dynamics between the two of you."

Unexpectedly, Basil held up a sudden index finger as a thought came to him. "She liked to pull practical jokes."

"What?" Samantha was unsure if she had heard correctly.

"She had this uncanny ability to catch me off guard," he mused. "I have always been much too serious and she wanted to see me smile more, to be startled and recognize the funny side of things. So she found ways to do that. I never knew when something would come jumping out at me, or the salt and sugar would be switched. Things like that."

Samantha laughed out loud at this unanticipated side to her mother. "She never writes about that in her journal!"

Her father nodded and his expression sobered. "Of course, when she did not feel well, the practical jokes disappeared for a while. Enough time would pass that I would forget to be on the lookout for something unexpected, and as soon as she was back on her feet, she would startle me again. We had many good laughs over those little stunts of hers."

"And that was the whole purpose, so she succeeded in her efforts."

"She did," Basil smiled from ear to ear, "indeed she did." Samantha realized with a happy skip of her heart that that was the first full smile she remembered seeing on his face.

For days afterward, she contemplated this unexpected side of her mother and every time the thought delighted her. *My mother, the trickster! Who would have thought?*

***

Yes, it was nice to be home, but Samantha's heart ached with the separation from Sterling. She thought back on how she had pictured it and realized that this was much harder than she had imagined. She had thought it would be similarly difficult to last time, but this was completely different. Their last separation was before they had professed their love for each other, spent countless hours together, talked about everything under the sun (and stars), and came to know each other's hearts and minds nearly as well as they knew themselves. She missed feeling his fingers entwined in hers, the loss of his strong arm around her, and the tenderness of his kisses. She pictured the way his brown eyes looked deeply into hers and understood what she couldn't say, and she heard his infectious laughter rumble deep in his chest. Samantha missed the perpetually unruly lock of wavy hair over his forehead and how his gaze made her feel beautiful, somehow. She craved to feel the presence of his spontaneity near her, his energy and zest for life that brightened her own. And she yearned for their long and deep conversations on so many topics. She would catch herself thinking, "Oh, I must tell Sterling that when he comes," or "Sterling would love to read this when I see him later"—and then remember with a jolt that she actually wouldn't be seeing him that day, or that week, or even that month. And every time, her heart would fall with a painful thud.

She tried to be strong, stay positive, and not think about how long it was till Christmas. Writing letters to him did help, so she wrote often: long and descriptive missives that probably rambled, she realized, but she didn't care. The action helped assuage some of the pain of his absence, and helped her feel more connected to him across the miles. At least once a week, often more, she received a letter from him in return. And as she felt the thick letter inside each unopened envelope, she would smile and remember that time months ago when they had promised to write each other "exceedingly long letters." She supposed having a writing teacher for a beau had its advantages.

One letter even contained a series of dots and dashes that made her smile. She knew without even deciphering it what it said: *I miss you and you are too far away*. She remembered their twilight walk among fireflies and their discussion about light. Sterling was most definitely too far away, but like the fireflies, she and he also carried light within them—Jesus' light—which would strengthen them during their time apart. That realization was a comfort.

***

For a while after her return, Samantha felt she had an excess of time, so she used it to at last finish *Jane Eyre*. Brimming with beautiful words from the book, she felt compelled to write some of them to Sterling, as they so perfectly described some of her own feelings. She loved when Mr. Rochester described to Jane how intricately they were connected, because she related to it so well:

September 27, 1902

Sterling,

The month passes and my ache for you does not dissipate. I am happily busy and life is good. But I feel that part of me is missing and I cannot enjoy a fullness of joy until we are together again. It puts me in mind of how Mr. Rochester describes his connection to Jane. Now I completely understand what he means:

"...It is as if I had a string somewhere under my left ribs, tightly and inextricably knotted to a similar string situated in the corresponding quarter of your...frame. And if that boisterous channel, and two hundred miles or so of land come broad between us, I am afraid that cord of communion will be snapt; and then I've a nervous notion I should take to bleeding inwardly..."[1]

Sometimes I do feel as if I am bleeding inwardly, missing you. However, a decided advantage I have over Mr. Rochester is that 1) we are not two hundred miles apart with a channel in between (though one hundred miles is far enough!), and 2) I know we will be together again, that I have only to be patient and keep up the work I am doing. Knowing that you return my love makes all the difference: it comforts me, cheers me, and helps me continue moving forward.

---

1. Charlotte Bronte, *Jane Eyre* (New York: Grosset & Dunlap Publishers, 1983), 305.

I suppose you heard about the Shiloh Baptist Church stampede in Birmingham, Alabama,[2] earlier this month. Thinking about it still haunts me. I am sure Mr. Booker T. Washington was horrified to be a witness to 115 people's deaths, after having given what was undoubtedly a motivating and enlightening speech to some 3,000 people. Such a tragedy, especially as it would have been entirely preventable, if only the people had heeded those who were shouting that there was no danger. It is so terrible that "quiet" and "fight" were misinterpreted as "fire" and everyone immediately reacted in fear as a result. Words are so powerful, for both good and ill! I pray for the families of the victims that they may find peace at this difficult time.

How are your students? Do you find teaching easier this year? I can clearly picture you in front of the classroom, your clothing neat, your dark hair unruly, and your eyes flashing with excitement. Those boys are lucky to have you, and so am I.

Faithfully yours,

Samantha

***

A week later, she received Sterling's return letter and tore it open eagerly, as she always did. Partway down he had written:

I am glad you reminded me of Mr. Rochester's words. Would that I were so eloquent! The feelings of your soul are reciprocated perfectly in my own heart and I wonder how long it can withstand our absence from one another. I, too, will continue working hard and enjoying the life I have here—as much as I can without you. Whenever I feel that things are too difficult, I picture you in my mind: your tall, slim figure, your brilliant mind, and ready smile, and I tell myself to be strong like you are.

I recently came across another line in Jane Eyre, which expresses exactly how I feel about you, my dearest:

"…I have for the first time found what I can truly love—I have found you. You are my sympathy—my better self—my good angel—I am bound to you with a strong attachment. I think you good, gifted, lovely: a fervent, a solemn passion is conceived in my heart; it leans to

---

2. https://bit.ly/4c2qUmE

you, draws you to my centre and spring of life, wraps my existence about you—and, kindling in pure, powerful flame, fuses you and me in one."[3]

I felt my own center melting as I read those beautifully vivid descriptions and I agree completely. Remember when I told you I am as a moth to your flame? Even from here I can see that flame in my mind's eye, and I am drawn to you, body and soul.

I did read about the church stampede in Alabama and it saddened me too. You are right: the pen is mighty. In happier news, I found it inspiring what occurred in Australia earlier this month. Perhaps you have heard? The country was experiencing severe drought which killed livestock and threatened crops, so the whole nation observed a "day of humiliation" and prayed for rain. Three days later, God began to open the heavens. He is so good! I am relieved for that country to finally receive the life-giving water it needs. The story puts me fondly in mind of our conversations on rain last year, and on your poem. "Let us not waste heaven's tears." There is so much of life to be savored.

This teaching profession of mine is rigorous, no doubt about it. But it is also fulfilling as I see young minds learning new things that open and brighten their world. I enjoy it immensely, even as I miss you.

Never forget that you are my everything!

Always in my prayers,

Sterling

---

3. Charlotte Bronte, *Jane Eyre* (New York: Grosset & Dunlap Publishers, 1983), 383.

Chapter 14

RESTORATION and PLANNING

October 1902

As the weather gradually cooled and all the green foliage and grass began to change to autumn's brilliant display, Samantha decided it was as good a time as any to begin reorganizing her father's library. She had previously realized how important it would be to have all the books in a logical and uniform order for the future school so that anyone, including children, could find what he or she needed. She had not discussed the school idea with her father yet, but was relieved he'd given his permission for a tidied library.

Donning her spectacles, she stood in the middle of the room and perused it slowly, notebook and pencil in hand. She contemplated all the logistics and mapped out where the different subjects should be placed among the shelves, and which books should be put where small hands could most easily reach them. Then she set to work, knowing she probably had a couple of weeks of organization ahead of her.

To her surprise, she ended up with many helpers over the next several days and it didn't take quite as long as she expected. Mrs. Dolittle stopped in a couple of times to help on the lower shelves, and Samantha had the distinct feeling that the housekeeper was thrilled that this overdue project was finally happening. Claire put in several hours climbing the ladder, handing down armfuls of books, dusting, and re-shelving, commenting on how neglected the housekeeping in this room had been, judging from the amount of dust they inadvertently stirred up. As a child, Samantha had never noticed the dust, but now she wholeheartedly agreed that they must never allow it to return to its former condition.

When Katherine dropped in one afternoon and saw what Samantha was doing, she cheerfully jumped in to help as well, and they spent a pleasant and productive few hours bringing Samantha's vision for the library to fruition. Even Martin came in for a peek at "what all the womenfolk" were up to and looked around in wonder at the changes.

At last, feeling that every book was in its proper place and nothing could be improved upon, Samantha tiredly smiled to herself and brushed a stray lock of hair out of her face as she performed one last circuit of the room.

Father needs to see this! she realized. Without overthinking it, she took the long walk upstairs to her father's room and knocked on the door.

"You finished already?" he asked in surprise, when he heard her news about the completed project.

"With the help of many hands, I was able to complete it faster than anticipated. Even so, it was a monumental task." Suddenly she felt her fatigue and looked up at her father with a tired smile. "Do you know how many books you have, Father?" she asked as she blew a wayward strand of hair out of her eyes.

He pursed his lips together in thought and then shook his head. "No, do you?"

It had been meant as a rhetorical question, so she laughed at his serious consideration. "Too many. But combined, they are a powerful resource of information on a vast array of subjects. I am weary, but it was a very worthwhile project."

He nodded in agreement, his hooded eyes lighting up with what was probably the memory of countless hours of preparation and teaching from many of those very books.

"And now they are all arranged in a more accessible, logical, well-organized manner—and dust free! I know it will take some getting used to, but I think it will be much better in the long run. Won't you come with me and see it?" she asked eagerly.

In spite of himself, Basil found that he was curious to see the transformation his daughter had worked so hard on for over a week. He followed her down the stairs and indeed, it was a transformation worthy of taking special note. After perusing books for a while, he was startled to find that an hour had passed as he lost himself in exploring the shelves. They were all the same books as before and yet, with this fresh organization, different titles leapt out at him, pleading for him to pick them up and see them with new eyes. Basil thought perhaps he might spend more time in this room and not quite so much up in his own little bedroom. He liked the cozy look of the rearranged furniture in the middle of the room and how the late afternoon light streamed through the autumn leaves of the maple tree outside the window on the far side.

"Thank you, daughter," he said softly in his gruff way, turning to her at his side. "This is wonderful work."

She simply smiled at him. "I like it better too. And you are welcome."

***

Library organization complete, Samantha felt she should devote more time to correspondence and wrote letters to Aunt Irene, Aunt Eleanor, and Grandmother Julia. In no time at all, she received an influx of mail in return. Nearly every day she had a letter from someone. Aunt Phoebe and Uncle Samuel wrote her as well, and even Mary wrote her a delightfully awkward and emotion-filled letter brimming with her young joys and tragedies, asking for advice and confiding her secret affection for a boy in her Sunday School class. Samantha loved reading every one of these letters and wrote back as quickly as she could. Soon it seemed any spare time was taken up with reading and writing letters and she reveled in the connection with so many family members—and the fact that they wanted to stay in touch.

Sometimes she second-guessed herself, wondering if she should move to Worthington after all. There were more people to pull her there now than there were in Oberlin, it was true. But in the end she felt she had made the right decision to stay where she was, to be the constancy her father needed, to check in on him daily and coax him to talk and interact with her. Slowly, bit by bit, she could sense him changing, looking forward to her visits, and allowing the invisible wall between them to quietly dissolve. It felt good to know she was in the right place and that she was helping him. And it was a relief to let frustration and anger from the neglect she had experienced in the past be gradually replaced by a sense of positive connection. They didn't yet have the relationship she would like, but seeing progress strengthened her to patiently continue her efforts.

***

One afternoon, Samantha found Mrs. Dolittle sitting in the kitchen taking some time off her feet while chicken and potatoes baked in the oven.

"How are you?" she asked, sitting across from her. "You look tired."

"I am tired," Mrs. Dolittle admitted. "Claire told me to take a rest while supper cooks, and she went to pick some fresh greens from the garden before they freeze. I can feel in my bones that the first frost is coming."

Samantha nodded. "I am glad Claire is here to watch over you a little. Father and I don't do that well enough."

Mrs. Dolittle clucked and waved a hand to discount her concern. "I'll be just fine after a few minutes. You needn't worry about me. It's true your father isn't usually one to concern himself with my well being, but he is coming out of his shell more and more lately, isn't he?"

"You've noticed?" Samantha asked. Sometimes it was easy to wonder if she had just imagined it when the changes happened so gradually.

"I certainly have!" Mrs. Dolittle said emphatically. "You are performing something quite miraculous, my dear. It may not seem incredible right now, but change and progress are happening. And it is *long* overdue."

"It is," Samantha agreed. "I am glad you can see it too. But it isn't really me. God is in the details."

"Indeed, He is," the older woman smiled.

Abruptly, Samantha switched topics to one that had been on her mind. "I was actually looking for you because I have a question."

"All right. What is it you want to know, child?"

"Have you ever wished you had other options for earning a living?"

Mrs. Dolittle looked taken aback. "Well, I...I don't know," she replied slowly. "I suppose I did decades ago, but this is my life now and I am satisfied by it."

Samantha nodded impatiently. "Satisfied, yes, but stimulated? Are you doing what you really want to do with your life?"

"I don't know. I haven't thought about that in quite some time. I'm getting old, but I've had a good life." Mrs. Dolittle looked directly at her and asked outright, "What are you driving at, Samantha, dear?"

"Oh, it's an idea I have been playing around with for a while, just a vision at this point. I've discussed it with Sterling at length, but haven't yet talked to Father." She paused and thought how best to explain. "I know my mother always had a dream to turn this big place into a school for children and I would love to make her dream a reality. There are so many details and logistics to work out, but I wonder... Might you consider teaching a class or two, assuming we can bring this idea to fruition?"

Throughout Samantha's explanation, Mrs. Dolittle's face changed from confusion to realization to amazement, and she inhaled sharply at the question. "Me?" she asked in surprise. "A teacher? I don't feel qualified to do that, I'm afraid. It's been decades since I was a student myself... Though," she mused softly, "I always did enjoy teaching Mother and her friends the things I learned..."

"You are more qualified than I am," Samantha pointed out. "I think it would all come back to you. And Sterling and my father would probably have some pointers for you, as well, if you wanted them. You could start with one class and see how it went..."

"Me, a teacher," Mrs. Dolittle intoned softly, shaking her head in wonder. "My, my. Before I met Ambrose, I used to wonder what it might be like to awaken young minds to learning. But that was ages ago! Life is comfortable, my routine is set—I am nearly an old woman now!"

"Not so old," Samantha laughed. "And I know the children would love you! Anyway, you can think about it. As I said, it is only an idea at this point. But my vision has been further expanded by Booker T. Washington's book *Up from Slavery*. Have you read it?"

"No, not yet. But I want to."

"I'll lend you my copy," Samantha offered immediately. "And then we can discuss his experience and ideas together!"

Mrs. Dolittle looked thoughtful. "But if I did teach a class or two...how would I have enough time to do everything else I am responsible for here?"

"That is the beauty of Washington's system! Well, he didn't create it," she amended, "but he adopted it for himself and delineates it in his book. We will create a community of helpers here to assist each other with all the household chores. Sharing the load would help, don't you agree? And the children would learn important life skills as they worked."

"That does sound like an intelligent system," Mrs. Dolittle agreed, "once it was established. I can start the book right away, if you have it handy. I am intrigued now, my dear." She chuckled the warm laugh that was so much a part of her. "Mind you," she held up a hand to preempt a flow of enthusiasm from Samantha, "I still need some time to think about all this and wrap my head around it. I don't know if an old dog like me can learn new tricks, but I'll pray about it."

Samantha pared her enthusiasm down to just a brilliant smile. "Thank you."

***

Sterling walked with his characteristically long strides to school early one morning, thinking about the day's curriculum and what he needed to accomplish before the students arrived. He thought of how he would love to talk about his plans with Samantha and wished he could ask for her feedback and ideas. Her soft gray eyes would smile back at him, her sharp mind and vivid imagination helping him see things from a different perspective and improving his approach as a teacher.

Their frequent letters to each other kept him moving forward, and receiving hers was the best part of his week. But they didn't replace being in the same room together, or talking to her face to face, or holding her in his arms. He hated that she was so far away and he wouldn't see her until the Christmas holidays. But he gratefully held onto the promise of that December date.

In his quiet classroom that smelled of books and chalk dust, he distributed corrected work to each desk for the boys to see as soon as they arrived, then began writing a prompt on the board. He liked to start out each morning with a short writing session to get them all thinking and actively working. He loved writing along with them and then sharing with each other in discussion. He had noticed that a couple of the quieter boys were starting to find their voices—verbally as well as in writing—as they gained confidence. This realization gratified him and he held onto it like an ember, handling it carefully and encouraging its warmth to continue burning and glowing. If he could help all of his students recognize that their thoughts and perspectives had value, and to communicate their ideas in writing, they could really go far in their academic pursuits and, eventually, into their adult lives, whatever they chose to do.

In his neat, angular script, Sterling wrote a quote on the blackboard from the great writer Victor Hugo: *"In all his trials he was sustained and at times even exalted by a secret strength in himself. The soul aids the body and at moments uplifts it. It is the only bird that can endure a cage."*

Finished, he set the chalk down and looked at the words, considering how he would open the discussion, what he would share from his own experience to illustrate how he had found this strength within himself. He considered his privileged background in comparison with the boys of Worthington, many of whom had as humble an upbringing as Jerome, some of whom knew the reality of an empty stomach and parents concerned with how to make ends meet. He didn't know from experience what it felt like to go to bed hungry, or how hard it must be to watch parents struggle to provide necessities. No, his was a very different experience, and yet he, too, had faced difficulties that had forced him to find that inner, secret strength. And at times that "cage" around his soul had been suffocating.

He could remember very few times when he and his mother had agreed on anything. On the other hand, Father hadn't ever seemed to mind what interests Sterling chose to pursue—but he also didn't understand Sterling's lack of dedication to the family businesses. James' passion for horses and hemp manufacturing stood in stark contrast to Sterling's passion for writing and educating. Years of these discrepancies with his parents often left Sterling feeling very different and disconnected from the people he should have felt closest to. And while he loved Lucas as much as any brother could, as a boy it had often pained him to see how well Lucas shared their father's interests and passions, while he had inadvertently felt left out. It was a constant internal conflict: wanting to be part of the inner circle but also craving other things, wanting to feel understood by his family but also realizing he didn't fully understand *them*. And yet, looking back now, he realized the struggle had strengthened and deepened him, just as Samantha's differing struggle had strengthened and deepened her.

But at these boys' ages, it was hard for them to recognize that their struggles could be anything but a stumbling block to happiness. Actually, Sterling admitted to himself, even for adults it was hard to recognize positives in the trials of the moment because life could be so very hard.

It was like what Isaiah wrote in the Old Testament. He loved the poetry, vividness, and symbolism of his words. In Chapter 48, the Lord said, "I have refined thee...I have chosen thee in the furnace of affliction." Sterling knew that a smelter used the heat of fire to burn away impurities from silver. Sometimes that was how life felt, that it was a true furnace of affliction. And sometimes it felt that way for a very long time. Everything didn't always turn out all right, either, even when the sufferer was worthy and good.

There were some things these boys were going through that they might have to endure for years and it wouldn't help them for him to be idealistic about it. Sterling was optimistic by nature, but Samantha helped him look on the bright side while still coming down to earth, seeing the good and the hard in life a little more clearly. He acknowledged the harsh reality that sometimes bad things happened to good people. But the thought that everything might not turn out all right didn't scare him as much as it used to. Now he knew that because of Jesus, everything really would turn out for the best for those who followed Him, even if that looked different from what they expected. Even if it didn't happen until heaven. He guessed the challenge was to learn to see things from God's perspective while one was in the thick of things.

Sterling had read only a few days ago in Matthew 11, "My yoke is easy and my burden is light." He loved that. It gave him comfort to think about being yoked to Christ, walking with Him, and being helped to shoulder the load, like two oxen pulling a tremendous weight together. And he knew it was the specially made yoke that made the difference, because in reality the oxen were often not of equal size or strength—just as he and Christ were not equal in any way. But Jesus' promise was that He would meet Sterling where he was and help him along his path. He was so glad he had that knowledge now, that Samantha did too, and that they could be equally yoked with Christ as they continued on that journey together. It gave him immeasurable comfort to know that Jesus would give them strength to weather the storms of life.

Now, how to express the most important aspects of this quote on secret strength without preaching religion in school... Sterling thought about the possibilities for a few moments and jotted down ideas. Then he moved on to the next activity and put the final touches on the day's arithmetic lesson. Arithmetic would never be his favorite, but at least he knew different ways to explain the concepts after last year's classroom experience and time talking to fellow teachers. Not having to start lessons from scratch this year was making a big difference already!

***

One evening Samantha and Claire walked to a concert at the music conservatory on campus, talking and laughing as they enjoyed the cooling air, both wearing their best walking dresses. Samantha's was a simple flowered pattern that flattered her slim figure and ended in a wide ruffle around the hem. It was a light blue that deepened the gray of her eyes and complemented her pale coloring, cheeks pink with exercise. She wore her long fair hair in a large bun that was intricately twisted and pinned up under a dark hat with artificial flowers. Under a similar hat, Claire wore her thick black hair in a glossy braid that encircled her head, the dark pink of her dress complementing her brown complexion to perfection.

"I'm glad you can accompany me," Samantha told her older friend. "Katherine likes to go to musical events with me, but she and Rupert had other plans tonight. And it is much nicer to go to these things with a friend."

"I am glad to come with you!" Claire returned. "At first I wasn't sure I should come because I have barely dared go anywhere. But after all these weeks, I am beginning to think Phil has left Lorraine County for good and will actually leave me alone."

"Oh, I hope so!" Samantha said with feeling. After a beat she added, "You do seem happier these days."

"I am," Claire agreed. "Spending all this time with Mama has been good for me. And seeing that I am really, truly helping her with the work makes me feel like I have something to contribute after all." She shook her head. "I didn't realize how much of my self-respect Phil dissolved. I used to be so spunky and fierce but, over time, he turned me into a mouse without my even realizing it!"

"That is a terrible thing," Samantha said quietly. "I still wish we could have helped sooner somehow. But I'm very glad you are with us now."

"Yes, so am I," Claire returned. "I am beginning to think this all happened as it did just at the right time. Mama tries not to show it, but she is slowing down a little."

The thought made Samantha's heart squeeze, but she had noticed it too. "The mansion is just too much for one person to handle—even if that person had the energy of three! And you do make such a big difference. That is why I'm hoping..." She trailed off, uncertain if she should bring up the topic when she still hadn't talked about it with Father yet.

Claire looked at her expectantly as they walked in tandem in their black Regal[1] lace-up shoes. "You're hoping...?" she cued.

"Well," Samantha mused, "I haven't mentioned this to Father yet, so I may be putting the cart before the horse, but I am making plans to start a school."

Claire sucked in a surprised breath.

"Your mother didn't say anything to you about it, then?" Samantha asked.

"No."

"She knows I haven't spoken to Father and that I am just in the planning stages. But I did ask her to think about the idea of teaching a class."

"Mama? A teacher?" Claire asked, dumbfounded. But then her expression cleared. "Actually, she would be a great teacher! She was always so good at helping us all with our homework when we were children."

Samantha grinned. "I know she would be good at it and told her so. But what I am wondering is if you could stay on too."

"Oh, I am no teacher," Claire said, holding up both hands as if to stop the idea right then and there.

"Perhaps not." Samantha shrugged slightly. "You may surprise yourself. But I was thinking more along the lines of continuing your housekeeping efforts—with an added responsibility. I envision a school that teaches the children how to work and develop life skills, in addition to their academic studies. I want them to know how to clean house, cook, do laundry, plant and tend the garden, etc. But they will need to learn from an expert..." She left the sentence dangling, wondering how Claire would respond to the idea.

"Teaching children how to—Me?" Claire looked at her, large eyes wide. "I never had any children of my own, you know. I don't know the first thing about— Me?" she asked again.

"Just think about it," Samantha laughed. "Everything is still very much in the preliminary stages and nothing is certain yet. Except for the fact," she hurried to add, "that you are an indispensable part of this family and we are going to need you even more in the future than we do now. I hope you are all right with that!"

---

1. https://www.ebay.com/itm/275135935263

Claire linked arms with Samantha as they continued walking. "I am very much all right with that!" she crowed. "So yes, I will give it some thought. I might even come up with a few ideas of my own."

"Perfect!" Samantha exclaimed. "The more minds working together on this, the better."

Chapter 15

NEEDING FATHER

In mid October, Sterling's classroom rang with the sounds of young, exuberant voices as the boys worked on their autumn projects. It was the end of the day and they only had a few more minutes to finish their leaf displays. The room was filled with the musky-sweet odor of baskets of leaves, and their temporary color brightened the room everywhere Sterling looked. He swallowed down the scratchiness in his throat and smiled to see all the industry. Some boys were writing poems or stories about autumn leaves, reminding Sterling of the story Samantha had once told him of her childhood. She had gone outside with a large kitchen bowl and painstakingly collected the most beautiful leaves she could find, then brought them inside to sort and enjoy—forever, she had thought. What a disappointment when she learned that they quickly dried up and faded. Autumn leaves had to be enjoyed in the moment, and that was what Sterling hoped this project would provide them an opportunity to do.

Some of the boys were pasting leaves to paper in various designs to create works of art. Others were conducting experiments on how quickly specific types of leaves fell to the ground from different heights, and still others were researching and cataloging the kinds of leaves and the characteristics of the trees they came from.

Sterling was glad to see the students all so involved in their chosen projects, regardless of the noise. He was also glad the teachers on either side of his classroom had so far been tolerant of the occasional loud lessons like this one. As long as everyone was effectively engaged in his own work, Sterling felt that some noise now and then was acceptable, though he knew not all the teachers agreed with him on that point.

It was almost time to go, anyway, and he was relieved about that because he had a headache. He didn't think it was caused by the noise or by the strong smell of the leaves, and he had slept well the night before, so it wasn't fatigue. He hoped he wasn't coming down with something, though a couple of the boys had been out ill the past few days, so that was entirely possible.

Just before the big school bell rang outside in the school yard, Sterling called the class to attention and asked them to put their supplies and projects away to finish the next day. Then he thanked them for a great day and sent them on their way.

He left school a little earlier than usual to take supper at the Tomlinsons', then returned home and retired to bed a couple of hours early, hoping extra sleep was all he needed. Unfortunately, when he awoke the next morning, the headache had taken up more permanent residence and the scratchiness in his throat had given way to inflammation. He managed to teach his class adequately enough, but was exhausted by the end of school. His appetite waning, he didn't eat much dinner, praying that this time he would feel better upon awakening.

He didn't.

Again, he slogged through the day, wondering why his body was betraying him this way, why he kept getting worse and not feeling rested each morning.

The next day, he felt a growing heaviness in his chest and kept trying to clear it by coughing. He also felt warmer than usual and absently loosened his collar to compensate. By the fourth day, the students all noticed his bloodshot eyes and the hoarseness of his voice.

"Mr. Sterling, you don't look so good," one of the boys in the front offered.

"Yes," another one agreed. "Maybe you should go home and rest."

Sterling thanked them for their concern and declined, but while sitting at his desk later that morning, light-headed, he saw pinpricks of light on the periphery of his vision, gathering fast. Like tiny fireflies moving rapidly inward, they crowded his eyesight until he could see nothing and was not even aware he had passed out, his head on his desk. The students were on their feet in an instant and the boy from the front ran out the door, calling for Mr. Grover.

***

Samantha was researching in the library early one blustery afternoon in late October when Mrs. Dolittle hurried into the big room, a look of concern on her face. Samantha turned from a bookshelf. "What is it?" she asked, instantly feeling alarmed as she caught sight of the older woman's anxious expression.

Mrs. Dolittle held out a small yellow envelope. "A courier just brought this to the door."

Samantha's heart dropped to her stomach, then began to beat rapidly. *This could be something good,* she told herself, and took a deep breath to calm her whirling thoughts. *Remember that telegram last year?* But she knew that more often than not, telegrams brought bad news.

Mrs. Dolittle took one look at Samantha's face and grasped her by the elbow to guide her to the nearest sofa. "Let us sit down, shall we?" she said.

Samantha sank down onto the seat and Mrs. Dolittle sat beside her. With trembling fingers, Samantha slit open the Western Union envelope and lifted out the small paper inside:

Sterling very ill with pneumonia and asks for you.[1]

Samantha clamped a hand over her mouth to stifle a cry and turned to Mrs. Dolittle, who had read the message, silently, along with her. "Mrs... I can't... What should..."

Mrs. Dolittle faced her and grasped her hands, squeezing them tightly in her own. "Deep breaths," she instructed, and Samantha obeyed. "Again. There. Now, child, we must think things through and do what will help Sterling most, not go about in a panic."

"Yes," Samantha nodded, her heart pounding as if it would burst out of her chest, an alarming ringing in her ears. "I must go to him. There is no question of that." She thought for a moment, trying to slow her breathing. Reaching a sudden and impulsive decision, she stood abruptly. "I need Father!"

---

1. For an ambiguous discussion on the use and non-use of STOP in telegrams, see https://www.reddit.com/r/AskHistorians/comments/wm2152/why_did_tele grams_use_the_word_stop_instead_of_a/ -An.

Mrs. Dolittle stood, too, in her slow way. "Go to him. I will start packing for you."

"Thank you," Samantha whispered. She stood there, re-reading the telegram, shuddering involuntarily as she placed the paper back inside its envelope. Then she ran out of the library, into the long hallway, and up the great staircase. Telegram in one hand, skirts in the other, she sped up the stairs in time to her pounding heart until she reached the third floor. "Father!" she called as she dashed down the hallway. "Father!"

She reached his door and, to her surprise, it opened just before she grasped the knob. There he stood, tall and slightly stooped, his gray, wiry brows knit together in apprehension and alarm. She had never seen that expression on his face or known him to move that fast.

"Father!" She threw herself into his arms and let out the sobs she had been holding in since she saw the little yellow envelope. She felt him stiffen momentarily, then gradually relax, and his arms came around her gently, patting her back and hair, just letting her cry for a long minute.

When he spoke, his voice was dry and brittle. He cleared his throat and tried again. "What is it, daughter? What is wrong?"

She pulled away from him and looked up into his blue eyes with their slightly puckered eyelids, wrinkles radiating from the corners of each eye. He did not let go, but she was barely aware of this as she shakily began to explain. "Father, it's Sterling. He is terribly sick! I just received a telegram." She held it up. "He needs me! I must not delay. But I cannot go alone, Father. There is no time to make arrangements like last time I went to Worthington! What shall I do? I must go at once!" She stopped abruptly, knowing she was babbling, and dashed at the tears on her face. "I am sorry to barge in on you like this. I usually solve all my own problems, but this time I...I need you, Father." She buried her head in his chest again and the tears continued to fall. "I can't lose him!"

Basil's hold on his daughter tightened and he laid his grizzled head against hers as he stroked her back, waiting for her sobs to quiet while he gathered his thoughts. He knew what this felt like. Oh, how devastatingly familiar this was! He had re-lived those times over and over, of when he had heard a new diagnosis of his dear Lovenia's illnesses, and vividly remembered how the news had stabbed his heart and made him feel weak and helpless. If there was any way to soften the blow or ease Samantha's burden—or prevent history from repeating itself—he wanted to do it. As an old history professor, he knew all too well how history tended to repeat, and that could not happen here! He did not know how an old, used up man could make a difference, but he would try, for Lovenia's sake—and for their daughter's sake.

When Samantha quieted, Basil eased her away from him and handed her his hand-kerchief—shabby, but cleanly laundered. "Come, daughter," he said. "We will do this together. I will go with you to Worthington." Samantha inhaled with a start of surprise, but he quickly continued. "Mrs. Dolittle and Claire will help us pack our necessities and food for the journey." He fished around in his vest pocket for his pocket watch and checked the hour. "I believe we can be ready in time to catch the next train, if departure times are what they used to be."

Samantha sagged with relief and felt her father's arm reaching out instinctively again to give her support. To have the responsibility of planning this emergency trip suddenly lifted away from her, and the burden of concern shared, to feel lovingly cared for by the very man who had always seemed to take so little notice of her, felt miraculous. "Thank you, Father," she whispered, mopping again at the tears and wiping her nose. She gave him a tearful smile and reached up to kiss his cheek. "I will go help them pack."

***

This time, the journey to Worthington seemed to take much, much longer than it had before. Samantha finally forced herself to stop pulling out her little watch chain every few minutes, realizing that would not help the trip go any faster. She wanted to pace back and forth—to do anything but sit here!—but of course in these close quarters, and with so many passengers, she had no other option. Her mind couldn't settle, so writing was out of the question and reading was little better. But she found she could read a passage from her Bible here and there; focusing on the words calmed her mind a bit.

What she craved most was peace. And as she read the scriptures—even if she had to read a verse over and over to finally understand its meaning in the frazzled state she was in—she felt that peace. Comfort seemed to wrap around her like a warm blanket as she read in Joshua 1: "Be strong and of a good courage; be not dismayed: for the Lord thy God is with thee whithersoever thou goest." *He is with me*, she said to herself, closing her eyes and holding the words and the promise tightly to herself. *Wherever I go, He is with me. He can strengthen me and give me courage.*

A while later, when she randomly flipped to John 14, her faith felt strengthened with the words: "Let not your heart be troubled: ye believe in God, believe also in me... I am the way, the truth, and the life..." *He is the way,* she repeated to herself. *He is life and He can save life. He can inspire me to know how to help Sterling. And He can and will comfort us both through what lies ahead.*

She glanced at her father next to her and was glad to see that he was sleeping peacefully, his head bobbing softly on his chest. This would have been an opportune time to converse, to repair their relationship more fully and discuss things that had always been left unsaid, but right now she could not string those thoughts together long enough to form a coherent sentence anyway, so it was just as well that he rested.

In contrast to him, though, she felt restless and impatient, hating the enforced inactivity. Her legs longed to stretch, to have something else to focus her mind on. Finally, in desperation, she made her way to the end car where there was a small open-air place through a door. There she stood, holding the rail, watching trees and meadows dash by, the chill wind loosening her hair from its pins. She closed her eyes and took a deep breath, letting it out slowly. She pictured Sterling, suffering in bed and asking for her. Then she pictured strength flowing into him, an easing of his symptoms, and a healing sleep. *Would to God that would be the case!*

Father in Heaven, she prayed for the umpteenth time, *please bless Sterling to recover, to be healthy and strong again. And inspire me to know what to do to help him regain that strength. He is so dear to me. I know thou lovest him too, as thou lovest me. Thank thee for loving us both and for bringing us together. Please do not allow his life to be cut short, Father. He does so much good and is needed by so many. I need him...!*

In this moment she wished she were not so knowledgeable of facts and current scientific literature, for knowing that pneumonia was one of the leading causes of death in the United States did nothing to allay her fears or calm her heart.[2] She unwillingly remembered how the president of Oberlin College had died so unexpectedly of pneumonia only a few months before, and the thought chilled her more than the wind.

She forced her thoughts away from those treacherous waters and returned them instead to the gentle flow of the Bible's verses she had just read: "Be strong and of a good courage...

---

2. https://www.cdc.gov/nchs/data/dvs/lead1900_98.pdf

I am the way, the truth, and the life." She opened her eyes and grasped onto that last word as tightly as she had ever held to anything. *Life!*

"You must live, Sterling," she whispered. "You must!"

***

After what seemed an eternity, they finally arrived in Worthington and her father hailed a cab at the station. It wasn't until that moment that Samantha realized she could have sent a telegram to Uncle Samuel or Aunt Irene and someone from the family could have met them. Being so caught up in worry over Sterling and then occupied in prayer on his behalf, the thought hadn't even occurred to her. So instead, she gave the driver instructions to the boarding house where Sterling lived and they climbed inside the buggy. After his sleep on the train, Basil was wide awake and ready to take on whatever was needed. Samantha, on the other hand, felt like her emotions were completely unraveling and she was existing solely on nervous energy. But at least they were nearly at their destination now and had left that infernal train.

"How are you?" her father asked, looking at her perceptively from eyes that seemed sharper than she'd ever seen. "Sorry I slept so long and was such poor company."

She gave him a wan, lopsided smile, not knowing how to answer that question honestly, and he took her hand, patting it softly. "Things will be well," he told her, in his sparse, direct way.

"Do you really think so, Father?" she asked, her eyes and heart pleading for reassurance.

He held her hand firmly between his own and said simply, "Yes."

"Oh, I hope so!" She laid her head against his shoulder and he put an arm around her. For the first time in hours, she allowed herself to relax and almost fell asleep in the few minutes it took to arrive at the boarding house.

They alighted and her father paid the driver. Because of her time in Worthington the previous summer, Samantha knew which room was Sterling's and rushed around the front of the building to the correct side, her father close behind. Then suddenly, there were the stairs up to his room just as she remembered, and there at the landing was the lone door with its white paint beginning to peel. Her heart quickened at the sight of it, and at the anticipation of being so close. In her haste, she left her bag at the bottom of

168

the rickety stairs and ascended swiftly to the landing. She found the door unlocked and it groaned softly as she pushed it open. There she saw Thora blinking at her from a chair near Sterling's bed, having obviously just awakened at the sound of Samantha's steps on the stairs. She stood quickly and Samantha noted her disheveled appearance, her large auburn bun a little lopsided, her clothing wrinkled. Faint dark smudges showed beneath her eyes. The room smelled of sickness and despair.

"Samantha!" Thora exclaimed, opening her arms to embrace her. "I am so glad you're here!"

"Thank you for sending that telegram!" Samantha returned, looking past her to the still figure on the bed. "How long has he been ill?" She knelt at the bedside and her heart jumped into her throat. Sterling's strong, muscular form now looked haggard and almost gaunt. His handsome face was ravaged by illness, his cheeks hollow under a growing beard. The healthy tan of his skin had given way to a pallidness that alarmed her, and his breathing was ragged, shallow, and quick.

"I don't know for certain," Thora responded. "I think it came on suddenly. Last week, while at my house for dinner, he mentioned a headache and that he thought he might be coming down with something. My guess is he pushed himself too hard, because a few days later, Mr. Grover sent a messenger out to the farm to let me know Sterling had collapsed in his classroom during school."

"Poor Sterling," Samantha mourned, imagining it all. His forehead was hot to the touch and his hair was unkempt and tangled. Instinctively, she smoothed it back with gentle fingers, slowly, over and over again. "He must really have overdone it. I have heard pneumonia can sap all one's energy. Have you been here ever since, Thora?" She turned to the woman again and looked up at her with an expression full of gratitude.

"Most of the time," Thora acknowledged, "though Jerome has spelled me off a couple times, and even Mr. Grover stayed with him part of one day, so I could go home for a while." She looked tired enough to fall asleep on her feet and as Samantha glanced around the room, taking in its sparse furnishings, she wondered how the woman had managed to sleep sitting up in the only chair in the room.

"I didn't want to alarm you unnecessarily," Thora continued, stifling a yawn and rubbing briefly at her eyes. "But he hasn't improved at all, and this morning he started calling out your name in his delirium. I hoped that your presence might inspire him to fight." Her eyes showed love and pain and desperation all at once.

"Yes," Samantha said, rising. "You did right. Thank you." She grasped Thora's shoulders gently and firmly instructed, "You must go home now and sleep. Take care of yourself so you can take care of Jerome and your farm. I am here now and will stay with Sterling for as long as it takes."

Thora nodded gratefully. "I'll return when I can and will bring food with me. In the meantime, there are a few dishes there, brought by parents of his students." She indicated the desk in the corner and Samantha took note of a basket of rolls and a covered plate. "Anything you can persuade him to eat would be helpful. He has not eaten much in days."

Samantha looked back at Sterling's still, gray form and nodded. "I will do all I can to coax food down him. Did the doctor mention anything else we can do? Perhaps a bowl of broth would be beneficial."

"I thought of that as well," Thora said. "After I rest a few hours, I will make some broth and bring it. I would have made it sooner, but...I've been here." She gestured around the small room apologetically. "The doctor did not have much in the way of suggestions, other than to try and keep him comfortable and feed him as much as possible. He said some doctors like to try arsenic or strychnine to kill bacteria,[3] but he feels it is too risky."

Samantha shivered. She was very glad Sterling's doctor had not tried such poisons. Surely those would pose more risk than benefit! "Thank you, Thora," she said sincerely, hugging the older woman tightly. "I know you have done so much for him. We will pray and hope."

Thora hugged her back. "Having you here will make all the difference. I am sure of it!" She looked seriously into Samantha's eyes. "He needs to remember why he wants to live. And with that will, he can fight off this infection."

"Yes." A lump had formed in Samantha's throat and her voice came out in a whisper.

In a moment, Thora was gone and Samantha was alone with Sterling. She knelt again at his bedside and reached beneath the covers for his hand. "Sterling," she said quietly. "I am here. I will be with you as long as you need me. You *must* recover!" She stroked his hot hands and tears trailed down her cheeks. "Sterling, my love, you must fight! We have so many plans for a future together. There is so much good we want to accomplish and we need each other to do it. *I* need you." Her voice caught on a sob and she pressed his hand

---

3. https://bit.ly/4aXXPHO

to her lips. "Surely God does not need you yet." She knelt there, his hand clasped in both of hers, praying with all the energy of her soul until her knees ached. At one point, she heard her father come in with their luggage and then leave again.

About half an hour later, he returned to find her applying cool rags to Sterling's forehead. "How is he?" Basil asked quietly.

"He feels even hotter than when I arrived," she said, a line of worry marking her forehead as she looked up at her father. "I feel so inadequate to care for him—I am no nurse!—but after my prayer, this was the first thing that came to mind."

Her father nodded. "Follow those thoughts," he encouraged. "They may be inspiration from heaven and they cannot hurt anyway."

Samantha smiled wanly. "What have you been up to?"

"Well, I met Mrs. Tomlinson," he said. "Nice woman. Seemed very tired, as no doubt she was."

"Oh, I am sorry I did not introduce you," Samantha began, but Basil waved away her apology.

"We managed fine. Then, after I brought in our bags, I walked over to the Worthington Inn.[4] I asked if they had any extra cots we could rent. They did, so I secured us two, which I will go back and collect. We cannot have you sleeping in that hard chair, and this old man would never manage sleeping that way either," he said, indicating himself.

"Thank you, Father," Samantha returned quietly. "It means so much to me, to have you take care of these things." She still felt the relief of it.

"Of course," he replied. His voice was a little hoarse as he added, "I cannot undo all the ways I failed you in the past, but what I can do in the present to ease your way, I will." His voice was a bit gruff with what sounded like emotion.

She stood and placed a gentle hand on his arm, hoping he could see the forgiveness in her eyes.

"You are a better daughter than I deserve," he said finally, awkwardly.

Samantha embraced him for a long moment and said, "I am grateful to have my father here now."

---

4. https://worthingtoninn.com/about/

He swiped at his eyes quickly and cleared his throat. "Now then, before I retrieve the cots, what can I help you with?"

Samantha considered for a moment. "I feel like he should be propped up so he can breathe more easily. Could you help me get him into a sitting position?"

"Gladly," her father replied, looking a bit relieved to be given instructions. "He's a big man, but between the two of us, I think we can manage it."

It was a bit tricky, but they figured it out and soon had Sterling partially sitting with his back against the wall, cushioned by the one pillow. Samantha wished they had other pillows to work with, but they managed to roll up extra blankets and wedge them around him for support. Immediately, the ragged sound of his breathing eased a bit and Samantha felt sure they had done the right thing.

Her father left and she began applying cool rags to Sterling's forehead again. She hesitatingly unbuttoned his shirt to expose his neck and chest, then rolled up his sleeves and began rubbing him down there too. At first, she felt shy administering to him in this intimate way and seeing so much of his skin in the process, but she knew deep inside herself that cooling him down was of vital importance to his survival, so she pushed past the awkwardness. And he did seem to sleep more comfortably afterward, though his fever never stayed down for long. She was grateful her father would be able to help carry water from the pump outside, for she would need a constant supply of it as long as Sterling's fever lasted.

Sterling's face was no longer clean-cut, the way he liked to keep it. She saw the small mirror hanging on a hook on one wall, and a small bowl with soap, a brush, and a razor, and took a mental note to ask her father to help shave the dark beard that was growing along Sterling's jaw. But for now, she needed to focus on bringing his temperature down and helping him breathe more easily.

Chapter 16

CAREGIVING

Over the next two days, Samantha stayed by Sterling's side constantly, except for occasional breaks to use the privy and, a few times a day, to fetch water from the pump in the courtyard behind the boarding house. She needed those times to stretch her legs and feel the sunshine on her face for a few minutes, and was glad her father could stay with Sterling as she did so. But she never stayed away long; the situation was so tenuous, she couldn't bear to. If Sterling worsened while she was away, she would never forgive herself.

The day after Thora left, she returned with Jerome, as promised, bringing a large bowl of broth, other food items, and extra bedding. Samantha and her father had, by then, eaten up what remained of the food on the little table, and Samantha was starting to feel anxious that the only thing she had gotten down Sterling's throat was a bit of water every hour or so. But Thora commended Samantha's efforts, encouraging her with the observation that she thought Sterling looked a little better than he had when she left.

Thora herself looked refreshed in a clean and pressed brown dress, her auburn hair pulled back neatly in the usual bun, and her brown eyes bright. Jerome had grown taller and filled out a bit since Samantha last saw him, though it had only been a couple months. The extra pillows and blankets they brought were immediately used to make Sterling more comfortable and to outfit the two cots set side by side next to the bed for Samantha and Basil.

By the end of the second day, Samantha was able to persuade Sterling to swallow a good portion of the broth and felt relieved in that small success, though he remained unconscious through it all. She hoped she was not imagining an improved color in his complexion, though she suspected he would continue to look gaunt for a while. It seemed like his fever was not returning quite as often, and his breathing, though quicker than normal, did not sound as strained.

She held his hand and talked to him often, sharing passages of scripture she had discovered recently. Other times she read to him from a ragged copy of his favorite book, *Walden* by Henry David Thoreau, or from a lovely book of poems she found in the stack of books by his desk. She didn't know how much of these things he heard, but her voice did seem to calm him. Whenever he stirred in his sleep or called out in delirium, she rushed to his side and tried to soothe him, both day and night. Sometimes she fell asleep on her knees by the bed, and always she kept a prayer in her mind and heart, thanking God for the tiny successes and small progresses, continually pleading for blessings and inspiration. She felt that He was with her, watching over them and helping her to know little things to try for Sterling. But as improvement was so slow, she sometimes felt discouraged in spite of her efforts to maintain a positive outlook.

On the third day, Thora again brought a bowl of broth and, seeing how tired Samantha was, urged her to come home with her to catch a few hours of uninterrupted sleep. Samantha longed to do just that, but in the end refused, knowing she would worry more away from Sterling, which would not make for a good rest.

After Thora's afternoon visit, Sterling began calling out for Samantha in his fevered sleep. Samantha knew from experience that the fastest way to calm him was to hold firmly to his hand and verbally reassure him that she was there. His distress would ease at her touch and he would settle into deeper sleep. She decided to read to him again and pulled her hand gently out of his to find *Walden*, but as soon as she moved away, Sterling became agitated again. Quickly, she located the thin volume and hurried back to his side. She debated where to sit this time. The small space beside Sterling on the bed looked so incredibly inviting that she could not resist and made her way around the bed to sit next to him. *I do not remember ever being this tired in my entire life!* she thought, yawning hugely as she opened the book to the place she had last read. Sterling's head moved from side to side and he called her name again in a hoarse, thin voice. She grasped his hand with one of hers, held the book in her other hand, and began to read aloud. Soon, Sterling settled again and his breathing eased.

***

A couple hours later, feeling rested after a nap, Basil sat up from his cot and rose to check on his daughter. He found her curled up next to Sterling on the bed, her hand in his, a forgotten book discarded to one side. He looked down at them and his grizzled features lifted as he smiled at the tender picture they made. It might not be proper, but this was partly his fault for not being the best of chaperones. He did not care much for propriety just for the sake of propriety, however, and he knew that Samantha was safe with Sterling. Besides, the man had not awakened once since they'd arrived. Basil also had the feeling that they were both resting better this way than they would apart. And for now, sleep would probably help them both better than anything else. So, he pulled the blanket off Samantha's cot and tucked it around her on the bed, then quietly made his way over to the chair at the desk and picked up a book.

***

Hours later, Sterling woke slowly, blinking and drowsy, unsure of where he was. He looked around and recognized the room in the dim light cast from a lantern on the small bedside table. He felt a pressure in his chest and the answering pain in his head, and vaguely remembered the illness that had claimed him so completely. But he didn't feel quite as awful as he had in the schoolroom that one day...when had it been? He closed his eyes again and tried to remember, but he had no idea how much time had passed. He knew from the soreness in his whole body that he must have lain in this bed a long while, and he guessed from the extreme weakness he felt that he had been very sick.

But he seemed to remember something that did not quite fit with everything else. He became conscious of a form at his side and felt something soft and warm in his hand. He opened his eyes again and looked down to see a shape in shadow. When he traced the long fingers resting against his, his heart leapt and he smiled weakly to himself. He would know those fingers anywhere. Samantha was here, after all; he hadn't dreamed it! He turned his head to the other side of the room and noted the cot with a sleeping form on it as well. *Basil?*

With that small exertion, exhaustion rolled over him in a wave and he succumbed to a deeper, more healing sleep than he had yet experienced.

***

In the morning, as the sun shone through the window, Samantha opened her eyes and slowly stretched out her curled up legs. She felt truly rested for the first time since her arrival in Worthington. She luxuriated in the feeling for a moment, then realized that she had slept all night. Did that mean Sterling was...? She drew in a breath and looked up at him, still propped against the wall. To her surprise, he looked right back at her. Startled to see his eyes open, she instantly sat up and blinked. She reached forward and felt his forehead. Expecting the usual heat, she was thrilled to find it cool, and smiled in joyous relief. She brushed a lock of lank, limp hair back from his forehead and looked into his face, searching to know how he felt. He watched her with bloodshot eyes, but didn't reach for her and his smile was faint. He looked so devoid of strength and energy that it pained her to see it. But he was awake and no longer feverish! Surely that counted for something.

Finally, he slowly lifted his hand, as if it were heavy, and threaded his fingers through hers.

"You're awake!" she said, quietly, unnecessarily.

"And you," Sterling answered hoarsely. "I watched you...for a while." His words seemed to come with great effort and were slightly slurred with weakness. "You...looked so...peaceful."

"I didn't mean to fall asleep like that," she admitted. "I started out reading to you," she glanced down at the bed and saw a corner of the book peeking out from beneath the blanket, "and the next thing I know, it's morning." She stifled a yawn. "I guess the lack of sleep over the last few days caught up to me."

"Thank you...for coming," he rasped.

"Of course," she responded. "I am very glad to be here, and so glad Thora sent a telegram, or I would not have known you were sick."

"Yes. Her...timely telegrams." Sterling's attempt at a bigger smile turned into a grimace as he began to cough: a dry, hacking sound. "What day...?" he asked when the coughing subsided.

"Today is October 24th," she supplied. "It's been seven days since you collapsed at school, three days since I arrived."

He nodded weakly. "I guess I...was more ill than...I realized." The effort at conversation obviously exhausted him, so Samantha took over, tucking the blanket up higher around him, and relating everything she could think of that he might want to know of the past few days.

Basil awoke on the nearby cot and slowly sat up, rubbing a hand over his eyes and scratching his bearded chin. "You look improved," he said, appraising Sterling with a critical eye.

Sterling turned his head and acknowledged the older man with a slight nod. "Thank you for..." He gestured at Samantha weakly with one hand. "She made...the difference," he finished shortly.

"Yes," Basil agreed. "Love can do that." His tone sounded wistful and he gave a small smile. "Glad to see you back in the land of the living."

Sterling smiled wanly, but gratitude shone from his bloodshot eyes. "Not good for...much yet." He closed his eyes for a moment, as if he needed a rest from holding them open.

"I think you need more substantial food than the broth I keep spooning down you," Samantha decided, standing up. She tried to smooth her dress when she noticed how wrinkled it was, then gave up. She knew her hair must be a mess as well, and reached up to push in a few loose pins as she walked to the other side of the room. From the small assortment of food on the desk, she found a slice of bread and a little dish of butter, and quickly buttered the bread. She brought it to Sterling, along with a cup of water, which he downed with a shaking hand. Then he took a bite of the bread, his fingers trembling with fatigue as he brought it to his mouth. Seeing him too weak to properly feed himself smote Samantha's heart as she recalled his usual vitality and strength. He had a long way to go to regain that strength, but she would help him return to that place of health and vigor. With God's help, he would once again be all he wanted to be, she hoped.

Sterling thanked her for the bread and told her it was "delicious." In truth, he couldn't remember anything ever tasting better. He seemed to recall losing his appetite when he grew sick, and that food had not tasted appealing anymore. Everything had had a metallic taste to it, including water. But that was days ago—no wonder the body he glanced down at now looked so emaciated!

Samantha saw his glance and told him that the bread was almost the only thing he had eaten in about a week. "I hope you are ready to eat all day every day, to make up for it," she said, a challenge in her sparkling eyes. "We need to get your strength back and it starts with food and sleep."

He tried to smile and told her he would try. He didn't tell her he still felt terrible. After another coughing fit, he looked down at the half-eaten slice of bread and sighed. "No strength...to eat..." he apologized.

"It's all right," Samantha said, sitting on the edge of the bed. "I will help you. And then you can sleep again." She lifted the bread to his mouth and he took another bite, chewing slowly with his eyes closed. In a few minutes, the bread was gone and she gave him another long drink of water to end his meal. She felt grateful for this little progress and readied him for another rest. "Sweet dreams," she said, smoothing back his hair and kissing his forehead.

"Thank you," he whispered, and then he was asleep once more.

***

When he awoke a couple hours later, Samantha fed him again, this time with a chicken and vegetable soup that Thora had brought the night before, and which they warmed over the fire that cheerily took the chill out of the room. He did not have the energy to feed himself more than a few bites, but was able to eat a full bowl with Samantha's assistance. And once again, with the exertion of eating and the effects of having a full stomach, he fell right back to sleep.

Samantha's father took a trip to the outhouse and then insisted she take some time for herself. "I have the feeling he is going to sleep for a good long time now, so why don't you get out of this little room and go for a walk or something. I will be here, should he need anything." He stood near her and looked down fondly at this daughter of his who had acted the part of nurse so perfectly over the past three days.

Samantha thought about this offer for a long moment, realizing as she looked down at herself that she had not changed her clothing since she arrived. She had been so wrapped up in caring for Sterling and being present every time he needed her, that she had completely forgotten about doing even simple things for herself. She must look a fright! What she wanted more than anything, she suddenly realized, was a long bath and fresh clothes. Also, her stomach felt completely empty and she wanted to save the food they had for Sterling, now that he was eating again.

"Thank you, Father, I appreciate that. I do need to do a few things. Would you mind if I walked over to Aunt Irene's to beg the use of her bathtub?" She smiled. "She might even feed me, if I ask nicely." It might be a few hours before she returned, but she thought her father was correct that Sterling would sleep more soundly now and not notice her absence. And he seemed improved enough that she could spend a few hours away without worrying herself sick over him.

"Irene?" her father asked, eyes wide, as if he had not thought of her till this very moment. "Yes. Yes, of course." But he looked a little disconcerted.

"You may forget the Lewises, Father, but the Lewises have not forgotten you." Samantha laid a gentle hand on his arm and looked up into his face. "Whenever you are ready, they would love to see you again."

He swallowed hard and looked doubtful, but asked only, "Do you know the way? Can you walk there from here?"

"Yes and yes," Samantha returned. "It's been a couple months, but I know the way. Will you be all right here for a few hours?"

Basil nodded. "Take your time." He indicated Sterling's sleeping form. "We are not going anywhere."

***

On the walk, Samantha thought about all that had transpired since her return to Worthington. The experience had swung her emotions from one side of the pendulum to the other. This morning when Sterling awoke at long last, recognized her, and they were able to communicate, she was elated! Finally, he seemed to be making real progress and had even eaten twice! But at the same time, it was alarming to realize the extent of his frailty and how quickly he tired. And now, with time to think about it, the reality of his condition smote her heart further and made her feel weak at the knees. He had always been so physically strong and able, full of energy and seemingly untiring. Now he was reduced to needing to be fed like a baby, and it shocked her as she pictured his gaunt form in her mind. How could someone so big and strong become that diminished so quickly? And what was his prognosis? Could he fully recover and return to the man he was before? The time of recovery would undoubtedly be frustrating to him.

She had tried to be strong and optimistic in front of Sterling and even her father, but now alone, she was not quite so certain of that strength. *What if this illness has depleted him too much?* Tears pricked the corners of her eyes. She needed someone's advice! She had no qualifications to doctor anyone, and felt very inadequate to meet Sterling's needs. After all, she was only eighteen years old, and had never done anything like this before. Was she doing it right?

When Samantha walked up the path to Aunt Irene's little house, the chill air cooled her cheeks, but she felt warm from the long walk. She opened the gate of the white picket fence that surrounded the small front yard and closed it snugly behind her, then walked up the three stone steps to the recessed porch and knocked at the door. She looked at the bench near the door with its cheerful collection of colorful pillows and thought about what a comfortable spot that must be for Aunt Irene to rest in the evenings when the weather was pleasant.

All was quiet, so she knocked again. What if she had come all this way and Aunt Irene wasn't home? She pulled out her little watch chain and checked the time, then remembered that it was a weekday and Aunt Irene typically returned home from the university about 3:00. Samantha realized she had lost track of days and, to a great extent, of the time over the past few days. But it was just after 2:00 now, so she had less than an hour to wait. Now that she was here, she wanted to see Aunt Irene more than ever. She sat down and sighed, willing her body to release some of its tension.

The bench was quite comfortable, with armrests and all those pillows. As she eased back into their softness, she realized just how tired she was. Apparently, one good night's sleep was not enough to make up for a few nights of scanty sleep, topped with a great deal of worry and anxiety. So, she lay down on her side, pulled her knees up, and cocooned by pillows, soon drifted off to the soothing sound of a fall breeze blowing around the porch eaves.

***

What felt like only minutes later, Samantha awoke to someone calling her name. Her eyes snapped open and she quickly sat up, dazed and disoriented for a moment.

"Samantha," her aunt repeated, touching her shoulder and looking down at her in concern. "Are you all right? I didn't know you were back in town, so imagine my surprise to find you sleeping on my porch!"

Samantha blinked and ran a hand across her eyes. "I know. I'm sorry to show up like this, unannounced—" She stood as she began explaining.

"Nonsense, I am always happy to have you," Aunt Irene interrupted. "You are welcome to show up anytime, dear girl, but I sense this isn't just a social call..."

Samantha shook her head tiredly. "You are right, it isn't."

Aunt Irene pulled a key out of her reticule and moved to the door. "Well, come on in. Let's discuss whatever is on your mind over tea. I always like a bit of a snack when I return from work before I prepare supper."

Samantha's stomach growled loudly at the suggestion. Aunt Irene's eyebrows rose and she laughed. "It sounds like that was the right thing to say!"

Samantha exhaled a short laugh in return. "I guess it has been a while since I ate."

"I can certainly do something about that," her aunt smiled. The hallway was dim, but as Samantha followed her down the hall to the other side of the little house, they entered the cheery kitchen where the last sunshine of the day shone through the big window. Aunt Irene set down her reticule on the small kitchen table. "Would you like to wash up?" she asked, indicating the sink.

"I would. And actually, if it isn't too much trouble..." Samantha grimaced, "I could really use a bath."

Aunt Irene looked at her with an appraising eye and then slowly nodded. "You do look...worn, child. It appears you could use a change of clothes, as well."

Samantha held up the string bag that contained the few items she had brought with her.

"Ah." Aunt Irene nodded. "A bath it is. My home is yours, Samantha, so don't hesitate to ask for anything. Let's start heating a few pots on the stove and I'll fix us something to eat."

Samantha nodded and helped her aunt fill every large pot they could find with water from the kitchen pump. Then she started a fire in the cookstove while Aunt Irene busied herself with food preparation.

As they sat at the little table eating day-old currant muffins and waiting for the tea kettle to whistle, Aunt Irene turned to her, dark brows raised in curiosity and her characteristic directness. "So," she said. "What is going on? And how is that young man of yours? Are you in Worthington to see him?"

Samantha swallowed a delicious bite of muffin that seemed to melt in her mouth and considered which question to answer first. She decided on the last one. "Yes, I came here for Sterling. He has been very sick and I came to nurse him back to health. Father was so good to come with me, and Sterling woke up for the first time this morning and even ate twice, so that's all good news."

She didn't notice her aunt's start of surprise at the mention that Basil was in town, but she was aware that she was probably speaking too fast. Now that she'd started, though, it seemed impossible to slow down. "I should be nothing but happy and grateful. But I'm..." she swallowed down a lump in her throat and blinked back tears. "Aunt Irene, I'm scared! He is still so sick. I think... I think I almost lost him!" Her words were choked to a whisper and she looked pleadingly at the woman across the table from her. She hadn't admitted that to anyone and saying it out loud now made it more real.

"Oh, Samantha, I am so sorry!" Aunt Irene immediately reached out to grasp her hand. "I wish I had known sooner! Why didn't you send us word? I would—all the family would—be happy to help however we can. Don't carry this burden alone, all right? Will you let us help you? That's what family does!"

Samantha nodded tearfully and couldn't stop a little sobbing laugh of relief from slipping out. "Yes. Thank you! I am still unaccustomed to that. I should have sent word to you, only I've been so consumed with caring for him I couldn't focus on anything else. And I'm... I feel so inadequate to help him. He is incredibly weak and thin, and barely has the energy to swallow when I feed him, or to speak three words together."

Aunt Irene made a noise of incredulity and compassion. It was difficult for her to imagine the strapping young man in such a diminished condition. That must be extremely alarming for her niece to witness. "You poor child! No wonder you have dark smudges under your eyes and your clothing is all rumpled. Let us get you fed and freshened up, and I'll take you back there in my buggy and see what else can be done. Is my brother-in-law caring for him now, then?"

Samantha nodded, feeling a bit lighter already, just having her concern validated. "He told me to go do something for myself. Last night was my first full night of sleep since we arrived three days ago, but I haven't had a chance to even change clothes in all that time." She looked down at herself tiredly. "I actually didn't even think about it."

"Do you have enough food?" Aunt Irene asked suddenly.

"Thora has been bringing us some every day, and the parents of students bring food sometimes as well, but when I left to come here, it was mostly gone and I wanted to save it for Sterling, now that he's finally eating. The inn isn't far, though. I'm certain Father and I could purchase any meals we need there."

Aunt Irene shook her head decidedly and settled back into the chair with the air of a woman on a mission. "With so much family right here in the village, you have no need to buy hotel food. We can handle feeding three more people." She smiled reassuringly.

Samantha felt herself relax further and exhaled slowly, trying to smile back. "I know you have a busy schedule and I didn't want to trouble you, but we do need help. And when Father told me to take some time away, you were the one I wanted to see."

"I may not be the best of cooks," Aunt Irene laughed, "but I am very good at organizing." She held up one index finger for emphasis. "I can whip the Lewis family into shape and we will be at your service shortly. Here, have another muffin. You look half starved!"

"Thank you, these are delicious! I don't believe that about you not being a good cook."

"Well, as they say, 'hunger is the best sauce.'" Aunt Irene waved a dismissive hand and turned serious once again as Samantha filled her in on the last few days.

As the tea kettle began to whistle, Samantha admitted, "I really don't know what I'm doing, but I pray almost constantly. So far, the ideas I have had seem to be helping, but I still feel so deficient."

Aunt Irene removed the teapot from the stove and placed it on a green and brown knitted potholder on the table, then lifted the lid and dropped in a small silver infuser filled with herbs. "I am not a doctor either, of course, but I would say you are going about things in just the right way," she replied, setting the lid back on the pot. The small kitchen began to fill with the scent of mint and lemon balm. "And I understand your feelings of inadequacy. May I share with you what my father told me, back when I was struggling with the same feelings to such an extent that I didn't know how to move forward in my life?"

Samantha nodded. "Please! I want to hear everything about Grandfather."

"Well!" Aunt Irene spread her hands on the table and bent forward in anticipation. "Things had not gone the way I planned, with beaux and all, and during that period of my life I became very concerned that it was my fault. I thought that if I were just wiser or more spiritual, more attractive or had less of a forceful personality, my life's journey would go smoother. I blamed myself for not being like all my friends and just getting married. I blamed myself for being too picky as I courted men. Finally, I tearfully expressed as much to Father, and you know what he did?"

Samantha shook her head, all ears.

Aunt Irene was misty-eyed at the memory, and leaned back in her seat. "He took me in his arms, stroked my hair and let me cry, and told me that he loved me. He reminded me that my Father in Heaven loved me too, and that my trials were not a reflection of my worth. And then he related to me the story of Jesus and the loaves and fishes. Do you remember that story?"

"The one where he fed thousands with only a small amount of food?"

"That's the one. I had always considered that an obvious miracle and not thought much more about it, but Father shared with me his deeper perspective—and I have remembered his words countless times over the years. He said, 'Irene, I think what Jesus was telling His followers was that even if they did not have much, if they brought what they did have to Him, He would multiply it.'" She looked off into space as she remembered that time with her father. Then she blinked and looked back at Samantha. "Jesus knows we aren't perfect. In fact, He knows how incapable we really are! But *with* Him we can do everything He asks of us." Her voice was filled with conviction. "He can do amazing things for our lives as we give Him all that we have and are, even if it is only a few small loaves and fishes when thousands of empty stomachs need filling. *He* can fill us and strengthen us. He can provide enough and to spare."

"That's beautiful," Samantha said softly, her mind expanding with the concept. It was deep and wide and as she contemplated it, warmth entered her heart with the truth of it. "Have you found that to be true in your life?"

Aunt Irene's gaze returned to her niece, and she smiled ruefully. "I have, but it hasn't always been easy. I never felt I had the faith and goodness of your mother, the patient obedience of Eleanor, or the steady strength of Samuel. On top of all my other inadequacies, I felt inadequate in my spiritual life too. But when I stopped comparing myself to my siblings or anyone else and just focused on Jesus, I found that what my father said was right. Sometimes I still fought against God and, because of my strong will, I sometimes resented that He didn't always want for me what I wanted for myself. But I keep learning that the more I can let go and give Jesus my heart, the more I am able to see how He multiplies my strengths and helps things happen that are beyond what I could ever imagine." She gave a short laugh. "It's actually a much less difficult way of life than the one I used to live, because letting Him be in charge means I can let Him worry about all the details and I can just move forward, confident that He will work things out in the right way and time."

Samantha nodded appreciatively. "That takes a great deal of faith, I imagine."

"Indeed. Having faith like that can be quite difficult. But the results are worth it. For example, without the knowledge that He was with me and would support me in my desire for a college education, I would probably have given up the whole thing the first time one of my male classmates gave a disparaging comment, and that happened many times. Or when the college dean, himself, expressed his disapproval of me pursuing an advanced degree—and in entomology, of all things. During those rigorous educational years, every time someone would tell me to go home and get married, to 'stop playing with bugs and go have a family,'" she chuckled at the memory, "I would try to seethe quietly and remember that God had led me this far and He would not abandon me now. And he hasn't. Now," she clasped her hands together and looked directly into Samantha's eyes, "as for you, I can already tell that your faith is leagues ahead of where mine was at your age. But more importantly, I see that you are seeking God's will and inspiration and that He is sending it as you need it, line upon line. So trust in that, child. Trust Him. He loves you and Sterling both, and I am confident He has a plan for you. He can work miracles—"

"Oh, He already has!" Samantha interrupted. "He really has." It was good to remember that, to put things into proper perspective.

Aunt Irene nodded. "Expect more miracles as you go about your daily journey. I have the feeling He has many more in store for you."

"Thank you. I hope so!"

Samantha smiled and her aunt suddenly recalled a memory of her dear sister, Lovenia, smiling at her in just that way, full of faith and hope.

"You are just what I needed, Aunt Irene. Thank you for welcoming me unexpectedly like that."

"Anytime, child. I am glad you felt comfortable enough to come sleep on my porch!" Aunt Irene gave a slight chuckle and her eyes twinkled. She stood. "Now let us see about getting you that bath."

Chapter 17

PROGRESS BY DEGREES

October 1902

That evening when Samantha returned in Aunt Irene's wagon to Sterling's room, newly bathed and clothed in a ruffled cream blouse with a mustard-colored skirt, she found the doctor's horse and buggy waiting patiently at the hitching post at the bottom of the stairs. She experienced a momentary feeling of panic and silently looked at her aunt with wide eyes.

Aunt Irene placed a firm, calming hand on Samantha's arm. They both stepped down and Irene secured her horse to the post, then together they climbed the stairs. Samantha led the way, very anxious to know what the doctor would say about Sterling's condition. Her father stood near the door, out of the way, and smiled at her as she entered. But when he saw Irene right behind her, his face paled. He stared at his sister-in-law and she nodded shortly at him.

Samantha did not notice this interchange, fixed as she was on the doctor who was bending over Sterling with a stethoscope. To her surprise, Mr. Grover stood there as well, so the little room was crowded. The superintendent smiled brightly when he saw her and stepped forward to grasp her hand in a warm shake. "Miss Jennings," he said. "So good to see you again. Thank you for saving our boy here. It was touch and go there for a while before you arrived!"

"Oh, I didn't—" Samantha said, flustered. "It wasn't I who saved him. I just prayed night and day." She lifted her hands as if to show their emptiness and how much she lacked. "I am just grateful Sterling is finally improving." Tears glimmered in her eyes at the relief, and Mr. Grover smiled at her gently.

"He who has all knowledge gave you the knowledge you needed in the moment." It was a statement but also a question.

She nodded. "He did."

"Good woman," he said, still smiling, and patted her shoulder. He looked past her to Aunt Irene, and Samantha knew she should introduce them, but she couldn't bear to wait any longer.

"How is he? What does the doctor say?" she asked.

The doctor, an older, distinguished gentleman with gray hair and a well-groomed, close-cut beard, raised his head to look at her and removed the stethoscope from Sterling's chest, pulling the earpieces out of his ears and straightening up. "Hello, young lady. I am Dr. Nielsen, and your young man is surprisingly improved since last I checked on him, about four days ago. Whatever you are doing, keep doing it! His lungs are still congested, but sleeping propped up as he has seems to have helped drain things quite a bit. His fever is nearly gone and his pulse has slowed to normal." He turned back to Sterling. "How is the cough now?"

Sterling had been wearily watching Samantha and the superintendent, but now he looked at the doctor. "Frequent. But not...too bad."

"Do you still have a headache?"

"Yes, but...less."

The doctor nodded as if he had expected that answer. "Good. I think that means your lungs are pulling in more oxygen again, and that will soon help alleviate the headache. How about the muscle aches and chest pain?"

Sterling's hand went up to his chest involuntarily and he admitted that he still felt some pain there. "And I'm sore...from being...in bed."

"Yes. That is to be expected," the doctor told him. "As you feel up to it, push yourself to get up, walk around a bit, try to use your muscles and work out the knots. Just don't do too much too soon," he advised.

Sterling nodded. "Thank you, Doctor."

But the doctor shook his head. "Don't thank me," he said, looking down at his patient in all seriousness. "Your young lady here is the one who made all the difference. I didn't tell you before, but for a while there I really didn't know if you would make it, son." He paused, his expression grave. "Many patients with as bad a case of pneumonia as you've had don't pull through."

Samantha's heart shrank and she shivered at his words. So, her impression hadn't been off the mark!

"Pneumonia is a serious disease that can decimate even a healthy young person very quickly. But now that you are past the worst of it, I expect you to make a full recovery, as you have previously been strong and healthy."

Sterling looked relieved at this news, and Samantha exhaled with relief. *Thank You, God!*

"It will take time, though," the doctor cautioned, his voice and gaze firm. "You must only push yourself in small increments and listen to your body. There may be days when you wake up and feel like you can jump back into everything you used to do, and then you'll get out of bed and suddenly feel like you've hit a wall. It will be frustrating at times, but I assure you this is all a normal part of the healing process. Your body has expended so much strength and energy trying to fight off the illness that now you need to take it slow and give it what it needs to repair the damage and build back your strength." He turned to the superintendent. "I trust you can give him time, Mr. Grover, before he returns to the classroom?"

"Absolutely," Mr. Grover replied. "I have employed a temporary replacement until you are back on your feet, Sterling. When you are ready, you can ease back into teaching." He smiled as he buttoned up his coat to depart. "I will pop in on your class right now and tell them the good news. They will be relieved to know you are finally on the mend. They've been very worried about you. Oh, I almost forgot!" He stepped to a corner of the room and lifted a canvas bag from the floor. "I brought you some mail. Your students made get well cards and asked if I would deliver them to you." He set the bag by the bed.

Sterling smiled faintly. "Thank you. For everything."

When the two men had gone, Samantha moved to sit on the edge of the bed and took Sterling's hand in hers. He squeezed it slightly and looked at her through fatigue. His eyes were still bloodshot, she noticed, but seemed a little clearer than they had been that morning.

Her father came to stand behind her and placed a hand tentatively on her shoulder.

"Did you realize you were—" she looked at Sterling and swallowed, not wanting to finish the thought "—that close to not making it?"

He shook his head. "I don't think I...was aware...of much."

A lump rose in Samantha's throat as she considered all that had happened as opposed to all that *could* have. "I think it was actually a blessing you collapsed at school and not here in your room, where no one would have known. Dear Mr. Grover is such a good man, obtaining the help you needed right away. And without Thora's timely message, neither of us would be here." She turned to glance up at her father, "Of course, Father's willingness to bring me made it all possible."

Basil squeezed her shoulder gently in answering support, and Sterling patted her hand on the bed. "God is in...the details," he agreed hoarsely.

Samantha suddenly remembered her aunt still standing by the door and beckoned to her. "Sterling, I know you don't feel up to visitors yet, but Aunt Irene has just offered her help, and brought me back here from her house."

Irene stepped up to the bed beside Basil and smiled at Sterling. "I am headed to tell the other Lewises the news and to recruit meals for as long as needed. Now that we know you are here and in need, we can help." She cast a somewhat accusatory glance at Basil, clearly indicating that he should have told them sooner. But Samantha knew she wasn't really upset when she said, "We want to help. As I told Samantha, that's what family does."

"Thank you," Sterling replied faintly.

"You get better now, young man, you hear?" Aunt Irene told him sternly. "We'll all be praying for you, so you let our faith work on you and get your strength back. No disappointing Samantha! She has put a lot of time and energy into your care."

"Yes, ma'am," he replied with a slight smile. Then he began coughing again, and Samantha felt the bed shake with each cough. Aunt Irene and her father withdrew to the other side of the room and Samantha didn't hear their conversation as she focused on Sterling. Once the fit had passed and Sterling lay back against the pillows in exhaustion, Samantha fed him another meal of bread and butter and the last of the broth. Then she tucked him in and watched as he fell quickly back to sleep. By that time, her aunt and father had stepped out of the room and she could hear them conversing on the small landing outside. Their voices weren't raised, so she hoped that meant they were reconciling amicably. She paused in front of the slightly open door and listened for a moment.

"I can't begin to understand what you went through when she died, Basil," Aunt Irene was saying, "but I think it's time you realize what *we* went through. God took Lovenia home to Him and, from our viewpoint, you also took yourself and little Samantha from us. It hurt that you never allowed us to meet her—that you didn't even respond to our many letters! We have forgiven you over and over again, but I have to tell you, Basil, some members of the family have done that better than others. I am no saint, as you well know, and I have had my fair share of struggle with this. Now that Samantha has been restored to us, I believe healing is beginning to take place. And we want you back too. But I think it best you are aware that some will accept you more warmly than others. Eighteen years of pain and hard feelings takes time to mend."

"Yes." Her father's voice was sad. "I understand. I would not expect otherwise. I know I did not respond as I should have." He paused and Samantha knew him well enough now to know that he was searching for the right words to express his ordeal. He cleared his throat. "At first, I was lost in a sea of grief and the care of a newborn. Then guilt pushed down on me and I wondered why death took my wife instead of me, when she was the one everyone needed, particularly the baby. I felt like I was drowning in guilt. And the despair...!" Samantha heard her father blow his nose and then he cleared his throat once more. When he spoke again, his voice was raw with emotion. "A fierce melancholia gripped me, Irene, and would not let me go. It was a vicious cycle that I could not seem to pull out of. In all honesty, over the years I lost the will to break free of it—until Samantha came knocking on my bedroom door one day last year and everything began to change."

Samantha opened the door wider so she wouldn't feel like she was eavesdropping, but neither of them noticed her presence.

Aunt Irene touched Basil's shoulder and made a sound of compassion and regret. "It was not your fault she died, Basil," she said in her direct way. "You do believe that now, don't you?"

"I..." Basil looked at her with wide eyes and shrugged dejectedly.

"Women die in childbirth every day. It is a tragic fact of life. You know that. There was nothing you could have done to prevent it from happening. Even the doctor, trained for such things, could not prevent it."

"But if I had not given in to her wish to try again for another baby..." he trailed off helplessly and blinked at the mist in his eyes.

Aunt Irene nodded once, decisively. "Then Samantha would not be here. And most likely Lovenia would not be either. You know her health was never good. The possibility that she would live another eighteen years, regardless, is remote."

Basil looked at her as if he had never considered this truth before and said nothing.

"Don't blame yourself for taking her so far away from home, either. She *wanted* to go, she *wanted* to help you fulfill your dream. And I vividly recall how excited she was to do it just like the pioneers, carting all your books, belongings, and supplies in covered wagons. We couldn't talk her out of that adventure and neither could you. You tried, Basil, I remember!"

Basil nodded reluctantly.

"And then when it came time for you to help her fulfill *her* dream, she was so happy to again be with child. Her desires were uncomplicated and pure, just as she was. And she never blamed you for anything that happened. She always counted her blessings, and you were right there at the top of her list."

Samantha's throat tightened. She had the feeling these were all words that had needed to be said for a very, very long time. The barrier between her father and the Lewises was beginning to crumble.

Basil pulled a handkerchief from his pocket and mopped at his eyes. "She made me very happy too."

Samantha stepped forward between them and put her arms around her father. "She would want you to be happy again, Father, I'm sure of it. There is so much more to do and to be."

Basil nodded, wiping his nose. "Yes. I see that now and I am grateful. Thank you, both of you, for your patience with me."

Aunt Irene snorted. "I haven't been the least bit patient with you, Basil! But now that you have explained how it was, I understand you a little better and see what a difficult situation you were in. Perhaps it is time to let bygones be bygones and repair relationships that were severed for far too long."

Samantha tightened her embrace and willed her father to let go of regrets and allow himself to feel loved again. "Maybe God is turning this horrible ordeal with Sterling into good for you. He can make 'beauty for ashes' in your life too, Father."

Basil gave a watery smile and returned her embrace. "Thank you, daughter. You have your mother's faith. I don't know how God could forgive my neglect of so many people and things, but I am trying to be better."

"I think He already has forgiven you, Father. I know I have. Maybe it is you who need to forgive yourself."

Basil considered this. "You are probably right."

***

After Aunt Irene left, with the promise that she or another of the Lewises would be in touch soon, Samantha and her father re-entered Sterling's room. He slept soundly for two or three hours while they alternately read and conversed quietly. When a soft knock sounded at the door, Samantha opened it to find Thora standing there with a basket of food in her arms, the lowering sunlight glinting through the trees behind her. "I don't want to disturb him," she whispered, peering around Samantha to the bed, "but I figured you would be running out of food about now."

Samantha ushered her into the room, gratefully took the proffered basket, and set it on the little table. "Bless you, Thora. He is eating again today and just finished the last of the bread. He said it was the best meal he had ever eaten." She laughed quietly. "The doctor was here earlier and says he has passed the worst of it. Now he just needs to regain his strength."

Thora grasped Samantha's hands and beamed. "Such good news!" she exclaimed. "Oh, what a relief. I love him like a son, you know, and I couldn't bear thinking..." She trailed off, but her shimmering eyes told Samantha what her words could not. "Thank God he'll be alright." She spoke with feeling and wiped her eyes with a handkerchief. "I came to bring the food, but also to make an offer." She looked at Samantha and her father questioningly. "How would you feel about all three of you coming to stay at my home until Sterling is on his feet again? The accommodations would be much more comfortable, and we could rotate caring for him—and I wouldn't have to come all the way into the village every time I wanted to check in on him or bring food."

Samantha brightened and glanced at her father, who looked as if he were surprised at how much he liked the idea. "Oh, yes!" she cried. "That sounds like a wonderful arrangement—if you are certain you don't mind all of us invading your home."

"I would love to have you, and I know Jerome would be delighted. Really, I think it will make things easier for all of us. So it's settled!" She glanced over at Sterling and, seeing he was awake, put a hand to her mouth. "I'm sorry if I woke you," she apologized.

He shook his head and smiled, weakly holding out a hand to her. She crossed the room and took it, grasping it firmly in her hands and telling him how glad she was that he was on the mend. "Did you hear what we were discussing?" At his nod, she asked, "Is that alright with you?"

"Yes," he affirmed with a smile. "Thank you." He struggled to sit up straighter. "When?"

Thora turned to include everyone and asked, "How about first thing tomorrow morning?"

Sterling was concerned about how to make it down all the stairs outside his door, so Thora assured him she would bring Jerome with her. At Basil's expressed confidence that the two of them could help him down between them, he relaxed and nodded. "Thank you. Sorry I'm so..." he trailed off and began coughing.

"No need to apologize," Thora told him reassuringly, when the fit ended. "We are happy to help. We're just overjoyed you are improving!"

Sterling smiled weakly and said, "Me too." Then he added, "Did I...see food?"

Samantha caught a slight twinkle in his eyes and laughed in delight. She hadn't seen that twinkle in what seemed like ages, and it told her more than anything that the old Sterling was still in there, trying to come back.

She picked up the basket from the table and carried it to him just as Thora said, "You did! I've been cooking up everything I could think of that might tempt you."

Thora left them to enjoy supper together and went to retrieve Jerome from his after-school maintenance job and take him home. Together they would prepare rooms for Sterling and the Jenningses and return early the next morning, after Sterling had had a full night's sleep and regained enough strength to be moved.

Sterling was determined to sit in the chair at the table for the meal, so Basil and Samantha helped him settle himself there and he slowly and shakily ate the meal by himself. It felt good to sit in a chair, but by the end he felt worn and drawn and was barely able to walk back to the bed by himself before he collapsed. However, Samantha could tell he felt like he had accomplished something, and she was proud of him for trying.

For Sterling's part, he was alarmed at how quickly he tired and how little he could do for himself. It was disheartening, but he tried to remember what the doctor had said, and told himself this was normal and he just needed to take things slow. *I guess God wants me to learn patience again in another way,* he thought wearily, *for I would never willingly spend*

194

this much time resting. He hoped he could learn what God wanted him to, as quickly as possible.

Once Sterling slept again, Basil left to take a quick walk. While he was gone, Samantha tidied up the room and repacked their suitcases to be ready for the move in the morning. Unbeknownst to Samantha, her father was sending word to Irene of the change in their arrangements and that the Lewises would not need to provide meals after all, now that they would be lodging with the Tomlinsons. But he welcomed the family to visit them there anytime. In his note, he expressed his appreciation for their kind offer and expressed how much he, Samantha (and Sterling, if he were up to it) would enjoy seeing anyone who cared to drop in. His note was a small step in the right direction, he thought, though one that took more effort than it should have. He hoped this small communication from him would leave open the opportunity for the Lewises to do with it what they were ready to do, and over time re-build the bridge he had long since burned down.

Chapter 18

RECONCILIATION

November 1902

The next morning, as Samantha watched her father and Jerome support Sterling down the long rickety flight of stairs, one slow step at a time, her heart squeezed with dismay—yet again—to see her beloved reduced to such a state. He was as weak as a baby, and she could see that he felt shaken by his own inability to do simple things that used to take no effort. She forced herself to school her expression before Sterling could see her alarm, and reminded herself that it would take time, but the doctor had predicted a full recovery. By the time the trio finally made it down the last step, Samantha was composed with a ready smile. "You did it! The rest should be easy," she promised.

He stood there, grateful for her bright outlook and tried to smile back. But he had to stand still and rest for a moment, still carefully supported on either side, while he closed his eyes and focused on breathing. His heart raced with the effort of the descent and his head spun. For a moment he just stood there, trying not to sway or lose his footing. Then he opened his eyes and allowed his friends to help him into the back of the wagon. Samantha had made a cushioned area for him to sit on top of extra blankets, with pillows to rest his back on, and a couple quilts to pull over him. It would be a bumpy, exhausting ride, but he appreciated the effort to make him as comfortable as possible.

"Thank you so much, Jerome," Samantha said, hugging the boy before she climbed into the wagon bed next to Sterling. "We couldn't have done that without you."

Her tone was so sincere that Jerome's answering smile erased the disappointment in his expression. He did not want to attend school today with all that was going on at home, but his mother insisted. He straightened his shoulders. "Glad to," he said simply, and after one lingering look at them all, headed for school.

***

They traveled the two miles to the Tomlinson farm slowly, trying to make the trip as easy on Sterling as possible, but by the time they arrived, his face was gray with fatigue and he had started coughing again in the cold air. They bustled him inside and while Samantha settled him into his new room, Basil and Thora brought everything into the house from the wagon. Basil found himself increasingly impressed with the efficient and capable Thora Tomlinson and appreciated her generosity in bringing a stranger into her bright and comfortable home.

"Sorry we had to put you through that," Samantha apologized, sitting on the edge of the bed and smoothing back Sterling's limp hair. She pulled the quilt up around his chest and felt his forehead. To her relief, it was only a little warmer than usual, but his eyes were already closing. "Get some sleep," she said, kissing him on the cheek. "When you wake up, we'll bring you some food, and then maybe you'll even feel up to a bath and a shave!" She knew that would help him feel more human and a little more like his old self, and regretted that they hadn't yet been able to provide him that. But now, in this home, so much would be easier.

He opened his eyes for a moment to see her looking at him expectantly, eyes shining. He chuckled and coughed, closing his eyes again. "I need it," he said, scraping a knuckle over the dark beard that, by now, completely covered his lower face. And then slumber claimed him again.

***

Late that afternoon, Samantha took great pleasure in helping Thora cook supper while Basil and Jerome prepared a warm bath for Sterling and assisted him as needed. She hadn't

197

realized how much the days of constant vigilance and care in the confines of Sterling's little room had worn on her spirit until she entered the Tomlinson's cozy home with its rooms full of light and love. She also hadn't realized how much she missed having a real bed to sleep in and more than one room to move around in. She hadn't even recognized how much she missed female company and the ability to do something as simple as preparing nourishing food for people she loved. Bless Thora for bringing them into her home! Samantha knew it would be physically easier for them to provide Sterling the care he needed, but it felt also like they would all do better emotionally here as well.

After Sterling's bath, Samantha peered into the room briefly to check on him and found her father gently shaving off Sterling's beard while he sat quietly in a chair by the window. The autumn sunlight filtered in through the glass, highlighting both men's profiles and providing extra warmth for Sterling who sat, eyes closed, wrapped in one of Thora's colorful patchwork quilts. Neither of the men saw her watching them. Her heart melted as she watched her father tenderly ministering to the man she loved, and she thought about all her father had done to be a strength and a support to her and Sterling over the past few days. *Father really is a good man*, she thought, gratitude swelling. It suddenly occurred to her that she now naturally thought of him as "Father" instead of "Professor Jennings," and it was a glad realization. When she considered their collective progress over the past few months, it was truly stunning.

Sterling had wanted to join the rest of them in the dining room for supper, but the bath and shave had taken more energy than he anticipated—which seemed to be the case with everything these days, he thought woefully. So he submitted to being tucked back into bed and meekly eating what Samantha spooned into his mouth. It was a thick, creamy beef and vegetable stew that woke up his taste buds and warmed up his insides. The fact that food tasted good again felt like a miracle in itself. "Delicious," he said, as Samantha brought the spoon to his mouth again.

She smiled. "I'm glad you like it. Between Mrs. Dolittle and Thora, they may yet turn me into a good cook. Here, try a biscuit." She handed him one and he found that he could eat it himself. When he had finished, he wiped his face with the napkin she offered, and appreciated feeling his face smooth and clean-shaven again. It was frustrating how much the bath had drained what little energy he had, but he was grateful for how clean he felt now, and how comfortable this bed and this room were. And having Samantha here with him, too, was everything he could ask for. For now. He was truly a blessed man.

Now, if he could just manage to work up enough energy to get out of bed for more than half an hour a day, he would be making headway!

***

They all developed a routine over the next few days, rotating who checked on Sterling, who sat with and read to him, who helped him walk around as he started to regain strength. Together, they read through all the get well cards that had been so lovingly made by his students, teachers, and others at school. It seemed there were many who were concerned about him and that he was truly missed. That realization greatly warmed Sterling's heart and rekindled his love of teaching and his desire to get back to it.

Samantha was a great help to Thora in the kitchen and with the housework, and Basil made himself useful around the farm wherever he could. He was surprised to feel strength returning to his body, and pain working out of his joints more and more as his increased activity continued. He felt more alive here on this farm in Worthington than he had in his attic room in Oberlin in more years than he cared to remember! He found that he relished the brisk morning air and enjoyed basking in the brief warmth of the autumn afternoons.

***

Aunt Irene came by for a visit the Saturday morning after they were settled at the Tomlinsons and brought Aunt Eleanor and Grandmother Julia with her. Samantha met them at the door and all three women took turns giving her a loving embrace. Grandmother took Samantha's face in her hands and looked her over carefully. "You don't look any worse for the wear," she finally admitted with apparent relief. "Irene has been telling me everything you've done over the past week, but you seem to be pulling through." She gave her a kiss on the cheek and Samantha identified the scent of lavender that she had noted before.

"I appreciate your concern, Grandmother. I really am doing fine—much better than I was a few days ago when I saw Aunt Irene."

"Because Sterling is improving?" Aunt Irene inquired.

"Yes!" Samantha answered, a deep exhale showing her relief. "And we've all rested better here, which makes such a difference."

Grandmother joyously clasped her hands together. "Oh, I *am* glad to hear it. That young man is a treasure."

"Yes, he is." Samantha couldn't agree more.

Thora joined them, then, and was officially introduced. Worthington being the small village that it was, they had seen each other before but were not really acquainted.

They all moved to the front parlor and had an enjoyable visit. Samantha's female relatives were impressed with Thora's gracious hospitality and warm manner, and Thora, in turn, noted the obvious love they had for Samantha and Sterling.

After pleasantly chatting for a while, Aunt Irene asked if Basil was disposed to join them. Samantha noticed that her grandmother's face lost all color at this question, as did Aunt Eleanor's, but neither protested. Reaching across the coffee table, Samantha grasped Grandmother's hands. "I think he is ready to meet with you, if you are ready to see him. But if you need more time, we understand."

Grandmother dipped her gray head a moment, rubbing Samantha's fingers between her soft, slightly wrinkled hands. Then she looked up with firm resolve. "At my age I can't afford to take more time. Enough time has been wasted, as it is. I am ready, if he is."

Samantha looked into her brown eyes, noted the color returning to her face, and squeezed her hands. "All right. I will bring him in. Thank you, Grandmother. I know he regrets all the pain he caused you and wishes to make amends."

Grandmother nodded once and took a fortifying breath. Samantha let go and stood to fetch her father.

As she walked to the waiting ladies with a willing but pensive Basil a few minutes later, she felt him tense beside her. He stopped in the hallway just short of the room and looked at her, as if for confirmation, his wiry gray brows raised high above the blue eyes. "Would it be appropriate for me to stay with you?" Samantha asked him in a low voice. "I am more than willing, if it would ease the situation."

Basil nodded slowly and patted her hand on his arm. "Yes. Thank you."

She squeezed his arm and whispered, "It will be all right, Father. I know it."

He gave her a faint smile in reply, then stepped forward and they entered the parlor.

Thora excused herself quietly and Samantha and her father sat on the sofa across from the three Lewis women. He nodded to them gravely. "It is good to see all of you," he said in a voice gruff with emotion.

"And you, Basil," Aunt Irene responded, in her carrying, no-nonsense voice. She did not smile, but there was a distinct softening about the eyes that had not been there before their last encounter.

Aunt Eleanor nodded back at him and looked as if she wanted to say something but was afraid she would burst into tears. Grandmother looked upon him steadily for a long moment, taking in everything about him.

Her father looked down at his hands and Samantha noticed they were trembling. He clasped them together and let out a long breath.

Grandmother's quiet voice made Samantha and Basil both raise their heads. "I am glad to see you, at long last, Basil." Her tone held no accusation. "It has been too long."

Basil nodded, maintaining eye contact. "Yes, it has been much too long. I am sorry. I know that is my fault entirely. And I know that no amount of apology will make up for my failure to respond to your kind and well-meaning letters long ago. Or my keeping your granddaughter from you." He took a deep breath and Samantha felt the agony of that unfortunate omission radiating from him. "I never meant for things to turn out as they did, for Samantha to grow up without you—or much of me either..." His voice grew husky and he trailed off.

Grandmother Julia reached across the coffee table and he reached back to bridge the gap as she placed her small hands on either side of his large ones. "I know," she said. "Basil, I know." She pressed his hands more tightly, as if trying to press into him the feelings from her own heart. "There has been much pain and grief for many of us for a very long time. I feel it is time to forgive and move forward, to accept what is and enjoy what time we have left as a reunited family. Will you allow us to do that, my son-in-law?"

Basil opened his hands and enveloped Grandmother's hand in his. "Yes," he said, his voice cracking and a lone tear starting down his grizzled cheek. "Oh yes, Mother."

Grandmother stood slowly and came around the coffee table to stand next to him, dwarfed by his height as he stood to meet her. She held out her arms without a word, and he swallowed hard, his Adam's apple bobbing. Tenderly he bent to embrace her and they stood that way a long moment.

Samantha pulled a handkerchief from her pocket and wiped away tears as looked at her aunts, sitting side by side. Aunt Eleanor wept openly now and Aunt Irene, dry-eyed and smiling, handed her sister a handkerchief.

After another moment, Grandmother pulled back and looked up into Basil's face. She took a handkerchief from her dress pocket and carefully wiped away the wet track down his cheeks, as if he were a child.

Basil smiled at her and took the proffered handkerchief. "I have missed you," he said, wiping his nose. "I have missed all of you," he added, gesturing to his sisters-in-law.

"Have you *really* missed me?" Aunt Irene asked, one dark eyebrow raised. "I recall a few arguments in the distant past, and sensing definite distaste from you about your wife's overly opinionated sister."

Basil chuckled and Samantha started. She couldn't remember the last time she had heard her father laugh! "Yes, even you," he said. "I often heard your voice in my head these past years, chiding me—and you were always correct."

Aunt Irene returned his laugh and then, in mock indignance, replied, "Well, of course I was!"

Samantha's aunts stood to hug their newly restored brother-in-law, and Samantha felt a great relief in her spirit, as if an immense weight had been lifted from somewhere deep inside that she hadn't even known existed. As she looked up at her father, she saw the same relief reflected in his face. In fact, he suddenly looked several years younger and even stood a little straighter. She put an arm around his waist and hugged him with true affection, not wishing to be anywhere else in the world.

"If it weren't for Father taking charge of the situation when we received Thora's telegram, and bringing me here with him, we might not have arrived in time," she told the others. "I was panicked, but Father stayed level-headed and figured everything out. Very quickly he had us on the next train out. And now he is doing so much to help the Tomlinsons, I am not sure they will want him to leave!"

Basil chuckled again and wiped his eyes a final time. "You give me too much credit, daughter. I cannot do enough to make up for all I did not do in the past. But it is good to be useful and needed again." Then, with an unexpectedly vulnerable admission, he added, "I am beginning to feel like a man again, instead of just a shell of what I once was."

***

That reconciliation with the matriarchs of the family marked the beginning of reconciliation with all the Lewises. Full acceptance, forgiveness, and integration back into the family would take time, but now the door was fully open, and understanding and empathy were beginning to replace resentment, anger, and hurt. Every couple of days, one or two Lewis family members would stop by for a visit and gradually, one by one, Basil humbly apologized and asked for forgiveness from each member of the older generation. He didn't know the younger members of the family at all, of course, but that would come in time. It was a difficult process—Samantha could see just how difficult—but each visit left him a little lighter and brightened his aspect that much more.

It was an interesting transformation to witness and Samantha was grateful to watch it unfold. She shared some of these feelings with Sterling when he was awake and wanted company, and he drank in the gratitude and delight in her face, taking nourishment from the news of the miraculous emotional healing happening in her mother's family. Somehow, her joy helped in his own physical healing.

During one of their afternoon chats, Samantha asked Sterling if he had notified his family of his illness. He sat up in bed, pillows at his back, and she sat next to him on a chair, her hand in his.

He shook his head.

"Don't you think you should?" she asked gently. "They would want to know, wouldn't they?"

Sterling sighed. "I don't know. Perhaps. At any rate, there is nothing any of them can do for me now." He traced the lines of her long fingers and was quiet for a moment, looking at their connected hands, his skin smooth from enforced time indoors, hers a little work-worn and calloused from housework and gardening. "None of them could hold a candle to the way you have all taken care of me." He looked up, his brows pulled together in thought. "It might be nice to visit with Father and Lucas," he reflected, "but I don't want Mother here. Of course, I can't imagine her actually coming... More likely, she would demand that I go home to Lexington, where a hired nurse would care for me." His troubled expression suddenly melted into a wry chuckle. "Then I would expire of boredom and all your time and efforts would be wasted."

"Well, we certainly can't have that!" Samantha said, smiling at his returning sense of humor. But she wondered at a woman who would not visit a son who had been so very ill. Surely she should at least be told what had happened, shouldn't she?

***

One afternoon, Basil sat with Sterling on the front porch, both men rocking slowly in the old rocking chairs that sat on either side of the door. In comfortable silence, they watched a man walk by on the distant road, a knapsack over his shoulder, until he was out of sight. Sterling pulled the quilt up more snugly around his shoulders and sighed. "You know, I have learned the truthfulness of the saying that you don't fully appreciate what you have until it is gone." He thought about how good it was to breathe again without feeling a weight on his chest, how good to speak again without needing to pause for breath after every few words.

Basil nodded thoughtfully, continuing his slow rocking.

"I always took my strength for granted, counted on it, and never thought to be grateful for it. Growing up on a horse and hemp farm, I needed that strength every day, and it was always there." He was silent a moment. "Now, after almost losing my life and being reduced to an infantile state, I don't think I will ever take strength for granted again! Or forget to thank God for it."

"Yes," Basil mused. "Staring death in the face like that leaves one shaken and aware for a lifetime. It provides a completely different perspective on everything."

"It certainly does." Sterling looked over at the older man appreciatively, gratified that he understood. Well, of course he did. Basil knew much about loss and despair, after all. But it was good to hear him talk briefly about it.

Sterling turned back to the road, thinking about the travelers he had witnessed passing by while he sat in this old chair. "You know, as I watched that man walk by a minute ago, I was amazed at the ease with which he walked so quickly. If I could have spoken to him, I would have told him how much I admire his brilliant display of energy and his wonderful ability to walk so far." He shook his head and chuckled. "Yet all he was doing was walking down the road. Quite a normal activity and something I have done myself countless times! Only now, in my current weakness, I find him incredible."

Basil stopped rocking and looked at him seriously. "I think that expresses your level of frailty more than anything else you could have said."

Sterling returned his look and thought back on the events of the past two weeks. It was sobering to consider how quickly the illness had decimated his strength and sapped him of nearly everything: health, breath, consciousness, even—almost—the will to live. He shivered. "In all honesty, I don't know if I would have survived, had Samantha not coaxed me back. Her determination and persistence, her own strength of will, brought me to this point, such as it is." He looked down at his too-thin frame and grimaced.

"Love can do that," Basil acknowledged in a voice wistful with memories. He looked off into the distance and Sterling knew he was seeing events of past years, remembering hopes and griefs. After a moment, he blinked and turned back to Sterling. "But I can imagine how difficult it must be, particularly as a strong young man, to be to the point that all you can do is accept assistance."

"Yes," Sterling said heavily. "It is humbling, to say the least." He rubbed at his temples for a moment, remembering how bad the headaches had been for days, up until recently. It was a relief that his body no longer had to fight constant pain. In addition to the headache finally dissipating, his increased physical activity—even if it was only to sit in a chair instead of in bed—had eased much of the body aches.

Sterling knew this experience was not something he would ever wish to go through again—or wish upon anyone else—but he also knew he would never forget it. He hoped it would engender in him the empathy for others that he probably needed. At this point, it felt as if he would never regain his former strength and vitality. Progress seemed excruciatingly slow! But he kept reminding himself that progress *was* being made, and that he needed to recognize each step in the right direction.

As if reading his thoughts, Basil said quietly but reassuringly, "I have full confidence that you will completely recover, son. You are young and your body has always been strong and healthy, so there is no reason to suppose otherwise. These things just take time, and youth never wants to give time." He chuckled softly. "While I am no longer young and quick, I remember how it was to be so. I know it is difficult, but try to be patient and at peace with taking things slowly. Soon enough, you will be back to all your old responsibilities and hurtling through life at breakneck speed." His ironic smile was tinged with fondness.

Sterling nodded at him and tried to internalize his words, sensing the wisdom in them. Besides, once he felt strong enough, Samantha would go back to Oberlin, he realized, so there was no need to try to rush a recovery that went at its own pace anyway. Still, though, it went against his nature to sit here, bundled up on the porch like an old man, rocking away his afternoon.

Chapter 19

CALAMITY

NOVEMBER 1902

Early one evening shortly after they sat down for dinner, they heard hoofbeats pounding into the yard and a young voice shouting. The urgency in the tone propelled everyone but Sterling to their feet and they rushed to the front door. Thora was about to throw it open, but Basil closed his hand over hers on the latch and a look passed between them. Thora nodded and stood back a step. Basil pushed the door open and stood tall in the doorway, a sentinel.

Now they could hear the youth clearly, and what he shouted chilled Samantha's blood: "Samantha! Samantha! Uncle Basil! Come quickly! Grandmother's house is on fire!"

In the fading light Samantha saw the boy atop his horse and recognized her cousin. "Benjamin?!" she asked, heart pounding.

The boy brushed windblown blond hair back from his eyes with one hand while the other hand firmly adjusted the reins, trying to calm the blowing, stomping horse. His wide eyes showed fear and uncertainty, and a look of pleading. The chestnut gelding shifted restlessly under him, snorted, and stood breathing heavily.

Samantha ran to meet her cousin and in a moment stood, grasping the horse's bridle in the chill air and stroking his neck to calm the animal, even as her heart clutched with dread. "What happened?" she demanded. "Is the fire brigade there? Is Grandmother all right?" Now that she was closer, Samantha could see that Benjamin's face was streaked with cinders and tear tracks.

Her father stepped up behind her and laid a hand on the boy's knee. "What of your grandmother, lad? How can we help?"

The boy swallowed. "I don't *know* how she is," he said in obvious agony, his adolescent voice cracking. "I was only there a couple minutes before Mother told me to ride out here to tell you. They can use all the help they can get!"

"Is the fire spreading?" Basil asked.

"Fire Chief Jim[1] and his brigade are managing to keep it from spreading to other houses. But I don't know if they'll be able to save Grandmother's house."

"And you don't know if Grandmother escaped?"

Benjamin shook his head quickly, his eyes reflecting the same desperation Samantha felt.

"I'll saddle a horse and we'll follow you," Basil decided immediately, running for the barn.

Sterling appeared in the door at that moment, having slowly made his way there to see what the excitement was about. He leaned against the door jamb for support and shakily looked out into the dusk, wishing he, too, could jump on a horse and actually be useful.

By the time Basil returned a few short minutes later, Samantha had donned her coat and held her father's ready, and Benjamin had drained the cup of water Thora brought him. He handed it back down to her with a thank you, his face looking more composed but his eyes still pained.

"How is Uncle Samuel? Aunt Phoebe?" Samantha asked, hoping to redirect his focus. "Are they all right?"

Benjamin nodded quickly. "Father is worried, of course, but he just rolled up his sleeves and started helping the other volunteers. Mother is there with him and told me to come find you," he reiterated. "The rest of the children are at home with Mary."

"Bless Mary. I'm sure she is frantic with worry too."

Benjamin nodded.

---

1. A barber by trade, Jim Wagner actually served as Worthington's volunteer Fire Chief from 1906 to 1929. See https://www.worthington.org/DocumentCenter/View/1 95/History-of-the-Worthington-Fire-Department?bidId=

"Well, we will do all we can and pray Grandmother is all right." The words were brave, but Samantha felt anything but brave as she grasped Father's hand, placed one foot in the stirrup he offered, and swung into the saddle behind him. She waved grimly to the others, then clung to her father on the dash to town, praying mightily for her dear Grandmother Julia, hoping against hope that she had gotten out in time.

Fire was a dangerous and common adversary, as everyone knew, and often resulted in disaster and tragedy. It was started all too often by a wayward candle or a tipped lantern. Without meaning to, Samantha's mind went back to the stampede deaths at the Shiloh Baptist Church in Birmingham, Alabama. That panic was created by people simply *thinking* there was a fire! And there were plenty of well-known stories of horrific fires that didn't bear thinking of at a time like this. Yet think she did, and for once she hated that her memory retained numbers just as well as words, as she remembered the numerical devastation of the Great Chicago Fire[2] of 1871. Burning out of control for more than a day, it made one in three people homeless—90,000 residents—as it destroyed 17,500 buildings and 73 miles of street. Such knowledge was enough to make anyone feel panicky when a fire alarm sounded, and she did feel a sense of panic, even while she tried to take deep breaths and calm herself. Cincinnati, she knew, had started the first professional fire department[3] in the country nearly fifty years previously, but not all towns and cities had them yet. She was infinitely glad there were experienced volunteers at the scene now, but would that be enough?

***

Still over a mile from the center of town, Samantha and Basil saw dark gray smoke billowing above the houses. Samantha let out an involuntary cry and her heart jumped into her throat. Basil spurred the horse ever faster. How there could be that much smoke from one small home neither of them could fathom!

---

2. https://education.nationalgeographic.org/resource/chicago-fire-1871-and-great-re building/

3. https://www.cincinnati-oh.gov/fire/about-fire/history/

They were both filled with fear at the thought that Julia Lewis might not survive. They had not had enough time with her!

When they clattered into Grandmother's yard a few minutes later, all the shouting and scurrying around seemed pure chaos. Samantha dismounted and forced herself to focus on what she could do, while her father headed straight for the bucket brigade. Benjamin, still sitting on his horse, took the reins of the horse Basil had ridden and led both skittish animals away from the inferno to a safe distance, as instructed by Uncle Samuel, who also yelled something at Basil and made room for him in the line. Basil immediately began hefting buckets of water down the brigade and Samantha made a beeline to the women who were clustered together near the road. As she drew closer, one of the women cried out her name and pulled her into their midst. It took a moment before Samantha recognized the soot-blackened face of her aunt Phoebe.

"Did Grandmother get out?!" she demanded, breathless.

Phoebe nodded and coughed. "A neighbor boy saw the smoke and pounded on her door, which roused her. She had accidentally fallen asleep in her chair in the living room before putting out the candle on the kitchen windowsill. We think there was a draft that blew the curtains into the flame. The candle itself was still there, but the curtains burned to nothing."

Samantha shook her head in disbelief, patting her aunt's back as she began coughing again. Someone pressed a cup of water into Samantha's hands and she passed it to Aunt Phoebe, who drained it gratefully.

"Is Grandmother all right then? Where is she?" Samantha persisted.

Aunt Phoebe wiped her mouth with a clean corner of her apron. Then, seeing how much soot came off onto the apron, proceeded to wipe the rest of her face. "Irene arrived even before we did, just in time to see the neighbors carry your grandmother out. Irene sent Tommy—the boy who first saw the smoke—to fetch the doctor. In the meantime, his mother took Irene and Julia in. I think the doctor arrived a moment ago." She paused and tried to take a deep breath without coughing, grimacing at the bad taste in her mouth from all the smoke. "I tried to save a few knick-knacks and things I knew Julia would want, but the firemen pulled me out before I got very many. They said the roof is in danger of caving in. And Samuel was frantic." She began to cough again.

"Aunt Phoebe, you're hurt!" Samantha exclaimed, gingerly touching a cut on her cheek and noticing a burn mark on the opposite temple.

The coughing fit passed, and Aunt Phoebe touched her face in surprise. "Am I? Well, I suppose the doctor will need to check me over too. But I wanted to wait for you, so you would know what was happening. I knew you would come."

One of the other women in the group passed Phoebe another cup of water and a second offered her a damp cloth for her face. Phoebe murmured a thank you as she took both items, and quickly emptied the cup. When Samantha had helped her clean up her injuries as best she could, she took her aunt's arm and together they walked to the house across the street. A young boy of about ten years old met them at the door and held it wide for them to enter. He was a bit soot-dusted as well and peered up at Phoebe curiously, apparently calculating the extent of her injuries.

"Are you Tommy?" Samantha asked. At his nod, she asked, "May I shake your hand? I hear you are the one responsible for saving my grandmother's life!"

Tommy's puzzled expression turned to embarrassment as he grasped her extended hand for a momentary shake. "I just knocked on the door," he said matter-of-factly, shrugging his shoulders. "And when Mrs. Lewis didn't come right away, I went in and hollered for her. She came out of the living room, coughing, with a big cloud of smoke following behind. We got out of there quick!"

"You did exactly the right thing," Samantha told him. "Thank you for acting swiftly." And then in a sudden desire to explain to this young boy just how heroic she found him, she admitted, "I just found my grandmother a few months ago, you see, and I don't want to lose her already." She felt emotion rising in her throat at the verbal admission, but swallowed it back as she heard footsteps approaching.

"Samantha, is that you?" came Aunt Irene's voice down the hall, and then she was there beside them, grasping each of the other women by the hand.

"How is Grandmother? Is she all right? Was she hurt?" The questions tumbled out quickly in Samantha's anxiety to know of her grandparent's condition.

In answer, an uncharacteristically quiet and somber Aunt Irene turned and gestured for them to follow her down the hall to the back room. There, Grandmother reposed quietly on a bed. Someone had removed her shoes and she rested on top of the covers, her back against the wall. An afghan was tucked around her and a glass of water waited on the nightstand. The smell of smoke was strong in the room. Samantha recognized Dr. Nielsen as he bent over Grandmother with a stethoscope, listening quietly to her chest. Grandmother's eyes were closed and she looked somewhat singed. But her chest rose and fell regularly, and the doctor nodded as he straightened up and removed the earpieces, turning to them.

"She was lucky," he told the women quietly, without preamble. "She has a strong heart and I think she will recover in time, thanks to young Tommy's rapid action. But she may continue to be confused for a while. And she will need a great deal of rest. This accident may have quite a traumatic affect on Mrs. Lewis, both physically and mentally. She is getting on in years and will need assistance."

The aunts nodded in sober agreement at Dr. Nielson's words.

"Truth be told, I've been waiting for something like this to happen," Aunt Irene admitted in a small voice. "I've had visions of any number of accidents happening and worried that I wouldn't be able to get here in time..." She trailed off and brushed at her eyes, making a visible effort not to cry.

Aunt Phoebe put an arm around her. "We'll all help, Irene, don't you worry. As a family we will figure out what to do."

Samantha looked over at her grandmother again, to see if she heard the conversation or if she was really asleep, then cried out in alarm, "Doctor!"

Dr. Nielsen whipped his head around, then quickly reached into his big, open bag on the bed. He pulled out a clean white rag and reached to blot the blood trickling from Grandmother's nose.

Samantha stepped quickly to her grandmother's bedside and took over the job. "Why is her nose bleeding?" she asked, concerned.

"It does seem alarming," the doctor replied kindly, "but it is not uncommon for someone to have nosebleeds after going through a fire. Many little ash particles can be inhaled and irritate the inside of the nose, mouth, and eyes. We just need to give her body time to clean out the impurities and heal."

Aunt Phoebe began to cough and Dr. Nielsen turned his attention to her for the first time. While he applied a salve to her cut and burn, asking questions and scolding her for going inside the burning house, Aunt Irene joined Samantha at the bed and looked down at her mother whose nose still trickled with a slow stream of blood. Grandmother's eyes remained closed and her breathing was steady.

"I can't lose her yet," Aunt Irene whispered, her voice quavering. "I simply can't."

Samantha nodded and gave her aunt a firm hug. She had never seen this dear aunt close to tears even once, but she understood. As the two single, mature women in the family, they shared a special bond. And even now in her middle years, Irene relied on her mother's wisdom and advice. Surely, no daughter was ever truly ready to lose a good mother.

Samantha wiped away another stream of blood, folding the rag around itself to find a clean place in the cloth. "I can't lose her either—and we won't," she declared firmly. "As Aunt Phoebe said, we will figure out the best care for her together. Grandmother will recover, Aunt Irene. See if she doesn't!"

***

It was decided best not to move Grandmother Julia that night. Aunt Irene stayed with her and sent Aunt Phoebe and Samantha home. She told them she would take an emergency leave of absence from the university for now, and take Grandmother home with her as soon as she was stabilized. Aunt Phoebe volunteered to send word to Aunt Eleanor and Uncle Andrew in Columbus first thing the next morning. And Samantha told them she would return on the morrow to see how everyone was getting on. She was concerned about Aunt Phoebe's cough and cautioned her to care for herself and send someone for the doctor again if anything worsened.

By the time Samantha stepped outside, the dilapidated embers that had once been Grandmother's house glowed brightly against the darkness of the night. But the main fire was out, no one had been killed, and all other buildings were spared. The stench of smoke hung heavy in the air. Samantha bid her aunt Phoebe goodbye as she headed for home, then turned to find her father.

As they rode back to the Tomlinson's farm that night, reeking from smoke and exhausted from the physical and emotional toil of the last few hours, they said little, lost in their own thoughts. When they neared Thora's house, Samantha finally offered, "I am so very glad Grandmother is still with us, Father. I couldn't bear to lose her so soon after finding her. But I am sorry she lost her house. She had so many memories tied up in it." Her arms were around her father's waist as she sat behind him in the saddle, and she felt him nod.

"Yes," he said gravely. "Waking up to that revelation may be a hard blow. She will need all the love and support we can offer over the next little while."

"I'm glad I could see the house, particularly my mother's room, before this happened. That is a grace from God, at least." But Samantha's heart drooped with a deep sadness for her grandmother's loss.

***

Before bedding the horse in the stable, Basil let Samantha off at the back door of the house so she could wash up at the pump before entering. Once inside the lantern-lit room, she found pots of water boiling on the stove and Thora busy filling a large tin tub in the kitchen.

Thora looked up when she heard the door close, and her flushed face smiled sympathetically at Samantha. "I thought you and your father would want to bathe when you came home," she said, pushing a wayward strand of auburn hair behind her ear. The small room was warm and humid with all the steaming water. "Fighting fire leaves a mark."

Samantha wrinkled her nose and looked down at herself. "It certainly does. We both stink so much we hesitate to come in. I washed my hands and face at the pump, but..."

Thora waved away Samantha's apology. "Not to worry. I am only relieved you are both safe. Just leave your clothes in a pile on the floor and we will wash the laundry tomorrow. Let me refill this pot," she said, stepping to the sink, "and I will go outside and detain your father so you can bathe without interruption. Then we can all leave him be to do the same."

"Bless you, Thora!" Samantha said gratefully. "You think of everything." She gave a tired laugh. "I would kiss you, only I stink too much."

***

An hour later, a scrubbed Samantha and Basil sat at the table eating a long-delayed dinner, after dumping the tub contents outside. They were both subdued as they ate, thinking how close Grandmother Lewis had come to perishing in the flames, how Aunt Phoebe could have been killed by falling timbers, and how the old Lewis home was no more. "All those memories gone up in smoke," Samantha mourned. "I am so sorry, Father. It must

214

have been painful for you to see it all crumble to ashes, despite your best efforts. I know you courted Mother there."

Her father nodded thoughtfully. "Yes. And yet those memories live on." He tapped his head with a forefinger and then his heart. "And I am slowly making amends with the Lewis family, being restored to them, and moving forward. Only...thank God Julia's life was preserved."

"Yes." Samantha returned her attention to her re-warmed chicken and vegetable pot pie. "I have been thanking Him constantly over the past few hours—and asking Him to help in her recovery. And Aunt Phoebe's as well. I'm afraid both may have inhaled more smoke than they realize."

Basil nodded, his brows furrowed in concern. "We will visit them tomorrow and see how we can help."

"Perhaps dinner is in order," Thora suggested. "I would be happy to make extra to take to them."

Samantha agreed. "I'll help you." Then switching topics, "Are Jerome and Sterling already sleeping?"

"I believe Sterling is, but he insisted we wake him when you returned. He wants to know how your grandmother fared and if everyone is all right. I believe Jerome is out in the barn working on a project." Thora looked at Basil for confirmation, who nodded.

"I spoke to him briefly while I was out there," he said. "He is quite involved and I didn't want to disturb his concentration. That boy is a wonder with wood! I have said it before and I am sure I will say it again." Basil smiled at Thora and wiped his beard with a napkin. He pushed back his chair with a contented sigh and thanked her for the meal. "Delicious, as always. It is as if I never left home: your cooking is on par with Mrs. Dolittle's—and that is high praise."

Thora accepted the compliment graciously and offered, "I would like to meet this Mrs. Dolittle sometime and compare recipes. She sounds like quite the housekeeper."

"Indeed," Basil replied.

"And she has become one of my dearest friends," Samantha smiled. "As have you, Thora."

***

On their way to bed, Basil and Samantha checked in with Sterling, who had slept only fitfully and was very glad to see them returned unharmed, and relieved to learn that old Mrs. Lewis had not perished in the fire. After talking for only a few minutes, everyone retired for the night and slept the sleep of those who have worked hard and earned it.

Chapter 20

CONVALESCENCE

NOVEMBER 1902

The next day was much like the previous days, everyone helping Sterling however they could, in between the kitchen and farm work. In the afternoon, Samantha helped Thora cook a large dinner of beans and cornbread which Samantha and her father then took to town to check on Aunt Phoebe and Grandmother. Aunt Phoebe was ill in bed—much to her frustration—and the family was grateful for the unexpected meal. Phoebe wanted to be up and doing but felt so fatigued and sick she could only manage a wan smile, her normally rosy complexion now pale, except for the burn mark and cut that stood out in stark relief on her face. Samantha was concerned about the phlegmy cough that persisted and when she spoke to Uncle Samuel about it in private, he agreed with her, briefly confiding that he was worried about his wife's inability to rest because of it. With one look at Mary, who was near tears, Samantha knew she felt the weight of her mother's responsibilities as she tried to hold everyone and everything together in her absence, while her father continued his work at the post office. Mary's expression showed obvious relief to be presented with dinner and know she did not now have to make it on her own. Seeing this, Samantha asked Uncle Samuel for his pastor's address so she could pay him a visit before they returned to the Tomlinson's. She wanted to ask if their church community could bring in additional meals, so it would be easier for Mary to manage.

At Aunt Irene's house, Grandmother Julia was awake but weak and coughing frequently. She had had two more nosebleeds that day, Aunt Irene reported, and had coughed up quite a bit of gray and black matter, but though alarming, Irene took that as evidence that her mother's body was ridding itself of impurities. She planned to take the rest of the week off to care for her, by which time she hoped Grandmother would be strong enough to ride the train in to Columbus to Aunt Eleanor's house. Eleanor had insisted on taking over the caregiving at that point, and Irene relented, knowing she needed to continue her role at the university. Julia's relocation would allow both her daughters to be near her as Aunt Irene resumed her work.

"There are so many people needing care," Samantha worried aloud on their drive back to Thora's after visiting Aunt Phoebe, Grandmother, and the pastor. "How will we adequately help them all?"

Basil patted her hand and smiled grimly. "One person, one day at a time."

***

In between visiting her ill aunt and grandmother and caring for Sterling throughout the week, Samantha helped Thora process the abundance of apples from the orchard for winter storage, and learned more about cooking and managing a home. She appreciated the explanations Thora provided as she went cheerfully about her daily tasks, and the perspective their conversations gave her. Samantha realized she worried less about her ill loved ones as she stayed busy, and felt happier while she simply did what she could each day. As she and Thora worked together, their conversations turned to every conceivable topic: from how to make the perfect pie crust, to their most important educational moments in school, to how to recognize when God is speaking to one's heart.

One afternoon while Basil and Sterling conversed inside, Samantha and Thora donned colorful knit hats and pushed wheelbarrows through rows of decimated pumpkin vines that had withered in the recent frost. As they walked among the spent vegetation collecting the bright pumpkins that now stood out so conspicuously against the darkened, dead leaves, Samantha sensed Thora's tiredness and thought back to their conversation the past August. Soon her friend would have a winter's rest from the unrelenting work of the farm, but it was a cycle that could never end as long as she wanted to provide for herself. It was a blessing to be able to do so, but a burden nonetheless, and Samantha saw that Thora felt its heaviness some days more than others, despite her good cheer.

After cutting a large pumpkin free of its vine with a knife, Samantha hefted it in both arms and carried it to the wheelbarrow. She knew Thora would sell more than half of this harvest, then process the rest, some of which would be turned into tasty goodies which she would sell through the local bakery over the holiday season. All good things, but so much work!

What can I do to ease Thora's burdens in a meaningful way? she asked herself. Instinctively she knew the woman would not accept a monetary donation from the Jennings. That would not be a long-term solution anyway, and Samantha longed to help in a way that would ease and secure the future for her. Thora, of all people, should be able to relax a little in her later years, reaping the benefits of a lifetime of labor. She and Mrs. Dolittle, both.

The women continued moving through the garden, filling their wheelbarrows in silence for a few minutes. Then Samantha stopped in her tracks as an idea occurred to her. "Thora," she called suddenly. "Would you ever be open to selling this place and moving to Oberlin?"

Several yards away, Thora straightened abruptly and looked at her across the wilted pumpkin patch. "Oberlin?" she asked in surprise. She looked intently at Samantha and asked, "Where did that thought come from?"

"Oh, it's just part of an idea at this point." Samantha walked closer to Thora so she could continue in her normal voice. "Actually, it's part of a well-developed plan that Sterling and I have discussed at length. I want to bring my mother's dream for a children's school to fruition, and I just now had the thought that you might be the perfect person to help us."

"Me?" Thora asked, her surprise deepening. "A school?"

"Yes, at our mansion. It is much too big for us, and we have such a large plot of land to go with it, most of it unused. I want to follow Booker T. Washington's model of a school that teaches its students all the usual academic subjects but also teaches them the intricacies of real-life work: gardening, tool maintenance, cooking, food preservation, construction, sewing, laundry, etc. I think perhaps Mrs. Dolittle and Claire could help with many of those things, but you are the expert on gardening and maintaining an orchard, and Jerome is so good at building, repair, and maintenance. The two of you are the wealth of information and experience that this school needs."

Thora looked a little stunned by the idea.

"Students and faculty would provide a good deal of help, so the full burden of the work wouldn't be on your shoulders, as it is here. And with Mrs. Dolittle overseeing the housekeeping and cooking—which she would also receive assistance with from students—you wouldn't have those chores to worry about. Plus, you and Jerome would have a nice place to live, and we would see you every day!" Samantha realized she was a little breathless after this excited explanation and paused to calm her racing heart, startled at how right this sudden inspiration felt. But it wasn't her call to make.

Thora just stood there in the weak autumn sunlight, bewilderment and thoughtfulness chasing each other across her face, with just a hint of excitement, if Samantha interpreted correctly. "Oberlin..." she said at last, as if tasting the idea. "Selling this place..." She let out a long breath. "My! I don't—Samantha, that is such a generous offer! We would need—" She cleared her throat. "You leave me much to contemplate; I am not certain how to answer."

Samantha laughed, more at her own impetuosity than anything else. "Now I am acting like Sterling!" she giggled, putting a hand to her face in amusement. "Sorry. That came all at once out of nowhere. It surprised me too, but I love the idea! As I said, plans for the school are only in the beginning stages. But I would love for you to think about the possibility. If it were to work out, wouldn't that be a lovely arrangement?" Samantha was tentative as she appraised Thora breathlessly, wondering what the woman might be thinking.

"I..." Thora looked a little astonished. "Yes," she admitted with a laugh of her own. "Yes, I believe that just might be an excellent arrangement! You have certainly given me much to think and pray about. And you are right that I need to find a solution to this situation." She gazed at Samantha with great fondness in her smiling eyes. "I can see you are a dreamer too, Samantha, just like Sterling."

***

Samantha was at home several times when Jerome returned from school, frustrated over homework he didn't understand. Wanting to see if she could help him, Samantha looked over the materials he brought home and discovered that she remembered the concepts. She found that she liked explaining them to him in different ways until she saw his eyes come alive with understanding. With three extra adults temporarily available in his home, Jerome found many willing teachers, all with differing strengths and abilities, willing and able to help him, and he basked in it.

Once Sterling felt strong enough to sit through Sunday church services, he attended with them, and Samantha felt such peace and contentment sitting in the pew with her father on one side and Sterling on the other. Every time she thought back to how sick Sterling was when she arrived, the gray pallor of his skin, his labored breathing, his lack of awareness that she was even there, a chill crept over her, and she would say yet another prayer of gratitude. It would have been so easy for Sterling to cross over into that other realm, to pass on as so many others had of the same illness. She and Sterling were no more deserving of this great blessing of continued life and renewed health than anyone else, so she was eternally grateful that God had stayed the hand of death anyway.

She hoped that Grandmother would soon feel up to attending church with Aunt Eleanor and Uncle Andrew, and that Aunt Phoebe's strength would return so she could join her family as well.

***

As Sterling slowly regained his health, he was relieved to find that he didn't need to sleep quite so much. After several days with the Tomlinsons, he began waking with the sun and did not need to sleep again until after lunch, and then for only a couple of hours. This allowed him to share a morning devotional with Samantha each morning, which he enjoyed. Her depth of spiritual understanding continually surprised him, and she appreciated the thoughtful questions he posed that made them dive back into the Bible for answers.

Since Sterling could not physically do much, he spent the majority of his time reading, including reacquainting himself with news, thanks to newspapers his colleagues saved for him. He and Samantha were both relieved to learn that the five-month strike[1] in eastern Pennsylvania of United Mine Workers finally ended during the final days of October, which meant that coal would not be withheld from the public over the winter months,

---

1. https://en.wikipedia.org/wiki/Anthracite_coal_strike_of_1902

after all. Though the workers did not receive exactly what they asked for, the commission did agree to give them 10% more pay and a nine-hour workday (instead of ten). In the meantime, thirty thousand men had left that area, ten thousand of them heading back to Europe.

Sterling was sorry to hear of the death of Elizabeth Cady Stanton, a household name, who had done so much over her almost ninety years of life to further women's rights and abolish slavery. He was amused about a stuffed bear being named a "teddy bear" after President Teddy Roosevelt, wondering if it would really catch on. And he felt weary reading about the continuing conflict in the Philippines, confused with conflicting statements about the "water cure"[2] and other tortures American soldiers allegedly employed to gain information from Filipino soldiers. He was incensed about the so-called civilized world using such methods on other human beings. And yet, he knew from his past studies about war that politics, practices, and policies were always as complicated as the people involved. He wondered what the case was here and if such techniques could ever be considered justifiable.

Sterling was more than willing to help the writing committee when a tentative member paid a visit to see if he felt up to it. He told the man he would love to continue his efforts as a judge of entries, if the papers could be delivered to him, as he had not the strength to pick them up from the committee himself. Arrangements were made and Sterling felt an immense sense of satisfaction that he was still considered useful for something.

He also enjoyed reading the copy of *Up from Slavery* that Samantha checked out for him from the local library, at his request. With pride almost worthy of a village native, he told her that Worthington had intermittently had an unofficial library since 1803, and she was gratifyingly impressed. With the book fresh in their minds, they engaged in deep conversations about the stories and principles they learned from it. When they took short, slow walks, bundled up against the ever-cooling weather, they discussed what opening a large school for children would entail, what the focus should be, and how they could accomplish their goals for such an institution.

---

2. https://en.wikipedia.org/wiki/Water_cure_(torture)#Notes , https://apjjf.org/-Paul-A.-Kramer/2685/article.html

One afternoon, after they had been with the Tomlinsons for over two weeks, Samantha's father accompanied them on such a walk, and it suddenly felt to Samantha like the right time to ask his perspective on the matter. She no longer had any trepidation about talking to him, but she hoped she was broaching the subject sensitively enough. She held Sterling's right arm, matching her stride to his slow one, which was already much stronger than it had been only the week before. Her father walked on Sterling's left, ready to assist him, should he need it.

"Father?" she began, deciding to just ask with no more deliberation. "I've had a question for you for the longest time and have not known how to talk about it. But I feel it's something that needs to be asked and I hope it won't be too painful for you."

Basil looked over at her and his blue eyes widened briefly, but he nodded. "What is it?"

"Do you remember Mother's dream of turning our mansion into a school for children?"

He inhaled sharply, but inclined his head after a moment. "Yes. I had forgotten, but her journal reminded me."

"That's where I learned of it too," Samantha affirmed, "and the more I think about it, the more I feel like I need to help her dream become a reality. Serving the children of our community is such a worthwhile goal. And we have the means to do so."

Basil said nothing, but she could tell he was thinking deeply.

"I have been reading everything I can find about education in general, and also about how to help children learn to work and develop important life skills. My notebook is almost filled with all I have learned! I've had many questions about how such a school should be managed, how to find good teachers, how we could feed so many children, and so on. But the most fundamental of all these questions is...how would you feel about starting a school, Father? It is your home and I respect your authority over it. I would never want to presume to tell you what to do with it, or to push you into something you would resent. It is just that this is something that has been insistently nudging its way into my mind for months and won't leave me alone." She paused, hopeful but a little concerned she may have pushed too far. Basil's gray, wiry brows were drawn together in serious contemplation.

Sterling took her hand and squeezed it encouragingly.

They continued walking until Basil finally spoke. "Well now, I don't know. You have obviously put great time and thought into this proposition. I am afraid I don't have the benefit of either, so will you forgive me if I mull it over for a while?"

"Of course!" Samantha hurried to say. "I just didn't want to go on thinking and researching without asking you about it. Your opinion and your perspective matter a great deal to me."

Basil surprised her with a low chuckle. "There is quite a bit going on in that fair head of yours, isn't there?"

She couldn't remember him teasing her before, and she grinned back. "Always!"

Sterling smiled too. "I can vouch for that."

"You remind me of your mother," Basil continued, his smile unwavering.

Samantha's heart warmed. "I'm glad." He had said this before, but never given many details.

"Yes," Basil continued, "she was always thinking about many things, writing about them in her journal, and reading everything she could get her hands on. Sometimes she only had the energy to do those three things, but she did whatever she could to expand her mind and learn all she could. I am glad to see her legacy being passed on, in spite of myself." His tone was rueful and he looked down, his hands in his coat pockets as they ambled along the path.

Samantha knew he still regretted how he had handled things after her mother passed, and she didn't know how to ease his pain, but she did know how to show her love in the present. She stopped walking and let go of Sterling's hand, then put her arms around her father. "Thank you for being here, Father. I will never forget what you have done for us." She looked up at him and saw the happiness and gratitude in his blue eyes that were clearer than she had ever seen them. The time they had spent in Worthington appeared to have done him as much good as it had Sterling. "I love you," she added.

He hugged her back for a long moment and, with a choke in his voice said, "I love you, daughter." He swallowed. "Thank you for reminding me what is most valuable and helping me find joy again. It has been such a long time."

After a moment, Sterling cleared his throat. "Can I get in on this loving family moment too?" he asked.

Basil's chuckle sounded a little strangled with emotion, but Samantha laughed in delight as she pulled Sterling in to join their embrace.

***

When they had been at the Tomlinsons' for about three weeks, Mr. Grover came by for his weekly visit to check on Sterling and asked if he felt up to grading papers yet. Sterling visibly brightened. "Yes!" he exclaimed. "Actually, I was thinking along those lines before you arrived. I don't quite feel strong enough yet to be in the classroom all day, but I would love to start taking on what I can from here."

Mr. Grover nodded approvingly and held up a satchel that Sterling assumed contained the aforementioned papers. "I don't mind telling you that the substitute is finding your load heavy. He tells me it is hard to fill your shoes, but he is doing his best. I pitch in as often as I can, and it is obvious what a hole your absence makes. Your students are all eager to have you back, as soon as you feel up to it."

"Thank you," Sterling said. "I miss them, so it is good to be missed in return. Might it be possible for me to start out gradually? I think in another week I will feel up to teaching half days…"

"Excellent!" Mr. Grover exclaimed. "That sounds like a good plan."

"Sorry I am not able to jump in all at once, and sooner," Sterling grimaced. "This recovery tries my patience daily."

Mr. Grover's chuckle became a full belly laugh as he looked at Sterling, wrapped up in a colorful quilt on the parlor sofa, with a morose and annoyed expression on his face. "I am sure it does, son. I'm sure it does. Slowing down a young bull like you in the prime of life is no easy thing." He sobered, pushing his glasses back up his nose. "Remember, this won't last forever. We are just grateful you are on the mend!"

"Yes," Sterling acknowledged, "so am I."

"And, I have to say, you really do look much better than last week. Last time I came, I visited with you while you sat in bed, and this week," he spread his hands to indicate the room, "here we are in the parlor."

Sterling sighed. "You are right. Thank you for the reminder. Another week and I should feel strong enough to return for half days. I appreciate your patience with my recovery, and that you are holding my job for me."

"Of course, Sterling. Glad to do it. I try to keep good teachers as long as I can! And I'll be happy to report to your class the good news. With any luck, now they will stop pestering me about when you will return and I can get my own work done." He winked at Sterling and, turning to go, quipped, "I think I'll go see if Mrs. Tomlinson has any more of that delectable apple pie she offered me last week."

Sterling grinned as the older man left the room. The real question was whether Mr. Grover wanted to satisfy his sweet tooth or just spend time with Mrs. Tomlinson!

He turned to the satchel Mr. Grover had deposited next to him and opened it. The smell of leather filled his nostrils as he pulled out the stack of papers within. So many! Yet he actually found his heart picking up a bit with anticipation. Who would have thought he could ever feel excited about correcting papers! But this was something productive he could do, something that resembled his life before pneumonia, and as he began to go over each paper one by one, the rhythm of the familiar activity soothed him.

Samantha found him there after she sent Mr. Grover off with a large, wrapped slice of cake (as the pie had long since been consumed). He had spent nearly half an hour in the kitchen with her and Thora, the three of them chatting pleasantly while the women prepared the evening meal. She had her suspicions that the man was developing a particular fondness for Thora and not just for her delectable baking. She tucked the topic into the back of her mind to ask Thora about when the next opportunity presented itself.

When Samantha stepped into the parlor, she was surprised to see Sterling intently focused on a paper in his lap, a small stack of papers next to him on the sofa. When he looked up, she could see that his eyes were clear and alert and showed no signs of fatigue.

"Homework?" she asked.

"Yes, isn't it wonderful?" he grinned.

She stood in front of him and looked down at the papers covered in writing and laughed. "I am glad to see you so happy to be back in teacher mode."

"Like so many other things, in this, too, absence makes the heart grow fonder. What once felt like drudgery at times now feels like a privilege. This," he said, holding the paper up in a triumphant gesture, "this I can do."

Samantha smiled at him. "Yes. And soon you will be back to doing everything else you did before, too."

Sterling nodded, suddenly feeling more confident about that idea now than he had since the illness. "I really think I will. But there is one problem with that, you know."

"There is?" she asked, sitting next to him, on the side not occupied by papers. "What is that?"

"The fact that you will go back home and we'll be separated yet again."

"Oh," she exhaled, leaning back against the sofa. "You are right. I don't like thinking about that either." She bit her lip and her gaze dropped to the gleaming wood floor with its colorful rag rugs. "Letters are never as good as being together."

He took her hand and traced her fingers. "I hate the distance between us when we are in separate cities, and I don't know how much longer I can handle that."

She looked up at him. What was he saying exactly? "I know. It's hard for me too. But you must finish out the school year."

He nodded. "Yes. I just didn't realize it would be this difficult. You have to go back to Oberlin and my place is here for now, but this is not a tenable long-term arrangement." He grimaced as if in pain.

"No." She sat quietly, thinking. "But we'll be together at Christmas, so we have that to look forward to."

He nodded slowly and his hand tightened around hers. "Yes, you're right. Christmas is not so far away now—already next month. I still think we should go to Lexington, if you're agreeable to that. I want my family to meet you. And I want you to see where I grew up."

"All right. I would like to meet them too," she replied, kissing his cheek. "For now, let us enjoy the days we have left together. I want to see you back on your feet before Father and I head home."

Sterling's eyes twinkled with mischief. "Hmm, in that case, I think I'll just stay sitting," he teased. But the light of purpose was back in his eyes and she finally knew he would truly be all right.

***

From that day on, Sterling's progress went at a much faster pace. His walks grew longer, he kept up with the workload Jerome brought him each day from Mr. Grover, and his tall frame started filling out once again. His complexion was no longer sallow nor his eyes bloodshot, and his hands didn't shake anymore. The bright-eyed, quick, light-hearted young man Samantha knew and loved was returning, and she was grateful from the bottom of her heart for each improvement. But as the days drew closer to her return home, she felt a curious mixture of dread and anticipation. She cherished the time they'd had in the Tomlinson home, but she really did miss all the things and people that were so dear to her in Oberlin. She would miss Sterling more than she could even articulate, but she also looked forward to being in her own place again and returning to her old routines. This tug of war in her heart could be exhausting! She didn't know what the answer was to all this, or if there was any solution but time, so she just kept praying they would figure everything out in God's timing, and that He would help them through each separation.

Once Basil and Samantha assured themselves that Sterling truly could manage teaching half days and was ready to return to his little room at the boarding house, they planned their trip home. They went to one last dinner at Aunt Eleanor and Uncle Andrew's house in Columbus to express their love and say goodbye (though Sterling was invited to continue joining the weekly family dinner as often as he liked), and Samantha noticed that young Julia had warmed toward her a bit. Perhaps one day they might even be friends. Only time would tell.

Basil bought return train tickets and he and Samantha packed up their things. The evening before their departure, they bid a reluctant farewell to Thora and Jerome, feeling inadequate to express sufficient gratitude, but knowing the bond between them was now firmly cemented. They would all see each other again sometime soon, they would make certain of that.

Thora's embrace was long, firm, and tender, and Samantha knew her own eyes reflected the glittering tears in Thora's, but neither of them let the tears fall. They refused to think of this as goodbye. Basil clapped Jerome on the back and gave him a few more words of encouragement, which Jerome accepted with a nod and a grin. Then her father took Thora's hand in both of his as he sincerely thanked her for making her home theirs during the past few weeks. He didn't know how they could ever thank her for all she had been and done for them. Thora thanked them both in return, expressing gratitude for all the help outside and in. Did Basil's hands linger over hers for a little longer than necessary? Samantha noticed Thora didn't try to pull away.

∗∗∗

Samantha and her father spent their last night in Sterling's boarding house room, so as to be closer to the train station for their early departure the next morning. They helped him move everything back in and reorganize, remaking the bed with clean linens and even airing out the room briefly to rid it of any lingering evidence of illness. Basil treated them to a farewell meal at the nearby inn, and then retreated to the lobby where he could sit and read, yet keep an eye on the young couple through the doorway, knowing they needed some time to themselves. So Samantha and Sterling remained at the table another hour, talking, sharing memories, laughing, and trying not to think about how they would have to say goodbye the next morning. Finally, Sterling took her hands across the table and looked into her gray eyes. "Thank you," he said gravely.

Samantha studied him questioningly.

"Thank you for coming without delay when I needed you most. Thank you for saving my life, for helping me want to keep living." He looked down at her hands and rubbed slow circles across them with his thumbs, his mind deep in the difficult memory. Then he looked up again and his earnest eyes met hers. "I know you feel like God did the hard part, but you were instrumental in making it happen. So thank you for being His hands and for not giving up on me." He squeezed her hands tightly, as if willing his gratitude to be transmitted directly to her heart.

"Never," she whispered, eyes wet. "I could never give up on you."

Chapter 21

ANOTHER SEPARATION

November-December 1902

This time on the train, Samantha and her father spoke often and slept little. They were filled to the brim with experiences and relationships that needed discussing. Samantha had further questions for Basil about the backgrounds of Lewis family members, and she offered him insightful perspectives on those who still harbored negative feelings toward him and what he might do to assuage them. They also discussed their joy at Julia's continued recovery and the prospect that she might soon be ready to move into Irene's house to live with her. Although she was quite comfortable at Aunt Eleanor's, Grandmother still preferred little Worthington.

"But what about Aunt Phoebe?" Samantha asked, her fair brows furrowed. "She is slow to recover and her children need her so much!"

"I know," her father agreed, his own bushy brows drawn together. "It seems she has always had an asthmatic tendency and the smoke inhalation has triggered an allergic, inflammatory response." Seeing Samantha's look of simultaneous surprise and understanding, he nodded. "I spoke with the doctor privately a few days ago and he recommended that she hire a nurse for a week or two. Phoebe has been doing too much for everyone but herself, and in spite of Mary's efforts to do all she can to help, it has not been enough. Phoebe needs more rest and better nutrition or she will lose too much more weight and full recovery will be difficult."

Samantha's heart squeezed at the thought of this difficulty her aunt was going through as a simple result of trying to help her mother-in-law. "Can Uncle Samuel afford to hire a nurse?"

"No, but I can," Basil replied firmly. "Samuel did not want to take the money I offered, but I pressed him. His children need their mother back and Samuel needs her too." He smiled that grim, reminiscent smile that spoke of tender times. "I reminded him that I know what it is to have an ill wife, and if a live-in nurse could have made the difference for my dear one, it would have been worth any amount of money. In the end, he accepted my offer. I will write him next week and inquire as to the progress of our patient."

"And I will write dear little Mary as well, to see how she is getting on."

Basil patted her hand and nodded, then they were both quiet in their thoughts for a while. Samantha was gazing out at the dreary landscape of bare winter trees hurtling past them when he commented offhand, "That Thora Tomlinson is quite a woman, isn't she?" His tone was bright and affectionate.

Samantha turned back to him, curious. "She certainly is," she agreed. "The best of women, in my opinion. She has been through difficult trials, losing a child and then losing her husband all those years ago." Realizing who she was talking to, she added quietly, "Much like what you went through, Father."

"Yes, I suppose," Basil said slowly. "But she handles her lot much better than I ever have. And she is so strong and cheerful, withal."

"I don't know how she does it," Samantha agreed. "But I am ever so grateful she is like that. Thora has become the wise and gentle mother figure Sterling never had and was sorely in need of last year. And in the short time I have known her, she has become my dear friend and mentor as well. She fills so many roles with such grace and I am grateful to be part of her life."

"Yes." Her father nodded. "Yes." He cleared his throat. "Do you think she and Jerome might like to visit us in Oberlin some time?"

"I—yes!" Samantha was surprised her father's thoughts had jumped there already. "I think they would, especially if it's during a slow time on the farm."

Basil's bearded lips turned up in the memory of their time together. "That young Jerome is a character. I do not believe I have laughed that much since your mother died."

Samantha squeezed his arm. "He is quite something," she agreed.

"I would pay for their trip, of course."

"Of course," Samantha agreed. Was that excitement she sensed in her father's expression? And the color and strength of his countenance looked invigorated with the prospect. It seemed that over the past few weeks, the years had fallen away from him and she no longer thought of him as an old man.

Suddenly, she felt a twinge of conscience as she remembered her conversation with Thora about the children's school. "Actually, Father, there's something I should tell you."

He looked at her questioningly.

"I already spoke to Thora about the possibility of coming to Oberlin."

Basil's eyebrows rose, but he only waited for her to continue.

"One day when we were harvesting pumpkins, I saw how tired she was. I'd noticed that before and was concerned. She works so hard just to keep things running and it must be overwhelming at times."

Basil nodded slowly, obviously internalizing Samantha's words.

She told him how she wanted to help Thora in a meaningful way and how the idea came to her out of the blue, but why she felt like it was a good one. "I also think she and Mrs. Dolittle could be great friends!" she concluded, turning to face him again. Then she said tentatively, "I should probably have discussed it with you before I said anything to her, but it felt like inspiration and I--"

Her father placed a quieting hand on her knee. "I like the idea too," he said.

In the quiet that ensued over the next few minutes, Samantha watched her father discreetly, noticing how his brow wrinkled and his gaze shifted from one side to the other and back again, his thoughts deep and in need of careful perusal. Finally he offered, "If she could make a profit off the farm, that would put her in good stead... And if she had a way to use her skills but not be overworked..." He paused. "That really might be a good solution, daughter." He turned to her again. "I think you *were* inspired. What did she say?"

"She said she would think about it."

Basil nodded.

Samantha realized with sudden clarity how good this trip had been for him on so many levels. Not just reconnecting with her mother's family and asking for forgiveness, but also helping a widow and her son in ways that were truly needed and irreplaceable. And recognizing that he still had something to give—many things, in fact.

"Are you glad you came with me, Father?" she asked, looking up into his grizzled face.

He smiled affectionately through his beard. "I am," he answered without hesitation. "I truly am."

"There have been many hard things during these weeks, but you passed through them beautifully. I've said this before, but you were my rock when I needed you most."

"Well, the gratitude is mutual," he told her, his blue eyes twinkling and alive in a way she had never thought she would see. "I am socially exhausted," he admitted, chuckling at himself with real humor, "but I feel more myself than I have in longer than I can remember."

"Does it have anything to do with a certain Thora Tomlinson?" Samantha probed gently.

Seeing her father redden under his gray beard tickled her, but she hurried to say, "I am only teasing, Father. I know there are many reasons. But she is one of the big reasons I, at least, can look back with pleasant memories on this time."

"Indeed," he said cryptically. But his eyes generously agreed.

Samantha turned her face back to the window so he wouldn't see the size of her smile, and her heart beat a happy rhythm.

***

Sterling pulled up his coat collar against the chill breeze and pulled his hat down more tightly. He stepped past the Walnut Grove Cemetery gate and his pace slowed as he felt the peace of the place gradually distill into his being. The green grass had faded into its yellow winter coat in preparation for the weather that would soon come. Most of the leaves had fallen from all the large trees and they skittered across the yellowed, dormant grass with every cold breeze that blew through.

Here was where he had found solace time and time again last year, and where Samantha had reached the end of her search for her mother. This was also the place where he had unexpectedly laid eyes on Samantha when he never in his wildest dreams would have imagined finding her here.

As he made his way to Lovenia Lewis Jennings' headstone, he thought about that day: Samantha in a becoming green dress that brought out the auburn highlights in her blonde hair, and the attractive way it was piled up on her head, instead of in two braids down her back. She had resembled her old self just enough that he had recognized her, but the plain-clad girl with spectacles he left behind had become a poised and stylishly dressed woman in his absence. Her voice was still the same, her grace, intelligence, and perceptiveness were as much a part of her as they ever were. But her maturity and depth had captured his heart in that moment even more than her youth and naivete once had.

He shook his head to dismiss the image, glad for the hundredth time to be on this end of things. Now he sought the refuge of the cemetery as a way to connect with someone who was near and dear to Samantha's heart. Someone he had never addressed before.

He found the modest, gray headstone and noticed that someone had been here recently and tidied it up. A little pot of yellow and orange flowers rested against one side of the stone, adding a cheerful spot of color to the faded autumn landscape. He traced the neat lines of the words with an index finger and thought about how this woman had brought his Samantha into the world. Lovenia had wanted her so much and it had brought her great joy to know she was coming. Now he wanted to tell her about the joy he experienced in his life because of Samantha, and to thank Lovenia for her sacrifice. Slowly, he removed his hat in respect and introduced himself.

"My name is Lee Sterling," he began, mildly surprised not to feel silly talking to a stone. He was completely alone and this felt like a safe space to bare his heart, so he took the direct course. "I am in love with your daughter. I wish I could meet you in person, but this will have to do. On the chance that you may be listening from heaven, I need to tell you that Samantha is everything I have always dreamed of and more."

He paused, images of their summer together flashing through his mind, poignant moments when he had realized again and again all that Samantha was and how much she meant to him. He cleared his throat. "Recently, she saved my life. I don't know how she did it, but I am very glad because I am not ready to join you above just yet. I think Samantha needs me—I know I need her. And Basil needs her too." The corners of Sterling's mouth turned up as he thought fondly of the old professor and the talks they shared during his convalescence at the Tomlinsons. "He is doing better lately, thanks to her efforts. I am sure you know how he's been since your passing... Samantha is a forgiving and generous person and she doesn't give up on people." He rubbed his forehead, thinking about all she had done to nurse him back to health. "My, am I glad she doesn't give up!"

He paused again and exhaled slowly, lowering his hand. "Anyway, I am learning how much people need each other, even the most self-reliant of us. And that is a good thing. People like you leave a big hole in the lives of their loved ones when they pass on. That deep loss powerfully indicates how important you were in their lives and how much they love you. It's a blow that is difficult to recover from, and your family is no exception. They are still healing, even after all these years. But I think for the first time they are truly on the mend now. And it is all because of your daughter. She is really quite a remarkable young woman.

"I am confident you know that and you are proud of the life you brought into the world. She has become a light to so many of us! But I wanted you to hear it from me personally. I love her and I want to marry her. I want to raise a family with her and grow old together. I have wanted to ask her long before now; we have already had a longer courtship than most couples do. But with me here and her in Oberlin, and then with me so sick, the timing just hasn't been right."

He sighed again. "Somehow, I think you understand that too... Anyway, if you could just keep an eye on things from your place up there and help me know when the time is right, I would appreciate it. I keep asking God the same thing and am trying to follow His direction. And while I can't exactly ask for your approval," he smiled lopsidedly, "I hope I have it. I will seek permission from Basil, of course. He is a good man, as you know."

He touched the stone once more. "At any rate, I do hope you understand how sincere I am and can feel how much I truly love Samantha. She loves you very much and has taken your legacy to heart. So thank you for that. The way you always turned to Jesus in life and helped others find His light is something that has helped us too." He kissed his fingertips and rested them on top of the stone marker for a moment. Then he bowed his head and said, "May you rest well in Him."

***

Samantha luxuriated in being home again, but the pain of missing Sterling was real and endless, sometimes physical. And the quietness of the Jennings mansion seemed hollower now than it ever had before. She didn't realize how much she had grown to appreciate and enjoy a busy and bustling household until she was now removed from both the happy order of Thora's place and the loving chaos of the Lewis families.

Her father stayed in his room for a couple days upon their return and Samantha sensed that he needed time to himself, to recenter after their extended time with more people than he had associated with in nearly twenty years. She wished he didn't need that time, but she understood and didn't push him. In contrast, she herself itched for contact with other people, especially Katherine. So that week when, on Mrs. Dolittle's and Claire's day off, the snow clouds parted and the sun came out, Samantha decided to walk through the snow to her dear friend's house.

It had been several weeks since they last saw each other, and she felt a sense of anticipation as she took the long walk. The exercise was invigorating, but the way was bitterly cold, and when Samantha arrived on Katherine's front porch, her scarf was encrusted with ice from her breath. Her cheeks were pink with the frosty air, but her eyes sparkled when Katherine exclaimed her joy and pulled her quickly into the small house.

"Samantha!" Katherine cried, throwing her arms around her friend, heedless of the ice and snow clinging to her. "How are you? I haven't seen you in ages!"

Samantha hugged her back, laughing. "I know! Now that I'm back from Worthington, I had to come see you. Mrs. Dolittle and Claire are gone today and it is much too quiet at home. It seemed the perfect opportunity to take a walk and see if you were here. I am so glad you are!"

"I am too," Katherine said, her fine features bright with her smile, "but you walked?" She indicated the snow outside the window, as if Samantha hadn't seen it. "It's not exactly prime walking weather…"

"Oh, but there is sunshine today," Samantha said brightly, as if that made up for the cold and the several inches of snow on the ground.

Katherine laughed and shook her head, then grabbed her hand again and pulled her into the small parlor. She shut the door behind them and took Samantha's coat, hanging it on the coat tree in one corner, along with her scarf. They laid her mittens and hat on the floor near the fire in the hearth, which crackled with warmth. Then they sat in two armchairs facing each other across from the fireplace and Katherine handed her a blanket from a large basket on the floor. Another blanket draped over her armchair and a book lay open on the small table beside it, indicating to Samantha that her friend had been sitting here for a while, reading.

"All right," Katherine said, settling back into the armchair and pulling the blanket over her shoulders. "I want to hear all about what you've been up to."

"Well," Samantha exhaled slowly, thinking about all that had transpired since she last saw her friend in October. "How much do you know?"

Katherine's dark brows furrowed as she considered. "Not much, really. I came by sometime in October, not long after you left. Mrs. Dolittle told me about the telegram you received and that you and your father left for Worthington almost immediately. I was worried for all of you, with that terrible news! I checked back a week later and Mrs. Dolittle told me she had received a telegram a couple days before, letting her know you and your father arrived safely and were caring for Sterling, who was very ill but seemed to at last be out of danger. After that, I was able to relax a bit and just kept praying that he would recover and all would work out well."

"Thank you," Samantha said gratefully. "With God's help, it did. But what an experience!" She shivered involuntarily. "It still chills me to the bone every time I think about how close to death Sterling really came." She described what he looked like when she arrived and how little strength he had for weeks, even after his recovery had begun in earnest.

Katherine was incredulous, as everyone else who knew him had been, and expressed her amazement over what happened. She also expressed real concern over Samantha's grandmother and aunt, after Samantha told her about the fire, and even shed a few tears over Samantha's recital of the Lewis family's reconciliation with her father and how healing was taking place among them now.

"I don't think it was necessary for Sterling to fall deathly ill in order for that to happen," Samantha mused thoughtfully, "but at the same time, to me it is a dramatic demonstration of how God can help good things come from really bad situations. I hope He will help good to come from the fire as well."

Katherine nodded, eyes serious. "I agree. And what a remarkable story! I am so relieved it has all turned out well so far."

"Me too," returned Samantha, "more than I can say. We just need to keep praying for Aunt Phoebe, in particular. But now it's your turn, Katherine! What is the latest with you and Rupert?"

Katherine smiled and her cheeks flushed. She held out a hand and, for the first time, Samantha noticed a pretty silver band around her ring finger. Samantha inhaled in surprise. "Oh, Katherine, congratulations! It is going *very* well, I see." She laughed in delight. "You should have told me your news first!"

"I knew we would get to it," Katherine responded unconcernedly. "And yes, it is going very well." She sighed contentedly and they both laughed. "Rupert is wonderful. He is so kind and considerate, humble and big-hearted and selfless—and a hard worker. My family loves him."

"Even your father?" Samantha asked, knowing the man was a hard one to please when it came to suitors for his beautiful daughters.

"Even Father," Katherine acknowledged. "I have never been so happy."

"I am very glad," Samantha said. "Imagine...my two dearest friends, in love with each other," she mused aloud. "When did he propose?"

"In October. That was why I came to see you!"

Samantha cringed apologetically. "I am so sorry to have missed that! I would have loved to hear your big news!"

"I thought of writing you a letter, but I kept thinking you would be home soon. And I wanted to tell you about it in person anyway."

"And then you had to wait so long!" Samantha exclaimed, regretting she hadn't been there for her friend. She stood and took the few steps to Katherine's armchair, blanket trailing behind her, and gave her a tight, congratulatory hug.

"And you like his parents, as well?" she asked as they both settled back in their chairs.

"I do. They seemed a bit standoffish at first, but it didn't take them too long to warm up to me. They are quiet, careful folks and I think they wanted to make sure I was good for Rupert before they were ready to accept me."

"But now they have?"

She nodded, smiling. "They are really wonderful people, much like Rupert himself. I feel nothing but respect for the way they raised their children and live their lives. They adore Rupert and so do I—so right from the start we had something important in common!"

Samantha laughed with her friend and her heart swelled to see Katherine's obvious happiness. And to know that she had found love with one who had long been interested in her from afar, and who was also dear to Samantha... It just felt like the best thing that could have happened. She felt doubly glad that she had never encouraged Rupert's romantic interest in herself and had ultimately encouraged him in his pursuit of her friend instead, even though it had been a difficult decision at the time.

"What about you and Sterling?" Katherine asked. "He didn't propose in all that time you spent with him in Worthington this second time?"

"No," Samantha said, "he was too busy getting well! Believe me, recovering is an all-consuming occupation. But he did express to me, with a very pained expression, that he very much dislikes all this time we must spend apart. It is wearing on him and is 'not a tenable long-term arrangement.'"

"And you heartily agree, of course," Katherine supplied.

"Of course."

"So...?"

"Well, as I pointed out to him, he still has to finish out the school year. And I think Father needs me now more than ever. Leaving Father alone for months at a time is probably the worst thing I could do at this point, when he is finally learning to do and be more than he ever has in my lifetime!"

Katherine nodded in perfect agreement. "So when will you and Sterling see each other again?"

"Over the Christmas holidays. He wants to take me to his parents' home in Lexington."

"Oh, the 'meet the parents' event!" Katherine exclaimed. "That can be a little intimidating, as I know all too well."

"Yes, it is a little nerve-wracking," Samantha admitted. "Especially knowing that Sterling and his mother don't see eye-to-eye and that she is already predisposed to dislike me, considering her background and social station. But I have told him more than once that I still want to try, for his sake."

"Well, that does sound like a daunting task," Katherine answered, giving her a sympathetic look. "But if anyone can accomplish it, it's you. How could anyone not like you, anyway? I'm sure you will win her over."

Her complete confidence in such an outcome warmed Samantha's heart, but it didn't fully convert her. "I hope you're right, Katherine," she said with real concern, then gave a small sigh. "I think you might do a better job of it yourself. You are the one with the bright personality who wins everyone over! And you always know just what to say to bring out the best in people. I don't have that gift. At any rate, I will do my best and if she does not come to like me, it won't be for my lack of effort."

"I will pray it goes well," Katherine responded sincerely.

"I sense I will need your prayers, so thank you," Samantha replied. "Now tell me, when is this wedding to take place? And how can I help?"

They discussed the upcoming wedding, which was romantically set for Valentine's Day, and Katherine took her into the room where the fabric for her wedding dress was carefully folded, awaiting her mother's expert skills. Samantha listened with great interest, absorbing Katherine's delight with all the pleasure afforded her closest friend.

***

Samantha stayed busy at home with Claire and Mrs. Dolittle preparing for Thanksgiving, then Christmas, and out in the community with social, charity, and church events. But in quiet moments, her heart would catch as a memory forced itself into her mind at random moments. Flashes of despair and anguish swept across her consciousness as she involuntarily relived scenes of Sterling's illness. They exchanged letters constantly through the end of November and into December, so she knew his recovery continued steadily and surely and that he loved being back in the classroom again. In fact, by the middle of December he already felt back to his old self, he told her, with the exception of being more tired at the end of the day than usual. He reported that he tried to make up for that by retiring earlier in the evening—following doctor's orders—and that seemed to help, for he felt renewed again each morning and able to accomplish all he needed to each day. Samantha was relieved to read this and know that not only did his health continue to improve, but that he was taking care of himself. She was doubly relieved to learn from Uncle Samuel's letters to her father and Mary's letters to herself that Aunt Phoebe was finally feeling stronger and was able to keep up with her tasks again, though she was still too thin.

Sterling also reported to her that all was arranged for their trip to Lexington for the Christmas holidays. He had the details worked out and could hardly wait to see her again.

Chapter 22

LEXINGTON

December 1902

For Sterling, his month of separation from Samantha passed rapidly and agonizingly slowly all at once. However, after a couple weeks of struggling against an enigmatic nagging at the back of his brain, despite all the arrangements being settled, he finally acknowledged to himself that he felt some trepidation about taking Samantha to his parents' home. He knew that in all probability this would not be an easy visit and expressed as much to her in his letters.

Mother is a difficult woman, as I think I've told you before, he wrote. *But she is my mother and I do wish her to meet the woman I love. That said,* he hastened to add, *if you do not feel good about going, I completely understand and will not force the issue. Your comfort and well-being are at the forefront of my mind. I do not enjoy being with Mother, myself, but am used to her ways. You, however, know nothing of women like her and a part of me wishes that you never would. On the other hand, I anticipate you and Father and Lucas hitting it off quite nicely, and I would love to show you some of my favorite places. Please advise me. I do not wish you to walk into this blindly and I want us to be united in our decision, so I defer to your feelings on the matter.*

Samantha was a little surprised by the gravity of Sterling's letter and spent a few days taking stock of her heart. She prayed to know what was right, as she felt that Sterling's desires in this were good. In the process of this introspection, she felt that things could turn out well and that if this was what she wanted, God would support her in it. She did still want to see if she could get to know and understand Mrs. Sterling. This was the woman, after all, who had given birth to Samantha's beloved, and she felt she owed her that much for the wonderful man she had raised. Surely, having produced such a good young man, she could not be all bad herself. Besides, it would only be for ten days. So she wrote Sterling back and expressed her gratitude for his concern and for consulting her, but reassured him that she wanted to proceed with their plans.

For his part, Sterling was relieved she wanted to go through with the visit, but also had a deep sense that the way might not be easy. He would need to be vigilant and keep his thumb on the pulse of everything throughout their time there, no matter how challenging that might be.

***

A couple of days before Samantha left for Lexington, Basil joined her in the kitchen for a simple evening meal. Mrs. Dolittle and Claire were off visiting family for the evening, and Samantha had thrown supper together from leftovers. Her father walked in as she set the last dish on the table, and she smiled to see him. After his first couple reclusive days back from Worthington, he had ventured out of his room more and more, taking meals with her, joining her in the library, perusing the house with a thoughtful countenance as he appraised the rooms and tried to envision a school taking over the space. Every time he walked into a room where she was, Samantha felt that same surge of quiet happiness, a relief and a joy that his progress and happiness continued—and most of all, that he wanted to maintain connection with her.

"This looks delicious," he told her, folding his long frame into the chair across from hers and placing the napkin in his lap.

"Thank you. Mrs. Dolittle always leaves us well provided for, doesn't she?" Samantha sat across from him and placed her own napkin.

"She certainly does. And having Claire here seems to make a difference for her, I think."

"Without a doubt! The shared load increases her ability to accomplish tasks she hasn't had the time or strength to do alone. I've never seen the house so clean and glowing!"

"Indeed. There is much to be said for working together." He eyed her meaningfully. "I have had to relearn that recently myself, and it has been enlightening."

Samantha laid a hand on the table, palm up. "May I say grace?" she asked. Basil nodded and placed his hand in hers while she blessed the food.

After a few minutes of eating in companionable silence, Samantha asked, "Father, may I ask you a question? It has been on my mind since Sterling's illness and it keeps nagging at me."

He nodded, looking at her as he chewed a mouthful of food.

"I am sorry if it brings up painful memories for you..." she prefaced.

He quickly shook his head in response. "It is high time I talked about such things with you. Please, go on."

"Well," she put down her fork and thought how best to word what she'd been thinking. "I know you spent quite a bit of time nursing Mother back to health, whenever weakness or illness flared, and especially after she lost...my brother."

Basil nodded and swallowed his bite of food, his eyes intent on her face.

"Now that I know what it's like to almost lose the one I love, to spend all my strength nursing and willing him back to health, I have empathy for you that I never had before. That had to have been so difficult for you, Father. Especially as it happened repeatedly."

"Yes," he answered slowly. "But I would do it again. Would love to do it again, in fact..." Some of the old sorrow crept back into his face.

"I know," she said simply, understanding at least some of what he felt. "I would do it again too. But...how did you have the strength to go through that so many times? And you knew when you married Mother that she had health problems you would need to help her with, but you were willing to make that commitment. How did you keep going when things were so difficult?"

Basil blinked at her and said simply, "I loved her."

"Yes, I know, Father. And I love Sterling, and that made it easier to forget the work and fatigue and just keep pushing forward. But...after weeks of that, when your own physical and emotional exhaustion became too much, how did you keep going then?"

Basil put down his fork as he considered her words. "Well, that is a good question. I do not know if I have the answer for you, but while your mother lived, there was always the hope that she would recover..."

Samantha nodded contemplatively. "Hope can be a strong motivator."

"While she lived, my faith in God was also much greater. Turning to Him lifted me. Though I forgot that much too quickly after she..." He paused and swallowed. "But, too,

I think God gives us strength deep inside our beings that rises up in our extremities and surprises us with its tenacity."

Samantha resumed eating while she thought on those eloquent and powerful words. "That certainly was true for Jane Eyre," she finally offered. "Have you read Charlotte Bronte's novel?"

Basil shook his head. "I seem to recall your mother reading it, but I never did. Maybe I should."

"Oh, you should, Father! It is my new favorite; I am so glad to know Mother read it too." The realization thrilled and warmed her. "The protagonist, Jane, has such a hard lot in life, beginning in childhood, and yet she never loses her sense of who she is. She retains a strong moral character and a quiet dignity in all she experiences, and insists on respect from others, regardless of their station in life compared to her own. She is truly remarkable."

Basil nodded and his gray brows drew together as he sought the recesses of his brain for something long forgotten. "I think it was Victor Hugo who called it a 'secret strength' in his book *Les Miserables*. He said something like, 'The soul aids the body and at moments uplifts it. It is the only bird that can endure a cage.'"

"'The only bird that can endure a cage,'" Samantha repeated. "Sterling wrote me those words, too. I think he discussed it with his students. That is a powerful concept. Of course," she mused, "since God made us, it all goes back to Him anyway, doesn't it?"

Her father smiled at her fondly. "Yes, I suppose it does."

"So God made us strong—stronger than we know—but He also made us to need Him. Without a connection to Him, that strength can diminish and fail; it needs constant replenishing."

Her father's eyes shone. "You sound so much like your mother," he said. "I need to get back to that strong place, myself. She would want that for me, I think." His voice was raw with sudden emotion as he made this admission.

"She would, Father. And you *are* strong. Think of all you did for me when I needed you most. And all you did for Sterling, and the Tomlinsons—and Grandmother and Aunt Phoebe! It also took a lot of strength to repeatedly ask for forgiveness from Mother's family, to recognize that you had done wrong and needed to apologize. Sometimes that is the hardest strength to have."

"How do you know all this already?" Father asked, smiling and shaking his head. "You are wise beyond your years, my daughter. You are right, of course. Maybe I am stronger than I realize. I know I feel stronger now than I have since your mother...passed."

Samantha didn't miss his pause before the last word. It was still difficult for him to talk about Lovenia, even though it had been eighteen years. But now they had just had a conversation about her and it seemed to be getting easier for him. "I am so glad you feel stronger," Samantha told him. "And I'm glad to have you in my life again. I think we help each other be strong."

"Yes," her father replied thoughtfully. "Yes, I think so too."

***

Samantha took in the new sights from the beautifully polished black sleigh[1] with its red plush interior as it pulled away from the Lexington train station, through the bustling city streets, and out into the country. She was used to seeing cutters—smaller sleighs that typically fit only two passengers—but this sleigh was the height of luxury, even including a roof and a back panel. Two pure white horses pulled them down the snowy road at a brisk trot.

After a welcoming, deferential greeting from the driver when they stepped up into the sleigh, the man turned around to face forward in the seat in front of them, pulled his cap down over his ears, and said nothing more as he directed the horses to their destination. Samantha couldn't help thinking that if this were Martin and she were home, they would be chatting all along the way about the latest news. Apparently, the Sterling estate was not run the same way.

Turning her attention to the scenery, she imagined what it would look like without the dusting of snow: green fields as far as the eye could see, broken only by neat white fencing with horses in their respective fields, and the occasional ribbon of road. It would be beautiful, she was sure. In fact, it was beautiful now, in a different way. The dark outlines of winter trees here and there gave variety to the rolling hills, and the sharp

---

1. https://parkcityhistory.org/wp-content/uploads/2012/04/ Teacher-Background -Information.pdf (p. 6 discusses sleighs)

outlines of fences, barns, and houses were softened by the light covering of snow, which gave an almost magical quality to the landscape.

But exactly seven days before Christmas, it was cold and Samantha's booted feet hadn't warmed up all day, though now the foot warmer with its hot coals was beginning to help. Despite her layers of clothing, the rest of her was chilled as well. She rubbed her mittened hands together, hoping to generate a little heat, and tried to keep her teeth from chattering.

Sterling spread a lap robe embroidered with horses over her legs, tucking it in around her and smiling. "Maybe that will warm you a bit."

She smiled back at him gratefully. "This cold has a way of seeping right through all my layers." She shivered involuntarily.

"It certainly does," he agreed. "But we'll be there soon. Just another few miles." He put an arm around her and drew her close, trying to warm them both. Samantha snuggled against him and felt content, despite her trepidation at meeting his family. They had enjoyed their time together on the train, reacquainting themselves with each other's lives in Oberlin and Worthington, and the people they had grown to love in both places. Samantha learned that Sterling had celebrated his twenty-fifth birthday with the Tomlinsons, and that he had continued visiting a few of the Lewises. All of them sent her their love. Samantha, in turn, expressed her father's greetings and desire that Sterling come visit them again very soon.

Samantha had noted with relief the returned healthy coloring in Sterling's complexion and how his frame had filled out again to the strong and virile physique she remembered. Gone was the gaunt form and hollow cheeks, and the shadows beneath his eyes had vanished. The lank droop of his hair was now again the buoyant, unruly waves she liked so much. The only lingering sign of his recent wrestle with death was a depth to his eyes that sometimes spoke of the experience more profoundly than words could articulate, as if he were in the brief throes of remembering the time when his spirit had so closely lingered near the line between this world and the next. She knew the ordeal had changed his perspective. It had changed hers also, and she hoped that she would never forget the precious nature of life.

She sat with her head on his shoulder and breathed in the cold air, feeling its bite through her teeth as the sleigh rushed them along. She would sit in the cold with Sterling any day, she realized, if it meant more time with him. It was so good to be reunited once again!

After a moment she raised her head and observed, "This great expanse of fields is quite striking. Even in winter I can see why Kentucky is perfect horse country."

"Indeed," Sterling agreed. "You should see it in high summer!"

"What is it that makes the grass grow so green and thick here, providing such perfect nourishment for the horses?"

Sterling's eyes brightened. "That is a great question! And I think you may find the answer as fascinating as I did as a schoolboy."

"Oh good," she smiled, snuggling closer into him. "Do tell."

"My hometown of Lexington sits on top of a limestone shelf," he said, sounding like the teacher he was. "Limestone contains calcium which filters into the grass—"

"Which strengthens the horses' bones!"[2] Samantha interrupted, understanding the connection immediately.

"Exactly. Have you ever heard of 'Big Lex'?"

"No, I don't think so."

"He was a champion racehorse born here in 1850. People claim that he turned blue from eating the rich Lexington bluegrass."

Samantha grinned. "That is a fascinating legend."

"For sixteen years, Big Lex was also the leading sire for famous champion offspring. In fact, the favorite horse of

General Ulysses S. Grant during the Civil War was a colt sired by Blue Lex."[3]

"I didn't know that!"

Sterling was honestly surprised, since Samantha knew so much about a vast array of topics. It felt good to present her with new information, so he kept going. "How about this question: Do you know how the town got its name?"

"That I do know," Samantha supplied. "It was named after Lexington, Massachusetts, the site where the Revolutionary War began."

---

2. https://www.visitlex.com/guides/post/lexingtons-equine-history/

3. https://equisearch.com/all-about-horses/lexingtons-symbolic-big-lex-horse-has-the-blues-thats-what-its-all-about/

"Correct." He paused, then chuckled. "All right, my quiz is over. You are an excellent student, dearest."

"Thank you! But I have a few more questions..."

They discussed other facts of local interest and then, just as Samantha was at last starting to feel a little warmer, the driver took a right turn off the main road and they traveled onto a smaller road that ran between two white rail fences. After another few minutes, the fencing ended and the vista opened up before them on both sides. Soon they crested a small rise. From this higher position, she could see a beautiful, wide expanse fronted by a large frozen pond, behind which sat the huge house with barns and paddocks beyond. Samantha thought she also detected a walled-in garden behind the house, and even a pagoda or two. The road ahead of them descended gradually, eventually curving around the pond and heading toward the house, where it swooped around the spacious drive to the wide front doors.

Samantha studied the mansion as they drew closer. It was evident that everything on the Sterling estate was meticulously maintained in top condition from the fencing to the outbuildings, but the house was the icing on the cake. It was the most beautiful building she had ever seen! It was built in the Federal style with tall white columns at the center front from ground to roof. But where most Federal style houses she had seen were box-like regardless of their size, this one spread out along both sides in graceful wings. The house itself was a very light yellow with the window shutters a complementary shade of blue so dark they looked almost black. It was stunning now in the snow, but she could picture how attractive it must also look with the green backdrop of summer grass and trees in full leaf. In that moment, she realized how neglected her family's mansion looked in comparison. She had never thought her spacious house could look small, but as she looked at the sprawling Sterling estate, the Jennings mansion seemed quite conservative.

She must have inhaled more sharply than she meant to because Sterling glanced at her questioningly.

"How does your mother maintain a house this size?" she asked in wonder.

Sterling chuckled dryly. "She employs many servants and keeps them on a tight schedule. Mostly she oversees others, preferring not to do any of the actual work if she can avoid it." His mouth quirked in an ironic smile.

"It's so beautiful!" Samantha couldn't stop looking, trying to soak in the regal vertical lines and the elegant horizontal planes, which gave the whole place a look of harmony and confident prosperity. After a moment, they drew close enough that she could no longer see the entire house as they curved around the long drive.

"Yes. Mother is nothing if not vigilant about keeping up appearances. She has the outside repainted regularly every couple of years, and the inside is spotless. Nothing makes her happier than hosting a large social event and receiving praise for her beautiful estate."

"Oh, Sterling, the 'Jennings' mansion' must seem like such a farce to you, in comparison to the real mansion you grew up in!" For the first time, Samantha felt embarrassed by her small-town perception.

Sterling's dark brows bunched together in sincere thought. "No," he said honestly. "I don't like to make such comparisons because there are so many factors to consider. It is a different world in Oberlin and I like it. Your mansion feels comfortable and lived in. This mansion is beautiful, yes, but it feels more like a museum one must tiptoe through, being careful not to touch anything without white gloves."

"Form versus function?" Samantha offered faintly, feeling only slightly reassured.

Sterling nodded decisively. "Precisely. I could never imagine this house being turned into a school or serving any other productive purpose for the community, other than as a social gathering place. But your father's house has very usable, sensible space that could easily be transformed into a school. Personally, I would rather have function over form any day."

"Unless it were possible to have both," Samantha mused, her mind already whirling with possibilities of improving the appearance of the house she had grown up in.

They were pulling up near the front door, and Sterling momentarily tightened his grasp around her shoulders. "Are you ready for this?" he asked. "I feel to warn you—again—that my mother is not an easy woman to understand, to get along with, or to please."

Samantha glanced at the driver to see what he thought of all this talk of his employer, but he remained facing forward and gave no indication of having heard.

"Although, ready or not, I suppose at this point it is too late to change your mind," Sterling quipped, the wry smile back.

Samantha willed the butterflies in her stomach to still and took a deep breath to fortify herself. "And I remain firm in my willingness to try. We decided this must be done, that it is important for me to meet your family."

Sterling nodded in agreement and removed his arm from around her as they pulled to a stop in front of the doors. "Yes, we did decide that. I guess I am a bit nervous."

Samantha swallowed a lump of apprehension. "Then imagine my nervousness…"

"I will be right here with you," he said, thinking maybe he shouldn't have mentioned his mother again. "Thank you for being willing to come, to try Christmas in Lexington for me."

"Of course." The brightness of her smile belied her trepidation.

Sterling loved her for her courage. He kissed her lightly, pressed his forehead to hers, eyes closed for a moment, then smiled at her warmly as she refolded the lap robe.

He helped her down and reached inside for their luggage, which he placed on the skiff of snow at their feet. Just then, the front door of the mansion opened and an elderly man with gray hair and equally gray trousers, black suit coat, and a black tie emerged and hurried toward them.

"Master Lee," he said with barely disguised warmth. The two men shook hands vigorously.

Samantha hadn't heard Sterling's given name used for so long, the sound of it struck her as odd.

"It is so good to have you home. We knew you were coming, but not what time you might arrive." The servant's voice was deep and authoritative, but held an obvious warmth for his young master. His eyelids, loose and wrinkled, puckered over kind eyes.

"Yes, Wilson. I was unsure myself until departure. Allow me to introduce Samantha Jennings from Oberlin, Ohio." Sterling placed a gentle hand on her back. Wilson's eyebrows began to rise, but he quickly stopped their ascent and bowed to her.

She curtsied, blushing a little, and the butler's hooded eyes seemed to warm further.

"Please announce us to my parents," Sterling instructed. "We will be in the front parlor."

Samantha observed Sterling's role with this senior male servant with interest. It was a side of Sterling she had not seen before, but he responded automatically and naturally, as if he had been doing it all his life. Indeed he had, she realized. For her part, she was not sure how to act toward servants. After all, Mrs. Dolittle, Claire, and Martin were more like members of the family.

They stepped inside the spacious entryway and Samantha caught her breath again. The polished white marble floor shone with a perfect luster from one end of the room to the other, all the way to a great double staircase that curved in graceful parallel lines to join at the upper floor. The black ornate balustrade contrasted beautifully against the white marble of the stairs, and its curlicue design complemented the curve of the stairs themselves, continuing all around the upper landing in a great circle. Suspended from the center of this circle was an exquisite chandelier at least as wide and tall as Sterling's height. Samantha was speechless and could only stare in awe for a few moments. Conscious that her mouth was open, she closed it quickly and took a deep, fortifying breath. She had known in theory of the affluence of the Sterling family, but now in these first few minutes she was utterly overwhelmed by the visual evidence of it.

Sterling set their luggage beside the large mat in front of the door and Samantha wiped her feet thoroughly. She did not want to leave a wet trail of footprints across the perfect floor as her first impression to the Sterling family! Sterling did the same and a maid took their coats, hats, scarves, and mittens and whisked them away. He guided Samantha across the floor to a smaller, carpeted room, leaving their luggage behind, and she had the sense hers would reappear in her assigned room later. Seeing a warm fire crackling cheerfully in the hearth, Sterling led her across the plush carpeting and fashionable furnishings to stand before it.

"A fire, at last," she said gratefully, standing as close to it as she dared. She rubbed her hands together and held them up to the warmth at intervals, Sterling doing the same, and a companionable silence settled over them. After a day of travel, they had finally arrived.

Chapter 23

DIFFICULT EXPECTATIONS

DECEMBER 1902

A few minutes later, Mrs. Sterling swept into the room, followed by her husband and a young man. Sterling and Samantha turned to greet them and while Sterling made introductions all around, Samantha observed each member of the family to gauge how this stay with them might go.

Cordelia Sterling was a tall woman for her generation, in fact the same height as her husband, and her figure was shapely with generous curves. Her waist had thickened now in later years, but she was still very beautiful with bright, shrewd, dark-lashed brown eyes, and elegant dark brows, full lips, and a creamy complexion with only a hint of fine lines around her mouth. As a young woman, she must have been the perfect example of a Gibson Girl.[1] Her abundant white hair glistened, done up expertly in a fashionable pompadour, and her dress was the very height of style—in fact, the gathers, embroidery, and embellishments on her day dress were far fancier than any evening gown Samantha owned. At this realization, Samantha's insides shrank a bit. How would she fit into this society at all, if she couldn't even look the part, much less feel it?

As Samantha continued to discreetly study Sterling's mother, she immediately recognized that he had inherited his beauty from her. She also noted during their introduction

---

1. https://en.wikipedia.org/wiki/Gibson_Girl

that there was a tightening of the woman's mouth and a critical glint to the eye when she looked upon her. Samantha hoped she had imagined it, but was afraid she had not.

James Sterling was of below-average height for a man, and quite handsome with a wiry build. He walked with a slight rolling gait that Samantha decided must have more to do with a life of constantly riding horses than with rheumatism. His thinning hair was gray like his mustache, and his eyes were blue above a straight nose. As she was introduced to him, she noted the kindness in those blue eyes when he looked at her, and the way his mustache turned up when he smiled. She instantly felt a little more at ease.

The other man was Sterling's younger brother, Lucas, and the two young men embraced with much back-slapping and apparent gladness. Samantha knew they had not seen each other for at least two years, as last year when Sterling had come home for Christmas, Lucas had been away on business. Samantha observed that Lucas was more reserved than Sterling. He seemed good-natured and looked upon Samantha with evident curiosity, but held his feelings in check and she could read very little else in his manner. He was also a few inches shorter than Sterling, though still taller than his parents, and of a more wiry build. His brown hair was a shade or two lighter than Sterling's, and completely straight. His blue eyes and straight nose immediately identified him as his father's son, but his chin was more rounded, like his mother's. Lucas didn't look much like Sterling, she decided, though they did look related.

Samantha took in all these observations in a few moments of quiet fascination. Family resemblances interested her now more than they ever had, after seeing herself in her mother's portrait a few months before.

Tea was brought in and Samantha realized how hungry she was after the long day of travel. Sterling guided her to a sofa near the tea tray and was about to sit beside her when his mother asked, "Lee, dear, won't you sit here beside me? I have a few questions for you." He complied and crossed the room to sit beside her, balancing a small plate on his knee while he ate, casting apologetic glances Samantha's way every few minutes.

Samantha tried not to mind and willed herself to relax as she ate from her own plate, attempting small talk with Mr. Sterling and Lucas. Neither was very talkative and once she had exhausted her meager questions for them, her naturally reserved nature took over and an awkward silence fell over them. She continued eating the food in small bites, in order to keep herself busy, but she found that her appetite was waning. After a moment, she tried once more. "Mr. Sterling, is there still quite a bit of work to do in the stables, even in winter?"

"Yes," he responded, focusing his gaze on his food. "On a horse farm this size, there is always plenty to keep one busy."

She nodded. "But you have a winter rest from the hemp side of the business?"

"From the growing and rope-making, yes." He swallowed a bite and glanced up at her. "There is always planning to do. Currently, Lucas is working on a projection for next year's crops. Best ways to increase production over last year and all that." Samantha sensed that James was as economizing in his words as in his business practices. She could certainly respect a man who was careful with his finances, particularly when he had more and to spare. She found herself suddenly wondering how her father and this man might get along. It seemed they had a few things in common.

"I see," she said. "It does sound like enough work to keep you both busy!"

"It is," Lucas concurred.

"Do you enjoy it?" she asked, turning her attention to Sterling's younger brother in her desire to keep the conversation going.

"I do," Lucas said simply, while his father nodded.

"In that sense—in your love for your work—you and Sterling are very similar," she mused, looking over at her beloved, who was in apparent deep conversation with his mother on the other side of the room. "He enjoys teaching and is always thinking of ways to teach more effectively and work more efficiently. He has the need to constantly be doing something productive." She turned back to the men nearest her and offered, "You seem to be that way too: never idle."

Lucas seemed a little surprised by such an astute observation made so shortly after their acquaintance. "That is true," he agreed. And then, apparently to redirect the topic, he said, "Sterling says you met in Oberlin, Ohio...?"

Samantha patted her mouth with her napkin before answering, relieved that the conversation continued to flow for the time being. "Yes. He was my writing teacher for a short time. I owe him much for all that he taught me." Unbidden, the memory of their time writing together at the old warped table in the school yard and their lively discussions during pleasant walks near the fields filled her inner sight. Those were such happy, bright, discovering times. She was grateful to have those memories to remind her of how she and Sterling had started out.

James cleared his throat quietly and offered, "Surely your debt does not necessitate such a visit...?" He indicated the room with a sweep of the hand. His eyebrows raised in a question and Samantha felt a little panicky. What was he really saying? But then she saw the twinkle in his eyes and a lopsided lift to his mustache. He was teasing her!

Her panic instantly subsided and she laughed softly. "No. I came because Sterling wanted me to meet his family and see where he grew up. Our roles are much different now, after... spending more time together." She paused, not sure how much to say, but feeling this much might be sufficient.

"And we are glad you came," Lucas said suddenly, then reddened slightly. "He has never brought a young woman home before," he hurried to explain, "so I knew you must be different from other girls he's courted." He smiled at her briefly, then dug back into the remaining food on his plate in an apparent attempt to distract himself.

Samantha returned her attention to her own plate, murmuring a thank you because she didn't know what more to say either.

After their small meal, Samantha was shown to the room that would be hers. As she turned to follow the maid upstairs, Sterling stopped her with a touch of his hand and an encouraging smile. "I'll see you at dinner?" he asked.

She nodded, returning his smile, then noticed his mother's expression.

"We always dress for dinner," Mrs. Sterling stated firmly, in a tone that tolerated no nonsense. "I trust you have something appropriate." As she looked Samantha over, her expression showed how highly she doubted it, though her voice sounded pleasant enough. The dichotomy was disorienting.

Samantha followed the maid out of the room without a word, not noticing Sterling's frown, and made her way up the great staircase to the second floor. At the landing, they turned left and she counted rooms as they walked past them. Every room was open to view, clean and bright, each one decorated distinctly from the others, as if many people with distinct personalities and preferences lived here and maintained them personally. Such a contrast to the dark and dusty Jennings' mansion! She swallowed.

The maid turned in at the fifth door on the right and Samantha stepped inside. Like all the others, it was a beautiful room, tastefully organized and artfully decorated, this one in creams and pinks, the floor covered by a carpet of dark green with intricate pink and white flowers spiraling across it. Unconsciously, Samantha clasped her hands together and stood there taking it all in with pleasure. She appreciated that even though Sterling's mother clearly did not think much of her yet, she had still given her a pleasing room where she could be comfortable.

"Do you like it, Miss?" the perceptive young maid asked her, smiling.

"I do, indeed," Samantha responded. "I have never slept in a room like this before!" She turned in a slow circle and her gaze traveled around the room, taking in the broad fireplace on one wall with a plush pink armchair and writing desk before it, the floor-to-ceiling window on the outside wall with a glazed, flower-painted porcelain pitcher on a washstand in front of it, and the large pink canopied bed across the room. As she had expected, there near the bed sat her luggage.

"The bed's real comfortable," the maid offered. Then in a whisper behind her hand, "I tried it myself once, when I was tidying the room. But don't tell Mistress."

Samantha laughed, startled at her openness. "It is all very pleasant. Thank you. What is your name? I suppose you know I am Samantha Jennings."

The maid nodded. "I'm Hannah, Miss." She bobbed a little curtsy. "Pleased to make your acquaintance. When Mistress told us you were coming with Master Lee, I imagined quite a different lady." She cocked her head slightly and appraised Samantha for a moment. "You brought no lady's maid..." Her gaze was non-judgmental and honest, which took away any sting from the implication of her words. Samantha found herself liking the girl already. She couldn't be older than fifteen, with brown hair pulled back in a braid beneath her maid's cap. Her cheeks were rosy and her blue eyes bright.

"No, I am afraid I wouldn't know what to do with a lady's maid. I have never had one, you see." Samantha felt a little chagrined, in spite of herself.

"That's all right. We will figure things out. I already like you lots better than who I imagined."

Samantha's eyebrows rose in surprise at the girl's continued frankness. "Well, thank you. I'm glad I have made a favorable impression. Though I am not certain Mrs. Sterling would agree."

Hannah made a face and lowered her voice, speaking almost in a whisper as she leaned forward confidentially. "She is hard to please, and don't I know it! I've been afraid of being sacked half a dozen times in only a year. But those of us who can harden ourselves to her moods can learn to live with things." She straightened up and spoke a little louder. "The pay is good and helps out my family, so I keep 'sticking it out,' as my mother says." She put a hand to her mouth and apologized. "I'm sorry, I've probably said way more than

I should. My mouth does run on so. One of those things Mistress disapproves of." She grimaced and shrugged. "You be needing anything, Miss, before I go?"

"No, I don't think so," Samantha replied, smiling. She loved the cadence of Hannah's speech and her candid manner. Then, remembering Mrs. Sterling's words when they parted, she sobered and reconsidered. "Actually, would you mind telling me how Mrs. Sterling expects me to dress for dinner? I don't have anything fancy."

"Silk or velvet—with lace—is always a safe choice,"[2] Hannah responded, matter-of-factly.

"But I have neither!" Samantha exclaimed, her heart sinking. "Whatever shall I wear?"

Hannah thought a moment. "Let's see what you brought with you," she offered practically, turning to Samantha's suitcase and helping her heft it onto the bed.

Samantha opened it and began pulling out the contents while Hannah walked to the wardrobe standing against one wall, opened the heavy door, and pulled out a hanger.

Soon they stood in front of the wardrobe looking at Samantha's few dresses hanging inside. "These are of fine quality and cut," the maid told her. "You need not be ashamed of your clothing, Miss. To be sure, they are of a simpler design than the Mistress prefers. But all of them are serviceable day dresses."

Samantha fingered a dark purple gown. "In Oberlin this is appropriate for evening wear, and it is the best I have."

"It will do for tonight," Hannah decided. "And tomorrow we'll see what we can do about fashioning a couple of evening gowns that will meet Mistress' standard." At Samantha's protest, Hannah said, "I am sure she will insist on it, once she knows you don't have what she thinks necessary. Now don't fret yourself, Miss! It will be no trouble."

"I am sure it will be trouble for someone! You all have plenty to do already, without me causing more work for you."

Hannah patted her hand. "Don't you worry, we will work it out. Don't you want to meet with Mrs. Sterling's approval—and impress Master Lee into the bargain? Well," she giggled, "I am sure you already do that without dressing fancy, seeing as he thinks so much

---

2. https://etiquipedia.blogspot.com/2013/10/the-etiquette-of-gilded-age-dinner-and.html

of you as to bring you home. But he will be dressed elegantly himself…" She trailed off and looked at Samantha meaningfully.

"All right," Samantha conceded with a sigh. "You are right." She smiled. "Thank you, Hannah. I appreciate your help. This is all a bit intimidating for me."

Hannah nodded in understanding. "You will catch on. And I am happy to give advice anytime. My mother says I do that a little too well." She grinned and a little dimple peeked around the right side of her mouth.

Samantha smiled back. "I am sure it will be needed, in my case."

"Now, before I leave, may I draw you a bath, Miss?"

"Oh, yes, that would be wonderful!" Besides feeling fatigued from traveling all day, Samantha suddenly realized how nice it would be to wash off the travel dirt and work out the aches in her muscles—not to mention finish warming her cold toes!

The maid nodded decisively. "I will have a tub ready for you in about half an hour, if the water heats as fast as it usually does."

And, true to Hannah's word, Samantha soon had a metal tub full of steaming water waiting for her behind a paper screen in one corner of the large room, a towel, washcloth, soap, and shampoo set neatly on a nearby washstand.

***

When Samantha descended the stairs late in the evening, holding up the hem of her deep purple gown, she felt thoroughly clean, warm, and ready for the evening, eager to be with Sterling again. But when she reached the main floor, no one was there to greet her and she had no idea where to go. She stood there for a few minutes in the spacious, ornate, sterile hall, waiting for a servant to happen by, feeling more awkward by the moment. To her relief, she soon heard footsteps on the stairs and turned to see who it was. Sterling stepped down quickly, smoothing hands along his vest and smiling at her as he descended. Her heart flipped in her chest as she noted his perfectly pressed dark suit, which flawlessly fit his broad shoulders. The matching dark pants hugged his lean hips and angled down to meet shiny black shoes. The vest beneath the suit was white, as was his bowtie. She had never seen him in such formal attire, and the effect made her breathless. His dark hair was still damp from a bath and combed back neatly, and his face was newly shaved. As he drew near, she could smell his pleasant signature scent of leather and spice. She knew the wave above his forehead, once dry, would spring back in its usual disheveled way, and she was glad of it.

Sterling reached her and took her hand. She clasped it gratefully and started breathing again.

"You look wonderful!" he said quietly. "How are you? Is the staff taking care of you?"

"Yes, they are. Hannah has been most helpful."

"Good. Please tell me if that changes or if you need anything."

Samantha hesitated, unsure if she should mention the short conversation she had had with the girl when she'd brought in the bath essentials.

"What is it?" Sterling asked, noting at once the slight pucker between her brows.

"Well, it's just…" Samantha's gaze dropped to the smooth, polished floor. "She seemed surprised I didn't bring a lady's maid with me. But I have never… I don't…" She gestured with the hand not holding Sterling's and looked up at him. "I have always been independent—and our servants are not the same class as yours anyway. I do not quite know how to respond to the servants here. As far as a lady's maid, Hannah says she can help me, but I know she already has many responsibilities. I accepted her help, though I do not feel I need it, as she seemed to think it necessary. But what do you think I should do?" She searched his face for confirmation that she had done the right thing, and found it as he smiled gently down at her.

Softly, he traced the side of her face with one thumb and said softly, "My independent, yet sensitive and considerate Samantha. I appreciate that your clothing is not so elaborate that you have need of a lady's maid." He dropped his hand and pulled back a step, looking at her seriously. "But yes, you did the right thing. Hannah is the one most qualified to help you in this household at the moment, and I am sure Mother will expect your level of dress and coiffure to be different from what you are used to. I hope you know that sort of thing means nothing to me, but here it is Mother's standard we all adhere to, to keep the peace…"

His apologetic tone soothed Samantha's worried heart and she nodded. "Yes, I see. Already I feel so keenly the difference between your world and mine. I don't belong, but I will try to meet it with grace, the best I can."

"You are already doing wonderfully well," he assured her.

Standing there next to him, she felt better about everything and was grateful for his stabilizing and calming presence. So far, it seemed things would be all right after all in this posh, high society place.

"Shall we?" he asked, offering his arm.

Samantha placed her gloved hand in the crook of his elbow and he led the way to the dining room, where Mr. and Mrs. Sterling were already seated. Sterling offered her the chair to his left and when she raised her eyes to glance around the beautifully set table before she sat, she saw Mrs. Sterling's gaze travel the length of her in disapproval, mouth pursed as if she tasted something unpleasant. Quickly, Samantha looked away and busied herself sitting, while Sterling pushed in her chair. A moment later, she glanced right into the face of Mr. Sterling, whose eyes were crinkled at the corners to match his upturned mustache. She appreciated his welcome reception, in contrast to his wife's apparent distaste.

Lucas arrived, a little out of breath, as if he had run from the other side of the house. Now, with Mr. Sterling at the head, Cordelia to his right, and Lucas beside her, with Samantha and Sterling on the opposite side of the table, their party was complete and the table stretched on beyond them, empty. Samantha had never seen a table so long, nor a dining room so large. Soon the servants were serving the food and Samantha was relieved for something to do with her hands other than twist the napkin in her lap. Her stomach grumbled, their earlier light tea only a memory. The portions were small but there were several courses, all of them delicious: creamed soup, roast beef, potatoes, beets, rolls and cheese. They just kept coming until Samantha could not hold another bite.

Mr. Sterling and Lucas discussed current horse farming concerns, and Sterling's mother told him specifics about the large Christmas ball she would host two days before Christmas. Samantha ate as unobtrusively as possible, saying little. Partway through the meal, Sterling tried to steer the conversation to better include Samantha, and mentioned her desire to turn the Jennings mansion into a school for children. Cordelia seemed uninterested in the school but perked up at the mention of a mansion.

"Who is your father?" she asked, her eyes sharp. "Anyone I should know?"

"He was a history professor who taught at The Ohio State University and then Oberlin College. He bought the mansion when he inherited his brother's money, before I was born."

"I see. New wealth, then." Her mouth turned down a bit.

"Yes." Samantha nodded. One thing could be said for Mrs. Sterling: At the moment she was not trying to hide how she felt beneath a facade of manners, so Samantha knew by her derisive expression and the tone of voice exactly how she felt about the Jennings' status.

"And your mother?" Mrs. Sterling's lips were pursed.

"She...she died when I was born." Samantha answered, a little unsteadily. She felt as if she were being interrogated and evaluated all at once. And already she was not measuring up. "Like my father, she was born and raised in Worthington and moved to Oberlin a few years after they married."

"I see," Mrs. Sterling said, as if the topic already bored her. But then half-heartedly offered, "I think I have heard of Oberlin College. I believe they were the first college in the country to accept Black students. And now—of all things—they even give bachelor's degrees to women, I am told.[3] Both ridiculous notions, in my opinion," she continued, without waiting for Samantha's response.

Sterling glanced at Samantha apologetically and she knew she would have to be patient with this woman's bigoted and unprogressive views.

"We all have our place in society," Sterling's mother continued, warming to her subject. "That is the natural order of things. We should be content with our lot in life and stay in our places." She said this decisively, raising a hand to emphasize her point. "The poor have our pity, of course, but it is not our fault we were born at the top, with a good pedigree." She pointed at Sterling, as if calling him out, "And we need not feel guilty for it." She shook her head. "I never understood the need for educating Blacks,[4] or servants, or common workers. It does not do them any favors and only makes them discontent. And what need has a woman for a college degree? After all, she can manage home affairs without a 'high and mighty' college education—as I have done for more than twenty years."

---

3. https://www.oberlin.edu/about-oberlin/oberlin-history

4. This is currently considered the correct way to write this term, according to the Chicago Manual of Style.

Social Darwinism![5] thought Samantha incredulously. *Cordelia Sterling actually believes in Social Darwinism!* She had read about the philosophy a few times. It had become very popular several years before and was, for obvious reasons, particularly preferred by the wealthy and elite to justify their position and negate the need for helping the unfortunate. Samantha felt sick inside to realize that this woman, the mother of her beloved Sterling, would honestly believe such an idea.

Sterling did not miss Samantha's stricken expression as she glanced at him, and knew she was near panic. He cleared his throat and set down his fork, wondering what he could say to ease the atmosphere. He looked across the table at his mother and, with as much lightness as he could muster, said, "Education is a blessing to everyone, Mother, regardless of their race or role in society." Sterling wished they did not have to have this conversation again. He knew from experience that it would go nowhere and would only succeed in frustrating him almost beyond endurance.

Samantha thought about Mrs. Dolittle, Claire, and her other Black friends in Oberlin. All were very capable, intelligent people who did not deserve to be relegated to the 'common workers' category or denied opportunities for education or anything else that would impede their success. Growing up in a progressive little town where it was normal to believe that anyone could and should receive an education, the contrast now of this woman's ideas startled her.

With her characteristically impressive memory, Samantha also remembered something Charlotte Bronte had written in *Jane Eyre* that she agreed with wholeheartedly: "Prejudices, it is well known, are most difficult to eradicate from the heart whose soil has never been loosened or fertilized by education: they grow there, firm as weeds among stones." That certainly seemed to be true here.

Sterling thought of his early conversations with Samantha about women's rights and recognition, feminism and fulfillment, and tried not to seethe.

"Oh, well, you would say that," Cordelia quipped airily, "seeing as you are a teacher." Samantha sensed that if his mother could have reached Sterling across the table, she would have patted his hand condescendingly. "Teachers and their call to educate the masses..." She made a sound nearly like a scoff. "It's admirable, I'm sure, but not practical."

5. https://www.history.com/topics/early-20th-century-us/social-darwinism

Sterling's mouth tightened, and Samantha could tell he did not care one bit for his mother's view on the matter. She also recognized this was not a new argument, and one he was probably tired of discussing. As she glanced at Lucas and James Sterling, she saw further confirmation of the correctness of this assumption. They both looked at their plates uncomfortably, moving their food around with their forks. What could she say to defuse the situation, she wondered.

"This food is delicious," she offered, the turn of topic sounding awkward even to her ears. "Thank you so much. It was a long, cold trip today and a warm meal is just what we needed." She looked at Sterling for affirmation.

"It certainly is," he jumped in quickly. "Travel food is never as satisfying as warm food at home."

James and Lucas chimed in, then, to add their approval of the meal, and Lucas asked his mother a question about her plans for the upcoming party.

Samantha willed her pulse to slow and forced herself to take another bite of roll, for something to do. She felt Sterling's foot brush against hers and remain there, as if to reassure her of his presence and support. She looked at him gratefully and gave him a fleeting smile. She had the feeling this was only the beginning of uncomfortable dealings with Cordelia, and she prayed that God would strengthen her through them. She would need it!

Chapter 24

THE LIBRARY

The next morning, Samantha slept later than intended, but awoke feeling that she had slept a few hours at last. It had taken her a long while to fall asleep, the unfamiliar bed and surroundings combining with her inability to turn off the repetition of their dinner conversation in her mind, complete with Cordelia's disdainful expression and condescending comments that had seemed to extend to her personally. Samantha did not wish to take offense whether or not offense was intended, and tried to dismiss it from her thoughts. *I knew the woman would be difficult, so last night was really no surprise, right?*

She turned her face to the daylight spilling from behind the white lace curtained window. Time would tell if there would be true sunshine or not. It was very cold in the room and she was glad for the warm quilts and blankets piled on the bed. Not wanting to brave the cold quite yet, she looked around at the beautifully wallpapered and carpeted room, noting not a single book, though there was room for several bookshelves.

A light knock sounded at the door and she started. Sitting up, she pulled the covers up with her, then called, "Enter."

A young girl in a chambermaid's[1] cap peeked her head around the door and gave a quick curtsy. "May I light you a fire, Miss? I'm sure it's awful cold in here."

---

1. https://www.nps.gov/articles/000/household-management-at-hyde-park.htm

"Oh, yes, thank you!" Samantha responded. "I appreciate that. It *is* very cold." She was so used to starting her own fires each morning throughout the winter that she had not thought to realize there would be a servant for that here. But of course there was. "What is your name?" she asked.

The girl stepped inside and closed the door behind her. "Tabitha," she answered shyly. "And you are Miss Jennings."

"I am," Samantha replied. "But at home, we don't stand on formalities and our servants call us by our first names."

Tabitha's eyes widened. "Oh, Mistress wouldn't like that one bit, Miss." She hesitated and her expression softened as she offered, "Though I would like to." She advanced across the room, holding the handle of a bucket of supplies in one hand and an envelope in the other. Reaching the bed, she held out the envelope. "This is for you, Miss."

"Thank you," Samantha said in surprise, taking it. She instantly recognized the neat, angular script and tore it open.

Dearest Samantha, it read, *my father and Lucas are eager to show me their newest horses this morning, so I am breakfasting quickly in my room and heading out. I hope you slept comfortably and are well. The maids can bring breakfast to your room, if you desire. Mother always sleeps late, so breakfast is a casual and individual affair, which is a nice reprieve.*

I would like to show you the library when I return in an hour or two, if you are willing. It is not as wonderfully intriguing as your father's, but it has great value to me and has always been my pet project, so I want to introduce you to each other.

Samantha smiled at that. She understood the sentiment exactly!

I want to see you now. This house is too big.

Lovingly yours,

Sterling

Still smiling, Samantha shivered and placed the letter back inside the envelope, then rubbed her hands along her arms to warm them. Though her arms and hands were cold, Sterling's letter had warmed her insides and helped her feel more confident, somehow.

The maid worked quickly and efficiently at the fireplace and soon had a cheery fire crackling in the grate.

"Thank you, Tabitha," Samantha said gratefully. "That will do nicely."

Tabitha stood and bobbed another curtsy, then offered to bring her a breakfast tray. When it arrived a short time later, Samantha was deep into her daily Bible study, still under the covers, and the room was slowly warming. The eggs, bacon, and potatoes were delicious and filling. She felt thankful for this time of quiet solitude and the grounding she felt as she read the verses that were now so dear to her.

This time, as she read in Mark Chapter Two about the man with palsy and his friends who dismantled a roof to lower him bodily into the room where Jesus was, she was touched by the determination and love of the friends. And she noted how Jesus immediately recognized their faith as they did this. He was not upset that they had made a hole in the roof or interrupted his sermon; instead, he tenderly reached out and healed the man on the spot—both physically and spiritually. She wanted to be like that, she decided: to see people's true intentions, to understand their hearts, and to love them as Jesus would. She would certainly like to understand Cordelia Sterling better! Smiling ironically to herself as she pictured the woman's dour expression, she had the feeling these next few days would bring many opportunities to put that desire into action.

***

Dressed for the day in the now tolerably warm room, Samantha sat at the intricately carved vanity, brushing her waist-length hair and wondering about the library Sterling wanted to show her. A knock sounded at the door and Hannah entered at her call, followed by two more servants. One of them carried a bristling pincushion and a measuring tape, and the other a few heavy dresses, which she quickly set down on the bed.

Samantha stood in surprise. They looked like they meant business!

Hannah looked her squarely in the eyes and smiled brightly, the dimple at the corner of her mouth winking prettily. "You need evening gowns," she stated simply. "I am learning to be a seamstress and need the practice, especially with alterations. So Mrs. Sterling has authorized her lady's maid[2] to help me." She gestured at the older woman, whom Samantha judged to be in her mid-thirties. She had curly brown hair caught up in a tight bun and wore a plain gray dress with black and white piping. She was a plain woman and her expression very serious, but she had nice brown eyes, Samantha decided.

---

2. https://hair-and-makeup-artist.com/ladys-maid/

"Miss Moore, this is Miss Jennings—Miss Jennings, Miss Moore," Hannah introduced them. Miss Moore inclined her head and Samantha did likewise. Then the women set to work. The dresses were apparently castoffs from Cordelia herself, and Miss Moore made quick work of helping Samantha into and out of them, measuring her, pinning, and taking notes. A few times she clicked her tongue and shook her head as the rich folds of the dark evening gowns dwarfed Samantha's slender frame. Samantha had no idea how they were going to make these ill-fitting dresses look suitable on her, but she fervently hoped they could! She had never touched such sumptuous clothing, much less worn it!

When the fitting was complete and Samantha was once again dressed in her own clothing, the other two women left, taking the extra dresses with them, and Hannah stayed to help Samantha with her hair. Samantha would have preferred to do it on her own, but acquiesced when Hannah insisted in her practical way that if she was going to style Samantha's hair for social events over the next few days, she might as well practice now.

Despite the maid's young age, she was very capable. Samantha was impressed by how quickly Hannah determined what styles would look best with her facial structure and hair texture. Hannah finished by shaping Samantha's hair into a loose pompadour, as was so much in fashion. Samantha was unsure it would stay in place, since she was used to pinning or braiding her hair tighter, but agreed to try it for the day. She did like how the shorter locks that fell around her face and neck curled so readily, complimenting the swirling mass of hair above. And she was surprised at how much the hairstyle softened the angles of her face and somehow brought more attention to her eyes.

"Thank you, Hannah," she said, patting her puffed up hair experimentally. "You really have a knack for this, I think." She looked up at the girl in the mirror behind her. "Someday you will make a wonderful lady's maid!"

"You really think so, Miss?" Hannah asked, gratified. At Samantha's affirmative nod, she beamed and said, "Thank you for saying so. I make a muddle of so many things, it's good to know there's something I can do well."

"I also want to thank you for arranging the dress fitting, and for the dresses themselves. You made quick work of all that, Hannah, which takes organization and prioritization."

"Such big words, Miss!" Hannah giggled, suddenly bashful but delighted. "I'm glad I could do that for you. Mrs. Sterling wants you outfitted properly, which helped my case. I hope you don't mind wearing her old gowns—" she cupped a hand around her mouth and whispered confidentially, "though they are anything but old, truth be told." Samantha assumed that meant the woman's wardrobe was extensive and the age of the dresses in it were completely relative. "Without time to order fabric and create brand new gowns, this will be the fastest way to do it," Hannah finished explaining.

"Oh, I don't mind at all," Samantha replied honestly. "I have no idea in the world how you will make them fit me properly, but I am sure they will be the most beautiful gowns I have ever worn and more than adequate for the occasions. In fact," she confided, "in spite of myself, I feel some excitement about seeing the alterations when they are finished. I do hope it will not be too much work for all of you!"

"Like I said before, don't worry about us," Hannah laughed. "This will be a nice change from our usual duties. It's not often I get to help create something new."

***

A short time later, after she had received instructions on how to find the library, Samantha walked carefully through the broad, red carpeted hallways, hoping she was going the right direction. She noted beautifully painted portraits on the walls and stopped occasionally to look up at one in contemplation, trying to guess Sterling's relation to the person pictured. In a few of the paintings, slaves were shown in the background. She knew some of Sterling's ancestors had had slaves before the Civil War, which he viewed as a shameful part of his family history. She kept walking and soon saw the double doors that she assumed led into the library. One door was open and she was about to step through when she heard Cordelia's raised voice from within. Something about its tone gave her pause. Quickly, she moved to one side and pressed herself against the wall, scanning the hallway and wondering if she should head back the way she had come.

"I am sure I don't know what you see in her, Lee. Such a plain, common girl—nothing like the young women of Lexington society that you have always known. She is *so* far beneath you I don't know how you ever even took note of her. There is certainly nothing striking about her. Why," she added derisively, "she doesn't even own appropriate evening wear—to say nothing of the fact that she has no lady's maid!"

Samantha's heart dropped. Apparently, her efforts so far had fallen very short of the good impression she had hoped to make.

"Mother," Sterling said tightly, his voice quieter and more controlled than his mother's, but still obviously upset. "I don't expect you to fully understand. But I love her. And I would appreciate it if you would give her the chance that she is giving you. You are not making things easy for her—or for me."

Cordelia gave what sounded like a harumph.

"I hoped that after being absent for a year I could come home for Christmas, bringing the woman I love, and find acceptance and tolerance for the short time we will be here. It really won't be long and we will take our leave—perhaps for another few years," he said drily. "All I ask is that you be civil and tolerant. I am the one who invited Samantha here to see where I came from—including my family. She knew she might not fit in, but she agreed to come for me—because she is good and brave and patient. Please don't make things any more difficult than they already are."

Samantha's heart pounded and she stayed where she was, acutely uncomfortable, wondering what would happen next and if she should run.

"Me? Difficult!" Cordelia scoffed. "I have done nothing but bend over backwards for you and your common girl. I gave her the best room, detailed the best menus during your stay, and even offered a few of my old gowns for alteration. I have spared no expense—"

"Yes, Mother," Sterling interrupted placatingly. "You have done all that and we are grate—"

"Though I have my doubts as to whether or not even our skilled maids can remake them to fit such a scrawny frame." Even from the hallway, Samantha could hear her cluck of consternation. "She is certainly no Gibson Girl, is she?"

"Mother..." Sterling spoke quietly but there was an edge of warning to his voice. "You will speak respectfully of her, regardless of your personal views. I love her the way she is and ask that you remember that, if you remember nothing else."

After a long, tense silence, Cordelia finally offered a tight, "Very well."

Suddenly Samantha heard swishing skirts headed toward her across the library carpet and she ducked behind the open door to hide in the shadows, hoping she could not be seen from that vantage point. She had not meant to eavesdrop! Indeed, she would not want to happen upon such a conversation on purpose and, in fact, wished she could unhear it. She was not used to being talked about behind her back, particularly not in such a derogatory fashion.

In a moment, Mrs. Sterling had breezed past Samantha down the hallway in the opposite direction, trailing a faint floral scent behind her. But even in the woman's elegance, there was a tightness to her stride and an anger in her bearing. Samantha remained where she was for a couple minutes, closing her eyes and working to slow her pulse and calm her troubled thoughts.

When she felt ready, she glanced around the door and, finding herself still alone in the hallway, proceeded around the door and into the library. She saw Sterling immediately, his tall and elegantly clad figure silhouetted against a big picture window, facing out at the cloudy, wintry landscape. His hands were clasped behind his back and his broad shoulders slumped, his head bent forward. Pain rose up in her heart at the sight of him hurting on her account. She made her way to him, nearly soundless, and placed a gentle hand on his arm. He startled slightly and turned, his eyes lighting up at the sight of her. Putting one arm around her, he drew her close, so they could both gaze out at the scene side by side. He kissed the top of her head and said into her hair, "Thank you for meeting me here. I've missed you."

"I've missed you too," she said. "Your note was right: this house is too big." She turned to face him, deciding not to mention that she had overheard the heated conversation between him and his mother. She wanted to help him feel better, to erase the distress visible in those deep brown eyes. "Are you all right?" she asked, reaching up to finger a tendril of his dark, wayward hair.

He sighed and closed his eyes for a long moment, then opened them and looked at her. "I will be. Mother and I had an argument. It wasn't the first and it won't be the last, but I hate the conflict."

"I'm sorry," she said simply, dropping her hand. "Just sensing the tension your mother carries around with her everywhere is enough for me."

"Yes," Sterling agreed, his eyes harking back to previous conflicts throughout his life.

Samantha reached both arms around him in an embrace. Her cheek pressed against his chest, hoping he could feel her empathy. "You had much to deal with, growing up! Most people probably only see the affluence and the privilege. But you had your share of hard things, too."

"I did. But so did you," he said, hugging her back. "At least I had one loving parent, though he was always too submissive for the sake of peace. But we all have our trials. Even

Mother. That's what I keep reminding myself. She is a troubled woman, though I don't know why. And while I can't fix any of that, I can be patient and compassionate."

"But sometimes even that is really difficult," Samantha guessed.

She felt Sterling relax a little at last as he began to chuckle, the vibrations tickling her cheek. "Very," he replied. "One thing about Mother: dealing with her difficulties has taught me patience. But I am still not as patient as I need to be, apparently."

"That's all right," Samantha quipped, pulling back from him slightly. "You have a long life to acquire the patience you desire."

"Thanks to you," he intoned quietly, pulling her close again and kissing her slowly. Then he added, "Mother doesn't know about my illness."

"You still haven't told her?" she asked, stepping back in surprise.

He shook his head. "This place feels like a completely separate world from my world in Worthington. It's difficult to reconcile the two."

"I feel that disparity also. Still," Samantha replied thoughtfully, "she is your mother. For all her rough edges, I think her mother's heart deserves to know you...almost died."

Sterling nodded slowly. "You are probably right." He cupped her chin with one hand and traced the curve of her cheek with his thumb. "How did you get so wise?" he asked.

Samantha smiled and placed her hand over his. "The same way you gained patience," she offered. "Life."

"Yes," Sterling agreed, a bit sadly. "Life has the tendency to teach us things, whether we want to learn them or not."

"But if we let Him, God can turn all things for our good," Samantha reminded him.

Light filled his eyes again and he nodded in agreement. "Yes, He can." Then, in a change of topic, he suddenly noticed, "You've done your hair differently."

Samantha smiled shyly. "Hannah wanted to experiment this morning."

"I like it."

"Thank you." She touched it gingerly, wondering how the loose style was faring, and found that it was still in place.

In her concern for Sterling, Samantha had not really seen the library she stepped into, other than to notice the elderly woman sitting in one corner, knitting. Throughout their exchange, she seemed oblivious to them, which Samantha was glad of. Vaguely, she wondered how the woman came to be there, but assumed someone had apprised her of Sterling's meeting here and she had come to chaperone.

Now Samantha took a good look at the wonderful room as Sterling led her around the library by the hand, showing her all the books he loved so well. His great-grandfather had started the collection, he told her, and each succeeding generation had done their part. In his teen years he, himself, had taken on the responsibility of organizing and cataloging what, by then, was a confusing mess of authors, titles, and genres. He had carefully separated the genres, alphabetized the authors, and meticulously cataloged them all in his neat hand in a thick ledger that still held a place of honor on a gleaming wooden pedestal, easily accessible to anyone wishing to know where a particular book might be. Samantha leafed through it briefly and noted the care with which Sterling had kept the records. Having recently completed her own library organization, she could more fully appreciate all he had done.

The height of the room was about thirty feet, she guessed, and books covered most of the four walls. She was fascinated by the beautiful dark paneling of the built-in floor-to-ceiling bookshelves, and the ingenious built-in ladders that ran on tracks on wheels, which made it easy to reach any book anywhere.

"This room was my haven for many years," Sterling confided, reaching to pull down a beautifully illustrated copy of Shakespeare's *Hamlet* and handing it to her to look through. "At a young age, I found that the care and organization here fulfilled me in a way that the work I did with Father did not. It was my first conscious indication that the life my parents had in mind was not the right kind of life for me."

"And you made many new friends here as well," she guessed, tracing the lines of a detailed painting of the tragic figure of Ophelia. The bright and varied colors across the glossy page were striking. Knowing the Shakespearean play as she did, she could tell that the beauty of the pictures complemented the drama of the story and brought it to life in a new way.

"I did," Sterling agreed. "I probably read half of the time I spent here, when I meant to be organizing. It was hard not to!"

"So many books, so little time?" Samantha suggested with a wry smile.

"Exactly."

She closed the book and handed it back for him to lift back up onto the high shelf where it belonged. Sterling watched her turn in a slow circle, head tilted back to see the highest shelves. When she laughed, the remaining heaviness in his heart lifted.

"I thought my father's library was extensive and the most incredible of libraries, but so is this one! And it is so beautiful!" She spread a hand from one side to the other, her eyes wide in admiration as she continued to gaze around the room. "Being here and seeing this has given me new ideas about what I can do with his library. I never realized that two libraries could be so different from one another and both still be so...wonderful!"

Sterling nodded, watching her with smiling eyes. How he loved that she appreciated books the way he did! He thought back to when she had shown him her library and how he had felt to see that magnificent collection. She was right: they were equally impressive, even in their distinctness.

"Oh, Sterling, how could you not lose yourself in here for hours at a time? I love it!"

He grinned that lopsided smile she loved so well. "I *have* lost myself in here countless times. In fact, my family knows that if I am not to be found anywhere else, I am probably here." He frowned slightly. "But that common knowledge has its disadvantages..."

"In other words, you can't actually hide," Samantha concluded.

"Right. More's the pity. Here," he offered suddenly, moving to another shelf. "I thought you might like to see our copy of your currently favorite book." He moved his finger quickly along the spines until he reached the B's, then pulled out a green velvet-covered version of *Jane Eyre*.

"Oh!" she breathed, taking it from him reverently. "What a beautiful edition!" She turned the thick, gilt-edged pages and smiled at the familiar words. "Are all your books as lavish and gorgeous as these two you've shown me?"

Sterling chuckled. "Many of them are, but not all. For example..." he moved to the D's and handed her a battered copy of *A Christmas Carol* by Charles Dickens. "I read this one over and over as a boy and it's rather the worse for wear. The theme of redemption and change appealed to me more than anything, I think."

"And hope," Samantha agreed. "Definitely a classic story." She turned the pages, noting smudges and places where the corners were turned down, apparently by a boy who was sometimes a little dirty, and sometimes too hurried to find a bookmark. The image made her smile.

She handed it back to him and asked, "What about *Walden*—your favorite?" Since she had bought him a new copy for Christmas, knowing of the battered condition of the one in his room in Worthington, she hoped he would tell her he didn't have another copy.

But this was apparently not the case, for he quickly walked away from the fiction area to a different section of shelves. When he found Thoreau, he held it up. "My personal, battered copy is in Worthington, as you know, but I bought this edition to remain here, as I decided this library ought to always retain a copy of it."

In that case, she still hoped he would welcome a nice new copy for his room. "Indeed," she agreed, fingering the stiff pages which had obviously not had much wear as of yet. She looked up at him and smiled, quoting: 'Books are the treasured wealth of the world and the fit inheritance of generations and nations.'"

Sterling smiled back, offering another *Walden* quote: "'If one advances confidently in the direction of his dreams, and endeavors to live the life he has imagined, he will meet with a success unexpected in common hours.'" His eyes were soft as he looked at her and she knew he was thinking of all they had been through together over the past year as they kept their dreams in sight.

"Yes," she said simply. "I learned to love Thoreau almost as much as you do. But on that topic, I still think Goethe said it best: 'Dream no small dreams, for they have no power to move the hearts of men.'"

"I agree completely, along with Mrs. Tomlinson, who reminded me of those words when I needed them most." Sterling replaced *Walden* on the shelf as she handed it to him, then showed her the complete works of Goethe, in English. "Someday I would love to own copies in the original German, but before I do that I should probably learn the language." He gave a wry smile. "No sense owning something I can't read."

"True," Samantha laughed. "I am glad you are so practical."

"You must be rubbing off on me," he replied, winking.

***

Later, they stood in front of the section which contained works by philosophers and scientists, deep in conversation about Aristotle's principles of correct reasoning, when a footman entered the library with a message for Sterling to join his mother in her rooms. Polite, as always, Sterling thanked the footman, but when he left, Sterling turned to Samantha with a grimace, saying apologetically, "I am fairly certain this is just a pretense.

I doubt there is anything she actually needs my help with. But," he sighed, "this is how it is. And like a dutiful son, I go, to keep the peace."

"That's all right," she said, squeezing his hand. "I will be fine." Then she added regretfully, "It has been lovely here with you, though." She glanced at the elderly servant in the corner who had fallen asleep half an hour before. "Thank you for showing me your haven. It is truly a library to be proud of; an ongoing work and a labor of love."

Sterling smiled fondly, feeling the familiar gratitude rising in his heart that this wonderful young woman understood him so well. "I am very glad you could experience it with me. You showed me your library and now I have shown you mine. But consider this yours as well, whenever you like." He squeezed her hand back, kissed her softly, and left, though he hated to do it.

Samantha amused herself in the library for a couple more hours, perusing the shelves, climbing the innovative ladders that slid effortlessly from side to side wherever she pulled them, and taking out a book here and there to leaf through it. She appreciated the thoroughness of the collection. There was always more to add to a library, of course, but the span of subjects, authors, and genres here was surprisingly comprehensive. It wasn't her library and didn't feel as comfortable, but it would do while she was away from her own.

Chapter 25

WAITING

By lunchtime Samantha was back in her room again and, not having heard from Sterling, ate alone, as she had eaten breakfast. A couple of hours before dinner, Hannah and Miss Moore arrived, the latter carefully holding aloft the first of the dresses that had been altered. Samantha was struck with how different it looked from that morning—and how wonderful! She'd had no idea the women could make such quick work of the extensive alterations, nor that they could make such a complete transformation with the dress. It seemed as though fully half the width had been removed, leaving it looking more sleek and elegant than Samantha could have imagined. She wore it with the S-shaped corset they provided (apparently borrowed from Hannah's older sister, who was near Samantha's size), which created the silhouette so fashionable these days, but which Samantha had never tried before.

The dress was a scintillating dark blue satin with embroidered dark blue flowers on the bodice and along the skirt's hem. The sleeves were very short now, where they had been long before (which was appropriate for an older woman), with matching satin gloves that pulled up above the elbows. The square neckline was much lower[1] than Samantha was accustomed to, but she noticed that the women had added dark blue lace to raise it an

---

1. https://fashionhistory.fitnyc.edu/1900-1909/

inch or two. The maids helped her try it on and cinched all the small buttons up the back, then Hannah gently turned her around to face the tall mirror by the wardrobe and Samantha gasped in surprise. She hardly recognized herself! She had never worn a gown this beautiful, becoming, or fashionable! It completely covered her feet and trailed behind her in a graceful whirl. She hoped the black slippers she had brought with her and worn last night would continue to be adequate with the new gowns, and not detract from their beauty and grace. The slippers were the only footwear she had, besides her usual lace-up boots, so they would have to do.

She glanced at Hannah in astonishment and looked back at the mirror, wondering at the slender young woman looking back at her. The embroidered bodice hugged her small bosom snugly and lace draped from the front of it to her waist. The wide neckline showed off part of her shoulders and the fabric at her waist clung gracefully in folds past her slim hips to accentuate a figure she hadn't really known she had.

Hannah giggled, watching her reaction, and Samantha realized her jaw had dropped. She closed her mouth and shook her head. "How did you do it?" she asked. "It was absolutely splendid before—only too large—but now it is magnificent!"

"It now fits you perfectly. That makes all the difference," Hannah agreed.

"Thank you. You worked magic!"

"Miss Moore is the magician," Hannah said without hesitation. "I learn everything from her." She looked at the older woman beside her in appreciation and Miss Moore inclined her head.

"You are very welcome. I enjoyed the challenge," the older woman said, her brown eyes warm, though her mouth remained unsmiling. "Let us see you walk in it now, to be sure your movement is not too restricted. It must be functional for dancing, as it will need to double as a ball gown."

Samantha obliged, turning away from the mirror, lifting the hem of the dress, and walking forward until she reached the other side of the room. Then she turned back, dipped a slow curtsy, and returned to the maids. When Miss Moore had tweaked a thing here or there and the three women agreed that nothing more needed to be done, they helped Samantha out of the gown and she put her day dress back on.

"Thank you again, so much. Both of you," she said to them, hoping they could feel the depth of her gratitude in those simple words. "I appreciate all you are doing for me. I didn't know how it was possible to make the gown fit me properly, but that just goes to show how little I know! In my eyes, you worked a miracle."

Hannah beamed at her and bobbed a little curtsy in acknowledgement, and even Miss Moore's mouth tilted slightly upward at the corners when she nodded in reply. Hannah told her she would bring the dress back in approximately an hour, after the final small alterations, and help her change for dinner then.

After they left, Samantha sat at the vanity and began removing pins until her hair spilled down in a chaotic profusion. The new hairstyle had given her a slight headache and she knew Hannah would want to restyle it when she returned anyway. As she brushed her hair out smoothly, feeling the relief of a head free of pins, she wondered at the new gown that had made her actually feel pretty. It was a strange, but not unwelcome, sensation. But then, unbidden, Cordelia's words echoed in her mind: *I'm sure I don't know what you see in her... Such a plain, common girl.*

How could two people see her so completely differently? At her core, Samantha was the same girl she had always been, wasn't she? She knew she had grown in many important ways since that fateful day in May last year, but she felt basically the same, just...improved. At least, she hoped she was becoming a better person. Mrs. Dolittle had seen the changes and applauded them. Samantha knew that improvement was one aim of a Christian life—to become more like Jesus, the only perfect being—and she was striving to do that, though she knew she would never master it. She was sure Sterling saw all of that in her, as she saw in him all the ways he was always trying to better himself and help those around him. But his mother apparently saw only a nondescript girl of no consequence from a lower station in life, not worthy of her son.

So who was right?

Samantha knew she *was* of no consequence—she had never claimed to be otherwise. But Sterling made her feel special and wonderful, that her goals and dreams were of value and worthy to be reached, and that she made a positive difference in others' lives. That was enough for her.

But now that she had time and space to think about the confrontation in the library, the dichotomy between Sterling's and his mother's views jarred her in a way little else had in her life. She had always thought of herself as plain Samantha the bookworm, the quiet scholar, the overlooked and unseen girl at the fringes of society. And she had felt comfortable there, though lonely, as she discovered later. When Katherine and Rupert had taught her the meaning and joy of true friendship and integrated her into their society of friends, involving her in church and town events, she had started feeling seen for the first time. She generally felt accepted and that she was appreciated by her new circle of friends, which was a beautiful thing to experience.

But now she was faced with the very uncomfortable perspective that someone whose acceptance and appreciation mattered to her saw her as nothing more than an annoyance and a hindrance to her son's proper place in society. Samantha did not want to hold Sterling back in any way! She had always felt secure and confident in who she was, but she was afraid this formidable woman might undermine that. And Samantha was unsure of what to do about it.

She tried to brush away these distressing thoughts as she brushed the tangles out of her long hair, and willed her mind to fill with positive sentiments instead. "Peace I leave with you," she quoted silently to herself from John. "My peace I give unto you: not as the world giveth, give I unto you. Let not your heart be troubled, neither let it be afraid."

Jesus' words comforted her, but she had the feeling she would have to repeat them to herself often in the days to come.

***

That evening's meal was as uncomfortable as the previous night's, with everyone dressed in their best and exercising their best manners, but no one feeling relaxed. Being around Cordelia Sterling was like trying to walk on eggshells without breaking them, or across hot coals without being burned. And to make matters worse, Samantha was now seated across from Sterling instead of beside him. The table was too wide for even his foot to reach hers, and she felt bereft at the physical distance between them. Last night had been difficult, but at least she had been close enough to hear him breathe and feel his calming and fortifying presence beside her.

She tried to tune into the conversation, to add a little here and there, but it felt like Cordelia was purposely steering the discussion away from her, to topics she knew nothing of. She ate little, pushing food around on her plate, hoping the woman would think she had eaten sufficiently. She did catch Sterling's appreciative eyes on her across the table multiple times and knew that he liked her new dress and that he loved her as much as ever, so she held to that knowledge and made it through the meal.

During their time in the drawing room after dinner, Cordelia monopolized all of Sterling's time and attention, making him unable to sit by Samantha at all. Samantha could tell it irked him but that if he protested, it would cause a scene. She tried her best to make conversation with the other two men, and even learned to play whist to pass the hours until bedtime. Lucas was kind enough to sit by her and explain why he played each card. She silently blessed him for his patience and was relieved for the time this activity consumed, which effectively distracted her from the strain of the situation.

At long last, it was time to retire. Samantha felt exhausted after the evening's emotional tension and could scarcely believe she had been here only one day. She was immensely grateful when Sterling broke free of his mother to escort her up the curving front staircase to her room. She held his arm close as they ascended, instantly feeling a bit stronger just by being close to him again. When they stopped outside her door, in the dimly lit corridor, he pulled her into his arms and she rested her head on his chest, feeling his steady heartbeat through the side of her temple. She closed her eyes and they stood there holding each other for a few silent minutes.

"Are you all right?" he asked at last, kissing the top of her head. "You seem unhappy."

She pulled away and looked up at him. "I will be fine. It has been a long day."

"Indeed it has." He rubbed a hand over his eyes and down his face and she saw his weariness too. But she thought this obvious tiredness on his part might be a residual effect of his illness.

"Thank you again for showing me your inspiring library, Sterling. That was the highlight of my day."

"And mine," he replied, smiling tiredly. "I wish it could have lasted longer." He sighed. "Another time."

She nodded, then stood on tiptoe to kiss him. "Good night."

"Good night," he said. "I love you, Samantha. I know this feels like a losing battle, here in this house... My mother... But you are doing splendidly. May tomorrow give us more time together."

***

But it didn't. After a somewhat restless night, despite her fatigue, Samantha breakfasted in her room as before and had Bible study alone. She would have liked to have met with Sterling to enjoy such study together on this Sabbath day, especially knowing she would miss formal worship, as the Sterlings did not attend any church. But when she sent a note via Hannah to enquire about the possibility of meeting with Sterling, she received a response back that he was, regrettably, unable to do so. There was little detail in the note to explain why, and Samantha felt destitute with the omission, though she tried to stifle the reaction. No doubt his mother had him tied up with preparations for the Christmas ball they would be hosting in three days. If that was the case, why could she not help as well? Samantha tried to soothe her disappointment by telling herself that his mother's time with him was limited and she was just trying to spend as much time with him as she could. Knowing that she, herself, would be leaving with Sterling in a week's time and would again have him all to herself, gave her surprising comfort, which she tucked up close in her heart. She just had to bide her time and eventually this already long week would come to an end.

After another lunch alone, she decided to make her way down to the library, hoping she might see Sterling along the way. She imagined finding him there and the thought quickened her pulse. But when she entered the spacious room, it was empty, though a fire crackled in the walk-in fireplace in the center of the room, as if to welcome her. But Samantha was tired of reading and tired of being alone. With a sigh, she turned back to the door and retraced her steps up the great staircase, wondering how she should occupy the long hours until dinner. Then, remembering the wall behind the house that she had noticed upon arrival, which hinted at a garden, she determined to explore it. She needed fresh air and exercise anyway; both might raise her spirits. Not knowing where to find her coat and gloves, she returned to her room and pulled the bell for Hannah, apologizing when the maid arrived. "I am sorry to call you from your regular duties, Hannah. It is just that I desire to go out and have no idea where to find my coat."

"Oh, not to worry, Miss. I was in need of an interruption to my routine anyhow. Would you care to follow me and I'll show you where the outdoor gear is kept? That way, you can have it anytime you need it."

Samantha nodded gratefully. "I would appreciate that. The more self-reliant I can be, the better."

Hannah's intelligent blue eyes were sharp with observation. "I *thought* you were the independent type."

Samantha followed Hannah back down the staircase, across the expansive foyer, and into a back hallway that led to the coatroom, just off the back door to the house. As Samantha donned her coat, she asked Hannah, "Is there a garden here?"

"Yes, Miss!"

"Would it be all right, do you think, if I explored it a bit?"

"I'm sure that would be fine. It can be a nice stroll, as long as you're bundled up."

"Thank you. I'll try that."

Hannah curtsied and left and Samantha finished buttoning up her coat, then found an extra hat and pulled her gloves on. As she walked out, she pulled a scarf snugly around her neck, noting that the temperature was not bitingly cold. She stood on the top step, looking out at the white landscape before her and saw a large covered patio to her right, complete with outdoor furniture protectively covered for winter. The space looked like a wonderful gathering place for small groups on warm summer nights and she imagined what that might look like, with cheerfully clad people laughing and chatting together, plates of hors d'oeuvres in their laps. Several yards in front of her stood the brown brick wall she had noticed before, its squares interspersed with various shades of lichen. She saw a door in the wall and walked down the steps toward it, making the first footprints on a path that was covered by a light layer of snow.

When she reached the door in the wall and tried to push it open it didn't budge, so she tried again, this time harder. It yielded with a prolonged squeak and she stepped inside. Like everything else she had seen here, the garden was vast and supremely organized and tidy. The snow softened everything and blurred all the lines, but she could still tell that a skilled gardener had sculpted the bushes to look like a variety of animals. She had read of British topiary gardens before, of course, but never seen one herself, so she was delighted. The place must be wonderful in the summertime when the bushes were filled out with greenery! She wanted to see it all and began walking briskly through the light skiff of snow to warm herself. She noted a bear, a wolf, a lion, a deer, and many other readily recognizable animals, as well as fanciful creatures like a unicorn and a phoenix. Benches were placed throughout the garden, and she imagined how nice it would be to sit out here in pleasant weather and enjoy the sunshine and birdsong. She wished both were present on this cold, gray day.

Walking quickly, she saw the entire garden in about fifteen minutes. The whole effect was artful and whimsical, even in the winter, but she was disappointed that there was no area to actually grow a vegetable garden. That was what she had expected, she realized: an orchard and a traditional kitchen garden. Oh, what she and Mrs. Dolittle could do with a walled garden of this size! But she came from a different world and knew she could not look at this world through the same lens. Truly, she must remember that often, she told herself, particularly here in Lexington, on this opulent, pristine estate.

By the time she made her way back around to the entrance of the garden, she felt thoroughly exercised and her hands and feet were chilled through. She knew she needed to go back inside, but she hated the thought, not knowing how else to fill her day now.

On the outside of the wall, she pulled the door shut again, finding that she appreciated its squeak—it was one tiny imperfection that, rather than marring the place, gave it character. She followed her own footprints back up the path and ascended the few stairs leading to the door.

When she stepped inside, she was surprised to see Sterling stride into the room from the hallway. "There you are!" he exclaimed, pulling her farther into the room by one hand. "All glowing and rosy from a walk about the garden, Hannah tells me."

"Yes," Samantha laughed, a little out of breath. "It is a lovely garden. What have you been up to all day?"

"Missing you," he smiled, removing her gloves and rubbing her cold hands between his warm ones.

"I have missed you too."

He met her gaze, his expression regretful and pained. "I am sorry things are going this way today," he said. Then, lowering his voice, he added, "I keep trying to get away and my mother keeps thinking of other things for me to do—none of which need to actually be done by *me*." He continued rubbing her hands as he detailed his duties with a grimace. "I have helped draw up the seating chart for dinner, approved Mother's menu, as if she needs me to do that, verified that the musicians are coming, counted the silver and overseen its polishing—I mean, what do we have Wilson for, if I am doing his job?" His voice inadvertently rose as he detailed these grievances.

"That sounds frustrating."

"And all the while, I am wanting to be with you!" He looked behind him at the door and lowered his voice again. "I am beginning to think Mother is deliberately trying to keep us apart as much as possible."

Samantha nodded, but said nothing. She had had that same feeling since they arrived. Her hands feeling a bit warmer, she unbuttoned her coat and pulled off the scarf, and Sterling took them both from her to hang them exactly where they had been before. She guessed it must be some kind of systematic organization he was accustomed to.

"Have you had a good Sunday?" she asked, wanting to lighten the mood, but also thinking of their missed Bible study.

"Not really," he admitted. "Mother never rises earlier than ten, but somehow today she needed me about the same time as I received your note, around nine o'clock. This has not been a day of rest in any way."

"I am sorry," she offered. "You have too much to—"

"Inane, unnecessary things," he clarified.

"While I have started going mad with inactivity!" she continued, drawing closer to him, wanting him to understand. She kept her voice low with effort. "We need to do something about that. Meet in the middle somehow. I would love to help—with anything at all." She knew she sounded desperate, but that was how she felt.

He looked at her compassionately and touched her face. "I will mention it to Mother. As it is, this is stolen time and I don't know how long we have. But I wanted to find you." He put his arms around her and she leaned into him. "Thank goodness I ran into Hannah and she knew where you had gone. I wish I could have taken that walk with you!"

"Hmm," Samantha murmured, suddenly realizing how tired she was after two nights of interrupted sleep. "We need to figure out how to steal more time."

"Agreed!" He eased her away from him and bent to kiss her, gently and slowly, her cold lips warming with his touch. "I'll figure something out," he promised, resting his forehead on hers. "But first I have to get back to Mother before she comes looking for me."

"Indeed," said a voice from the doorway.

Sterling sighed and turned to face his mother.

"Whatever are you doing in the coat room, Lee?" Cordelia looked at him sternly and a bit quizzically. "Have you already finished adjusting the star on the tree in the front hall? We don't want it crooked on Tuesday when our guests arrive, you know."

"Of course. I will do that, Mother. But first, I was speaking with Samantha. I haven't seen her all day." He hoped he had succeeded in keeping a whine out of his voice, and hated that though he was a grown man, his mother could make him feel like a petulant schoolboy caught putting a frog in the teacher's desk.

"Ah," Cordelia stepped inside and peered around Sterling's tall frame. "I see. The two of you alone in this small room... That doesn't look good now, does it." There was no question in the statement, nor any warmth. Her tone was all steel, yet said so lightly that one uninvolved in the situation would not have noticed her judgment.

How could Samantha feel guilty when she had done nothing wrong? And yet, at the woman's tone she felt almost obligated to feel that way. Samantha tried to deflect the negativity and suspicion by offering, "I just took a walk in your walled garden, Mrs. Sterling. It is absolutely beautiful! I love its whimsy and art."

Cordelia pursed her lips and inclined her head. "Yes, our gardener is the best in the state, and creates whatever I dictate. In summer, we receive many visitors to see it, so it must be kept in top shape at all times. Bushes grow so fast, after all. They take constant trimming." She spoke as if this were highly inconvenient and she, alone, were responsible for the garden's upkeep.

"I am sure they do," Samantha said haltingly. Then she tried another angle. "Mrs. Sterling, might I be of assistance in your preparations for the ball? I do not have much to occupy my time and would love to be of help in any way I can."

Cordelia laughed, but there was no mirth in it. "Put our guest to work? I would not think of it! You are here to enjoy yourself and relax, Miss Jennings, to be waited upon, not to do the waiting." And that seemed to be the end of the matter.

But I am waiting, Samantha wanted to cry. *Waiting to be of use to someone while you are putting your son unnecessarily to work in your efforts to keep us apart!* The whole convoluted situation confused and saddened her. Was she really so offensive to Cordelia? What had she done? And how could she repair this ever-widening gap?

Sterling squeezed her hand quickly, then left with his mother, and Samantha slowly walked back upstairs, her feet heavy.

***

The next day passed much the same for Samantha: a couple glimpses of Sterling, stolen moments for brief conversation, and much too much time alone.

Cordelia kept Sterling so mindlessly busy that at times he thought he might go mad with nothing to engage his intellect besides her gossip. He greatly missed Samantha and kept wracking his brain to figure out how to change their situation. At one point after lunch, he happened to glance out a window from the second floor at just the right moment and saw her making her way through the snow to the walled garden. Her tread was slow, he noted, and even from his high vantage point he could tell that her shoulders were rounded in dejection. But when his mother followed his gaze, her lips tightened, her eyes flashed, and she all but refused to let him go after her. He distinctly felt that if he defied his mother, he would only bring more angst down on Samantha. And he was loath to do anything that would make the time here harder for her. Maybe if his mother recognized how compliant and dutiful he was being, she would soften toward Samantha. He could hope...

***

When Samantha had spent as long out in the cold as she could handle, she returned to her room, wondering how to occupy the rest of her day. But when she arrived in the hall outside her bedroom door, she saw that the door was open and Hannah and Miss Moore were just leaving.

"Oh, this is good!" Hannah said when she saw her, clasping her hands together in happiness. "We came to help you try on the second dress and see what further alterations need to be made. Is now a good time?"

"Yes. Yes, of course." Samantha stepped inside and closed the door.

Another wonderful creation lay on the bed, this one a green satin with a darker green overlay of lace shaped like holly leaves. Around the hem in a width of about two inches sparkled hundreds of tiny sequins made of pounded steel circles. At the bodice's front was pinned an imitation sprig of red holly, complete with glossy green leaves.

"Oh, it's exquisite!" Samantha breathed. "What a perfect dress for the season! I assume this is for tomorrow's ball?"

Miss Moore nodded and Samantha noted that her slight smile was quicker now than it had been a couple days ago.

The women helped her try the gown on, finishing the effect with white gloves, which also sparkled with silver sequins. Like the first dress, this one, too, was transformative. The green color brought out the red strands in Samantha's golden hair and she felt like the belle of the ball here in her own bedroom. "Thank you! I thought this dress was absolutely beautiful before, but now it is somehow even more stunning."

"It helps when the gown fits properly," Miss Moore said drily, reminding Samantha of their conversation about the last dress, but her eyes twinkled as she said it.

And it did fit properly—perfectly, in fact. This time, there was no need for a second alteration. For the first time, Samantha felt a sense of excitement about attending the ball. Maybe such a social event would not be quite the painful experience she had anticipated. And, of course, spending time with Sterling was something to look forward to.

When the maids left, Samantha stood there in the middle of the room and sighed. There was so much time on her hands, so much space in this vast residence, and so little with which to occupy her mind and hands. Now that she knew what it was to be useful to others, to work, serve, and converse, this enforced idleness felt demeaning and suffocating.

Finally, she decided she could write, which was something she had not done in days. She removed her cold boots, tucked her feet under her, and wrapped herself up in a blanket, then made an effort to see how effective her pen might be at a time like this.

An hour later, warm and spent, she sat in a chair at the desk, her head resting on her arms on the small table's surface. Her heart had eased a little with her cathartic efforts with the pencil and her breaths came soft and slow, regular in sleep, as the fatigue finally overtook her. Her diary lay open beside her, a long entry within, concluded by a new poem written neatly on the page:

BEREFT

I am an autumn leaf
Soon to blow off course
A brilliant crimson flag
But fading, an echo of what was
Like the shrinking sun
Each day shorter than the last
Night nudging with frosted fingers.
I remember better days
Ebullient, emerald, warm
Encircled by others with
A common purpose
An understood identity.
Now I stand alone.
Soon to fall
This brittle
failing
leaf.

Chapter 26

UNJUST ASSUMPTIONS

When Hannah came in to help Samantha dress for dinner, she found her asleep at the desk. Smiling down at her fondly, Hannah softly closed the diary and put a gentle hand on her shoulder. Stirring, Samantha raised her head and blinked up at the maid.

"Sorry to disturb your rest, Miss, but it's time to change for dinner."

"Oh! Thank you!" Samantha rubbed her eyes and yawned. "I didn't realize I fell asleep." She untangled herself from the blanket and stood, moving to the wardrobe where she again chose the deep purple gown from home. *If Cordelia refuses to approve of me regardless of what I do or wear, I may as well enjoy my own familiar clothing*, she reasoned. And she was surprised by the sense of security the familiar garment gave her as she drew it over her head and down over her body. Hannah tried another new hairstyle, this one a large, loose bun with multiple twists. Samantha liked it and hoped she could remember how Hannah had done it so she could recreate it at home herself.

Sterling must have spoken firmly to his mother about the seating arrangement, for Samantha was again seated at his left. She was greatly relieved, but still did not have much appetite. Again, there was little for her to contribute to the conversation, but she also noted that the majority of the time, it included only Sterling and his mother and she wondered how to turn the talk to include the other men of the family. In a slight lull, she finally ventured a question for James Sterling. "How do the horses fare in the cold weather?" she asked, truly wanting to know.

He swallowed a bite of food and set down his fork. "They do well," he answered. "The barns are insulated and keep out much of the cold. And each horse has his own blanket."

"I see." She was not sure what else to say, but then asked, "Might I come see them sometime? I know a bit about horses and would love to meet them, if I could."

Cordelia looked on disapprovingly, but Lucas brightened and glanced at his father, who was taking another forkful of beef and potatoes. "Of course," Lucas answered for him, and she could see the enthusiasm in his eyes, even though his voice stayed even. "You are welcome in the barn anytime. If we had known you were interested, Father and I would have invited you earlier."

"Thank you," she smiled. "I have a horse of my own at home and have learned to care for him."

"Really?" Lucas asked, surprised. "I don't know any young women who care for their own horses."

Samantha blushed, realizing how out of place that must sound to someone in this society.

"Yes, and she does it well," Sterling interjected, cutting his beef in small, even bites. "Samantha has many talents and abilities. She is quite independent."

"What breed is your horse?" Lucas asked, his eyes bright with interest.

"I think Champion is an Arabian?" She looked at Sterling for confirmation and he nodded. Turning back to Lucas she added, "He is black and beautifully majestic—large, of course—full of energy and loves to run—but he's careful with me. He is a pleasure to ride." She was afraid she was talking too much now, but wanted to add one more thing. "Champion was Sterling's horse first, in Oberlin, and when Sterling left for Worthington, I bought him."

"That she did!" Sterling laughed. "I had no idea until I went back to Oberlin. She has a keen eye for good horse flesh and she does a marvelous job of caring for him. They are good for each other."

Samantha nodded in agreement at his last statement, until she caught a glimpse of Cordelia's frown, and decided maybe she had talked enough for one meal. But at least now the topic had settled on one of more interest to all but one person at the table. And she could tell that Sterling's father and brother were gratified to have been included.

***

That night, Samantha did not sleep any better than she had either of the previous two nights. She was beginning to feel that she must accept the lack of sleep and perhaps resign herself to additional short, involuntary naps like the one she had had earlier. When dawn came, she was already awake and went about setting her own fire so the room would warm faster. She did not want to trouble Tabitha and saw no reason to wait for her when she could light a fire perfectly well by herself. After her daily devotional she dressed, brushed her hair, and sat busily writing at the desk when Tabitha came in. It had been a hectic morning already for the poor girl, who showed her anxiety. She expressed her gratitude for not having to start Samantha's fire and Samantha hoped the saved time would put her back on schedule so that she would not be reprimanded.

Samantha took her breakfast a little earlier than previously, hoping she could catch all three men in the barn if she went first thing. She was not dressed for riding—indeed had somehow overlooked bringing her riding habit with her—but she could at least see the horses and gain a better view of the extensive and respected horse business the Sterling family ran.

When she entered the huge barn, James and Lucas greeted her with pleasure, which warmed her and helped dispel some of the negative feelings that clung to her from the house, despite her efforts to push them away. Lucas took her on a tour of the facility, introducing her to any of the horses she took an interest in as they walked past stall after stall. Each horse's name was written on a plaque on the door and Lucas was able to tell her not only the breed of every one, but also the parentage of each, and their individual strengths and characteristics. She was amazed at the breadth of his knowledge and understanding.

"You really love your work here with the horses, don't you, Lucas?" She noticed a familiar light in his eyes and a fervor in his speech that reminded her of Sterling when he discussed writing or literature or education.

He nodded. "It is all I have ever wanted to do. Horses are my life. And hemp, of course."

"That must be great to have in common with your father."

"It is," he said simply.

"How do you remember all the facts and figures about this business? I definitely see a similarity between you and Sterling in your abilities to retain vast information on the topics you are passionate about."

Lucas blushed a little and redirected the question. "I have heard that you do the same. Sterling says you can recite long passages from anything you read. And you've read hundreds of works."

"That used to be my only pastime," Samantha admitted, "growing up as I did. And I do remember many passages; somehow they just stay lodged in my brain once I've read them. Anything that makes a particular impression, that is. There are many passages I don't retain, of course."

Lucas nodded. "I've never been much for book learning or reading, but when I need to know something about the business, I read everything I can find on the topic in order to be as knowledgeable as possible. I want to be an asset to my father's good name in the industry. He is widely respected and I don't want to do anything to mar that."

"I am sure you are a credit to him in every way," Samantha assured him, patting a brown and white speckled head that poked through the bars as they passed. And that launched them into a discussion about horse breeds.

After passing a very nice hour in the extensive barns, Samantha returned to the house, a little lighter in her step. She was careful to clean her boots thoroughly with the brushes and bristle mats provided before taking the long staircase up to her room. But once there, she couldn't find a way to occupy herself. Realizing there were still two hours until lunchtime, she decided to make another visit to the library. Maybe she could find something else there to expand her vision about children's education. She pulled the bedroom door shut behind her and walked down the long carpeted hallway back to the double staircase. She was about to descend when, from a room farther down the hallway, she heard Cordelia's raised voice through an open door. Samantha froze on the top step, not wanting to hear but unable to move.

"I tell you, she's treasure hunting! What else could her motivation be?"

Samantha's breath caught in her throat. Motivation? Treasure hunting? What was the woman talking about?

"Her father is supposedly wealthy, but have you seen the state of her clothing? And how unaccustomed she is to servants? I believe that whole 'mansion' bit is just a ruse so Sterling doesn't suspect what she is actually up to."

She is talking about me! Samantha's heart sank. *Why does she suspect me of being conniving and grasping?* She felt a bit indignant in spite of herself, and warmth crept up her neck.

"And she has completely pulled the wool over his eyes!"

What? Samantha's heart dropped to the pit of her stomach. How could she ever change the mind and heart of someone so bent on seeing her in such a terrible light?

But the rant continued: "My son, who is supposedly such a brilliant scholar! Ha! It's enough to make a mother tear her hair out!"

Finally, shaking off her momentary paralysis and blinking back tears, Samantha fled down the stairs as quietly and quickly as she could. When she arrived at the library, she rushed in and stood before the big picture window, clenching her hands together tightly and trying to breathe evenly. She *would* think about this rationally and not become emotional! She would *not* cry! The woman simply did not know of what she spoke. She was making terrible assumptions based on her own life's experience, which were apparently very limited to the cutthroat mentality of the status-climbing elite.

She *would* not cry. She took another steadying breath and willed herself to be distracted by the wintry beauty outside. Snowflakes fell lightly and their unhurried, gentle movement gradually soothed something in Samantha's soul.

Carefully, she deliberated again. If what she had overheard was how Cordelia really thought of her, that was very unfortunate. But she was mistaken, and a mentality and life view such as hers was to be pitied. With such a perspective, the woman was surely missing out on so much joy! Simply overlooking the goodness in others—irrespective of their status—was a great loss in and of itself. As she thought along this vein, the indignation began to melt away, and she found herself feeling sorry for the woman instead, willing herself not to dwell on the hurt.

Feeling a little more grounded and stabilized with these thoughts, Samantha unclenched her hands and took a slow circuit about the room, wondering where to start in her research. After a lengthy perusal, she found what she was looking for in a slim volume about educational reform, women's suffrage, and racial equality, which included writings by Horace Mann, Catharine Beecher, and Emma Willard. She particularly appreciated Mann's comment that "Education...is the great equalizer of the conditions of men—the balance-wheel of the social machinery."[1] She couldn't agree more! That was why she

---

1. http://www.caggiasocialstudies.com/docs/AH104/Mann

wanted to help disadvantaged children rise above ignorance at an early age. It would make such a difference to their lives—in so many ways!

She did not wish to think ill of Cordelia, but she couldn't help thinking that she, too, could use a good dose of education about social castes, economic injustices, and racial prejudice. Continued learning was so vital to an enlightened view of the world—and those who stopped learning stopped growing and improving and experiencing wonder. Samantha vowed never to do that.

At lunchtime she returned cautiously to her room, not wanting to run into Cordelia on the way. She didn't quite feel strong enough for that. The anxiety of the last couple of hours had tied her stomach in knots, but she figured she should try to eat something anyway, so she didn't risk fainting from lack of nourishment. Cordelia would probably chalk that up to using feminine wiles, or some such thing, and Samantha did not want to add any fuel to the fire. When she closed the door behind her, she noticed a small envelope with familiar handwriting on the bedside table and eagerly ran to snatch it up.

Dearest Samantha, it read.

Only one more day until the ball, and then I pray my mother's "need" of me will let up a bit. I ache to see you, to do more with my time than the mindless chores Mother thinks up. It is hard to believe we are living in the same house when I am kept from even glimpses of you. How is it that I am seeing less of you today than yesterday? This is not right, my dearest. I am racking my brain to figure out a solution.

Please reserve most of your dance card for me, as I want to dance with you the whole night through, if possible. And no, I don't care what others may think: their assumptions will be correct. I know you believe you are not a good dancer, but I am not worried. You will do well: your knowledge is sufficient and you are graceful and lovely besides.

Samantha, let it be known that I have no wish to dance with anyone else, so why not be transparent to all and sundry? I love you. Please don't forget that. I want to tell you this in person. Will you join me tonight for an evening of music and drama? While I do not feel Lexington is my home any longer, I do love many things about this city, and the Lexington Opera House is one of them. After all, this is the 'Athens of the West'[2] and theater has a long history here. I would forever regret if, in bringing you here, I did not give you the opportunity

---

2. https://www.nps.gov/nr/travel/lexington/athens.htm

to experience a night at the opera. It is truly magical, and being with you will make it doubly so for me. Please say yes!

Yours,

Sterling

She held the letter to her heart, closed her eyes, and exhaled in gratitude. For a moment, it had felt like Sterling was right here beside her. Carefully she tucked the letter into her journal, pulled out a fresh sheet of paper and wrote:

My Sterling,

I would be delighted to join you this evening and will be waiting with great anticipation to enjoy my first night at the opera.

Love,

Your Samantha

Chapter 27

THE OPERA

As soon as Samantha had finished an obligatory lunch, Hannah swept in with the final dress, and Samantha decided she would debut it that evening for her night at the theater. It was an elegant black silk with three tiered layers of long ruffles around the bottom, edged in deep purple lace. The front of the bodice to a point below the waist was purple satin covered by a light layer of black lace through which the purple showed. The dress was simpler now than it had been before the alterations and Samantha liked it better without all the extra decorations. To add to the ensemble was a thick black opera cape that fell below her waist, complete with a dark fur ruff that reached from one hand, up the arm and behind the neck, and down to the other hand. Hannah showed her how to clip on a pair of purple garnet earrings that dangled two inches below her earlobes and glistened as they turned in the light. A matching long purple necklace with five glistening garnets completed the look, and the unaccustomed small weight against her sternum felt strange. She was sure the jewelry was worth a fortune, which was confirmed when Hannah mentioned that they were on loan from Cordelia's private collection. Samantha wondered why the woman would lend her something so valuable if she despised her so much. As she mused on it, she decided the only logical answer was that Cordelia was motivated by a desire for the Sterling family to show up in the best light publicly. Her sole motivation in sharing her jewelry was, no doubt, to assure herself that Samantha would not embarrass the family name. This realization was not comforting.

That evening they ate dinner a bit earlier than usual so they would be on time to the opera. Samantha had hoped she and Sterling might be able to attend alone, though of course they could not be unaccompanied. But she was dismayed when she learned that

Sterling's mother would be the one to chaperone them. Why couldn't it have been James or Lucas—or even that aged servant who had chaperoned them in the library? Suddenly the evening's prospects lost all luster.

When Cordelia saw Samantha's latest gown as she arrived at dinner, one of her elegant brows rose in obvious evaluation before her lips compressed into a straight line that seemed to indicate disapproval. But then she smiled slightly to herself, as if satisfied about something. Samantha did not know what to make of such a mixed reaction and decided to ignore it. Maybe the woman regretted letting the maids remake these old dresses of hers...? More than likely she simply disapproved of Samantha herself and it was not the gown at all. Samantha's head ached with the worry that had quickly become an ever-present part of each day.

As she picked at her food, she realized that more than anything else she felt an overwhelming anxiety about this outing. She almost wanted to beg off on account of the headache, and retire early. But even more than her physical fatigue, she was mentally and emotionally weary of being cooped up indoors, alone, and she did want to spend time with Sterling, even if his mother was present.

In the carriage on the way to the Opera House, Sterling sat beside Samantha while his mother sat across from them. It was so dark this time of night that they could barely see anything, and Samantha was glad of the reprieve from Cordelia's constant displeased expression. She was also glad for a better sense of privacy as Sterling's fingers gently closed around hers. All the way there, she said little but listened as Sterling and his mother discussed operas they had previously attended.

Opera was not something Samantha and Sterling had ever discussed, nor anything she was at all familiar with, but she learned a few things about opera etiquette as she listened. From Cordelia's comments, she also learned that how a woman dressed at one of these occasions was as important, almost, as the opera itself. Women's attire and jewelry were supposed to add to the opulence of the experience for everyone. Samantha found herself feeling even more relieved that she had heeded Hannah's advice to wear the jewelry and allowed her hair to be pulled up in a fancy style with ringlets around her face and a glittering purple flower hairpin tucked into one side. At least she wouldn't look woefully underdressed for the lavish occasion, thanks to Hannah's services.

Sterling explained that they would be watching *Carmen* by Georges Bizet tonight: not one of his favorite stories, he admitted, but definitely some of his favorite music. And it was a good opera for someone new to the scene. The whole story would be sung in French, so he would explain it to her as they listened. "Of course, I only know rudimentary French," he said, answering her unspoken question, "but I know the story well enough to help you understand what is happening."

The rest of their conversation Samantha lost track of, as Cordelia spoke about prominent families in the area who might be at the opera that night. Only one name stood out to her, as Cordelia mentioned it a few times: a Miss Fairfield. She spoke very highly of the young woman, told Sterling the girl had asked after him on more than one occasion over the past two years, and that she would be very pleased to see him if she happened to be there. Sterling responded noncommittally and eventually turned the conversation to someone else.

The front of the tall brown brick edifice was ablaze with many large gaslights and Samantha tried not to gape at all the beautiful people moving toward the entrance, alighting from opulent carriages pulled by perfectly groomed horses. Jewelry flashed and sparkled and the magnificence took her breath away.

Sterling noticed her expression and gave a low chuckle, bending to whisper in her ear, "Wait till you see inside!"

Indeed, as they crossed the carpeted foyer, the grandeur of the place and the people in it were a sight to behold. Cordelia greeted several people by name and exchanged pleasantries as they made their way toward the grand staircase. The press of people grew, and Samantha took a firm hold on Sterling's arm. Many people greeted him and seemed genuinely happy to see him, commenting on his long absence from the community. The men glanced at her curiously, and some of the women eyed her with suspicion. Several young women even stared at her with obvious disdain, then looked away with a condescending uplift of the chin. She pulled closer to Sterling in confusion and tried not to let the negativity and judgment bother her. He smiled down at her in encouragement, untroubled, and the sincere gesture reassured her.

Finally, when they had apparently greeted everyone, they ascended the stairs to the second floor. She heard the rustle of skirts and smelled the variety of perfumes around her, noting how many different colors of gowns the women wore, some virtually dripping with embroidery, lace, or jewels—or all three. Suddenly, her beautiful gown did not seem so fine, and she realized with a sinking heart that its dark coloring was too somber and subdued for the occasion. Had she chosen the wrong gown, or would it have mattered?

It was not as if she had a whole closetful to choose from, nor that she would ever have occasion to dress this way again, so she willed herself not to be concerned. After all, there was no one here she needed to impress. But she couldn't help noticing that only the older women dressed in darker tones, while the women her age wore lighter, more showy colors, like pinks and blues. *I guess that is what I risk, wearing an older woman's discarded clothing*, she thought. *But*, she reminded herself, *it is still a very handsome dress and it seemed more than adequate before we arrived, so I refuse to change my mind on that point. I don't need anything fancier.* She caught Cordelia watching her, and by her look of satisfaction, Samantha noted that she had correctly observed Samantha's train of thought, and that she was pleased with her discomfort. Samantha willed herself not to flush or visibly deflate. She straightened her shoulders.

They reached a door, which Sterling held open for the ladies to enter ahead of him. It was a small box seat and Samantha was glad of the privacy it offered, away from the press of people below and above them. Sterling indicated one of the front seats and Samantha settled herself there. He sat beside her, and Cordelia sat in a seat behind them. The box was perched out nearly above the stage and offered a perfect view of the activity below. A few musicians were visible under the stage and, judging by the sounds of instruments warming up, Samantha guessed there were many others she could not see. The pleasant cacophony of strings, woodwinds, and brass lent an expectant air to the hall.

"What do you think so far?" Sterling asked quietly, leaning close so they could speak without his mother overhearing.

"It...it's magnificent," Samantha told him with wide eyes. "The hall, the people, it's not something I have ever experienced before." She tried not to let herself think about how this was all normal for Sterling, part of his usual lifestyle until a few years ago. Tried not to dwell on how very different their backgrounds were from each other, and how out of place she felt. She pushed away the uncomfortable feelings and focused on enjoying the new experience, trying to absorb it all.

"I know it's probably a great deal to take in," he said, "but I hope you can enjoy it. I like to look at opera as an extensive poem with many moods. It is loaded with drama and emotion. Sometimes it is more about the experience than about understanding every word or nuance. And it is up to the viewer to recognize meaning and make connections. So it is both a collective and a personal experience."

This was just what Samantha needed to hear to feel grounded and in familiar territory. She loved poetry, so perhaps opera would not be too far out of her league after all. She nodded gratefully.

Sterling pulled something out of his pocket and placed it in her hands. "These are my opera glasses and I want you to use them as much as you like. Have you ever used binoculars before?"

She shook her head as she lifted the metal contraption in one hand and noted the two eyepieces.

"Here, before it starts, let me show you how they work." He put one arm around her and with the other hand helped her raise the glasses to her face, then adjust them with the middle knob, until she could see things clearly. He turned to his mother to make sure she was settled and noticed how intently she watched the crowd with her own opera glasses. "Do you see people I know, Mother?" he asked dryly. He knew she was certainly not the only person here spying on everyone else, but the practice still irked him.

"Yes. Most everyone who is anyone is here tonight," she returned matter-of-factly. "It is a pity your father and brother couldn't join us. They really should be here too." She said all this while gazing through the opera glasses.

"You know they aren't much for opera," he reminded her.

"Oh, I know. But it would be nice if they made an effort every now and then, for my sake—and for their own social standing."

"They have plenty of social standing without attending the opera," Sterling said tiredly, the argument old and stale.

"Hmm, I suppose," she replied absently, still scanning the crowd. "Oh! I see Miss Fairfield! She doesn't appear to be here with anyone but her parents. Maybe she would care to sit with us after intermission. We have an extra seat, after all."

Sterling, unseen by his mother, rolled his eyes at Samantha, and she held back a smile.

"Wouldn't that be nice to see her again?" his mother needled when he said nothing.

"Uh, sure, Mother. Whatever you like. If you need a seat mate, that's your prerogative, I suppose."

"But wouldn't you like to see her, Lee?" Cordelia persisted, lowering the glasses to look at him. "She is considered one of the most eligible young women in the county. And so beautiful!" She gave Sterling a meaningful look, but with his back to her, he missed it.

"Not particularly, Mother. But as I said, if you would like someone to sit with, that is fine by me. I already have who I want sitting here with me." He smiled at Samantha and laced their fingers together.

Samantha thought she heard his mother sniff from behind her, as if she hadn't cared for that last comment. But where Samantha had felt chilled from the weather a few minutes before, she now felt warmed from head to toe.

As the house lights went out and the stage lights rose, Samantha felt an almost palpable sense of excitement. The atmosphere was unlike anything she had experienced before. As the orchestra began playing, the hairs on the back of her neck rose and she shivered. The music was incredibly, unbelievably beautiful! Since becoming friends with Katherine, she had enjoyed attending many musical events in Oberlin put on by talented local musicians, but this was in another class entirely!

Sterling squeezed Samantha's hand, and when a woman stepped out on stage to join all the men gathered there singing, he explained briefly what they were discussing in their song. Samantha was enthralled. She had never heard a full professional orchestra before and she thrilled at the breadth and depth of music it played, seamlessly complementing the singers. The strings sang almost like human voices and the flutes danced sweetly above them. The bold brass and percussion instruments proclaimed their parts in triumph, and it electrified her to the core. It was like being transported into another world, the colors more vivid, the emotion more powerful than the ones in her own. She sat riveted.

At intermission, Sterling rose and Samantha followed him to stand at the back of the box to stretch their legs. Cordelia had disappeared as soon as the curtain fell and the house lights rose. Off to socialize, Samantha supposed.

"What do you think of opera so far?" Sterling asked, smiling in question. "I know there is some provocative subject matter; it is certainly not a story of straight-laced people like ourselves." He chuckled and raised his eyebrows. "Opera tends to be like that."

"Oh, there is so much to enjoy! It really is wonderful," Samantha replied honestly. "I wish I could understand the words, but the whole effect is breathtaking!" She paused, trying to summon adequate words to express her experience. "The music is ethereal and transportive. I don't know how to describe it—it is beyond beautiful! Thank you for this experience, Sterling. I will never forget it." Unbidden, the thought came to her that it might be a memory she would always hold close in her heart because it would be one of the few things she had of him.

As the box was small and they stood closely side by side, it was easy for Sterling to pull her even closer with one hand gently around her shoulder. "I am so glad," he said softly into her ear. "I've never enjoyed opera as much as I have tonight, having you here with me."

His breath tickled her cheek and she smiled, mentally pushing away the negative thought of a moment before and allowing herself to feel loved and appreciated in a way she had almost forgotten with all the loneliness and tension she had felt at the Sterling estate.

"Would you like a drink or refreshment?" he asked.

"No, thank you." Samantha shook her head. "I am still full from dinner."

"Hmm. I noticed you didn't eat very much," Sterling countered, looking at her doubtfully.

She had hoped he hadn't seen that. "That's true," she admitted. She looked up into his deep, brown eyes and her mouth turned up wryly on one side. "I haven't had much appetite the last few days. But I am fine," she hurried to add, as worry lines showed between his brows. "Is eating what most people do during intermission?"

"Many do, yes. But even more of the crowd peers around at everyone else with their opera glasses, trying to gauge who is who among those in attendance, and trying to be seen by the most important." His expression was playful, but also honest.

"Ah," she nodded sagely, her eyes twinkling. "Is that why we're standing back here, away from prying eyes?"

"But of course!" he responded jovially, then sobered. "I thought you might be more comfortable without everyone's eyes on you. And I don't care for the public spectacle, myself."

"Agreed," she said, suddenly serious. "I've been trying not to pay attention to it, but ever since we arrived, I have felt as if all eyes are on us, watching our every move—or at least mine. I am not normally self-conscious, but in this circumstance I can't help it. They can tell, Sterling."

"Can tell what?" he asked, kissing the top of her head. "That I am in love with you? I hope so."

"No," she said, pulling slightly away and looking away from him, out at the sumptuous theater. "That I don't belong here. That we are from two completely different classes of society. That I am an imposter."

"Samantha," he said compassionately. When she remained turned away from him, he said her name again. "Please look at me."

Finally, she dragged her gaze away from the glitter and glamor of the vast hall to meet his eyes, and he saw her pain.

He sighed resignedly. "I see that my mother is getting to you. But you must remember that nothing she says is a reflection of my own feelings. This *used* to be my life, though it always chafed at me and never felt right: the excess, the public show, the glamor and facade." In his earnestness for her to understand him, he had angled his body to face hers. "Please don't internalize anything Mother says, dearest." He cupped her face in one hand and ran his thumb along her cheek. "I know that you are true and good. You could never be an imposter. Remember, you are the secret dream of my heart and I feel most at home when I am with you. I care nothing for what my mother thinks. She is wrong anyway. About so much."

Samantha looked up at him gratefully, deciding against telling him what, exactly, she had overheard his mother say about her—on two different occasions now. He already carried burdens and she didn't want to add to them. But the heaviness in her own heart was lightened a little at his words. Suddenly, she felt the fatigue of a late evening compounded with multiple restless nights and emotionally stressful days. She lifted her hand to his, still cupping her face, and sighed, closing her eyes for a moment. When she opened them and looked up at him, it felt like her heart grew again in love for him. He was wholly good and ever true to her, and she recognized the love shining back at her from his own eyes. She would hold onto that and somehow she would make it through the rest of this visit.

When Cordelia returned, they were holding hands, standing side by side again, looking out at the theater and discussing Carmen's behavior. They turned as one when Cordelia cleared her throat. She was not alone.

"Lee, look who I found!" she exclaimed with evident pleasure, even as her eyes blazed at Samantha. "Isn't it just our fortune that Miss Fairfield is not otherwise engaged? She was gracious enough to agree to join us in our box for the second half. I know you were eager to see her again." Her smile was beautiful but seemed to Samantha a little wolfish.

Cordelia had not exaggerated Miss Fairbank's beauty, Samantha noticed. The young woman's dark, shiny hair was done up in perfect ringlets all around her face, and the soft pink of her gown complimented her exquisitely fair and rosy complexion to perfection.

She was small of stature with generous curves, and carried herself with confidence and poise. Her jeweled necklace and earrings sparkled like her enchanting blue eyes and her full, pink lips smiled seductively at Sterling as if he were the only person in the hall. Samantha felt excessively tall, decidedly angular, and positively plain next to her.

Sterling inclined his head to the young woman, smiled half-heartedly, and intoned, "A pleasure, Miss Fairfield." His mild tone suggested nothing but politeness.

Samantha was infinitely gratified that with this exchange he neither let go of her hand nor moved toward the other woman. She straightened her spine as she smiled at Miss Fairfield. "Hello," she offered.

Miss Fairfield's gaze flitted over Samantha, indicating in the briefest of moments how little she thought of her, then rested once again on Sterling. She didn't try to hide the admiration in her eyes as she looked up at him, and Samantha watched her sizing him up with pleasure, as if he were a delicious meal to be eaten and savored very slowly. The look made Samantha uncomfortable and she felt herself shrinking inside. Sterling's fingers tightened slightly around hers, and she took a steadying breath.

One impossibly graceful dark eyebrow rose delicately on Miss Fairfield's white forehead as she asked in rich, perfectly modulated tones, "How are you, Master Sterling? I have missed you these past two years."

"I am well, Miss Fairfield, thank you," he responded vaguely. "And you?"

"Very well, now that I see you again," the beautiful young woman responded suggestively. "It has been far too long. How are you enjoying the opera tonight? I think it the best rendition of *Carmen* I have yet seen!"

Sterling nodded gravely. "It is very well done, to be sure. The Opera House always produces top-notch performances." After a brief pause, he changed the subject by saying, "Miss Fairfield, please allow me to introduce Miss Samantha Jennings of Ohio." He indicated Samantha at his side and Miss Fairfield's expression gradually hardened as she more fully internalized their locked hands.

"Miss Jennings," the young woman intoned with a small, reluctant curtsy and obligatory bow of the head, but she did not smile.

Samantha responded with her own curtsy and felt a small twinge of sympathy for the gorgeous woman who had obviously intended a very different response to this meeting. Fortuitously, the lights began to dim at that moment, and they moved to their seats before the near-darkness engulfed them.

Samantha allowed herself to again be swept away in the drama of another world throughout the remainder of the performance. While she felt no special affection for the character Carmen, she did feel sympathy for her circumstances. And the ending felt truly tragic for both Carmen and Don Jose. The whole performance spoke dramatically of the shared human condition and the juxtaposition of each person's power and frailty, and of temptation and passion gone awry. Samantha did not feel uplifted by the devastating story, per se, but the grandeur of song and costume, the magnificent talents of the musicians and opera singers, had truly educated her in a new way. And, even though she could have wished for a better situation in which to be with Sterling, she was grateful to have been able to spend this time with him, to feel his unfailing love, and be bolstered by his strength. She vowed to try to hold on to that throughout the coming days, and not doubt her place by his side.

Of course, this vow was tried almost immediately, in the face of Miss Fairfield's beautiful coldness and Cordelia's obvious frustration with and disappointment in her son. On the ride home, despite the cold, Samantha felt herself nodding off, wrapped in a blanket and pressed close to Sterling's side.

After the "disaster" of the evening from Cordelia's perspective, she seemed ill inclined to carry on a conversation. Samantha did not really feel like conversing either, but she did thank them both for inviting her to accompany them—even though she knew the invitation had come exclusively from Sterling.

She also mentioned the little poem she had remembered by Walt Whitman that he wrote to an opera singer, as it seemed appropriate tonight. "I fully understand that poem for the first time now," she admitted. "Having just experienced the opera, I feel a similar gratitude and kinship, somehow, with the singers who lived their roles for all of us to see, out in the open like that. There is a sense of vulnerability in that action, a special kind of gift that is as deserving of reward as a 'hero, speaker, or general.'"

"I agree," Sterling responded.

Cordelia let out a breath of derision. "Such riddles. Whatever do you mean?" she asked irritably, as if she hated to ask, but was curious in spite of herself.

"We're speaking of Walt Whitman's poem entitled 'To a Certain Cantatrice'," Sterling explained. "*Cantatrice*, Mother, is an old word for 'opera singer.' Like many of his works, the poem is short, but redolent with emotion. Let me see... Samantha, you'll have to help me, but I'll take a stab at it."

He began:

> *"Here, take this gift,*
> *I was reserving it for some hero,*
> *speaker or general,*
> *One who should…"*

Samantha felt him turn toward her as he searched for the next words, and she was happy to be able to supply them:

> *"One who should serve the good old*
> *cause, the great idea, the progress*
> *and freedom of the race,*
> *Some brave confronter of despots,*
> *some daring rebel;*
> *But I see that what I was reserving*
> *belongs to you just as much as to*
> *any."*

Cordelia was silent in the dark carriage and Samantha wished she could see inside the woman's mind. After a moment, she said in a flat voice, "Well, what does it mean? It sounds like a lot of nonsense to me."

"That is a good question, Mother. It takes some pondering and working it out in one's mind to discover meanings in poetry." Samantha noted the lack of condescension in his voice, or of impatience or ridicule, any of which would have been easy to justify. In this moment, he was only a teacher trying to impart information to a new pupil. "But as I have studied it, to me it has come to mean that people of all ranks and roles have equal value. All have great things to contribute to society and are equally deserving of our respect."

"Yes," agreed Samantha. "I felt that tonight as I watched the opera, and as I benefited from so many others' talents that are so different from my own."

"Hmph," was the only thing Cordelia offered.

After that, the lateness of the evening and her accumulating sleep deprivation overcame Samantha and she dozed on Sterling's shoulder, his arm wrapped around her. He walked her upstairs when they returned, and as she glanced through the open door of her room, she was glad to see a fire crackling cheerily in the grate.

"I am so glad you accepted my invitation tonight," Sterling said softly, as he drew her into his arms. "It was much more enjoyable with you there."

"Thank you for the invitation," she responded, trying not to yawn against his chest. "It was a wonderful experience." But she couldn't help ending with an honest: "With a few exceptions."

"Indeed." Sterling sighed. "You have now had a taste of what I have despised for so long. But it helped, having you there, you know. A layer of protection, somehow."

"Me? Protecting you?" Samantha eased away from him in surprise, looking up into his shadowed face in the dim corridor.

"Yes, you. As always, you helped me feel stronger."

"Ah," Samantha said, at once understanding what he didn't say. "My presence kept the beautiful wolf from swallowing you whole." Suddenly, a laugh bubbled out of her before she could stop it, and she pressed a hand to her mouth. "Imagine, a sheep saving the lion from the wolf." She shook her head and another giggle spilled out.

"You, a sheep?" he asked, drawing closer to her again. "Hardly. Nor am I a lion—"

She placed a finger on his lips. "The king of beasts? Of course you are. By all appearances, you are the most eligible bachelor in all of Lexington, perhaps in all of Kentucky. I would say the description is accurate."

"Ah, but there you are wrong," he said, grasping her hand and pulling it gently down. "Because I am no longer an eligible bachelor. I am yours, and you have full claim upon my heart forever."

The air between them had suddenly gone from playful to serious and tender, and she searched his eyes in the dimness, unsure all over again how she, a common small-town girl had gained his notice and secured his affections over a woman as striking and vivacious as Miss Fairfield.

"I am glad," she whispered, swallowing down emotion, "because this sheep loves you wholly and completely. And I will do my best to protect you against all the wolves there are sure to be tomorrow night."

Sterling grimaced. "You are right. It will probably not be an easy evening." He stroked her hair and kissed the top of her head, then her ear. He pressed his lips to her forehead and Samantha felt the wall against her back. "I hate these social games," he said under his breath, his deep voice a growl. "After this week, I swear this will be the last time I will play them. Thank heavens I don't have to in Worthington or Oberlin!" He kissed her mouth slowly but insistently and she felt herself melting. "Good night," he said against her hair, and then he was gone and she stumbled into her room and closed the door, ready to sleep for an age.

As she prepared for bed, Hannah helping her make quick work of things, she reminded herself that this period of turmoil, tension, anxiety, and loneliness would not last forever. There would be an end to this visit and a return home next week. She could hold on that long, couldn't she? After all, what was the alternative?

Chapter 28

A VISUAL STATEMENT

December 1902

The next day, the 23rd of December, dawned bright and clear, and Samantha found that, even after her late night, she could not sleep through the sun. The snow sparkled like so many tiny, colored jewels and she sat on the window seat, enjoying the view for a few minutes, until the cold seeping through the pane chilled her and she moved away.

Tonight was the Christmas ball. She realized that more than anything she felt the desire for it to be over. The household had been preparing for weeks and, though Sterling had promised to dance as many dances with her as possible, she knew he would also be playing host, which was his responsibility as the oldest son of the hosting family. So, she tried not to expect too much. She was also concerned about her dancing ability (in spite of Sterling's reassurances), and whether she had what it took to not look a fool among the wealthy and privileged in attendance. After last night's experience with the social elite, she had little desire to be in the thick of it.

She sighed, forcing herself to consider one thing at a time. Sterling would be there and valued her protection from the "wolves." The thought made her smile, as she ran a finger along her lips where he had kissed her the night before. More important was knowing that he considered this a game he had to play for his mother's sake, but which his heart was not in—for his heart belonged to her. And at the end of all this, he would take her home and she could relax once again and not constantly feel as if she were falling woefully short of someone else's standard. These thoughts calmed her troubled heart and helped to ground her as she set about preparing for the day and studying scripture.

Over breakfast, she penned a few lines in her journal about her impressions of the opera, and then decided to brush up on dance steps the best she could. Katherine had been a good and patient dance teacher the year before, and the practice Samantha had had previously at Oberlin dances had helped. But she was certain tonight's dance would not be at all like those country dances!

She kept trying to talk herself out of her apprehension, but she still felt anxiety about being surrounded by those who had been raised to impress. *I will be a minnow afloat in a sea of salmon*, she thought. *They all know where they're going and how to swim upstream together, but I may flounder. This is nothing like my native waters.* She tried not to dwell on this vision of herself contrasted with everyone else, and tried to ignore the knot that tightened and grew in her stomach as the day progressed. She would just be herself, as she always was, but she knew that would not be enough for Sterling's mother, and possibly not for her guests either. However, Samantha also knew now that it would not matter how much she *did* do, it would never be enough for Cordelia—so she shouldn't focus on her. *I will just have to do the best I can and pray I don't embarrass Sterling. He is who matters here, after all.*

After her solo dance practice, Samantha made her way carefully down to the kitchens. She had deduced where this must be and hoped Sterling's mother would not catch her before she found it, as she would undoubtedly disapprove. Fortunately, she made it there in a few minutes after only one wrong turn, and without any resistance from anyone. Unfortunately, the kitchen staff informed her that Mrs. Sterling would not allow any unauthorized help. They had things well in hand. Again, Cordelia had stopped her before she even began.

More and more, Samantha felt hemmed in on every side. In the hallway outside the closed kitchen door, she took a deep breath and let it out slowly, thinking through her options. She didn't expect to see Sterling this morning, perhaps not at all until the ball, and Cordelia would allow her to do nothing to help, so her choices of occupations were small, as usual. In fact, she could see nothing more to do all day but take another turn about the snowy garden or research in the library. Thinking that the garden might be more comfortable in the afternoon when the temperature warmed up a little, she decided to go to the library this morning and see how much time she could take up. It was going to be a long day, she thought wearily.

Longing to be useful to someone, she bit back tears of frustration and resigned herself to hours in the library. The irony wasn't lost on her that in her old life she would have been perfectly happy reading in the library all day. Now she ached for contact with other people—excluding Cordelia. In her old life, she hadn't known or understood the comfort of regular connection with other human beings. Now that she did, there was no one to be found. Added to this was the constant necessity, when outside her room, to step cautiously and be vigilant lest Cordelia catch her unawares. She wished she didn't feel that way about the situation, but there it was. The ever-present tension, the need to be ever watchful, wore on her nerves—but she preferred to be on her guard than to unwarily come upon Cordelia around a corner.

There was just no comfortable way to *be* in this house! Samantha was fatigued with inactivity, loneliness, and worry, but was too tense to sleep well at night or nap much during the day. The food was excellent, but she could not manage to eat more than the token bit to fill up the ache around the knot that seemed to have taken up permanent residence in the pit of her stomach. Had it really only been five days since they arrived? How could she endure another five? The realization that she was only halfway through their stay almost filled her with despair.

She walked quietly down the carpeted hallway leading to the library, knowing her shoulders were hunched, but not caring. Putting a bright face on things when in the presence of others was hard enough, but pretending to herself was impossible. She hoped she could find something in the library that would distract her mind in a positive way.

***

Later, after lunch in her room and then a few turns about the solitary walled garden for as long as she could endure the cold, but enjoying a few minutes of the sun's rays on her upturned face, she returned to the house for a warm bath and to prepare herself for the ball.

The bath was wonderfully splendid and Samantha held onto that positive aspect of her day. Not having to haul the water or heat it on the stove herself was luxury enough, but then there was the generous size of the tub and the lovely soaps and shampoos available to her as well. As she allowed the water's delicious warmth to cover her chilled body, she willed herself to think of nothing but this moment and how good it was to enjoy a warm, aromatic bath on a cold winter's day.

Maybe one day I shall write a poem about this, she mused to herself. *Ode to a Bath...* She giggled softly to herself, surprised she could still find humor in her situation. God bless Hannah for arranging this bath and for her regular ministrations as the fill-in lady's maid! At least Samantha knew she would see *someone* each day, even if it were only for a few minutes at a time.

As she soaked, feeling the tension in her shoulders relax for a while, she thought about what it must have been like for Sterling to grow up here. Her own childhood had been lonely and sparse, but as she compared the two difficult situations, she found herself preferring her own. *I am not sure I would have survived the climate in this beautiful mansion*, she thought. *I would rather be neglected and allowed my freedom than hounded and pushed and compelled to fill Cordelia's impossible expectations.* Samantha had had a surprising amount of free rein in her own little world, she realized, not for the first time. And Sterling, even as a man with all his social status and wealth, had, until recent years, lacked the liberty to truly be his own person and grow in the ways he needed to.

She understood more completely now why he had had to leave home as early as possible, to be on his own and figure out who he was and who he wanted to be. She perceived now what he had been up against and why he had no desire to be the professional gentleman his mother wished.

But all of these realizations over the last few days had also distilled into a bleak picture of the very stark contrast between his background and hers. She had known their upbringings were very different, but now she truly understood just how much. Away from Lexington, it seemed they had many things in common—all the things that mattered, anyway. Here, she wasn't so certain.

Now there were long moments every day when she doubted their compatibility. How could Sterling forsake all of this beautiful life forever? And should he? Surely the privileges, culture, and sophistication were worth something, despite his words to the contrary. And though he had seen so much of the negative side of the elite, surely there were many good people of means here as well. Sterling, being the person he was, could do a great deal of good if he were to accept his share of his family's wealth. But to live this lifestyle, to accomplish that good, he couldn't do it with someone like her at his side.

This sudden realization hit her like a slap in the face, but she knew it was true. She would never thrive in such a life, with all the frills and jewels, manners and polish. Though she loved Sterling with every part of her being, she also knew that love could not flourish the way it needed to in the wrong setting. He always said he would never live here again, that he was much happier in Worthington and Oberlin, working for his own keep and learning alongside his students. But what if he didn't have to choose between teaching and living the life he was raised to live? She hated to think that he might be giving up something truly important for her sake and that he might one day resent her for it. That didn't bear thinking of, yet she had to acknowledge the possibility.

Samantha groaned within herself and covered her face with wet hands. Maybe she and Sterling were just too different. Maybe their dreams together would never work.

***

Hannah came in to do her hair late that afternoon and Samantha was glad for the distraction from her distressing thoughts. She enjoyed listening to the girl's chatter and felt some of the gloom lift. As she saw her reflection in the vanity's wide mirror, watched how Hannah brushed and twisted and pinned her hair, she wondered at her own situation. A year ago, she would never have believed she would one day stay on a sumptuous estate where servants took care of her everyday needs and she was dressed in a gown such as this. She looked at her bare shoulders, at the defined lines of her collarbones and the small hollow between them. Below that hung more borrowed jewels—an exquisite necklace of diamonds and rubies, with an emerald in the center—which perfectly complimented her gown. The matching earrings clipped to her earlobes hung heavy and she hoped they would not slip off and go flying away during the dance. If she lost anything belonging to Cordelia, it would be disastrous! It made her uncomfortable to show so much skin, so she adjusted the gauzy wisp of a scarf around her shoulders, which helped her feel a little less exposed.

Hannah noticed and said apologetically, "I know you're not accustomed to showing decolletage, Miss, but with this dress we found we could not raise it any more than we did without ruining the fabric. And we also didn't want you to stand out by being dressed too differently from everyone else. We hoped the scarf would add enough of a discreet layer to help you feel comfortable." She looked pensively at Samantha's reflection in the mirror.

"Thank you, Hannah, it does help," she reassured the girl. "I am just not used to being on display." She blushed slightly and looked away from Hannah's kind eyes in the mirror.

Hannah nodded. "The other servants and I know things are different here than you are used to, but we admire you for trying. You have been willing to do new things, for Sterling's sake, and we respect you for your efforts."

"The servants talk about me?" Samantha asked hesitantly, not sure if she felt more flattered or embarrassed.

"Oh, indeed," Hannah laughed. "We talk over many things below stairs. The overall consensus is that the two of you are good for each other and that you make him happy. So you have our full support. Not that you need it," she added hastily.

"But we hardly see each other," Samantha said, puzzled at how the servants could have observed all of that when the two of them were rarely together.

"Oh, don't I know it!" Hannah lowered her voice. "Mistress makes sure to keep him too busy to attend to you as he would like." Straightening, she added, "But you didn't hear it from me!"

All of this gratified Samantha, but it didn't change anything. "Do you think I might see him before the ball starts?" she asked with trepidation.

"Oh, yes! I almost forgot. He asked me to arrange to meet you before the guests arrive." Samantha's heart skipped a beat. "He did?"

Hannah nodded with a smile. "He misses you. He told me to tell you..." She paused in concentration. "Let me see if I can remember it all... He said that he is 'determined to break away at a quarter of six' and to 'disappear so completely' that his mother will not know where he is for a 'full fifteen minutes' time, which he will spend with you."

Samantha smiled. That did sound like him. "Where shall I meet him?"

"Here, actually. His mother will be so involved downstairs with the finishing touches that he will 'whisk his way up here to your room and escort you down personally.'" She said this last part triumphantly, as if proud of herself for remembering the right words.

Samantha nodded and smoothed her gown as she stood. "Thank you, Hannah. For everything." She grasped the girl's hand and squeezed. "You have been the perfect lady's maid for me and I have really appreciated your company as well."

"Oh! Of course!" Hannah looked surprised at the compliment, then pleased. "I'm happy to serve, Miss. Very happy to serve." Her dimple winked, and Samantha smiled back.

***

By the time Sterling's light knock finally sounded on her door, Samantha was a bundle of very tightly wound nerves. Without intending to, she had gone over and over what she thought was every possible negative scenario, and the exercise had done nothing to calm her worries. But seeing his handsome face there in the doorway, his expressive brown eyes, and lithe, smiling mouth, instantly calmed the worst of it, and the tension in her frame relaxed. She wasn't sure how his mere presence did that to her, but she was grateful it did. He seemed the same as ever, though possibly more handsome than she had ever seen him.

Sterling, for his part, did not miss the anxiety present in Samantha's features, and tried to put her at ease. "Good evening." He held out his large, gentle hands and she took them with her trembling, gloved ones, then he held her at arm's length, the better to admire her. His smile brightened. "You look wonderful!"

"Really?" she asked doubtfully.

"Really and truly," he assured, looking intently into her eyes. "But I would be happy to have you on my arm all night even if you were dressed in sackcloth." His tone was very serious, but his eyes twinkled.

She giggled and swatted his arm. "Oh, Sterling. Quit teasing." But his quip had done the trick and she suddenly felt much lighter than she had only moments before.

"Actually," he added in a confidential tone, giving her the once over, from head to toe, "You look delicious."

"Sterling!" she whispered in consternation, glancing down the hallway in both directions to be sure he hadn't been overheard.

"What?" he whispered back, leaning closer, both eyebrows raised. "I'm just being honest."

She could feel color warming her cheeks, but decided to focus on him instead—which wasn't difficult. He looked even more impeccably turned out than usual, aside from the wayward locks. Beneath his black single-breasted tuxedo, she was surprised to note that the shade of his vest perfectly matched the dark green of her dress, and his cranberry red bowtie was the same shade as the red she wore. She noticed the bowtie itself was a bit askew. How had he missed that?

"May I?" she asked, reaching up to straighten the stiff, red fabric, then looked up at him, laying a gloved hand on the front of his white-collared shirt. "There. Perfect."

He had watched her tidy him with obvious pleasure.

"How did you arrange...this?" she gestured at their matching colors.

"I wish it was my idea, but it was actually Hannah's," he admitted. "She offered to make the vest and bowtie for me. Apparently, there was quite a bit of fabric left over from the original dress after the alteration, and she thought it might be a good use of it."

"I agree," Samantha nodded, noting how perfectly the white shirt fit his broad chest and the green vest his trim waist, the dark tuxedo perfectly matching the dark pants and gleaming black shoes. She thought the effect was undoubtedly the best use for extra fabric that could be imagined.

She must have looked him over a little too long because he asked her, "What is it?" his brows drawn together.

"Oh." She blinked and looked up at him, blushing slightly. "You just look so handsome, Sterling." The fine clothing that he wore so naturally each day here made his good looks even more striking, and sometimes it quite took her breath away. Particularly tonight.

He grinned lopsidedly. "You shouldn't say such things. I might get a big head."

Samantha laughed, but quickly sobered. Very quietly she asked, "What will your mother think of us making a statement like this? Won't Hannah be reprimanded—or worse?" She fingered his green satin vest and he grasped her worrying fingers in his own.

"It's our secret that Hannah was involved in the scheme," he replied in equally low tones. "I will tell Mother it was all my idea—because once Hannah suggested it, I realized a visual statement would be perfect."

"But won't your mother be angry?" Samantha whispered, again glancing down the hall to be sure they were still alone.

"Perhaps, but that anger should be directed at me. And this statement we are making is just a continuation of the verbal statements I have repeatedly made since we arrived."

He yearned to ease her worries, convince her of his steadiness, and erase the pucker on her brow that indicated her earnest concern. "Now it will just be more public," he explained. But she remained tense. "Samantha, please let me worry about this. You have done nothing wrong and making this statement isn't wrong either, despite anything my mother may think to the contrary." He grasped her other hand, and she felt the warmth of his touch even from inside her gloves. She hadn't realized until that moment how cold her fingers were.

"I stubbornly persist in believing that if I say it often enough, Mother will finally realize I am serious."

Samantha smiled wanly, but her eyes wandered away from his. "What if she's right? Maybe tonight's ball is the perfect time for you to meet someone more suited to—"

"Samantha." Sterling spoke gently but firmly and her gaze returned to his face. "We are perfectly suited." He saw the pain in her eyes, and the doubt that didn't used to be there, and he ached at the sight. He squeezed her hands, willing her to feel how rock solid his belief in the two of them was. "Mother is just blinded by her own prejudices. I pray she comes around—but even if she does not, that should have no bearing on our feelings for one another." In spite of himself, the words came out sounding a little pleading. He wanted so much for her to feel the same conviction he felt, to be comforted in the knowledge that things were the way they had ever been, that for him nothing had changed.

Samantha let out a pent up breath. "I don't want it to, but she somehow has that effect on me. I do love you. You are so strong, Sterling. I want to be like that. I used to be stronger…" she almost said *a year ago*, but caught herself as she realized it had really only been a few days. *How* had it only been a few days?!

In her doubt, her gaze dropped to the floor again and he let go of her hand to raise her chin with gentle fingers. "You *are* strong, dearest. And you will feel strong again once we leave this house, I feel sure." He hadn't realized it until it came out of his mouth, but now he knew that might be what it would take. He sighed, the exhalation heavy with all he wished were different. "I am sorry this time feels so interminable. Only a few more days. Surely things will improve over the next few days." He said it for her benefit, but it was just as much to reassure himself. He rested his hand on her thin shoulder, hoping he wasn't overly optimistic, but sensing she needed to hear hope. Her shoulder blade felt thin, like a bird's wing, and he wondered if she were thinner than she had been a few days ago. She seemed so fragile and he felt even more the need to be strong for her. "What is that time compared to a lifetime together?" he asked, searching her face.

She took in a fortifying breath and let it out slowly. *A lifetime together.* They were not officially engaged, but there it was, his vision of their future. The thought warmed her through. "You are right. I must think positively. Thank you for believing in me—in us."

"Always, Samantha. Always. Now, I took the liberty of choosing you a dance card…" He pulled from his pocket a small booklet with an attached pencil on a string and handed it to her. "I hope you don't mind that I filled it almost completely with my name." He winked at her.

"Oh!" She took the booklet from him and turned its few pages, looking at the list of dances for the evening and all the lines signed with *Lee Sterling* in his neat, upright hand. "No, of course I don't mind. Thank you." The card she held suddenly felt like a lifeline. She hoped this meant she wouldn't be a wallflower too much of the evening. Then she remembered again how rudimentary her dancing ability was compared to his. "I hope I don't embarrass you tonight."

"You won't," he assured her, softly pulling on one of the golden curls Hannah had so carefully molded with the curling tongs. He let go and it sprang back into place. "You could never embarrass me. I can't tell you how much I have been looking forward to holding you in my arms tonight." He put his arms around her and kissed her. Her lips smiled against his.

She looked up at him and smoothed a lock of dark hair from his forehead. "I like these stolen moments," she said. "They are all the more precious for their rarity."

Sterling smiled back, his chest squeezing with the love he felt for her. "There's my Samantha," he said. "And I agree. They are indeed precious." He kissed her nose, which made her laugh, and then her hair. Then he sighed and took a step back, fishing in his pockets and withdrawing a pair of white kid gloves. "We really need more of these moments." He gave her a pained expression and pulled the gloves on quickly. "But for now, we must descend to the masses and join the crowd before Mother sends someone looking for me." He squared his shoulders and held out an elbow. "Miss Jennings?"

She took his arm and walked at his side down the hallway toward the stairs. Her skirts swished with each step and she concentrated on the rhythm of their unhurried stride and on taking slow, regular breaths so she wouldn't focus on the frantic pace of her heart. *I have done many difficult things in my life*, she told herself firmly, *and I can do this too. I have been dancing before, I have faced all kinds of people, and things turned out all right. This will not last forever*, she reminded herself. She would do this for Sterling.

He spoke to her in a low voice as they descended the stairs, distracting her from noticing his mother's eyes on her. But as they walked across the spotless white marble of the front hall, her smile dissipated as if it had never been there.

Cordelia did not look pleased. Those shrewd eyes missed nothing.

In a tone he had employed countless times in such situations, Sterling called out to her cheerfully as her eyes roved from him to Samantha and back again. "Is everything ready, Mother?" he called. "'Tis the hour we've all been waiting for!"

"Indeed," she said coldly, as they stopped in front of her, her lips set in a firm line.

Samantha felt herself shrinking inside. *She believes this was my idea, and regardless of what Sterling tells her, she will continue to believe that,* she realized.

Armed with that knowledge, and the recognition that nothing she could say or do would dissuade Cordelia from believing the worst of her, Samantha determined to enjoy the evening anyway. She would mentally package up this very uncomfortable feeling, the figurative daggers Cordelia shot her way, and set them aside in some remote corner of her brain, where they could be ignored for a while. *I am not at fault*, Samantha reminded herself, *and have nothing to feel guilty about*. Sterling had said as much, and she knew it was true. The thought was fortifying, but as she would discover time and time again throughout the evening, her resolution was much too easy to dissolve and took a great deal of effort to repeatedly rebuild.

Sterling could see from his mother's expression that this potential conflict was something he needed to address right now, at the outset, before guests began arriving at any moment. He did not like the way she looked at Samantha, and the anger that flared in response smoldered hot within him. But he tamped it down. They could not have a family row now, so he tried to quell the flame and schooled his expression to one of casual good-naturedness. "How do you like our matching attire, Mother? Isn't it brilliant—and so festive for your special occasion? I asked our resident seamstresses to make mine match Samantha's and I think they pulled it off beautifully. I surprised Samantha with it just ten minutes ago."

Cordelia's eyes narrowed doubtfully, but her mouth relaxed a fraction.

"And she is a picture, don't you agree?" Sterling put an arm around Samantha's waist and looked down at her appreciatively.

Samantha disliked the attention and was grateful for his arm to hold her up.

"It's high time we had a ball around here, isn't it, Mother! You have worked so hard for this night and now it is about to unfold." Sterling swept an arm around the room to indicate the gorgeous tree, the lights that reflected in the highly polished floors, the pristine beauty of everything around them. Samantha noticed he said nothing about his own involvement in all the preparations.

At that moment, a clatter of hooves could be heard at the front doors and Cordelia signaled to Wilson to open them. Lucas joined them hurriedly, smoothing down his hair and straightening his bow tie. James emerged from the ballroom and walked toward them with that particular gait that made Samantha smile inwardly. She did not know the man well, but all she had seen of him thus far made her wonder how he and Cordelia had ever gotten together. They were so very different! Samantha appreciated his low-key manner and slow, easy smile. He turned that smile on her now and gave a small bow. "Good evening," he said.

She gave a small curtsy and returned the greeting, thinking how odd his gnarled, work-worn hands looked in elegant gloves. He appeared a bit uncomfortable in his dark tailcoat, a large diamond stickpin in his cravat encrusted with tiny rubies and emeralds. Samantha guessed his attire was chosen by his wife and that he would have been much more comfortable in his work clothes. In that moment, she felt a kinship for Sterling's father that she had not felt before. She knew what it was to attend a large social function for someone else, to dress up in clothes that were very different from the preferred attire, and to feel uncomfortable stepping into a different role. Seeing James do the very same for his wife calmed her heart and gave her courage in a new way. If he could do it—had been doing it for well over twenty years—she could do it tonight. And the next night and the next, as long as their visit lasted. *As long as it won't be years for me...*she thought. But she felt a pinch in her heart at that realization, knowing her mental list of all that was different between her and Sterling was growing, despite her attempts to squelch it, and in spite of all Sterling's reassurances.

Chapter 29

THE BALL

Samantha stood in the spacious entryway at Sterling's side as he greeted the guests, with Lucas on her left and James and Cordelia opposite them. Wilson greeted and directed guests while the two footmen took their coats to the coatroom and another servant directed them to the ballroom. Samantha smiled and nodded, curtsied, and offered her hand to gentlemen when indicated. Sterling seemed to know everyone and always said the right things to greet these elite members of Lexington, to acknowledge and welcome them for just the right length of time so that the crowd making its way through the doors continued at a steady pace. She didn't know how to make small talk like this, how to say something without saying much of anything. It felt so superficial to her, but she realized it was necessary in such a circumstance. She wondered how Sterling managed it, when in reality he so loved to delve deeply into a topic and discuss every angle of it. *This is a different kind of conversation in a different setting*, she decided. *And he probably doesn't care for it much more than I do.*

So she stood there and smiled, nodded, and offered what felt like hundreds of *it's a pleasure to meet you's*, knowing she would remember very few of the names. At last, the surge of people became a trickle and Sterling turned to escort her to the ballroom.

"Did I miss the wolf?" he whispered furtively.

"The—oh, you mean Miss Fairfield?" Samantha whispered back, trying to repress a smile with little success. "No, I haven't seen her."

"Good," he said, with an exaggerated show of relief. "That's already a positive beginning to our night."

She nodded, but her shoulders felt tight.

321

"I know it's overwhelming," he whispered in her ear. "Just try to relax and follow my lead."

She smiled at him gratefully.

Drawing nearer to the ballroom, she could hear the beautiful strains of the orchestral ensemble as they played the first of many songs. The "masterpiece" Christmas tree Sterling had told her about stood impressively in one corner, its tiny electric lights reflecting from the polished floor. Sterling led her through the crowded room, greeting people, stopping for a few minutes at a time to have longer conversations with those he knew better, generally ensuring that the guests were comfortable and happy. He was a good host, a skill he must have learned from his mother, who swept around the room, offering refreshments and dispelling compliments everywhere she went. Cordelia obviously thrived in this environment; Samantha had never seen her look so radiant or so completely in her element. Sterling's father, standing among a small knot of men his own age, small goblet in hand, watched his wife as she made the rounds, his mustache tipped up in a small smile and his eyes tender. *He loves her*, Samantha realized with a start. *He really loves her and that is why he puts up with all the upheaval in his household as she prepares for enormous social events, and why he tolerates the formal attire he must wear, and ultimately the event itself. He knows how much she thrives in this atmosphere and how much it means to her. And he wants her to be happy.* This small revelation momentarily took her breath away and James's stature rose in her eyes by several inches. For a few minutes, she heard very little of the conversation around her as she absorbed this new knowledge about James and Cordelia.

She tuned in again just as Sterling was introducing her to a small cluster of young men about his own age. He indicated them one by one and told Samantha their names. Most were horse breeders from the area, though one—by the name of Robert Richford—had left to attend college the same time as Sterling and was only home for Christmas. He was handsome—as indeed they all were, in their own ways—and had an open and friendly smile that reminded her of Sterling. But there the resemblance ended. Mr. Richford's auburn hair was slicked back in perfect neatness, and a plethora of freckles scattered across his nose reminded her of a star-strewn night sky. They also reminded her of Jerome Tomlinson, which made her nostalgic. He was tall and skinny, seemingly all arms and legs, even though he should have grown into them by his mid-twenties. But he was poised and graceful, so at least there was no remaining awkward gangliness of earlier years. Sterling was still the tallest of the group and, in her eyes of course, quite the handsomest. She held on to his arm and focused on what he was saying. He seemed to have a genuine affection for these young men with their shared history and memories, and she was glad to see him enjoy reacquainting himself with old friends.

A few minutes later, the music stopped and the crowd gradually hushed as Cordelia stood at the front of the room to officially welcome everyone to the annual Sterling Christmas Ball.[1] Her husky voice carried well, and she looked utterly at ease and in her element. James stood off to one side, smiling quietly at his wife enjoying the spotlight.

"Welcome, dear friends and neighbors!" She spread her arms gracefully, as if welcoming them all into a warm embrace. "We are so glad for your presence in our home to celebrate the season with us. It is my greatest wish that everyone has a wonderful evening and a very merry Christmas." There was a smattering of applause and then she held out a hand and elegantly gestured at Sterling. "Tonight's ball is held in honor of Christmas, of course, but also in honor of my son, Lee, who is home, at last." She made it sound as if he were home to stay.

At her second gesture, which was more insistent, Sterling sighed quietly and squeezed Samantha's hand on his arm. "I am sorry to leave you here," he whispered, "but I must heed the summons and I think you would rather not join me at the front."

"No," Samantha agreed, letting go of his arm. "It's all right; you go."

After reassuring her that he would return quickly, he strode to the front of the huge room to join his mother and looked out at the audience, smiling and seeming as at ease as Cordelia. He bowed to the room at large as they applauded him, and his mother laid an affectionate, gloved hand on his arm. "Lee has been living in Ohio, helping...unfortunate...children, and we are happy he has traveled all this way to be with us during this happy time of year. As you may recall, he attended this ball last year as well, but I failed to recognize him then, so I wanted to rectify that this year. We are happy he is here." She smiled and paused dramatically, then announced with a flourish, "Let the dancing begin!"

Uproarious applause nearly drowned out the music of the small orchestra as they began playing a rousing song, and couples all around the floor started forming up. Cordelia

---

1. https://www.historyextra.com/period/edwardian/could-you-survive-edwardian
-dinner-party-etiquette-downton-abbey/

turned to her son, and he obliged by dancing with her for a few minutes before adroitly passing her off to his father, who turned out to be quite a good dancer, Samantha noted, impressed.

She also realized she had never seen Sterling dance before now, though she had imagined it a hundred times, and somehow the reality was even better than she had imagined. He danced so gracefully and effortlessly, and now his movement through the crowd as he tried to make a beeline toward her was so poised that it mesmerized her. He was waylaid for quite some minutes as more well-wishers said hello. Samantha knew she was staring, but she couldn't help it. She felt clumsy and inexperienced in comparison and wondered how he would be able to mesh his perfect dancing and manners with her halting attempts.

She was so absorbed in watching Sterling through the first dance and into the second that she didn't notice Mr. Richford watching her until he touched her lightly on the elbow. "May I have this dance, Miss Jennings?" he asked.

She shook herself as if from a trance and turned to look at him. "Oh! Certainly, Mr. Richford. Thank you." He bowed, she curtsied, and then he whisked her into the middle of the dance floor and she wondered how Sterling would ever catch up to her now. Despite Mr. Richford's gangliness, he danced adeptly and Samantha had to focus on the steps and follow his lead to avoid stepping on his toes or moving in the wrong direction.

To Mr. Richford, her obvious concentration was endearing and he couldn't help but smile inwardly. Where had Sterling found such an innocent young flower? He wanted to ask her more about her connection to Sterling, but he sensed the conversation would throw off her steps, so he kept his silence and continued whirling her around the dance floor as the musicians kept up the waltz's quick pace. When the dance ended, Samantha was flushed and out of breath.

"Thank you, Mr. Richford," she said with a smile, her heart beating quickly from the exercise. "I am only sorry my skill does not match yours. I hope your toes do not regret you asking me to dance." She grimaced.

Mr. Richford only laughed. "It was a pleasure," he said, bowing again. Then he looked at someone behind her, grinned, and added, "I think you are wanted."

Samantha turned and Sterling was right there, close enough to have heard his friend.

"Thanks, Robert," he said, putting a hand on Samantha's back. "And I do want you," he said into her ear as they turned into dance position. Her cheeks warmed, but she was happy to have him back at her side.

Mr. Richford did not miss the exchange, though he did not hear what was said, and looked at Sterling, a smile lighting his freckled features. "You've found yourself a delightful partner, my friend." Then, turning to Samantha, he added, "Should you need any further assistance tonight, I would be happy to spin you around the room again."

"Thank you, Mr. Richford." Samantha inclined her head and willed her cheeks to cool. But before she could think about anything else, the music for a quadrille began and couples started forming into small groups. Sterling clasped her hand in his and they joined a nearby couple to form a square. This dance was a bit slower and involved exchanging partners, so it encouraged mingling but made conversation difficult. As Samantha's heart rate returned to normal, she found the rhythm of the movements and repetitions and began to relax a bit. She had just reached the point that she felt comfortable enough with the steps to feel Sterling's eyes on her from a few steps away and smile at him, when a now familiar—and unwelcome—voice immediately brought back all the tension she had felt before.

"Thank you, I don't mind if I do. I'm a bit late, but I always love a quadrille." And there, suddenly in Samantha's line of vision, was Miss Fairfield, taking another woman's place. She looked as exquisite as the night before, though this time she wore a light blue dress that matched her eyes to perfection and showed off rather more bosom than most of the ladies' low-cut dresses. The young man at her side seemed captivated by his new partner, but when Samantha glanced at Sterling, she saw his expression tighten.

The wolf had entered their midst after all and desired to pounce. That much was obvious to both Sterling and Samantha and they were wary throughout the remainder of the dance. Samantha was doubtful she could actually do anything to help the situation, but was determined to try. Sterling silently planned their escape route.

When the dance ended, Sterling expertly escorted Samantha away from the group and into a different crowd, which closed around them and effectively blocked Miss Fairfield from following them. It appeared that was what she had intended to do, for when Samantha glanced back for a moment, she noted Miss Fairfield's thwarted attempt to make her way through the people, and then saw her glare after them as she realized they had won this round. Somehow, even that expression did not mar her perfect beauty, but Samantha shivered at the thought of facing her anger.

Samantha refocused her attention on Sterling, who was speaking with an acquaintance who had asked him a question. He held firmly to her hand and when the next dance began, gracefully moved them into place among the other couples. It was another waltz, this one slower, and Samantha looked up at him, relieved.

He leaned in and asked in her ear, "What does that expression mean?"

"It means I'm glad to be with you for this dance—and that it's not another quadrille. I don't know what Miss Fairfield has in mind, but I have the feeling she has not given up."

Sterling sighed and began waltzing her slowly around the room. This time, she didn't feel as if she had to focus on every step and, instead, could simply follow Sterling's lead and relax into a conversation. "I fear you may be right," he acknowledged. "She has proven persistent in the past, but I had hoped I discouraged her enough last time. Apparently I was mistaken."

"I'm sorry I can't do more to help the situation," she apologized. "But if dancing with you like this provides you any assistance, I am happy to do more of it!"

He grinned in that lopsided way that spoke of both tenderness and humor, and his hand on her upper back drew her a fraction closer. "Oh, this is definitely assisting me. I have wanted to dance with you for a very, *very* long time." His gaze held hers and she felt a thrill move through her. His movements were so graceful that she felt as if they were gliding across the floor, and she didn't even have to think about not stepping on his toes. Dancing with someone who was this at home on the ballroom floor was exhilarating and she didn't want the waltz to end!

A bit breathless, she said, "Sterling, you know my experience is limited, but I must tell you that dancing with you is nothing like dancing with anyone else."

"Well, I should hope not," he teased. "I wouldn't want you to enjoy this so much with anyone else."

She laughed, feeling the tension ease once more, wishing it would stay away. "You are right: being with you is what makes this special. But you really are remarkably skilled. Thank you for being willing to dance with someone whose abilities are so inferior to your own."

"You are doing very well, dearest," he said low in her ear. "I think you may be a natural."

Samantha laughed at the ludicrous statement, but loved him for making it. "I highly doubt that, but you are kind to say so." She thought for a moment and then looked back up at him. "Maybe I just needed a man who could lead in the right way."

Sterling mused on this a moment as they continued their circuitous glide around the floor, Samantha's skirts swirling around them.

Samantha smiled up at him. "Thank you for making me look good."

Sterling dismissed this with a shake of the head. "Oh, no. You do that all on your own." He gave her an extra whirl and they spoke little for the remainder of the dance, just enjoyed being together.

All too soon, the dance was over and they parted reluctantly. Sterling kept hold of her hand and led them to the refreshment table, where he presented her with a lemonade, which she took gratefully, as her throat was parched. They settled on seats near the refreshment table and spoke together as they rested and sipped their drinks for a few minutes, watching the couples swirl past them. As Samantha drained her goblet and turned back toward Sterling, she saw someone making her way through the crowd toward them.

"Sterling," she warned in a low voice, placing a hand on his arm.

He looked in the direction of her gaze and saw Miss Fairfield moving closer, a determined air about her. He groaned. "Already?" After a heavy sigh, he stood resignedly and said, "Unfortunately, it appears this was inevitable."

Samantha set her goblet on the table and stood up as well. He touched her gloved fingers with his own and said apologetically, "I'm sorry to have to do this, but I think I had better dance with her and clear up this matter without any further delay."

"I think that's probably wise," Samantha agreed. But her stomach clenched with worry.

When Miss Fairfield arrived, Sterling was ready for her and Samantha moved off to one side to allow them privacy.

"Ah, there you are!" Miss Fairfield exclaimed, as if she had only now caught sight of him. "I've been looking all over for you! I seem to recall you promising me a dance years ago that I intend to claim tonight. You wouldn't want to go back on a promise, now would you, Lee?" she asked, shaking a finger at him, her pretty lips pouting slightly.

Sterling cleared his throat and reminded himself to be both patient and civil. "I will keep my promise, Audrey, if you will agree that this one dance will fulfill it, as I have no intention of extending it beyond that."

"Oh, Lee, you are such a rogue," she teased, swatting his arm playfully. "Every other man here is dying to dance with me and you play hard to get." She laughed a low chuckle that made Sterling's skin crawl. "But I see through your game. I know you want me as much as any man. You just act as if you are above all that." She sidled closer to him and looked up through her long, dark lashes. "You are a very attractive man, after all, and I am a beautiful woman. Why shouldn't we enjoy one another's company?"

Even in her removed position and with the noise of the music and the crowd, Samantha heard enough of the conversation to be shocked by the woman's behavior and her heart leapt into her throat. How would Sterling handle this?

Surreptitiously, she watched his hands tighten into fists at his side and then forcibly relax. His face, which had tightened also, loosened into a polite smile, but his eyes held no warmth. "I play no games, Audrey. Again: I will offer one dance and one only, as is appropriate."

"And yet you have danced twice already with that skinny thing from Ohio," she said airily, waving a dismissive hand. You two aren't engaged are you? Please tell me you wouldn't throw away your good looks and charm on something like *that*." The last word sounded like she meant to say *trash*, yet her tone was so benign and said with such an expression of apparent goodwill, that at first Samantha thought she must have heard wrong.

But Sterling's coloring heightened as he warned, "Audrey, there is no call for—"

Miss Fairfield held up one forefinger and said coquettishly, "One dance, Lee."

Sterling scrutinized her from beneath dark brows, his face completely serious. "And then you must let me alone."

Miss Fairfield's eyes flashed, but her flirtatious smile remained. "If you *really* want me to leave you alone." Her tone was disbelieving, but another look at Sterling's unyielding expression prompted her at last to say, "All right, just one dance."

Samantha watched them move off together and take their positions for the polka that had just begun. She fervently prayed for Sterling to have the wisdom he needed to handle this situation, and resolved not to watch them in worry the whole time. Back at the refreshment table, she selected a cookie and successfully willed herself to eat it, even though it didn't really fit around the knot in her stomach. A middle-aged gentleman asked her to dance, and she thanked him graciously afterward, hoping that maybe her skills were improving after all. But as her confidence rose a notch at this thought, she suddenly overheard a young woman laughingly tell her companions, "Well, I don't know about that, but *I* heard that the girl Master Sterling brought from Ohio is posing as a young heiress when she is, in actuality, a poor farmer's daughter. Somehow, she has pulled the wool over his eyes and he is blind to her faults. Though I don't know how. He was always so intelligent…"

"I heard that too!" one of her companions exclaimed. "What does he see in her, anyway? Any one of us is more attractive than *she* is!" They all tittered and continued their gossiping, but Samantha had heard enough and snuck away, mortified.

She walked quickly, head down, hoping no one would notice she had heard the conversation. The young women's words hurt, not just because they were unkind, but also because most of what they said was untrue. She found space behind a tall, potted plant in a recessed window and took a few minutes to allow her pulse to slow and the tears pricking her eyes to melt away. She took a deep breath and smoothed her skirt with both hands, willing their shaking to calm.

Why did these young women feel the need to gossip about her? Because she was the guest from another town, an outsider? Or because they were jealous of Sterling's obvious attentions to her? And why speak that way about their hostesses' oldest son, when they should feel honored to have been invited to one of Lexington's most coveted balls? Why such competition for Sterling? She knew he was quite the eligible bachelor and she'd noticed that all women seemed to admire him—but weren't there enough men to go around? And wasn't it unfair to the other young men that all the ladies were vying for Sterling's attention and favor? Many of the other young men were quite handsome too, as she had already noted.

Dashing at her eyes to catch any stray moisture, she squared her shoulders and discreetly looked around, a headache beginning to pound at her temples.

Where could Sterling be? Samantha didn't see him on the dance floor anymore, so she decided to make a slow circuit to find him. It would have been easy to miss him, with the number of people crowding the ballroom, and all the movement constantly changing everyone's positions.

She made it halfway around the room, somehow managing to smile and nod at people who greeted her, but still saw no sign of Sterling—or of Miss Fairfield, she realized with a sickening feeling. Another young man asked her to dance and she knew she couldn't refuse without offending him, so she tried to use the opportunity to scout out the rest of the room. By the end of the dance, she knew for certain that neither Sterling nor Miss Fairfield was here. She felt she should do something, but didn't know what. Not only was this not her house, she didn't know all the rules of society—in fact, she probably was not even accepted or respected by most of these people. She had no power or clout here at all.

Think, she commanded herself. *There must be something I can do!* The only advantage she had that she could think of was that she could usually blend into the background, that when she wasn't with Sterling she was not constantly watched. *I think I could slip in and out of here without anyone noticing*, she decided.

As she stood there, uncertain as to her route but trying to be invisible, she overheard an older gentleman tell the man at his side, "Personally, I think the young man should be free to choose whomever he wants for a wife, regardless of where she comes from. He has a good head on his shoulders and has been out in the world for a few years now. He ought to know his own mind."

"I agree with you there, I just never pictured him choosing such an ordinary-looking girl. I'm not certain what he sees in her, but..."

Samantha felt her cheeks flame, realizing that once again she and Sterling were the topic of conversation. Suddenly the spacious ballroom felt much too small, and she thought she might suffocate in the press of people and noise. She made a beeline for the large doorway and prayed no one would see and stop her. Forcing herself to walk in what she hoped was a casual manner, she arrived at the giant ballroom doors which were open into the foyer, and turned to look back, feeling someone's eyes on her. For a moment she caught sight of Cordelia looking directly at her with a satisfied half-smile on her face, and had the sickening thought that she was the one who had started the rumor about Samantha being a poor farmer's daughter. Or, if she hadn't, perhaps Miss Fairfield had. It was well within Miss Fairfield's capability to spread untruths like that far and wide, and she and Cordelia *had* sat together for the last half of the opera last night. Maybe the two women had planned all this.

Samantha inwardly shook her head. She had no proof and she didn't like thinking this way. It was speculative and degrading and she didn't want to lower herself—even in her thoughts—to the level of some of the people she had met tonight.

She squared her shoulders once more, gave a grim, unflinching look back at Cordelia, and slipped out of the large ballroom.

Chapter 30

THE WOLF AND THE LAMB

December 1902

Samantha nodded at the footmen on either side of the huge doors and thought to ask them if they had seen Sterling recently. At first, she was afraid they wouldn't answer her, but then one of them furtively told her he had noticed Master Lee pass by with a young woman about twenty minutes before, and that she had mentioned the library.

Samantha thanked him hurriedly and tried to keep herself from running. Suddenly, she instinctively knew the library was the right direction to go, but had no idea what she would find or what she should do once she arrived. The pain at her temples pulsed and her palms grew damp. Once out of sight of anyone else, she did run until she could see the library doors. One was partially open and through it she could hear Miss Fairfield's laughter. But it was not a good-humored laugh and when she heard the conversation inside, the hair stood up on the back of her neck.

"Audrey, I told you no two years ago—and more than once!" Sterling's raised voice sounded exceedingly frustrated. "I have tried my utmost *not* to give you the wrong impression, but you persist in willfully misunderstanding me!"

"Oh, you are worth being persistent for." Miss Fairfield's sultry voice carried easily to where Samantha stood in the doorway. "I know what you want. I know what every man wants. You just like playing that you don't, so I will pursue you all the more. I know what will make you happy and I can give it to you."

Sterling's voice rose louder than before. "Your assumptions are entirely baseless. My answer is still no! I kindly ask that you leave and return to the ballroom. There are plenty of other men there who would love to dance with you."

"But you are the only one I want." Miss Fairfield's voice was low, seductive, and a little pouty. "And I always get what I want." Then there was the sound of a chair crashing to the floor and a grunt.

"Imagine, Lee. Just imagine, when we are discovered here, all alone together, and I tell my side of the story, complete with tears. How will that make you look?" She laughed again and the sound grated on Samantha's ears. "You don't really want a forced wedding and a stain on your pristine reputation, now do you? Just agree to an engagement and none of that has to happen. We can go back out to the ball, no one the wiser. Think what a beautiful pair we will make! Everyone expects us to be together anyway, you know."

As she spoke, Samantha, with pounding heart and sweating palms, pulled the door fully open and stepped inside to find Sterling sprawled on the couch with Miss Fairfield in his lap. Samantha's face flamed and she felt indignation on Sterling's behalf. How dare this woman pressure Sterling and try to force his hand! Lies, selfishness, manipulation—she couldn't believe that even someone like Miss Fairfield would stoop so low.

The expression on Sterling's face was an alarming mixture of anger and fear, and seeing fear in him for the first time, Samantha knew now was the time to act. She allowed her indignation to give her courage and strength. As Sterling tried to disentangle himself from Miss Fairfield's clinging embrace, Samantha said firmly but quietly, "Miss Fairfield, what do you think you're doing?"

The dark-haired young woman started and whirled around, standing quickly and straightening her dress, which gaped alarmingly at the front. In only a moment she had recovered her poise and said airily, "Why, Miss Jennings. Fancy meeting you here. Coming to check on your rich heir? I hate to tell you, but he is being very naughty. Would you believe, he—"

"No," Samantha interrupted, her eyes spitting fire.

Sterling rose quietly from the couch and ran a hand through his hair, his mind whirling, trying to gather his wits about him. Had this really just happened?!

Samantha felt a surprisingly strong surge of anger rise up within her—an entirely unfamiliar feeling. "No, I wouldn't. Because I know him. I heard you and I know what you're trying to do." Her voice shook, but she clenched her fists and kept on, firm as a rock anchored in cement. "I would advise you to accept Sterling's refusal and set your sights elsewhere."

"And if I don't?" Miss Fairfield's beautiful blue eyes glinted with challenge.

"Then I will be forced to tell everyone what I saw and heard here, and it will be *your* reputation ruined."

"You wouldn't dare!"

Samantha drew herself up to her full height, several inches taller than Miss Fairfield, which for once felt like an advantage. She clung to the feeling. "I would and I shall—but only if you press me. If you leave now and desist forever in this ridiculous and disgusting display of feminine wiles, I will say nothing of it to anyone."

Miss Fairfield sniffed and patted her hair, but she looked more subdued than a moment before. "I didn't think you had it in you, little mouse." She eyed Samantha disdainfully, but there was a tinge of respect there now. "Very well. Consider me gone and that this never happened." She swept out of the room and the scent of her perfume wafted after her.

After she heard the other woman cross the threshold, Samantha let out the breath she didn't know she'd been holding and forced herself to relax her clenched hands. She saw the chair that had fallen near the couch and moved to right it, realizing her hands were shaking. As she set it upright, she realized something else that she would never have thought possible: she was still angry, but now her anger was directed at Sterling. She remained turned away from him, hands on the back of the chair, trying to collect her thoughts. The headache flared and she closed her eyes.

"Samantha?" Sterling touched her gently on the shoulder. She opened her eyes and turned slowly around, but she didn't look at him.

"Am I ever glad you came when you did! If I had known what she was up to, I never would have agreed to come in here with her! You were wonderful."

His words barely touched her. She stood there, trembling, refusing to meet his gaze, hating that she felt as she did, but knowing they needed to address this *now*. "I don't understand, Sterling."

"What do you mean..." he trailed off, his eyes widening. Did she actually believe he had done something unseemly? Was she doubting that she knew him, as she had told Audrey she did?

"Why did you agree to go *anywhere* with her? That doesn't make any sense to me." She looked up at him, finally, and her gray eyes snapped. "You knew what kind of woman she is. I know you did! You were on a first-name basis. You have a history. Surely you knew what she was capable of!"

Sterling took a step backward in surprise at her obvious indignation. "I—yes, I should have known better," he acknowledged heavily. "I should have been more careful. I don't know why I let my guard down!" He ran a hand through his hair again in agitation, feeling angry at himself and baffled by the whole situation. Why hadn't he seen any of this coming? And now Samantha, his beloved, was angry—at him! And she had every right to be.

"And why would you allow her to trap you in a room without a chaperone, after all you went through with me on that very omission?" Samantha's chest heaved as her heart pounded and she fought to gain control of this emotion she was so unaccustomed to feeling.

Sterling's eyes darted around the library with an expression akin to panic. When he saw the empty sofa where the elderly servant had sat to chaperone them previously, the color drained from his face. "You are right," he said hoarsely, his glance falling on hers again, his face stricken. "She was assigned to be there all evening, in case any of our guests desired a respite from the busy ballroom. In my hurry to get in and out of here, and then Audrey's...advances, I completely failed to notice my old nurse's absence! Whatever could have happened to have prompted her to vacate her post?"

As the answer hit them, their eyes widened simultaneously.

Sterling had only to say one word: "Mother!" Surely it had all been arranged and orchestrated with assistance from the lady of the house, or Audrey's machinations would not have been so nearly successful. He closed his eyes and shook his head in disbelief. He really had been a naive idiot!

Seeing his bewilderment, contrition, and distress, Samantha felt a bit of her anger ease away and her pulse slowed as she exhaled, trying to put together all the pieces that contributed to the almost-fiasco. "What exactly happened?" she asked quietly.

Instantly he grasped onto this olive branch and opened his eyes to assess her expression. Was she still angry with him? She should be. He saw her color still heightened but her expression open and wanting to understand, so he took a fortifying breath and thought back on the sequence of the past half hour.

Running a tired hand down his face, he said, "She told me she needed to borrow a book that her parents hadn't been able to find anywhere and which I knew I had. I believed her, but I obviously shouldn't have." His self-recrimination was obvious. "You are right: I knew better and should have been suspicious. I think I must be out of practice at this sort of thing." He shrugged his shoulders in acute apology. "I trust people more easily than I once did and now accept them at face value—which was not how I was raised..." His anguished expression spoke volumes.

Samantha felt her heart softening as she realized what a terrible reality he spoke of. No one should have to feel guilty for not being suspicious and untrusting. No one should upbraid himself for expecting others to be honest and chaste.

He sighed and looked at the floor, his frame dejected. "I thank you, Samantha, for coming just when you did. You saved me. Again!" He looked up, his pained gaze tentatively touching hers. "But I am very sorry I allowed myself to be put in a position that required rescue. I knew the wolf was in our midst and circling, and I still..." He looked away.

If he were a cursing man, he would have cursed in that moment. He hated himself for being weak, for letting his guard down, for not heeding that little voice in the back of his mind that had warned him not to leave the ballroom. He didn't blame Samantha one bit for feeling angry with him. He was angry with himself!

Samantha looked at his tall, miserable form, his broad shoulders slumped, and felt all the anger drain out of her—and the extra strength it had given her. In a rush, the reality of what could have happened flooded over her: how easily someone could have found him and Audrey here alone, made assumptions, and believed Audrey. She felt sick to her stomach.

"Sterling, what if I hadn't come in time?" she asked in a whisper, grabbing hold of the chair at her side to steady herself. She felt so tired now and the headache had lodged itself sharply behind her eyes. "She would have ruined you, and then we—" her voice choked and she couldn't finish the thought.

Sterling's eyes flitted back to her face. Seeing her distress, which mirrored his own, he instantly stepped forward and took her in his arms, relieved when she let him. "I know! It doesn't bear thinking of. I am so sorry. So very sorry! It will never happen again. You...you're shaking, dearest." He drew back and looked at her, noting the anguish in her eyes, which shimmered with unshed tears. "Are you all right?"

She took a deep breath. "I will be." She was relieved the anger was gone, that she and Sterling were reconciled, but now she felt weak with exhaustion. "But I don't think I can go back in there yet. And we can't stay in here either."

"I know the perfect place," he said. Grasping her hand, he gently pulled her out of the room and back down the hallway. Instead of heading back to the ballroom, he turned left and led her to a wing of the mansion she had never seen before. Soon they saw another couple walking ahead of them and Samantha watched as they opened a glass door at the end of the hall and stepped inside. The smell of damp earth and foliage seeped out after them and Samantha looked inside, curious in spite of her fatigue.

"Is this...?"

"The conservatory? Yes." They walked up to the door and he held it open for her. "I've been meaning to bring you here since we arrived, but like so many of my good intentions, it never materialized." His voice sagged with regret.

The door shut behind them and Samantha caught his hand in hers again as they began to walk around the high-ceilinged glass room. She hoped he could feel through her touch that she wanted to be in accord with him again. The large space was well lit, but with the darkness outside and the lamps low, there were still many corners where the light did not reach. The air was moist and warmed by unobtrusive wood stoves. She imagined what the space might look like during the daytime and hoped she could come back and find out. She luxuriated in the atmosphere of green tropical plants and the feeling that they had suddenly jumped forward into summer.

"I am sorry I was angry with you," she said softly. "I'm not anymore. Mostly. I see now what a difficult situation you were in."

He looked at her beside him and gave a sad smile. "You had every right to be angry; I am angry with myself. But I do learn from mistakes and I promise never to allow myself to be compromised like that again."

She nodded and squeezed his hand. "You told me before about how some of the society women are, but it wasn't until tonight that I fully grasped what you meant."

"Hmm. Yes. I hate that you had to find out this way. I hope that will be the end of it."

Samantha gave him a doubtful look before turning away to admire a gorgeous white rose bush, but he didn't miss her expression and pulled her to a stop in front of the flowers.

"Tell me," he asked, "has something else happened?"

"I…" She sighed. "I don't know. It is probably just speculation on my part. I probably shouldn't say." She grimaced inwardly, touching the velvet petals with one finger. She had managed not to tell him about all the things she had overheard over the past few days, so why hadn't she kept this to herself as well? It must be the fatigue and the headache, which made proper thinking difficult.

"Shouldn't say what, Samantha?"

A middle-aged couple walked past them and Sterling gave a little bow and a murmured greeting in acknowledgement, then turned back to her. "With you, I very much doubt it's speculation. What happened?"

"I don't—I don't know. It's probably nothing." She couldn't meet his eyes as she thought about what she had overheard in the ballroom.

Her hand cupped one of the soft roses and he placed a hand under hers, drawing it toward him, along with her other hand. He faced her directly. "Please tell me. I can see it's something upsetting."

"I am trying really hard not to let it bother me, but…" She looked up at him and saw the care and concern in his brown eyes. "People are saying things about me that are not true, Sterling. And I have the feeling that Miss Fairfield and…and your mother are the ones who started the rumors." She hated how petty that sounded out loud and rushed to finish. "But I don't want to think that way about them, because I have no proof." She shook her head, then winced at the headache that pulsed with the beat of her heart. "I know what they're saying in there is not true, so it should not bother me. I wish it didn't."

Sterling's mouth tightened and his dark eyebrows drew together. "What are they saying?"

"I…I shouldn't implicate your mother. I'm sorry." She took in a deep breath and let it out slowly. "Miss Fairfield is one thing—we've just seen what she can do—but I shouldn't speak negatively of my hostess."

Sterling put his hands on her shoulders and pressed gently, noting again how thin and fragile she seemed. "Don't worry about that. We both know Audrey's schemes could not have been as successful as they were without Mother's help. I know what my mother is capable of and I don't think this will surprise me, whatever it is."

She swallowed and willed herself to speak nonchalantly, as if it didn't pain her to think about the unkind words. "People are saying I am really a poor farmer's daughter who has pulled the wool over your eyes and made you believe I am a rich heiress."

For the second time in only a few minutes, Sterling almost wished he were a cursing man, for he would have let loose a stream of profanity at the absurdity of such accusations. As it was, all he could do was stare at her in consternation, fire raging in his eyes. She put a hand on his chest, as if to calm him, and he took a leveling breath.

"I don't think I would mind being a poor farmer's daughter." She shrugged slightly, a gesture of resignation that squeezed at his heart. "That doesn't bother me. But it distresses me to think that anyone might believe I really have deceived you and am not who I claim to be. Dishonesty and facades go against my very nature, Sterling!"

"Yes, they do," he agreed.

"And I also don't like people believing you are foolishly deceived when they *know* you are a highly intelligent person. It just doesn't make sense." She realized she had now said that twice in only a short time.

"Dear Samantha." He pulled her close and put his arms firmly around her. "Any falsehoods currently circulating will be discredited over time, and my reputation—which you have single-handedly saved tonight—will bear the test of time."

She nodded against his chest and closed her eyes. Why couldn't she just stay here like this for the rest of the night? Greater fatigue was creeping over her fast and the headache showed no signs of abating. "But *I* have no reputation here. I am dispensable, and I think your mother is banking on that."

Sterling groaned in misery and she felt it deep in his chest. "I am so sorry," he said again. "I keep saying that, as if that could erase all the bad that has been done, even as I know it changes nothing. I wish I *could* change it all." He rubbed her back in a comforting motion and they stood silent for a few moments.

Finally, Sterling asked, "Why do you think the rumor was started deliberately by my mother and Miss Fairfield? I am sure you have good reason to believe that."

Samantha spoke with her cheek pressed against his chest and without opening her eyes. "Oh, I... I can't be sure, but the expression on your mother's face as I left the ballroom looked...triumphant. But," she paused, trying to think through the fog in her brain, to articulate what she had sensed. "I can't see her actually passing on the rumor herself while her son is involved and she is the hostess of the ball."

Sterling growled low in his throat. "You are right about that. So that is probably where Miss Fairfield comes in."

"Yes, and they were—"

"Together last night at the opera."

"Exactly." Samantha sighed. "Oh, Sterling, I don't want to believe it, but I feel it's true." She opened her eyes and drew back to look up at him. "I just want to curl up in a ball and hide from this until it all goes away, but I know that won't help. I know I need to be strong for you and that I have to go back out there and pretend like nothing is wrong."

"Because *they* are wrong—the rumor is wrong—not you."

"Yes," Samantha said in a small voice. And then after a moment, as if to herself, said, "I have done many hard things before, I can do this too."

"You have and you can," Sterling said gently, rubbing her back again. "Another few days and we will be gone from this place and all its hurtful rumors and deceitful pretenses. But I am sorry you have to go through this. There I go again: apologizing but changing nothing! I probably should not have dragged you into this to begin with. You should be at home with Mrs. Dolittle, Claire, and your father, enjoying a quiet night reading by the fire!"

"That sounds lovely," she admitted. "But Mrs. Dolittle and Claire are visiting family in Amherst, and Father isn't always much company anyway. And I would have missed you dreadfully if I had stayed behind!"

"So you don't actually regret coming?" He spoke tentatively, not certain he had heard her correctly.

She answered slowly and haltingly, distractedly adjusting his bow tie. "I don't regret being here with you...though we haven't spent much time together." Sterling made as if to speak, but she hurried on. "I don't like to complain, but it really has been difficult, Sterling." Her voice was tired but firm, and he saw nothing but stark honesty in her features. "I must confess, the days have been interminably long." She paused for a long moment and he waited for her to continue. "It is hard to fully express how trapped I have felt in this huge place with all its extra rooms. It's ironic, really..."

Sterling's heart dropped. It appeared things had been even more difficult for her than he had realized. "You have been left too much on your own and that isn't fair to you." His expression was pained and he put an arm around her as they began walking again.

They didn't talk for some minutes while Sterling thought and Samantha tried not to. She felt like she was in another world, here in this tropical climate with its lush plants and the rich scent of fertility. It was an oasis in the midst of a tense and stressful day, and she was grateful for the reprieve, though she knew it would be brief.

At the far end of the conservatory, they found an unoccupied bench and she sank down gratefully, Sterling beside her. He put his arm around her and she leaned her head on his shoulder. "I am so tired," she admitted, unable to stifle a yawn.

"You are not used to such late nights," Sterling observed. "How well have you been sleeping? Are your accommodations comfortable?"

She closed her eyes. "Everything is very comfortable, but I don't think I've had a good night's sleep since I left home."

Sterling squeezed her shoulder, feeling grim. She was suffering more than he had been aware and he felt terrible for not recognizing to what extent. "How about food? When was the last time you ate a good meal?"

She raised her head in surprise and tried to remember, her fair brows knitted together in thought. "I-I don't really remember. All the food has been delicious, but I have not had an appetite. I did try to eat breakfast and lunch today. At least, I think I did..."

"Hmm." He had the feeling she wasn't eating much of anything, but as he had spent so little time with her, that was mostly conjecture. And it shouldn't be. He *should* know; he should have been taking most, if not all, his meals with her. She really did seem thinner lately. He rubbed her arm and she laid her head back on his shoulder.

"Remember how you took such good care of me when I had pneumonia?" he asked.

"Of course," she murmured. "How could I forget?"

"Well, I want to do the same for you now. I want you to try to forget all the negative things you heard tonight, all the unpleasantness with Miss Fairfield, and just relax, if you can. Dinner will be served in about half an hour, and I want you to try to eat as much as you can. I have arranged for us to sit together and if Mother has changed seating arrangements, I will change them back. I am watching over you tonight and I won't leave your side. Mother can try to send me on any errand she contrives, or introduce me to anyone she wishes, but on this I will stand firm. You have had enough time in your life to be alone, you don't need to feel alone anymore. Besides, you're wasting away, dearest." He caressed her face with his thumb, feeling the contours of her cheekbones and her small chin.

She murmured something, half asleep against him. A tear glistened at the tips of her golden lashes, but she looked relaxed at last—a state he realized he hadn't seen her in for days. He looked at her, marveling at how strong she really was, even though she didn't feel like it at present. He decided to let her rest for a few minutes in this chaperoned sanctuary before they joined the crowd for dinner. As they sat there, he contemplated what he could change, if he should confront his mother when this event was over, and what he could do to provide a buffer for Samantha for the remainder of their stay. He wanted to give her that—he owed it to her—but he also hoped that through his actions, the statement he had wished to make tonight would be further solidified and make things easier for them moving forward.

***

The small nap did Samantha a world of good, and when she left the conservatory with Sterling, she realized the headache had abated enough to bear.

When they arrived at the head of the huge banquet table near Sterling's mother—his father sitting at the opposite head—Samantha didn't miss Sterling's subtle switch of Miss Fairfield's name card for her own at their plates. When Cordelia asked him in icy undertones, but with a perfectly pleasant expression, where he had been, he responded evenly that it was none of her concern and not to worry herself about it. When Samantha glanced around the table, she was surprised to note that she did not see Miss Fairfield there anywhere, and the dread she'd felt in the pit of her stomach melted away.

"Did you send Miss Fairfield away?" Cordelia hissed, turning to her son as all their guests noisily took their seats.

"In a manner of speaking, Mother, yes." Sterling responded, in a low voice. "But no, I did not tell her to leave the party." His jawline was taut. "She must have grasped that wish of mine all on her own. At long last."

Cordelia harrumphed, then said nothing more about it throughout the meal as she went back to acting the gracious hostess.

Sterling turned his full attention to Samantha as the servants brought in dish after dish. He offered her small portions of the choicest cuts of meat and fish, the creamiest potatoes and butteriest roasted vegetables. He encouraged her to try the soups and sweetbreads, and anything else he thought she might particularly enjoy.

The guests sitting closest to them chatted pleasantly with their seat partners, but they noticed Sterling's close attention to the young woman at his left, noted their matching attire, and couldn't miss the way they spoke to and looked at each other, as if they two were the only ones in the room. The guests couldn't help seeing their open and honest expressions and mannerisms, as if Sterling and the young woman were simply being themselves and not trying to impress each other. This gave the onlookers pause and provided food for thought long after the meal ended.

Cordelia unwillingly noticed all of this as well, looking on with great disapproval, but as she could do nothing about it under the public circumstances, she occupied herself by chatting with the guests nearest her, and tried to ignore the tender love manifesting itself at her elbow. Why, oh why, did her boy have to choose a girl like that?!

Samantha still had little appetite, but she ate to please Sterling and found that the headache receded and the hollow ache in her stomach dissipated completely. The only thing she turned down was the wine, as did Sterling. By the end of the meal, her corset felt very tight against her ribs. When he offered her dessert, she quietly but laughingly pleaded for him to desist.

"Truly, Sterling, I can't eat another bite. I think I just ate as much in this one meal as I did the rest of the week combined."

"Good," Sterling said with satisfaction and touched the toe of his shoe to hers. "I don't want you to be light-headed as we finish the ball."

"You don't care for fainting ladies?" she teased under her breath.

"I would care for you, regardless, but I do want you to be comfortable and well so you can dance with me."

"Ah, I see," Samantha responded. "Well, I am afraid I am much too full to be comfortable, but I can promise you that I will not faint. Although, I can't promise to stay awake." She wiped daintily at her lips with a napkin, then folded it and laid it beside her plate. "With all this food sitting heavy in my stomach, I am suddenly more tired than ever. What time is it, anyway?"

"It must be near ten," Sterling said.

"So early?" she asked, stifling a yawn. "I don't know how much longer I can last."

"Well, the nice thing about a ball happening in the house where you are staying is that you can easily bow out early, if you are not the host or hostess. Some society dinners don't begin until midnight, so in that sense, the night is still young." Samantha shook her head in disbelief and he chuckled. "I am no longer used to keeping such hours myself, now that I am a seasoned teacher with a teacher's early schedule."

Samantha's fair brows raised in amusement. "Seasoned, are you? I *thought* I glimpsed a few gray hairs there among all the dark ones, but I wasn't certain."

"Oh no," Sterling disagreed with feigned seriousness. "I wasn't referring to my still perfectly uniformly dark hair as befitting someone of my youth, but to my vast experience of teaching at the boys' school. You know, I have an entire year under my belt now." His sudden lopsided grin as he poked fun at himself made her heart skip a beat.

But she returned his banter by nodding sagely and replying, "Ah yes, quite the vast experience. One year is definitely extensive." Her quick humor in response to his own tickled him and he was silently amazed that after all she had been through here, with his mother only a few feet away, she could still be lighthearted.

As they all stood to return to the ballroom and the dancing, Samantha hoped the servants would be able to clean up early enough to still get several hours of sleep that night, but as she surveyed the enormous table and the vast array of dishes, she had the feeling there would be little sleep for them. She hoped they would at least be allowed the leftovers from the sumptuous dinner. When she asked Sterling about it, he assured her that the food would not be thrown out and that the servants were allowed their own party below stairs.

Back in the ballroom, with Samantha on his arm, Sterling walked slowly around the perimeter of the room and greeted the people he had not yet spoken to. Even after the music started up again, he continued to mingle with the other guests who were not dancing, introducing Samantha as "the esteemed Professor Jennings' daughter from Ohio." He was courteous but kept conversations short, and made sure they always included her. More often than not, he lightly remarked with geniality that he would offer the ladies a dance, except that he had promised them all to "his" Miss Jennings, and asked that they please excuse him the usual courtesy.

After a few minutes of this, it dawned on Samantha's tired brain what he was doing, and her gratitude for him grew in leaps and bounds. In a calculated but gracious and efficient way, he was simultaneously correcting assumptions and raising her status, while also giving people an opportunity to meet her for themselves, observe her countenance and manner, and recognize where they might have erred. Without Miss Fairfield here to embellish upon any rumors she had begun, those very rumors were being put to rest before they ever had a chance to grow outside the mansion and become ugly.

At last, Sterling turned to her and asked, "Have we walked around enough that your stomach would feel comfortable dancing now? Mine is not quite so full," he offered, patting his own trim front.

She smiled. "Yes, I am recovered." And then in a lower voice, "Thank you for what you just did, Sterling. That was so kind."

"It was my honor, dearest," he whispered into her ear. "And I do think it will help." As another waltz began to play, he swept her back to the dance floor before she could even think of where to put her feet. Indeed, she didn't have to think about it, didn't have to worry about a misstep or an awkward moment. Just as before, waltzing with him was elevated to an experience as easy as breathing.

"I do have a confession to make," he said after a few moments.

"You do?"

He smiled at her. "While that part about promising you all the dances was certainly correct, I made sure to tell everyone that because I want you all to myself, without all the interruptions."

"Really?" she asked, playing along. "So you mean, you wanted to make sure no more middle-aged men cut in?"

"Or young men."

"Hmm. But I was under the impression that the purpose of balls was to meet people, and that dancing more than two dances with the same woman is cause for conjecture and discussion."

"You are correct on both counts."

"But people will assume we're courting."

"Correct again, my lady. My, you *are* quick." His brown eyes twinkled as he looked down at her and spun her in the opposite direction.

She pretended to consider. "But by common courtesy, if another man asks me to dance, I am not supposed to decline..."

"Yes. Which is why I made sure to tell as many women as I could—within men's hearing—that I will be dancing with you."

"Ah... So was that preempting invitations or staking your claim?"

"Both," Sterling admitted with a laugh. "I hope you don't mind."

"Mind? It's a relief," Samantha replied gratefully. "Thank you for that also."

He pulled her a little closer and spun them in a circle. "You are very welcome."

***

The rest of the night passed quickly with Sterling at her side. She heard no more whispers about her, and whether this was due to her proximity to Sterling and people's lack of gossip around him, or whether it was because the rumors had truly stopped, she didn't know. But she was very glad. She felt that people were more friendly toward her in general—though she still caught some haughty or hostile looks from some of the women—and the whole scene was less awkward than it had been before.

She truly enjoyed herself until the moment exhaustion swept over her so completely that she nearly stumbled and had to admit to Sterling that she could not continue. He recognized her fatigue and promptly agreed to escort her to her room. As they walked up the long staircase together, he was relieved at the way the night had turned out and hoped that she felt that too.

She climbed wearily, one step in front of the other, her right hand tucked into the crook of his arm, her left hand holding up the hem of her dress. "Thank you for a wonderful night, Sterling. The last half was the best night I've had here. Thank you for somehow turning a mess into a pleasant situation. I wouldn't have thought that possible."

"Well, I would never have had the chance to get that far if it hadn't been for your intuition and quick thinking in following me to the library." He shook his head soberly. "That was much too close of a call; it chills me to recognize just how close."

She shivered. "It really was awful. It disgusts me to realize there are actually women who will stoop to such measures." She looked up at him briefly, and then back at the stairs as they continued their climb. "In my Bible study, I have read about Potiphar's wife with Joseph, but I didn't realize that sort of thing could still happen to good men in today's world."

"Oh, that's right!" he said in surprise. "I forgot that story. Where can I find it?"

"Genesis Chapter 39. Only, Joseph didn't achieve his happy ending for many, many years."

Sterling nodded. "I seem to remember he went to prison for quite a while."

"Yes, for several years."

"I guess he didn't have a Samantha to save him," Sterling mused quietly.

"No, he had no one but God for a long time. And, as it turned out, God was in no hurry to free him, though he did bless him in surprising ways while he remained there. And when Joseph was released, he prospered in ways that were truly remarkable. His is an incredible story."

"I would like to read it. Thank you for reminding me."

Samantha hesitated, then finished her train of thought. "I guess if—heaven forbid—you were ever faced with a similar circumstance, you could do as Joseph did. Perhaps there are times when that is the only recourse." She thought a moment as she remembered someone else who had had a similar reaction. "Jane Eyre essentially resorted to that method too, when her marriage to Mr. Rochester was thwarted by the news that he was a married man."

Sterling looked at her, a bit puzzled. "I remember she left Thornfield Hall. She told Mr. Rochester that if she gave in to him, *she* would know—even if no one else did—and it would erode the core of her being. But I'm not remembering how Joseph's story went..."

"He ran," Samantha supplied.

"Ah. That's right." He cleared his throat. "You know, that was actually what I was contemplating doing when you entered the room."

She tightened her grip on his arm. "Good."

"I would have done it, too."

"I know."

"Anything to get away from her." He felt his skin crawl as he again pictured the scene that could have so easily been his undoing.

Finally, they reached the landing and turned left.

"How long will the ball go on, do you suppose?" she asked, trying not to drag her feet as they walked down the long hallway to her room.

"Not too much longer, I wouldn't think. It's past midnight now, so guests will begin to trickle out soon."

Even through her exhaustion, she felt a sudden rush of gratitude for this strong, good man beside her. "Thank you for making me eat, and dispelling a rumor for me, and showing me what real dancing should feel like. The last half of the ball really was lovely."

"*You* are lovely, Samantha," he responded quietly. "I had a wonderful time too, being with you. Thank *you* for dispelling the wolf." He looked at her affectionately and reflected, "My little lamb can be quite fierce when she needs to be."

Samantha laughed tiredly, but was too weary even to blush. "I still don't know how I did that, other than the fact that I was terrified something utterly terrible would happen if I did not."

"Miss Fairfield is a force of nature when she has her sights set on something."

"Indeed."

"But let us not talk of her again. I think we have seen the last of her."

"I certainly hope so."

They arrived at Samantha's door and she let go of his arm to face him. "Good night," she said, looking up at him through bleary eyes.

"Good night. Will you ring Hannah to help you prepare for bed?"

"Oh, I don't wish to disturb her sleep for that. It is so late. I shall manage fine on my own; I always did before coming here."

Sterling placed gentle hands on her shoulders and kissed her forehead. "You are very competent, dearest, but you didn't wear a dress like that in Oberlin."

She blushed as she pulled the scarf up higher to more fully cover her bare shoulders and decolletage. "You are right; I may have to ask for help."

"Get some rest and I will see you tomorrow."

Samantha nodded, hoping it was true that she would see him, and opened her door. She smiled at Sterling one last time and closed the door behind her. When she glimpsed the bed, she felt as if she could not stand up another moment. But she knew if she went to bed dressed as she was, she would be sore for days. A slight rustling sounded near the hearth and she startled. Turning toward it, she saw Hannah straighten from the armchair. The maid rubbed her eyes and smiled at Samantha.

"Hello," she said, yawning behind her hand. "I hope you don't mind me waiting here in your room. I knew you would need help out of that dress, but wouldn't want to call for me, so I decided to make it easy for you." The girl was in a dressing gown and slippers, with her hair in one long braid down her back.

"Oh, Hannah, thank you. You are so considerate. I was just debating what to do. I didn't want to wake you at such a late hour."

Hannah reached for the scarf and Samantha slid it off and handed it to her. "You must remember, I am used to this sort of thing, Miss. And I can sleep anywhere, so it's really no hardship. Here, you look ready to drop. Let's get this dress off you."

Hannah gently and efficiently helped Samantha divest herself of the gorgeous but complicated gown, then the corset. Samantha slipped on the nightgown Hannah handed her, which she had apparently kept folded over the bed warmer, for it was warm and cozy.

By the time Hannah finished removing the pins in Samantha's hair and brushing out all the curls she had so carefully formed only a few hours before, Samantha couldn't keep her eyes open any longer. She sat at the vanity with her eyes closed and felt the tug and pull as Hannah braided her hair in a long braid like the one down her own back. A few moments later, Hannah helped Samantha into bed and bid her goodnight. As Hannah turned down the lights and let herself out of the room, Samantha had time only for a brief whispered prayer of thanks before she plunged into sleep.

Chapter 31

ULTIMATUM

December 1902

Samantha slept late the next morning, waking to weak sunlight shining feebly through the windows. She did not feel as rested as she would have liked, but much better than the night before. The headache that had plagued her most of the previous day was only a suggestion behind her temples. She sat up and immediately noticed a cheery fire crackling in the grate and breakfast on a tray on the bedside table. It appeared that Hannah had been busy already this morning, as if she had not had any disruption to her sleep the night before. Samantha was surprised to have slept through the small noises of Hannah's chores, but supposed that fact alone indicated her level of exhaustion.

Samantha managed to put away more of the breakfast than usual, then prepared herself for the day. She appreciated the touch of her own clothing against her skin and knew that Sterling would notice the blue dress from home. She brushed out her long hair and braided it up in a twist at the back of her head, careful not to bind it too tightly, hoping that the headache would not flare up again. Finishing her toilette, she sat in the armchair by the fire and pulled a blanket over herself while she read from the Bible and wrote in her journal.

She was greatly comforted by something in Romans 13:12. "Let us put on the armor of light," it said. She loved the vivid image those words brought to her mind, and the thought of being physically protected by light was a powerful, transcendent idea.

Spending time with Sterling last night, having him smooth the way for her and correct misunderstandings, had greatly improved her situation and her feeling of well being. But she still remained in the Sterling household, where tension and disapproval reigned. She was quite certain Cordelia's feelings for her had not changed one iota. Indeed, she could only hope they were not more strongly against her after last night's events. And as long as that strain remained between them, Samantha knew she could not fully relax or feel at ease here. So she clung to the idea of light providing her protection.

Jesus Christ is my light, she wrote in her journal. *John 1 tells us that the true Light "lighteth every man that cometh into the world." And in Verse 12 it says that to those who receive Him "He gives power to become the sons of God, even to them that believe on his name." I want more than anything to belong to God and to be called His daughter!*

As I face these hostile feelings in Lexington society and from Cordelia herself, I must try to remember these concepts. I want to be a conduit of His light for others to see, but also to allow His light into my life when things get particularly hard. And I feel the difficulties are not over yet; I will need God's light and strength to pass through them safely. How is it that these things are so easy to forget?

She was just finishing her morning devotional when she heard a light knock at the door. Hurrying to open it, she found Sterling standing there, dark hair newly wet with comb tracks through it, smiling at her. "How are you this morning?" he asked. She noticed that his clothing was simpler than what he had worn throughout their stay, though still immaculate. He obviously had not just come in from the stables.

"I am well," she smiled back. "What are your plans for the day?" She stepped out into the hallway, closing the bedroom door behind her, and looked up at him. He smelled of soap and she could see that he had shaved away the dark stubble that always shadowed his face by evening.

"Well," he reached for her hand and held it in both of his. "I would like to take you sledding after lunch, if you're up to it. Lucas says he'll join us."

"Sledding?" she exclaimed in delight.

"You like the idea?" He looked pleased.

"I love it."

"Good." A pause. "I like that color on you, by the way."

"I know. Thank you."

He chuckled. "Is there anything you would like to do this morning?" His thumb made slow circles on her palm.

She thought a moment. "Actually, yes. I would love to see the conservatory in the daylight."

"Ah. Perfect idea." He let go and then offered his hand to her again, palm up. "Miss, your escort awaits."

She took his hand and he tucked it into his other elbow, continuing to hold it as they walked down the hall.

"How are you feeling today?" he inquired in a lower voice. "Were you able to sleep all right?"

"I did sleep quite well, thank you, just not long enough."

He nodded. "Mother can sleep in for a long time after very late social events, but not so the rest of us. Did you eat breakfast?"

"I did, and you would be proud of me," she said. "I ate almost all of it!"

"Very good," he laughed. "Oh, I almost forgot. Happy Christmas Eve."

Her eyebrows rose in surprise. "That's right! Merry Christmas Eve." She thought for a moment as they descended the stairs, and then asked, "Is there a nativity service in Lexington? I would very much like to attend one."

"Yes! And I was thinking the same thing. I need that reminder of truly why we celebrate."

Samantha nodded. "I need to feel that spirit of Christmas right now. Without it, the season just isn't the same."

"Plan on it. I'll make some inquiries."

"Thank you, Sterling."

"My pleasure, dearest."

"I love it when you call me that."

He grinned at her.

The conservatory, while pleasant and enjoyable at night, was truly awe-inspiring during the day, with light streaming in through the glass, brightening every corner. She took a deep breath of the moist, earthy-scented atmosphere as they walked in, and immediately relaxed.

Two servants, one young and the other advanced in years, nodded at them respectfully and continued their work. It appeared they were tidying up after last night's visitors, though Samantha thought everything looked beautiful already. She admired the tropical shrubbery, flowers, and trees as they meandered through the large space, and asked more questions than Sterling could answer.

"I am sorry I'm not a botanist," he laughed, after she asked the fifth question he had no answer for. "Now that you ask about all these plants, I want to know the answers myself. We could ask Travers and Charlie. They might know."

He turned in the servants' direction, but she declined the offer. "That's all right. I'd rather spend this time with you, if you don't mind. My questions can wait. I am just so intrigued by all this flora and fauna. Remember, I know only what grows in Ohio. All of this," she waved a hand to indicate the plants around them, "seems so exotic."

Sterling nodded. "I suppose that is the point," he mused. "When she and Father designed the mansion, Mother wanted a place to house exotic plants that no one for miles around would have seen, let alone grow on their property. And it *has* succeeded in drawing people here. Mother always loves the novelty of it for others—and the attention it brings her, of course."

"Hmm," Samantha mused. "She certainly has an eye for beauty in everything she does, I can honestly say that for her. And I have a lot of respect for that. I imagine it takes a keen inner eye to make a plan blossom into reality like this." She gestured with one hand at the foliage around them.

"You are probably right," he conceded.

"And when it comes to architecture and design, I can't even imagine beauty I have never seen, let alone plan and create it. I think that must take particular talent as well."

"Bless you for seeing good in my mother," Sterling replied, a little taken aback. "She did, indeed, plan the additions and the garden, among other things. You are quite right, I'm sure, but it amazes me that you still look for it, after all she has put you through."

Samantha considered for a moment, and Sterling could tell her mind was processing a difficult thought. "Maybe there is a hurt somewhere deep inside her that is the root cause of her...perspective on life and people."

Sterling cocked his head. "I've never thought about that. She has simply always been this way. But it is true there is much I don't know about her, and if I did, I might understand her better."

"Yes. That is usually the way it works. Humans are complicated creatures."

"Indeed."

352

"There is so much going on under the surface that we never know."

They stopped and sat on the same bench as the night before. Sterling put an arm around her as he had last night and she affectionately laid her head on his shoulder.

"What is going on under your surface?" he asked.

"Hmm," she thought aloud. "I am just trying to live in the moment right now. So I am enjoying being with you early in the day. That hasn't happened for a long time."

"It hasn't, and I am sorry."

She lifted her head and looked up at him. "I don't blame you for it, Sterling. It has been an all around difficult situation for both of us."

"Yes," he agreed. "And a situation that I do not want to put us through again."

Suddenly they heard a commotion at the door, then feet running toward them. Sterling's brows knitted together in concern and he stood to meet the stablehand who appeared before them, out of breath. "Quickly, Master Lee!"

Samantha stood beside Sterling, wondering what could have made the man so agitated. He held his hat in his hands and turned it by the brim in quick, anxious movements.

"What is it, John?" Sterling asked. "How can I help?"

"It's one of the horses, sir. Your father thinks he may have a twisted bowel[1] and Lucas is away this morning, running Christmas errands."

Sterling needed to hear no more. He dismissed John with a quick nod. "Tell my father I'll be right there." The man sped back the way he had come and Sterling turned to Samantha apologetically.

"I understand. It's all right," she said quickly, grasping his arm. "Emergencies happen. You must go!"

"Bless you." He bent to kiss her quickly. "I'll find you when this is over." He started to run down the path, then turned and pointed at her. "And I'm still planning on that sledding outing!" He was off again and quickly out of sight. A moment later, she heard the conservatory door shut with a bang.

She looked in the direction he had gone for a moment and sighed. It seemed there was always something to keep them apart here. At least this time, it was a legitimate crisis.

---

1. https://www.irongateequine.com/education/equine-emergencies-and-how-to-tre at-them

She supposed she could enjoy the conservatory for a while longer, so she did so, then found her way to the library, planning to do more research.

But instead of reading more essays on education, she found a book of the collected works of William Wordsworth and lost herself in it. She was familiar with his poems but hadn't read them all, so she was intrigued and delighted. So many of them spoke to something deep inside her that after a while, she found herself sitting at the table in front of the window, writing down the lines she particularly wanted to read over again. Even though she could have easily committed them to memory, there was something about writing them in her own hand and re-reading the words that brought her pleasure. Like the words that reminded her of Sterling's first lesson about writing, back when they first met: "Fill your paper with the breathings of your heart." [2] She loved that! She felt a kinship to Wordsworth as she read it, for she had lived that truth. And writing from her heart had ultimately changed everything.

When she read Wordsworth's ode "Intimations on Mortality" she had a sudden memory of herself standing in front of the schoolroom as a young girl, reciting the poem for her classmates:

"Our birth is but a sleep and a forgetting:
The soul that rises with us, our life's Star,
Hath had elsewhere its setting,
And cometh from afar:
Not in entire forgetfulness,
And not in utter nakedness,
But trailing clouds of glory do we come
From God, who is our home..."

Her teacher had given her full marks, and that was the day Samantha realized she had a talent for recitation, that she could easily remember long passages from anything she read. This ability had come in handy throughout her school years, and then again more recently

---

2. https://www.brainyquote.com/authors/william-wordsworth-quotes

during the friendly debates she and Sterling engaged in last summer. Both memories made her smile.

Now, as she read the poem again, she understood and appreciated it more fully, and as a new Christian, believed what it taught. Once her spiritual eyes were opened, there were so many evidences of Him all around her!

She turned to the next page: "There is a comfort in the strength of love; 'Twill makes a thing endurable, which else would overset the brain, or break the heart."[3] She copied that as well, wanting to share it with Sterling, for that was what she had found in him and their love for each other—especially as it had been sorely tried over the past several days. Surely without the reassurance of his love, her heart would have broken by now! That, and God's comfort and light, were what had kept her going.

***

It was near lunchtime when Samantha heard someone enter the library and looked up to see Cordelia walking toward her. She wore a lovely velvet green gown, and a look of determination.

Samantha's heart dropped to her shoes and a sudden panic fluttered inside her. She was the only person in the room, so this visit could mean only one thing. And by the woman's expression, Samantha guessed it was *not* to have a nice female chat.

"Hello," Samantha said, standing in respect and removing her glasses to slip them into the pocket of her dress.

Cordelia stopped in front of her and pursed her lips. "I came to speak to you," she said unnecessarily.

Samantha nodded. "Let me bring a chair over for you." She realized as she said it that they could have just as easily moved to the sofas in the middle of the room, but somehow comfort didn't seem appropriate for the conversation that was about to take place. As she walked to retrieve another wooden chair a few yards away, her back to the other woman, she took a deep, stabilizing breath and willed her heartbeat to slow. She would

---

3. https://www.overallmotivation.com/quotes/william-wordsworth-quotes/

have preferred to go her whole life without having this confrontation! Returning with the chair, she placed it opposite her own and stood there, unsure what to do next.

Cordelia held out a commanding hand to indicate Samantha's chair. "Sit, if you please." They both sat. And then, without any further preamble, Cordelia launched into her reason for seeking Samantha out. "I am going to be frank with you, Miss Jennings. As you are my guest here, I did not want to have to have this conversation with you. But after the events of last evening, I fear I must."

"La-last evening?" Samantha stammered. What did the woman think had happened? Did she have any idea that her son had been in serious danger of having his reputation irrevocably damaged, his future forever altered? She wasn't entirely certain where this conversation was headed, but she knew in the pit of her stomach that it wasn't good.

"Yes," Cordelia said dryly. "First, your very obvious statement through your coordinated clothing—which my son claims was his idea, but what man thinks of such a thing on his own? Then there was your removal of him from the ballroom for nigh unto an hour, and his refusal to dance with anyone else when you both returned. And lastly, there was the sudden disappearance of my esteemed guest, Miss Fairfield, which I believe you also had something to do with." Her graceful eyebrows lifted and she gave Samantha a pointed look, as if challenging her to deny any of it. "It's enough to cause a scandal and I will not be made the talk of this city!"

Samantha felt a little indignant that the woman had failed to acknowledge how well the night had turned out, in spite of everything, and that all evil rumors seemed to have been put to rest. "But I... He—"

Cordelia held up a hand to stop her. "I was certain you would come up with all manner of excuses. I know you think you are in the right, but I need you to understand two things." She held up an index finger. "One, my son was not raised to marry a no-account girl from some backwoods town. And two," she raised the next finger, "as I have already lost in my effort to make a proper gentleman of Lee in the family business, I will *not* fail in my efforts to see him married into a family of money and good breeding. You have managed to sink your claws into him while he was away from my influence, but you *will not win*." She paused slightly between each of the last three words, strongly emphasizing them, her mouth set in a grim line and her eyes flashing.

"Many a young woman has tried to gain his attention over the years, and for reasons I will *never* understand," her voice rose, "he has turned them all away. Including the divinely beautiful Miss Fairfield, who would be the perfect match for him!" She threw up her hands in exasperation and Samantha flinched. "My Lee is a fickle young man and has some very strange ideas, but he is still my son and I know what is best for him." She pointed at Samantha. "And it is not you."

She stood. "That is all. I hesitated to deliver this message on Christmas Eve and while you are still a guest in my home, but after your embarrassing display together at the ball—which I held in Lee's honor," she said as she put a hand to her bosom in horror, "I realized I could not let this go unaddressed. I will not disgrace any of us by sending you away, as I have given my word to my son to provide you hospitality for the duration of your visit, but I do not expect you to return to visit us again. Nor do I care to know you better while you are here. I will never comprehend how you thought you could win my son over when women of much higher status and much more...shall we say—appeal—could not do so, but that disaster must end now. Good day." She inclined her head in a gesture of feigned cordiality and swept from the room.

Stunned, Samantha remained seated. She did not move for many minutes, shaking but too shocked to cry. She had never been the target of anyone's hatred and anger before, nor ever been so thoroughly castigated for something she had not done. It felt as if she had been physically attacked. The pain was a deep, gashing wound that caught her completely off guard, and she felt it so acutely that she looked down, half expecting to see herself bleeding all over the floor.

She didn't understand Cordelia's fury. Sterling had saved the evening so adeptly after she succeeded in saving him from Miss Fairfield, and then this morning things had gone so well—even with his emergency summons to the stables—that this blow completely blindsided Samantha. She'd known Cordelia's opinion of her had not changed, but with how things seemed to be improving in the last several hours, Samantha had failed to be watchful.

What should I do? she wondered in horror. If only this wound *were* a physical gash, copiously bleeding to show its need to be appropriately addressed. Then it could be staunched and stitched and eventually healed. She didn't know how she would recover from this invisible emotional pain.

Samantha yearned for home with her dear confidantes Mrs. Dolittle and Claire, and her sometimes still removed father—but a father who, she now knew, loved her deeply. Home with Champion and Martin in the barn, with its earthy smells of hay and manure, and its quiet peace. Home to the place where she could be herself without fear of the unjust accusation of being someone she was not.

Please help me, God, she pleaded. *I need you now more than ever! Please give me wisdom. I so badly need that light I read about this morning.* As she thought upon it, imagined it in her mind, as sunshine streaming down on a bright day to warm her head and shoulders, she felt a measure of warmth steal into her shattered heart and ease the pain of it just enough to think a little more clearly.

Unbidden, the story of Joseph of Egypt came to her mind, the one she had told Sterling about the night before. She thought of Joseph's unjust imprisonment and how painful that must have been for him, and recognized that she was not the first to be unfairly accused. Of course she wasn't. Even the Savior of the world had been unjustly condemned! But somehow these thoughts did little to comfort her.

I am afraid of Cordelia, she thought, allowing herself to admit it for the first time. *And while I want to explain and be understood more than anything, after that verbal attack, I have not even the gumption to leave this room.*

But leave it she did—eventually—as soundlessly as possible, heart pounding as she expected Cordelia to appear at every corner. Inside her room again, she closed the door and leaned back against it, trying not to think or feel, but unable to stop from doing both. She slid slowly down the door and sank to the floor, dropping what she held and hugging her knees up against her chest.

Suddenly she felt the overwhelming urge to write what this internal, bleeding ache felt like, to vomit it all over the page in the midst of her anguish—to rid it from her, if possible. She grabbed the paper with Wordsworth's beautiful words from the floor, took the pencil in her other hand, and pulled the book close to use as a desk. Flipping the paper over, she wrote with a desperation that gouged into the paper, intermittently creating small holes in her haste. She was vaguely aware that her shaking hand spoiled her penmanship, but that was of little importance.

It took her all of two minutes to get the poem out, and then she shoved away the paper, book, and pencil to fall again to the floor. She didn't really feel any better, but the shaking had eased a bit. Samantha rested her forehead on her knees and curled up against herself, as if that position could protect and soothe her heart. She longed, as she had many times before, for a loving Mother's embrace and kind words of wisdom. She felt so alone and she had no idea what to do about any of this. How had Jane Eyre done it? Or had she survived her aloneness and all the injustices done to her because she was a fictional character and Bronte had simply willed her to?

Cordelia's words reverberated inside Samantha's skull and she hated the ugly image of herself they created. It was at times like these that she cursed her imagination, for she clearly saw in her mind's eye the person Cordelia must see in her: conniving and controlling, selfish and unworthy. It was an ugly, bitter picture and she wanted to banish it, to erase it somehow. She wouldn't want such a young woman for her son, either! She felt sick to her stomach.

But I am not any of those things, her soul cried out. *They are all untrue!* She took a shaky breath and felt hot tears track down her cheeks.

What was she to do now? How could she go on? Indeed, how could she and Sterling go on? His mother wanted her gone and to be brutally honest, she wanted to quit this place even more than Cordelia wished her to!

The stabbing pain behind her eyes made her wince and she closed her eyes. So tired...! How could she break free of this cage? She remembered her father's words during their conversation about inner strength. She did not see a way out, though she longed for relief and freedom. In her torment, hope was a nice concept, but seemed entirely foreign now. She felt utterly isolated and powerless. How had this all turned out so horribly wrong when it had begun so beautifully?

Finally, realizing the light from the window was making the intensity of the headache worse, she gathered enough strength to stand and walk across the room to close the curtains. Then she took the blanket off the armchair as she walked past it to the bed, and wrapped herself up in its softness. She fell onto the bed and allowed herself to be swallowed up in blissful, numbing sleep.

Chapter 32

NATIVITY

December 1902

Later, a light knock on Samantha's door was not enough to rouse her from deep slumber, and when Hannah stepped in to check on her, the maid was surprised to find not only a book, paper, and pencil on the floor by the door, but also Samantha soundly asleep on the bed, wrapped in a blanket, her back to the door and her legs pulled up like a young child's. Hannah smiled affectionately, picked up the items from the floor, and set them carefully and quietly on the bedside table. After a moment's hesitation, she retrieved the paper and silently let herself out. She had just closed the door behind her when Sterling joined her in the hallway. She looked up at the young master and told him, "She's sleeping, sir."

His expression was surprised, then concerned. "Sleeping?"

Hannaha nodded. "I expect she isn't used to keeping such late nights and needs to make up for lost hours."

Sterling nodded slowly. "You are probably right." And then, as if to himself, "We were going to go sledding..."

"Well, she didn't eat any lunch, as far as I know, and now she's sleeping, so I don't think she's going sledding. Sorry, sir."

"Right. Hmm. Do you suppose she is well?"

"I imagine she's just tuckered out, Master Lee. Would you like me to check back on her in an hour and let you know?"

"Uh, no. Thank you, Hannah. I will check back myself." He blinked, as if coming to and looked at her more closely. "What is that you're holding?"

The maid looked down at her hands in surprise. "Oh! I found this on her floor. I don't read too well and thought it might be something for you. I...I hope I didn't do wrong!" Her expression showed her sudden trepidation.

Sterling quietly took the paper from her and made a cursory glance at the gouged paper, Samantha's writing distorted in a way he had never seen before. It made his gut clench. "No, Hannah, I think you did just right," he reassured her.

Hannah nodded, relieved. As she headed off down the hall toward her next duties, Sterling called after her, "Thank you for your careful attendance to Samantha. You have truly been a godsend, and we are both grateful to you."

"Of course, sir," Hannah stopped and curtsied. "It's my pleasure." She hesitated a moment and then added, "She is easy to love."

Sterling looked at the young maid's face and saw nothing but true regard. "She certainly is," he agreed with a smile.

He returned to his room, disappointed not to be following through with their plans for the day, but glad Samantha could rest. He hoped she would still want to attend the nativity now that he had made the arrangements. But he still had an uneasy feeling that all was not right with her, especially after seeing the paper in his hand.

He sat in an easy chair by the fire and contemplated the poem written there:

BURDEN

Heavy, so heavy
This burden on my heart
Weighs me down daily
Pushes moment by moment
Dragging, sagging
Each eternal day.
I hope for hope
Faith latent, an ember
But wonder: Are both lost?

"Help thou my unbelief."
God, my anchor
Christ, my hope.
Please, You who walked on water
Let me not drown.
Do You still love me,
Aware of my burden?
Heavy, Lord, it crushes.
I hold to You
Knowing Yours, the ultimate burden
You, the Burdened One
Gives slight light in this darkness
Small lifting of this weight
Thoughts of You, an exhale
To relieve the held breath
Of this heavy, so heavy
Burden on my heart.

Sterling read it through twice more, stunned. He grieved. What was this burden she felt? Why such despair that she even doubted God's love and was losing hope and faith? She still appeared to be clinging to the God she loved, and begging for confirmation of His care and concern, but there was a certain desperateness to her pleadings, as if she were on the edge of something terrible.

He willed his gut to unclench and his anxious heart to slow. Turning the paper over, he noted her usual neat and concise handwriting. Wordsworth. The words of the beloved poet on writing, God, and love were exquisitely familiar to him. He could see the volume in his mind's eye, right where it rested on the shelf. Sterling knew Samantha must have recently spent time in the library and found the book of Wordsworth's collected poems he, himself, had placed there. He also knew why these lines resonated with her, for they resonated with him too.

So what had happened between one side of the page and the other?

He knew with even stronger certainty that Samantha was not just tired from last evening's events. Something had surely occurred in the interim and she was *not* all right.

***

When he returned an hour later to her door, he knocked lightly and called out her name.

A few moments later, he knocked again and heard a rustling on the other side of the door. "Yes?" her voice was choked and short.

"Samantha, it's Sterling. I came to see how you are. Hannah told me you were sleeping; are you feeling all right?"

"Oh, Sterling, we've missed sledding, haven't we?" A cleared throat. "I'm sorry."

"Don't worry about it for a moment," he responded. "Your rest was more important. Do you want a plate sent up from the kitchen?"

"I- No, I'm not hungry. But thank you."

He frowned. She shouldn't be skipping meals. His instincts told him something was very wrong. She had always opened the door before. This talking through the door was not very conducive to conversation. Quietly, he asked, "How are you, dearest?"

He thought he heard a low, muffled cry, but after a moment, she said simply, "I have a terrible headache, Sterling. I think I will just rest until dinner."

"All-all right." Sterling stammered in his concern for her welfare. "Can I do anything for you?"

Silence, then what sounded like a sniffle and another throat clearing. "Pray for me, Sterling. Please, just pray for me."

"I will, Samantha. I will." He looked at the blasted door in between them and wished he could see through it. "Do you still want to attend the nativity tonight? If you feel up to it, I have everything arranged."

After a momentary silence he heard, "Yes, I think I can do that. Thank you."

He left her, though he hated to do it, and the weight that had started to settle over him now lodged in his throat. What was really wrong and what did she need? *She says she needs prayers.*

Returning to his room, he knelt at his bed, forehead on clasped fists, pushing against his knuckles until his head hurt. Into his mind flashed the memory of himself in a similar situation last spring, kneeling at a hotel bed in Oberlin, pleading for direction on how to find Samantha and what to do when he did. That had turned out well, he reminded himself. Better, in fact, than he could have ever hoped.

But now…?

God, he began praying in his heart, *I know I'm still new to praying and that I am a novice at Bible reading, faith, and all the rest. But I've been trying. I can't deny how You helped me in the past, and how You inspired Samantha in saving my life a couple months ago. I have to believe my life was spared for a reason, and that she and I are meant to be together.*

Father, when I am with her I want to improve. Her influence makes me a better man. And she relies on me, on my strength and friendship and love. But something is not right and I don't know what it is! I don't know how to help her. Please help me to know what to do—for her and for us.

He ended his prayer and then, craving more contact with the Almighty, hefted his Bible from the bedside table and sat in the overstuffed chair by the warm hearth.

Mother had had him so "busy" over the past several days that he hadn't focused on daily scripture study as he ought to have. He turned to the Gospel of John and began reading. He found it enlightening and immensely satisfying, and when he reached chapter four, everything jumped out at him. It was all about love: how God is love, how we can better love Him and others, how God demonstrated His love for us by sending His Son to be the Savior of the world. This was powerful stuff! He realized these were concepts that would take a while to digest and perhaps a lifetime to fully comprehend and apply in his own life. But for now, verse eighteen stuck out to him more than any other: "Perfect love casteth out fear."

He sat there with the large tome in his lap, staring into space and thinking about that concept. He knew he loved Samantha—that wasn't something he had to even think about. And he felt sure she loved him too—she had told him and shown him as much, many times. He was starting to truly feel God's love for them both as well, but he also feared many things in this moment: worry over what was ailing Samantha, apprehension that his mother's disapproval and interference would permanently damage his relationship with Samantha, and concern that he wasn't who he needed to be for the one he loved most.

Everything had seemed so clear before they came here, their future as bright and certain as the sunrise. Why did he feel that something had changed over the past several days, and that a negative shift had occurred very recently without his being aware?

He looked again at the verse in his lap that seemed to supersede all those anxieties and to distill everything into one word: Love.

God loved them perfectly and Jesus had lived as a man to demonstrate that love to the fullest extent, so the least Sterling could do was focus on his own growing love for God and the strength of his love for Samantha. Feeling compelled to make sense of something—anything—he made a list in his journal of all the things he could do to show love to Samantha and to God. The exercise illuminated his mind and humbled his spirit, and he suddenly understood why Samantha often took notes during her Bible study.

Before he knew it, he barely had time to change before dinner. Then he dashed back down the hallway to Samantha's room and knocked on the door once again. This time, to his relief, she opened it. She looked pale and drawn, but her eyes were steady, though shadowed and resigned. She wore a freshly pressed dress of lavender and her hair was smoothed back neatly into a simple bun. In her lovely simplicity, she looked more like the Oberlin girl he knew, and he loved her for it. He smiled and she took his arm to walk with him down to the dining room. But she didn't smile, and her subdued and withdrawn manner made the weight and worry descend over him again.

"Were you able to rest?" he asked quietly as they walked.

"Yes, thank you."

"How is the headache?"

She shut her eyes for a second and he saw pain there when she opened them again.

"Samantha, I think you need to eat. That should help."

She nodded reluctantly. Her expression was suddenly so woeful that he stopped and turned to her. He pulled her into his arms, relieved when she didn't resist, and asked, "What is it? I know something is wrong and I want to help."

She grasped his lapels and buried her face in his chest, but she didn't cry. The fact that she didn't worried him more than if she had. He stroked her back and waited to see if she would offer anything more. Finally, she pulled away and looked sadly up at him.

"What's wrong?"

She shook her head and looked away from him, blinking a few times, but staying silent.

"Hannah found your poem on the floor and gave it to me, not knowing what it was."

She started briefly in surprise, but remained turned away.

"I'm sorry... I don't know if you intended for me to see it, but I am glad I did. It's beautiful, but it pains my heart. What is this burden you write about, dearest? Can I help lift it? Please, tell me what I can do." He watched her profile, willing her to turn back to him and open her heart, as she had always done before.

She remained silent, trying to think of some way to explain to him that his mother truly hated her, that the atmosphere in this house was eroding everything that made her who she was, that the differences between them were irreconcilable, that she could never change enough to be acceptable, and that this lovely dream they had lived in since last May was now shattered and the shards of it were cutting her to pieces. But when she looked up into those beautiful brown eyes with their innocence and constancy, she couldn't put any of it into words. Not yet. It was too huge and too terrible. She looked away again and felt herself trembling.

Sterling grasped her elbows gently and willed her to turn back to him. "Samantha," he said quietly. When she finally turned, he said, "I love you." He was shocked to see doubt fully cloud her eyes at this proclamation. "I do!" he insisted. "You must know that!"

"I love you too," she responded in a choked whisper. *More than you know.*

He felt like the word 'but' hung unspoken, though she said nothing more.

Finally, she took a deep breath and turned to continue down the hall, and he let go. She wasn't going to tell him any more at all?! Deeply disappointed, he watched her move on ahead of him. Though concerned that she would still not let him share her burden, nor even express a portion of it to him, he also sensed this was not the time to push. She would tell him when she was ready. At least, he prayed she would.

He caught up to her in a few long strides and she placed her hand on his arm again, woodenly and without feeling. After a lengthy silence, she asked, "Is the horse all right?"

"I- Oh, the horse!" His mind raced to switch topics. "Yes, fortunately, Major just had a bad case of colic and there was no actual bowel twisting involved, thank goodness. It was a bit touch-and-go there for a while, but Father and I were able to pull him through. Major is one of Father's favorite horses, so I am relieved we didn't lose him."

"That's good," Samantha murmured. But she seemed so deflated and without her usual buoyancy and zest for life that it alarmed him. He knew it was more than the missed meal and the headache.

When they walked into the dining room, his mother and father were already there and Sterling noticed his mother's subtle look of surprise when she saw Samantha, before she covered it with a feigned look of indifference. She was maddeningly adept at putting on a facade when she wanted to, but he knew from her initial surprise that she had not expected

Samantha to come to the meal. Why would that be the case? Did she expect Samantha to request dinners sent to her room for the remainder of their stay? That was ludicrous! Samantha was their guest, not an embarrassment to hide away in isolation. Did she really think he would be all right with that?

Sterling took the seat on his mother's right and Samantha sat beside him. He noticed that she lifted her chin slightly, but avoided eye contact with his mother. This, too, seemed different from their previous encounters. Surely something had happened between them—but what?

Lucas hurried in the next moment and sat across from them, on his father's right. Throughout the meal, Sterling and his father told Lucas about their tenuous doctoring session of Major. Lucas berated himself for choosing that time to be gone, though he could not have known what would transpire in his absence. He promised to do the evening stable check himself, paying particular attention to Major's condition. No one mentioned the aborted plans for sledding.

Cordelia chatted on about Christmas events happening in the community and Sterling asked his family if anyone would like to join him and Samantha at the nativity service after dinner. His parents declined, but Lucas agreed to come. Samantha, who had said nothing up to this point, seemed to perk up a bit at the realization that his mother would not be coming with them. Still, she remained quiet and withdrawn and pushed more food around on her plate than she ate, but she did eat and drink enough that the color returned to her face. Softly, he touched the toe of her shoe with his a couple of times until she looked up at him and then he smiled and searched her face for a hint of what she was feeling. She offered him nothing but a faint, sad smile in return.

Throughout their sleigh ride to the nativity, Samantha said little. Because it was dark, Sterling had no visual cues to help him understand what was going through her mind, so he put his arm around her and held her close while he and Lucas maintained a conversation.

After they found their seats at the church, Lucas made eye contact with him over Samantha's downturned head and asked a question with his eyes. Sterling responded with a pained expression and a slight raise of the shoulders, grateful his brother was perceptive enough to have noticed the change in Samantha and that he, too, was concerned. Both sat there wishing they knew how to help.

The church was warm and snug with so many people crowded into it, and it smelled of scented candles and wet leather boots. Samantha closed her eyes to soak in the warmth, peace, and organ music for a moment. It felt good to be here. She took a deep breath to still her whirling thoughts and better focus on the present moment of being with like-minded people who desired to worship Jesus and remember His birth. She opened her eyes and looked up at the front wall, appreciating a beautiful painting of Christ and His apostles.

She was vaguely aware that Sterling and Lucas were concerned about her, but she could no more explain to them what troubled her than she could detail to herself what she ought to do. Her mind had considered every course, imagined every scenario, and succeeded only in pulling her down into a thick despondency she had never known. She could see no good outcome and wondered now how she had ever believed she could be a part of Sterling's life forever. It had been a delicious dream while it lasted, but maybe it was a dream that could never become reality, despite what Thoreau might say about that. They were from two disparate worlds and, from Cordelia's perspective, Samantha could never measure up. Samantha could not spend the whole rest of her life trying to reach that impossible standard, or overstretch and warp herself into becoming something and someone she was not. All these troubling thoughts only added to the ever-present headache, but she did not know how to stop them.

At least here in this church she might feel peace for an hour or so, and she desperately needed that. She kept praying, asking God for help, for insight and wisdom, for comfort. So far, she had only felt the latter—which was what kept her going. And along with that comfort were the words, repeatedly imprinted in her mind, to "hold on."

I am trying, she kept responding back, *I am really trying. But I don't see a way through this, Lord. My way is murky and dark and my future looks lonely and joyless. Surely You have a plan, don't You? I know I am no one special, but scripture has taught me that You love me, so that must count for something. Doesn't it?*

Again, the only thing she received in return was a warmth inside her, but it did give her a little strength and helped her relax enough to enjoy the music and the message. The recitation of the first Christmas story, so simple yet poignant, brought tears to her eyes as she considered what it might have been like to be an unassuming, ordinary shepherd and witness angels and a new baby Savior all in the same night. She found herself wishing she could have been there, to see the Babe with her own eyes and bow before Him in reverence.

That seemed like a simpler time and she craved to be there, away from her modern-day concerns and from Sterling's ubiquitous mother.

Beside her, Sterling felt Samantha relax and noted that the tension in her face smoothed. He was immeasurably grateful and prayed that the peace felt in this church would carry with them all when they left it. He enjoyed hearing the sweet details of the Christmas story and noted things he had forgotten or not known previously, determining to read the account in the Bible himself before the season was over.

They made their way slowly outside after the service, following the crowd of people wending their way through the aisles and down the front steps. Everyone buttoned coats, readjusted scarves, and pulled hats down more firmly.

On Sterling's arm, Samantha inhaled the cold air deeply. She was grateful to feel more grounded and calmer and hoped she would now have enough internal strength to make it through the rest of the week—though the thought of more days like this one was more than she could bear.

When they at last found their waiting sleigh near the street, something at the edge of Samantha's vision caught her attention. She turned her head to look and blinked in surprise. *What in the world?! But how...?*

In the skeletal trees around the church bobbed two small lights, blinking intermittently. Forward and up. Off. A pause. Forward and up. Off.

Fireflies! In winter? How...?!

One tiny light blinked brighter than the other. A male and a female. But how had they survived the cold so long?! This made no sense! *What would Aunt Irene say about this impossible scene?!*

She glanced quickly up at Sterling and over at Lucas to see if they had noticed the fireflies too, but they were conversing with the driver. Then Sterling reached to hand her up. Her heart quickened as she thought about what she had just witnessed, and looked back at the trees once more, still unsure if she had really seen what she thought she'd seen. There they were again, dancing upward in their quintessential J movement, just as they had last summer near Plum Creek in Oberlin. The swift reminder of that time of easy bliss warmed through her.

But how could such a thing be? The poor little insects should have died long before now! She was utterly astonished.

Sterling helped her up into the sleigh and she woodenly sat. The only thing that made sense to her was that it was a message straight from God to her. The symbolism wasn't lost on her, either; she and Sterling had discussed the metaphor of a firefly's light long ago. It must be that her Father in Heaven had remembered that conversation. Well, of course He had! She knew instantly that He wanted her to know there was still light in the world, even in the dark of night and the cold of winter. Light because of the Son He sent into the world. And hope could never completely fade as long as that was true.

Unbidden, Claire's words from months before filled her mind: "Ain't nobody a no-body."

She was as quiet on the way home as she had been before, but the heaviness felt easier to bear. She didn't know if it would last, but mentally drew the comfort around herself like a blanket, visualizing again the impossible sight of fireflies blinking in a winter night.

She was tired again, but the headache that had plagued her almost constantly for two days was not any worse. Her stomach felt hollow, but she still had no appetite and did not feel light-headed, so she assumed she had eaten enough dinner. *I will get through this*, she kept telling herself. *A few more days and I can go home to Oberlin and Father and Mrs. Dolittle and Claire and everyone and everything else that is so dear to me. Or nearly everyone...* She wouldn't allow herself to think beyond that, to the future that now seemed so bleak. *One day, one moment at a time*, she mentally repeated over and over again.

Sterling stroked her mittened hand, wondering how he could best help her. The church visit had helped, he could tell. It had helped him, too, in some indefinable way. But what to do now... He thought of the list he had made a few hours before and prayed for guidance.

***

When they pulled up to the front of the Sterling mansion, Lucas thanked Sterling for the invitation and bid them good night before alighting from the sleigh. Then Sterling directed the driver to take them around to the stables. Samantha looked at his dark form beside her questioningly, but said nothing.

"There's one more thing I would like to do tonight, if that's all right."

He felt her nod.

When they entered the stables, she inhaled the mingled scents of hay and manure, and instantly began to relax. If only she could sleep out here, she thought, she might actually sleep well!

Sterling led her by the hand to a stall situated in the center of the large building, with a shiny silver plaque on the stall door labeled *Major*. She perked up and took note of the animal. When he poked his sleek brown head over the door, she rubbed a gentle hand down his face and he snuffled at her.

"I think he likes you already," Sterling said gently.

She gave a small smile and rubbed the horse's fetlock. "I miss Champion," she said finally.

Sterling nodded. "Him and a great deal more, I would guess."

She swallowed, almost wishing he weren't so perceptive. "I'm glad you were able to save Major," she offered. "I know he means a great deal to your father. James is a good man." *And he tolerates much and loves greatly*, she added silently to herself.

"Yes, he is," Sterling replied. "He really is the best of men, which I haven't always recognized. But the older I get, the more I see it."

Samantha nodded.

They stood there in the peaceful stables for a few quiet minutes, stroking Major and listening to the night sounds of drowsing horses and the occasional shift of a floorboard or rafter.

Sterling waited for Samantha to speak and at last she said, "Thank you for taking me to the nativity. I needed that."

"So did I. Now it feels a little more like Christmas, doesn't it?" At her slight nod, he abruptly changed the subject, putting a hand on her shoulder. "Samantha, I know something is still wrong. I don't know what to do, but I want you to know I'm here for you."

She looked up at him gratefully, at last through a sheen of tears, and thanked him, wishing she could just lean into him and tell him everything that his mother had said throughout their visit, particularly her harsh words the day before. But the wound they had created in her was so raw and deep that she didn't know how to voice it yet. And a portion of her felt that Cordelia was right. Her continued association with Sterling would not help his social standing in any way, and she herself lacked the vibrancy and sophistication to be his equal. She *would not* shackle him to a lifetime in a backwoods town where his prospects for advancement or financial success would be severely limited.

Sterling continued. "You are probably wondering why I brought you here this late in the evening. It's simple, really. Regardless of the size of that house," he gestured behind them, "it is difficult to find a place to be alone together. Mostly because my mother's presence is everywhere and we never know when she will suddenly appear."

He let out a chuckled breath. "I can see by your expression that you completely agree with me, but haven't wanted to say as much. Well, I said it for you, so no need to feel guilty for thinking it. At any rate, I wanted to give you your Christmas gift in private, and I don't know what opportunity we will have to be alone tomorrow." He put a hand into his coat pocket, pulled out a small box tied with a tiny bow, and handed it to her. "Merry Christmas, dearest."

"Merry Christmas," she murmured in surprise, taking the gift and trying to savor the moment for future reflection. She might need to pull out this memory often in the days to come. "I have a gift for you too," she said, looking up at him. "But I didn't know the right time to give it to you either."

He nodded. "Open it."

She untied the bow and lifted the lid to reveal a silver heart-shaped locket with an intricate engraving of leaves on its front. In the center, an impossibly small ruby rose bud was nestled beside a tiny emerald in the shape of a leaf. "Oh!" she whispered, lifting it out. "It's beautiful! I've never owned anything so lovely."

"I thought of commissioning something more elaborate, but I knew you would want a simpler piece."

She nodded, appreciating his accurate understanding of her preferences. "It's perfect. Thank you!" She knew she would treasure this forever. He smiled as she inspected it. She found the clasp and opened the locket, curious whether anything would be inside. To her surprise, a small dark curl of Sterling's hair lay within, and beneath that were engraved the words *Love Forever* in tiny script. "Oh, Sterling. It's perfectly lovely."

"Here, let me help you put it on." He took it from her fingers and moved around behind her to fasten the chain's clasp around her neck. She felt the small weight of it against her breastbone and lifted it up to look at it again.

Sterling moved back around to face her. "I should have given something like this to you long ago." He put his arms around her and she returned his embrace, blinking back tears again. His thoughtfulness was not going to make their inevitably permanent separation easy, was it?

"Now, when we are separated again for a few months, you will have a part of me with you. And anytime you need to be reminded of my love, you can open the locket."

"I will cherish it," she whispered.

Lucas entered the stables then, his clothes changed, ready to do the nightly round. Samantha realized he was making good on his promise to check Major over before he retired for the night.

She and Sterling returned to the house.

That night, as she lay in bed, her mind still too active to allow sleep, she clasped a hand around the locket and felt its comforting weight and the significance of the message hidden within. *At least I will always have this small part of him*, she thought sadly but gratefully, *wherever I go.*

Chapter 33

TRUTH

December 1902

The next morning, after another night of little sleep, Samantha picked at the breakfast Hannah brought her, but managed to eat enough of it to ease the sharp ache in her stomach. *Merry Christmas*, she thought wryly to herself. It felt more like the end of the world than "merry." But yearning for more positive feelings, she picked up her Bible and opened it to Psalms, hoping that the holy, poetic words there might ease some of the pain in her heart.

"*The Lord is my light*," she read. "*Of whom shall I be afraid?*"

She believed that wholeheartedly in theory, but in this instance, how could she apply it? *I am striving to allow the Lord to be my light,* she anguished, *but I am still afraid of Sterling's mother. Even more than that, I am afraid of what she can do to us—what she has already done. And yet I have heard that fear and hope cannot exist simultaneously in a person's heart. I don't know if that is true, for I do very much feel both—and I don't know how to get rid of my fear! How do I hold only to hope?*

Samantha thought that once she left this place, she might eventually recover somehow, and perhaps full emotional healing would come with time. But more and more, as the hours passed since her confrontation with Cordelia, she was unsure of whether Sterling's and her relationship could endure under such conditions—and whether it should.

I still don't know what to do, Father, she prayed silently, her head bowed against her folded hands, elbows resting on the little table. *I don't want to jeopardize the future Sterling should have, not for anything. And I cannot endure more of this confrontation and conflict in my own life because of what it does to my spirit and my heart. But I love him as much as ever and I really do not want to lose him!* A tear leaked out and splotched the page in her lap. She dabbed at it with her sleeve and then at her eyes to dry them. Crying would fix nothing.

I am ready to accept Your will for my life, God, she promised with sudden conviction, *however painful and difficult. But if there is any way for Cordelia's inaccurate perspective and terrible accusations to be corrected, that would mean so very much to me. It pains me to see myself the way she does. I feel so much more whole and complete when I see myself the way You do.*

***

The staff had been given a half day off for Christmas, so those with family nearby left to spend time with them after morning chores were completed. The other servants enjoyed leisure time below stairs, which meant the Sterling family would be on their own for meals and everything else for the remainder of the day.

Sterling came to Samantha's door to collect her in the late morning, and they joined the rest of his family in the drawing room for a gift exchange. He helped her carry her stack of gifts downstairs, which was surprisingly heavy. She was not experienced in the art of gift-giving, so she hoped the items she had purchased and wrapped with care would be useful and appreciated, though she expected little response from Cordelia.

At the thought of being in the same room as the woman, dread sat in Samantha's chest like a living, clawed animal, stubborn and completely immutable. She passed through the hall beside Sterling as if toward her doom, hoping nothing, trying to feel nothing, quietly resigned to survive this day. Only the vision in her mind of two pinpricks of light blinking before her in the trees last night managed to lighten the burden in her heart a fraction.

Sterling's concern for her was not alleviated in the least when he noted the smudges below her eyes that surely indicated another night of poor sleep. He hoped she had eaten breakfast and prayed she could feel the love he felt for her, despite the oppression of the house.

Having expected no gifts, Samantha did not know how to respond when they were presented, particularly as Cordelia's face betrayed no softening of any kind. Why was she giving her anything, if she despised her so much? Samantha's weary mind was confused and troubled and she could only murmur her surprised thanks as she felt the weight in her palm of the string of pearls Cordelia and James had given her, noting how the light glistened off their opaque smoothness. They weren't practical, but they were very beautiful. She wanted to enjoy them, but wondered what they meant.

Sterling gave her a leather-bound notebook for her "most special writings," but it was Lucas' gift that almost undid her. When she pulled back the tissue and looked inside at the shiny metal plate inscribed in black script with the name *Champion*, she had to repeatedly swallow down the lump in her throat and command herself not to cry as a vision of her shiny black horse rose up in her mind. Lucas' thoughtfulness, the fact that he had remembered their conversation in the barn, was so like his brother's. With an almost physical effort, she pushed away the aching homesickness and took her turn at the gift-giving.

She was heartened by the delight that flooded James's eyes as he saw his gift: a custom-made saddle bag with extra pockets of many sizes. The sincere gratitude Lucas expressed for the large leather satchel (made by the same Oberlin leatherworker as the saddle bag) further bolstered her frayed nerves, especially as he seemed as excited as she had been about all the extra compartments which, she hoped, would be useful for all his projects and research efforts that kept the family businesses competitive. Cordelia said little more than a quipped, obligatory "thank you" for the painting Samantha had bought of ducks on a summer pond, but she was relieved that at least there was no derision in the woman's expression. Whether Cordelia would actually put the artwork on display remained to be seen, but if nothing else, Samantha knew the woman couldn't fault its artistry and beauty—or the obvious expense she had gone to in purchasing it.

It felt strange giving Sterling his gift with everyone watching, especially considering how carefully he had arranged to give his gift to her in private the night before. But she supposed this setting would do as well as any, considering the separation that must surely come. When Sterling saw the book before him, gilt-edged and smelling of new paper and ink, he grinned in pleasure. "This is a beautiful edition of *Walden*, Samantha! Thank you. You must have remembered the shabby condition of my copy."

She nodded, but thought of the gorgeous edition he had shown her that day he had introduced her to his library, and felt a little embarrassed that she had gotten him something he already owned, though she had thought it perfect at the time. She hoped he could still put it to use. "I know you already have a beautiful copy in your library here, so perhaps you don't need this one," she faltered. "But I thought for your personal use you could use one less likely to fall apart at the next reading."

"Most definitely! Thank you," he repeated. "I love it." He thumbed through it and she could tell by the way he caressed the crisp pages that he did. "This will be perfect to take back with me to Worthington." He shared some of his favorite passages with them all, and the words brought a flood of memories to Samantha:

"How vain it is to sit down to write when you have not stood up to live."

"Most men lead lives of quiet desperation and go to the grave with the song still in them."

"There is no remedy for love, but to love more."

How well he has followed Thoreau's advice, she thought, wanting to cry at the twin beauty of the words read and the heart of this man she loved so completely. *He has lived and written, sung and loved, with all that is in him. It will be impossible to ever forget him, to forget his zest for life, his quest to bring value to others' lives, or his pure love for me.*

And then her heart clenched with a sudden pang when he read aloud: "If one advances confidently in the direction of his dreams, and endeavors to live the life which he has imagined, he will meet with a success unexpected in common hours." He turned to her briefly as he read this and she knew he was remembering that time in the woods last year, and other times since then, when he had told her that *she* was his dream.

Another lump rose in her throat and she thought she might burst into tears right then and there. But the thought of so thoroughly disgracing herself in front of Cordelia checked her emotion and she swallowed it down with effort.

***

After the gift exchange, they helped themselves to a light luncheon of cold cuts, cheese, and bread from the kitchen, which they carried on plates to the dining room. It reminded Samantha of the picnics she had enjoyed with Rupert and then with Sterling, and as she thought about Mrs. Dolittle's help in those pleasant events, her eyes misted yet again. *One thing at a time,* she reminded herself. *Don't think about the future right now.* She was truly hungry by this point and forced herself to eat more than she wanted to, acknowledging that it really was all delicious and she needed the nutrients.

Sterling watched Samantha carefully throughout the morning and early afternoon, acutely aware that things were definitely not right. Where last night she had seemed devoid of emotion, today the emotion was very close to the surface. He longed to erase her burdens and worries, to comfort her and make things right again. But in front of his family, it was difficult to offer much more than a touch of the hand, a murmured word, a look that he hoped conveyed his concern for her. He prayed for an opportunity to discover the cause of her distress. It pained him to see her suffering, and it hurt him further to be of so little use in helping ease it.

After their meal, he took her on another walk through the conservatory, which she seemed to enjoy, but she remained distant and spoke little. He missed their open conversation, easy familiarity, and verbal sparring. Whatever could have happened to take away that spark and vitality that was so uniquely *her*?

After the conservatory, Sterling asked her if she would like to try again to go sledding. The thought of getting out of the house was definitely appealing, so though she didn't think she had the energy for the outing, she agreed. She headed to her room to put on more layers of clothing against the cold, promising to meet him in the front entrance in ten minutes. He needed to attend to something briefly in another area of the house, so she ascended the stairs alone. When she reached the top of the long staircase and was about to head left down the hallway to her room, she heard Cordelia's voice—more strident and upset than she had ever heard it—coming from one of the rooms on the right.

"I told that girl in no uncertain terms that she was not to continue her pursuit of Sterling! I expected her to be gone by now, crying home to her little backwoods town where she can disappear again into her father's 'mansion,' if indeed that really exists. Instead, she persists in coming to meals with us and going on outings with Sterling, and he is so blinded by his apparent 'love' for her"—she emphasized the word with obvious derision—"that he cannot see who she really is. It is positively maddening!"

Samantha's heart sank like a stone, but anger rose in her simultaneously. How dare this woman, who hardly knew her, defame her with such language—again! Hadn't she already endured enough?!

Before she even knew what was happening, Samantha found herself turning away from her room and heading the opposite direction, toward the voice. In fact, there was another voice, quieter, placating, but Samantha didn't hear it through the pounding of her heart. Her sole focus was to clear her name, to be understood, and to defend Sterling. She hoped this was what God intended for her to do, after all the "holding on" she had done, because she was on her way to do it, and she was terrified.

Heat spread up her body and she heard a pounding in her ears. It was an uncomfortable sensation, but propelled her forward. All rational thought departed, and she found herself moving forward through the doorway without consciously making the decision to do so. Her entrance visibly startled Cordelia, but by the time Samantha had advanced far enough into the room to stand a few feet from her, the woman wore an expression of superiority and barely suppressed triumph. Samantha scarcely had enough presence of mind to register that her own expression must have shown how utterly lacking in control she felt at that moment. Somewhere in her subconscious, she knew someone else was in the room, but her complete focus on Cordelia banished all other notice from her awareness.

She had no idea what would come out of her mouth. She only knew she could not endure this judgment and injustice another moment. Shaking, she stood before Cordelia and spoke in a clear voice that trembled with hurt and anger. "Mrs. Sterling, I do not know why you hate me so completely, nor why you persist in demeaning and belittling me. I came to Lexington hoping to get to know the mother of the man I love, hoping to be your friend.

"I have no ulterior motive. I am not a treasure hunter; money means nothing to me. I have no womanly wiles with which to ensnare your son. Surely you see me and know this is true. I am who I am regardless of who I am with, regardless of the setting I am in. This simple girl," she gestured at herself, "is who I am. I hide nothing, for I have nothing to hide." She spread her arms, to show Cordelia the whole of her person. "No subterfuge or conniving. The very idea disgusts me, and it wounds me to the core that you would consider me capable of even thinking of such games. As a simple girl, I have simple desires. My only 'design' on Sterling is to love him! To love him as he deserves and to return the love he so generously gives me. I wish to joy in his joys and share in his passion for literature and knowledge and helping others. I don't understand why you are certain it must be more complicated than that, or that there is some dark purpose to my intentions."

The tears in her voice were obvious now and she hated her lack of composure. She didn't know if she was making any sense or saying what was most important, but she couldn't stop now. Cordelia's expression had not softened one iota, but at least Samantha had her full attention.

"Confrontation is difficult for me. Loneliness is my old nemesis. You have made certain I experience both on a daily basis during my stay here. As I have sought to be strong and to keep my inner being from crumbling, you have sought to break me down, to pass cruel and false judgments upon me, and to make assumptions about my so-called motives. And then, after depriving me of honor, integrity, and even companionship, you have removed even the simplest opportunities for me to be useful during my stay here. I cannot express to you how distressing all of this is to me, and I cannot prevail another day without defending myself from your defamation, though I am a guest in your home."

Samantha dashed at the tears that leaked out despite her fierce effort not to cry and plunged on. "I see the doubt in your eyes whenever Sterling speaks of his love for me. You don't know how he could possibly want me, out of all the women who want him. You cannot know how often I have asked myself the same question!"

And then changing tack, she persisted, "But Mrs. Sterling, knowing your own son as you do, knowing his competence and intelligence, why do you fail to believe what he repeatedly tells you? Is he not fully capable of knowing his own mind and heart? Is he not intelligent enough to understand what he needs in a lifelong companion? Have you so little trust in him?" Her nose was running now and she felt sure she looked a disaster.

Feeling compelled to say one last thing, she hesitated for the time it took to inhale one more shaky breath. "I think he still has not told you of his near death this past autumn, and so I must."

At last, Cordelia's face registered something other than smugness. Her mouth opened slightly in surprise and her eyes widened.

"Your beloved son, the man I love, almost died of pneumonia a couple months ago, and it was me he cried out for in his delirium. I was who he wanted by his side. And I hurried to be there for him—it was the only place I wanted to be! We were over a hundred miles apart, but I rushed to his side as fast as I possibly could, and it was my privilege and relief to nurse him back to health. I was grateful to be the one to cool his fevered brow, to spoon broth inside his parched lips, to watch over him in his sleep, and finally to encourage his strength to return bit by bit. For weeks! Because I love him, Mrs. Sterling—deeply. Forever. And

I couldn't bear to lose him. I thank God every day that He showed me how to save your son. If that isn't proof of my true motives for Sterling, I don't know what will be. But it *is* the truth. I asked him to tell you about his illness, to express some of what he went through, but it appears he never did. It was not my place to tell you, but...for better or for worse, now I have."

Samantha sniffed and tried to stop shaking, but stood her ground to say one more thing. "I know I am nothing at all of what you want for your son, and if he decides the disparities in our backgrounds are too great, that we are no longer compatible..." Her voice broke and she was afraid the tears might threaten to choke her voice permanently. But she tried again, in a whisper. "I don't know how I will go on, but I will accept that decision because I never want to do anything to hold him back from doing or becoming all that he should." Then the tide of tears behind her eyelids pressed so suddenly and forcefully that she knew she could no longer remain in this room—or, indeed, in this house. She had said all she could.

As she fled, she did not notice Cordelia's ashen face or the shock etched into her features. Nor did she see Lucas run from the room, as if on a mission.

Chapter 34

HOLDING NOTHING BACK

December 1902

Samantha rushed from the house, pulling on her coat as she sped over the snow-skiffed lawns and past the wide expanse of skeletal-branched trees. She could barely see for the tears which—now that she let them—were falling fast. But it didn't really matter where she went, so she didn't care that everything looked a blur. All she knew was that if she did not get away from Cordelia, create the distance and solitude that would allow her to breathe, collect her thoughts, and find peace within herself again, she was going to break. Every bit of her nerves felt splayed and raw.

She bit back a sob and kept running.

She had always needed time and space to be alone, it was part of who she was—but this need was different. This was a deep demand, insistent and unable to be ignored, like hunger after a few days with no food. And yet, it was also more than that: it was a very real need to remove herself from Cordelia's disapproving and ubiquitous gaze. It did not seem to matter where in the house Samantha went or what activity she involved herself in, she felt that gaze ever upon her, condescending and disdainful. It followed her everywhere and weighed her down with its inky, clutching shadow. How had she thought she could put up with the woman for ten days? It was laughably naive of her to ever think she could win her over! The tears continued sliding down her cheeks, one upon another, chilling her face as the cold air breezed over them.

She ran and ran, her boots sliding in places, but not slowing her down. The need to get away was much stronger than her need for warmth and safety, so she kept going.

What did this mean, her inability to gain Cordelia's respect, much less make friends with her? And what did it mean for Samantha's relationship with Sterling?

Suddenly Samantha had a much different perspective on her own parent and a great swell of gratitude rose up in her heart for him. Though her father had been removed and uninvolved for too many years, things had begun to shift in the last few months in a wonderful and remarkable way. And from the start he had been respectful toward Sterling, quickly accepting him and believing his love for Samantha at face value. And then, during Sterling's illness, her father had become just the rock she needed and even helped her nurse Sterling back to health. *Bless Father!* Those were the kinds of things a parent did who truly loved his child and wanted the best for her. *Father loves me,* she realized again. *He really does!* With this remembrance came an even stronger pull to return home. Had she really arrived here only seven days ago? It felt like a lifetime!

She did not understand Cordelia—and oh, how she had tried! *What am I to do now?* she agonized. Not only had she not come to understand the woman at all, she had failed to gain her respect, much less her acceptance. Samantha felt like she had been bled dry of all her strengths and idealism and courage. What was left of herself was a mere shell, and all she wanted to do was completely cease to exist. Life was too heavy, complicated, and hopeless to bear!

Reaching the thicket of trees on the east side of the Sterling's estate, Samantha halted at last, chest heaving with the speed of her flight, and rested a hand against a tall oak. She grasped its rough, uneven bark under her fingers and felt of her smallness in comparison to the huge tree. Whether it was its size, solidity, or majesty, somehow it reminded her of her beloved maple tree back home.

Home. The word filled her heart with a longing as deep and gaping as the wound Cordelia had inflicted. Resting her forehead against her coat sleeves, Samantha leaned against the old tree for support, weeping in great gasping sobs, finally allowing herself to release all the pain, sorrow, disappointment, and loneliness she had lived for the past week. She wasn't certain how it would help anything, but she had no strength left to keep the suffering inside any longer.

She had tried everything she knew, hadn't she? She had been nothing but kind and respectful toward Cordelia, had given the woman the benefit of the doubt many times over and tried to respond with charity in every instance, so how had this whole visit gone so terribly wrong?

Just now in the house, she had probably said way more than she should have, but it was as if something else had taken over and she had been powerless to stop the flow of words.

She had only a vague recollection of what she had said, and didn't know how well she had expressed herself in the end. In the moment, she had felt like she was at last saying things that had long needed to be voiced and defended. But had the message gotten through at all? This second confrontation could not repair the damage the first had created, but she had yearned for the truth to be known.

What am I going to do? Samantha internally agonized. *How can I endure even another few days of this? I don't know how to get out of this by myself! I know no one outside this house, have very little money with me, and I can't walk far in this snow and cold.* She thought of Jane Eyre and her desperate journey on foot after she left Mr. Rochester, running out of money and food, and eventually strength and health. Jane had done what she had to do and was rescued in her extremity by the very people she needed in the moment. *But what should I do?* Samantha asked herself. *Who can possibly rescue me? Tomorrow, even if I were to persuade a servant to send Father a telegram, that would still take several hours and I don't think I can survive that long! And if I run away, what does that mean for Sterling and me? I do not want to just leave him—but would that be better, anyway, in the long run?*

Samantha pressed into the tree and allowed the sobs to overtake her anew, wishing desperately for relief. *Oh God,* she cried bitterly from the depths of her shattered heart, *why can You not just take me now to join thee? I fear I must give Sterling up, and I know I cannot live without him. What am I to do?*

A few moments later, she heard footsteps crunching the snow behind her and knew without turning who they belonged to. Her heart jumped. That long-legged run could only be Sterling's, but who would have told him where she was—and so quickly? She tried to calm her sobs before he arrived, but was unable to do so. She had held in the intensity of these emotions of frustration, injustice, and anguish for too long and now that she had opened the floodgates, there was no closing them until the storm had spent itself.

A strong, gentle hand pressed against her shoulder and a single, deep "Samantha?" was intoned with such concern and tenderness that she broke down further. Sterling turned her around and pulled her into his arms. His breath came in quick puffs and she could feel his heart beating rapidly from the run as she clung to him. But she had no words strong enough to push themselves past the sounds of her ragged heartbreak. And her mind was too numb to allow her to verbalize yet what her failure might mean for them both. So she just let Sterling hold her, taking comfort from the fact that he had come after her.

Sterling, for his part, was wild with worry. He had never seen Samantha like this! But some part of him also recognized that this release of emotion was a good thing. Even though it alarmed him, surely this was better than the recent periods of silence and emotional distance; surely he could get to the bottom of this now. He held her as tightly as he dared, willing her to feel his support, love, and strength, and to be uplifted by it.

After a few minutes, when she had calmed a little, he eased her away from him enough to reach a hand inside his coat and pull out a handkerchief. She took it from him and began mopping her face with it, unable to meet his eyes. Finally, she took in a breath and let it out unsteadily. "I'm sorry, Sterling."

"Sorry?" he asked, completely baffled. "Whatever for?" *For crying?* Surely their relationship was past that. But as he looked at her, he thought perhaps it wasn't the tears, for this seemed different. Samantha looked defeated and broken, two characteristics he had never seen in her before—never even imagined. Despite all she had been through, she had always remained strong and hopeful in adversity. This contrast alarmed him.

She took a shaky breath before offering a reply. "For not being all your mother wants me to be." Her voice muffled as she wiped her nose. "For not measuring up. For not even gaining her respect, much less her acceptance, in all the time we have been here." She willed the tears to stop flowing, but they continued coursing down her face. "I thought she could at least come to respect me, but such a result has proven beyond my capabilities. I wanted to form a connection with her, Sterling. I wanted her to like me, the way my father likes you! I realize now I wanted a mother figure, as I have missed my own all my life." Another sob escaped her lips and she pressed a fist to her mouth, but forced herself to continue after a moment. Now that the words were finally coming, she had to tell him everything.

"I'm sorry that I am not willing to become someone I am not, just to please her. I have never been able to pretend." She shrugged pathetically. "During primary school acting presentations, I could not pretend to be someone other than myself, even for fun." She laughed derisively and the sound jarred in his ears. "I cannot be dishonest with myself or then who would I be?" She realized she sounded frustrated to the point of anger and wished she could control herself better. But the strain of having controlled herself so closely over the past several days had stretched her to the breaking point.

Still she avoided his gaze, but he could clearly see the anguish in her eyes, and he also saw that she was shaking, whether from emotion or from the cold, he couldn't be sure.

"Samantha." He lifted her chin with gentle fingers until their eyes met, hers red-rimmed and still brimming. Tenderly, he smoothed a few stray locks back behind her ears. "You have nothing to apologize for. It is I who must apologize for bringing you here. I know precisely how my mother is; I should have known better than to inflict this experience on you! It's just that I wanted her to accept and love you, to see in you all that I see. But I know now that my desire was a mere fantasy. Sometimes even faith," he gestured at himself, "and hard work," he indicated Samantha, "are not enough to change something. Or someone."

He lowered his hand, but held her gaze. "Samantha, it is my mother who has limited capabilities, not you. You have been kindness and generosity and forgiveness personified!" He pulled her carefully back into his arms again and kissed her hair. "I would never want you to be who she thinks you should be to be 'worthy' of her son. I *love* who you are. It is *you* I love, and what she thinks matters not one whit to me. The truth of the matter is that it is *I* who have so much to do and become to be worthy of *you*! If her vision were not so blinded by pride and her mind so fixated on our family's place in society, it would be obvious to her as well."

Samantha rested against his chest and closed her eyes, suddenly so tired, physically and emotionally, that she sagged involuntarily, almost falling, and Sterling moved to brace her.

"Are you all right?" he asked when she was righted, his voice tight with worry.

"I..." her voice cracked and she swallowed. "No." She hated to make that admission, but it was true. "No, Sterling, I'm not. We have made a few good memories here, but mostly I have missed you so much over the past six days. And my home. It has seemed an eternity."

His grip on her tightened at those words and she drew in a trembling breath, unsure if she should continue. But the last of it came out in a tearful rush. "We have seen so little of each other since we arrived! I have felt more alone than ever in my life, here in this beautiful mansion, surrounded by all the comforts money and servants can provide.

"At the grand social events, I have seen all the admiring glances from beautiful, sophisticated women who are your equal. The attempts to separate us, the disdainful looks and cutting remarks spoken just loud enough to be overheard, the whispered conversations behind hands, with condescending looks cast my way..."

Her voice broke and he rubbed her back until she could compose herself enough to continue.

"I have always felt confident in myself, and comfortable with being different. I have always looked for and found the good in people; I guess I was naive to believe everyone would do the same for me. Here in this situation, I have felt myself...disappearing. Things your mother has said have made me wonder if I imagined everything between you and I. Did I make up all the wonderful and loving things you said to me—and seemed to feel for me?

"Being here has opened my eyes. I fear your mother is right! I am so far beneath your class, Sterling! That you would honestly feel anything for me seems ludicrous now, when I see what you could have." She drew away from him and swiped at her face again, the handkerchief nearly wet through.

He looked at her in astonishment, his heart plummeting. Was this the reason for her emotional withdrawal? Was this why he had felt her pulling away from him?

"I will never be glamorous or beautiful. I will never be good at planning and carrying out important social functions, or be the perfect, poised hostess. This is your life, Sterling! But it can never be mine." She looked up at him and in her gray eyes he saw so much pain that his heart seized. This must be the burden her poem had spoken of! And what a burden to carry alone.

At last, he grasped onto words he could say and spoke them hoarsely. "Oh, Samantha! I knew things were difficult and I have hated it all, have longed to make things better for you, but I had no idea you were actually doubting my love for you." And yet, he suddenly remembered that look in her eyes the day before. "I am so, so very sorry. I have greatly misjudged many things."

He drew her back to him and caressed her hair. "You imagined nothing, dearest. Everything we have experienced together, all the love we have confessed to each other, it is all real. And coming here, having this terrible experience, changes none of that. I fled home for college for many reasons, chief among them to get away from Mother, to find out who I really was, and to make my own future away from her aristocratic social ideals and pretenses. Once I left, I found that my head quickly cleared and I didn't want any of the things she wanted for me—including the 'glamorous and beautiful' women."

Samantha felt him shudder at the thought. She pulled away again and looked up at him, searching his eyes for truth. "But, Sterling, I have seen how all the unmarried women look at you—and even many of the married ones, particularly if they have a daughter within ten years of you! I have heard their whispers confirming what I know very well. You are a beautiful man." Her gaze swept up over his chiseled jaw, sculpted Greek nose, and high forehead framed by the dark, unruly waves of hair she so delighted in.

He colored slightly and started to speak, but she interrupted. "You are! It is obvious to anyone of the female gender, just as it is equally obvious that I am not beautiful nor ever will be. In that way, we are not well matched, even though I...I hate to say it." Her gaze dropped to the snow-covered ground. "Over the past several months, you have made me believe I am attractive—perhaps even pretty—but associating with the truly beautiful here in Lexington has made me realize that I am the same as I have always been. As plain as Jane Eyre." She looked up at him briefly. "It is easy to forget when I am with you. But here..." Again, her gaze fell and he sensed the despair in her. "It has never mattered before, so now that it does, I don't know what to do with the feeling."

Sterling grasped her cold hands and rubbed his thumbs over them again and again, willing her to believe him. "Samantha, look at me. Please." At last, she raised her head and he looked deep into the gray eyes that could hide nothing and didn't try to. He loved those eyes and the soul that shone from them.

"Good looks are the luck of the draw," he said slowly, wanting her to truly understand what was in his heart. "They are a gift from nature that is unearned—a blessing for the receiver, to be sure, but nothing to lord over others, as they were obtained through no effort or merit at all. It is therefore of little consequence compared to what a person makes of him or herself."

He thought for a moment, praying to know what words would help Samantha truly understand how he saw things and convince her of his love.

"I cannot help how women look at me, but the only gaze I care about is yours. As for *my* attraction to *you*, that is as real as the sun—or, or these trees around us." He looked up at the bare branches that spread generously over them.

"You have felt pretty because you are! When I look at you, I see everything I have always wanted in a woman. Do not let others' unkind and untrue comments take root in your heart. But please do believe me when I tell you that to me you truly are lovely."

He brought her hands to his lips and kissed them softly, one by one. The evening stubble on his chin tickled her fingers and she shivered, this time not from the cold.

"I will tell you that as many times as I need to, for as long as I need to. It will always be true." His voice grew husky with emotion and she caught a glint of tears in his eyes, as if he were willing his heart to speak directly to hers.

She stood there, her weeping stilled, searching those brown eyes for confirmation of his words. Could it still be true that he wanted them to be together? She used to believe it. But the last two days had so completely shaken the foundation of her understanding that even her hope in their love had felt tarnished and cheap. Was it possible the new perception was truly false?

For the first time in days, hope for their love seeped back into her being, like a sunrise gradually suffusing the horizon with light. She didn't know if she could trust it, but she wanted to.

Sterling felt himself relax a little as something in her despairing expression softened and a returning flicker of faith lighted it for a moment. "Just as Mr. Rochester found Jane lovely and irresistible, so I find you," he said quietly.

"But," Samantha hedged, "there is a great difference between us and them. Mr. Rochester and Jane were equally plain. You and I..." She shook her head, her expression still doubtful.

Sterling persisted, still rubbing her hands between his own, trying to warm them. "I want a woman who is unpretentious and kind, who always looks for and finds the good in others, someone who serves people around her and seeks to make connections wherever she goes. I want a woman who stands up for what she believes in—including herself—and bravely does what needs to be done, especially when it is difficult or uncomfortable or even terrifying! And, just as important, I want a woman who loves me for who I am—not for who society tells me I should be or for how I look. I need a woman with similar aspirations and goals for the future, with whom I can talk about anything and everything."

Gently he took her face in his hands and looked directly into her sad, gray eyes, willing her to feel his sincerity, to believe his love. "I have found all that—and more—in you."

At last, in a rush, her heart lightened completely. Something inside her told her she could let go of all the weight she had been carrying and allow the immense pain in her heart to melt away. And oh, how she wanted to release that burden.

She swiped at the tears again and swallowed hard. "Truly?" She realized she used to know all this without having to think about it. How had that certainty eroded so completely in only a few days?

"Really and truly." He grasped her gently by the shoulders. "Definitely and positively! You can always be confident in my love for you and trust that what we have is real and strong. I am so sorry for all you have endured over these past days." He spoke quietly and regret weighed down his words as he said, "I am sorry the woman who bore me is not the mother—and person—she should be. She has no right to treat you as she does. I wish I could change that! I should not have allowed her to separate us. I should have protected you better and been there for you more. It pains me to realize how much I have failed you. Can you ever forgive me?"

Samantha fingered the lapels of his coat and looked up at him. "It is not your fault, Sterling. You are not responsible for her actions. And you could not have known everything that went on when you were not present. I didn't tell you because I thought I could improve it on my own and did not want to complain. And then things became so bad I simply didn't know *what* to say! I am sorry I stopped trusting in your love. That was something I never thought could happen!" She shook her head. "I still don't understand it. I had no doubts when we arrived, but in only a few days…" Her lip trembled and she stopped talking, resting against him, not wanting to cry anymore.

Sterling's strong arms went around her again and his voice was hard as he said, "Mother has the amazing and terrible ability to twist everything around and manipulate it to her own ends. You have now experienced that—and for much too long." He willed his anger to dissipate, knowing it would help no one, least of all Samantha. When he felt calmer, he continued. "You have been exceedingly patient and brave." He rested his chin against her hair. "There is no doubt at all about that. Please don't concern yourself with any of this anymore." She was still trembling and his heart ached for her all over again.

"I think our visit here has been long enough," he decided suddenly and firmly, standing up straighter. "We will take the first train out tomorrow morning and I'll have you back in Oberlin by evening."

She inhaled sharply and pulled away from him to search his face. "That is days earlier than we planned. What will your mother say?" But the clear relief, the light in her eyes, confirmed to him that this was the right decision.

He shrugged. "It doesn't matter. We have both had enough, and I will not allow you to be mistreated or made to feel inferior any longer. You have been a saint to put up with her this long and no one can fault you for not being successful in your efforts. The failure is all on Mother's side. If she is going to allow her pride and biases to dictate how she views the woman I love, that is her loss. She will lose me too. We need to keep moving forward and not concern ourselves anymore with trying to win her approval."

Samantha nodded slightly, looking away from him in defeat. "It is still a shame how it all turned out. And there's something else I didn't tell you... I confronted her about everything just before I ran out here." She ventured a glance at him, still surprised that she had initiated that.

He nodded. "Lucas told me very briefly when he ran to find me. He..." Sterling's eyes probed hers and the corners of his mouth began to turn up. "He said you were magnificent." His expression was filled to the brim with pride and affection.

She was stunned. "He-he did?" She seemed to recall Sterling using that very word to describe her confrontation with Audrey.

"Yes. He called you the bravest and most truly good young woman he has ever met."

She blinked at him in surprise, unsure how to respond. Brave?! She didn't feel brave at all.

At last, she said very quietly, "Thank you, Sterling. For giving me a chance anyway, even though I'm nothing like the woman your mother always wanted for you."

"You are so much better than anything she imagined for me," Sterling told her softly, caressing her cheek with one cold knuckle. "Don't worry about it another moment, dearest. She has always been this way. You and I tried to improve things and that is all we can do. Either she will come around one day or she won't, and only she can decide that. Our time here is finished. I am only sorry it has taken me this long to recognize how hard it has been on you."

Samantha attempted a smile and reached up to smooth the soft, unruly curl at his forehead, feeling her heart growing lighter and freer every moment. "Maybe all this was necessary somehow?" she said, inflecting it like a question, her hand lingering on his face. "But it is a relief to know we are leaving early." Then in a whisper, "I thought I would break, Sterling—I think I did!" His hand closed over hers. "Thank you for loving me the way I am and not expecting more of me than I can give."

"Likewise," he replied with a lopsided grin. "I have so much to do to reach your level of kindness and forgiveness that it will keep me busy the rest of my life."

"And I hope it is a very long life," she whispered.

He bent to kiss her, long and deep, and then they both laughed at the taste of her tears.

"Oh, one more thing." He paused and cleared his throat. "I know this is unconventional, but everything about our history together has been that way, so this is probably fitting. It isn't the way I imagined doing this, but it feels like the right time." He wondered briefly if Lovenia in heaven might have just nudged him, and he hoped she was pleased.

He pulled something out of his coat pocket and knelt with one knee in the snow. "Samantha Jennings, will you marry me?" He held open a small velvet jewelry box and she gasped. Inside lay a beautiful engagement ring with a gold band and one simple, perfect diamond in the center.

She was so completely taken off guard that she stumbled back, but then the sudden flood of joy stabilized her and she tugged on his hand. "Yes! Yes, of course I will!" She laughed. "Please, please stand up. You'll get all wet; the snow is so cold."

He chuckled, relieved to hear that laugh he loved so well, and allowed her to pull him up.

He slipped the ring onto her finger and she looked at it in wonder as it winked at her in the waning sunlight. It fit perfectly. How had he gotten just the right size? The fact that this was a ring befitting one of higher social standing or affluence was not lost on her.[1] No one she knew, other than Aunt Eleanor and Cordelia, had a diamond engagement ring. "Oh, Sterling, it's absolutely beautiful. Thank you." She reached up on tiptoe and kissed him again. "I-I don't know what to think!"

"You mean, two pieces of jewelry in two days?" he teased.

She laughed again, and the sound warmed him from head to toe.

"No, I'm—I don't know! I'm just so amazed! An hour ago, I was convinced I had to give you up and now you're saying you want me for all time..." Her voice trailed off in wonder and she looked up at him with wide eyes. "I am not sure how this is possible! Am I dreaming?"

He chuckled a deep rumble and impulsively spun her in a circle. "I'm dreaming too," he said as he set her back on the ground. "I can't tell you how long I've wanted to ask you that question of all questions! But I didn't want to ask too soon, and then we were apart, and then I was too sick to think beyond living through the current moment." His eyes widened as a thought came to him. "I need to speak to your father tomorrow! I did things backwards, but I hope he will give us his blessing, anyway."

"Oh, he will," Samantha assured him. "He likes you, remember?"

---

1. https://michaelplatt.co.uk/history-engagement-ring-1900s-today/

"I like him too." Then, offering his arm, he said, "Come. I must get you back to the house before you grow any colder or more exhausted. You look ready to collapse."

Samantha gave a faint nod. She did feel depleted of all strength and wondered vaguely how she would make the long walk back to the mansion.

They began retracing their footprints back through the snow, she with one hand in the crook of his arm and the other in her pocket.

He guided her along, careful to match his pace to her slow one. "I'm certain there is a servant or two left who would help us pack up our things for the morning. With any luck, this time tomorrow, we will be back in the Jennings mansion eating a peaceful, secluded, and delicious supper provided by Mrs. Dolittle."

"Oh, but she has the rest of the week off, for Christmas!" Samantha remembered, her golden brows knit together.

"No matter," Sterling quipped. "We will manage with the leftovers I am sure she provided, and be all the better for our foraging." He winked at her and Samantha smiled.

"Foraging," she repeated ironically. "What a difficult life we lead, no?"

Sterling chuckled in response, but offered a sober, "Some things are more difficult than others and aren't to be discounted. But you are right, perspective is a good thing. What I don't want is for you to fall sick from being out here too long." He shivered. "I know from experience that pneumonia is not to be taken lightly."

Samantha nodded, the memories still very fresh in her mind. He had a point.

They continued walking as quickly as she could manage, and she was grateful for Sterling's strength beside her. Just by proximity, she felt some of his vitality seeping into her.

"At the moment, I can do nothing about your cold feet, but while we walk back, you can at least put your hand in here with mine." He drew her hand into his pocket, the new ring snagging for a second on the fabric, then their fingers entwined together. Soon she felt warmth creeping back into her hand as well as her heart. Gratitude suffused her whole being and she didn't want this moment to end, in spite of how much her toes were beginning to ache inside her boots.

"Oh!" she said suddenly. "We missed sledding again. I'm sorry."

Sterling had totally forgotten. "No matter. We'll sled another time. Let's go inside and warm you up!"

The moment they returned to the large house, Sterling took charge and a few servants were soon bustling around packing both of their belongings for the impromptu return trip. One of the kitchen maids even put together a bundle of food for them to take with them the following day to eat on the train.

When given the option to take the dresses that had been made to fit her, Samantha balked at the idea. Then she forced herself to think about the generous offer and the hours that Hannah and Miss Moore had spent remaking the dresses for her. They really were beautiful works of art, but the more she considered taking them home and hanging them in her wardrobe, the more she realized that her initial reaction was correct. That daily reminder each day of this difficult place was not something she needed. And they were too fancy to be useful in Oberlin anyway; she would never wear them there. She hoped that someday someone else of her build might enjoy them, but for her they had fulfilled their purpose and she was relieved to leave them behind.

Before she knew it, Samantha found herself in her nightclothes with her bare feet warming in a small enamel wash basin filled with hot water. She was snugly ensconced in a blanket, sitting on the armchair in her room, wondering how her life could have altered so completely in such a short time. The dramatic sweep of the pendulum from despair to joy made her almost dizzy. But the peace and light she sensed deep inside her soul told her that this change was real and lasting. Loving Sterling and receiving his love in return felt unequivocally right again, despite anything Cordelia might think or say to the contrary.

As she gazed out the window at the muted pinks and oranges of the sunset, she knew with sudden surety that they really were doing the right thing. The certainty she felt to her core with brilliant clarity was, she knew, God finally giving her His answer and assuring her that she was doing His will.

And what a humbling, beautiful thing that it was also what she most wanted.

A delicious and wonderful sense of well being flooded over her with this realization, making her truly relax for the first time since her arrival.

After all the weeping today, all the lack of sleep and the worry and tension of the past several days, exhaustion overcame her and she slept, sitting in the soft chair. She didn't notice when the water grew tepid, but she awoke slowly when large hands carefully lifted and dried them with a white, fluffy towel. She blinked in the dim room, now lit by gas lamps, and recognized Sterling kneeling on the floor, pulling soft, warm stockings over her bare feet. She started, surprised. He had never once entered her room in all the days they had been here, but now that they were engaged, here he was, ministering to her as if she were a baby. There was something so tender and cherishing in the action she was afraid she would cry again. But then he turned and situated the blanket more snugly around her feet.

"How is that?" he asked. "Are you feeling warmer now?"

"Oh, yes," she smiled, "much better. Thank you, Sterling." She freed an arm from the blanket and pressed her hand against his cheek. "I love you."

He covered her hand with his own and turned his face to kiss her palm. "I love you too. And I'm so glad you said yes."

"Of course I did!" She looked earnestly into his eyes, which were at a slightly lower level than her own as he knelt at her feet. "Yesterday, when I came to the conclusion that I would have to let you go, it felt as if my heart was being torn from my body. Imagining you absent from my life grieved me so that I almost couldn't breathe!" The emotion of it was still raw in her throat and her eyes were wet with the memory.

"Oh, dearest." He grasped both her hands in his own and pulled them to his heart. She felt it beating strong and sure beneath his shirt. "I never want to be absent from your life. I worried about you so much the last couple days. You were so distant that I felt you slipping away. And when I read that poem Hannah found, panic seized my heart. Not knowing what else to do or to whom to turn, I sought God's refuge and guidance."

"And what did He tell you?"

"I read in 1 John Chapter 4 that 'Perfect love casteth out all fear' and I knew that was what I needed to focus on. I didn't know what was wrong, I didn't know how to help you, but I did know I love you. And I knew I didn't need to fear that love. So I held to that, trusting that God would lead me in the next step."

She nodded.

"What did He tell *you*?" Sterling returned the question. "Did you find comfort in Him? You seemed so bereft of hope that it tore me up inside. And then your poem spoke of losing faith too, and not feeling God's love…!" he trailed off, an exclamation of disbelief that such an outcome could occur in one so faithful.

She shivered. "That was a very dark place to be in and I hope I never have to go there again. But I'm sorry I was unable to express what was happening and that my silence added to your concern. My mind was so confused and conflicted, after all your mother had said. I just didn't know *what* to believe! I wanted to do what was best, but I didn't know what that was. When I prayed for guidance, I didn't feel like I received many answers, but He comforted me and told me to 'hold on.'"

Sterling nodded contemplatively, waiting for her to continue.

"And then He gave me a remarkable sign after the nativity yesterday."

"He did?" Sterling looked at her intently.

"Yes." She paused and shook her head in wonder. "Two fireflies winked at me outside the church, just before we climbed into the sleigh."

"Fireflies in winter?" he asked, taken aback.

"I know."

"And *two* of them?"

"Exactly."

Sterling was silent a moment in reverent contemplation. "I am certain the symbolism isn't lost on you…"

Samantha shook her head, smiling.

"God is good, isn't He, Samantha?"

She smiled, agreeing fully. "Yes. He came through again. He is so very good, Sterling."

An even greater peace settled over Sterling as he considered this little miracle sent from a loving God in a way that Samantha would recognize and take to heart when her mind was clouded with doubt and confusion. And now God did the same with the retelling, for Sterling's sake. Such a tiny light and yet there it was, inspiring them both.

He stood and moved the other chair until it faced hers, as close as it could get. Retrieving a tray from the bedside table, he sat down with it in his lap. "Now for your supper, my dearest Samantha. You need a long sleep before we head home, but I am not going to let you retire for the night until you have eaten. I am afraid you've lost weight since we arrived, and I am determined to nurse you back to health."

He did sound determined, much like a mother, Samantha decided with a small smile—or like Mrs. Dolittle. His voice dropped and he gently continued. "You cannot go on this way, dearest. And you don't need any more of those headaches plaguing you, either."

She was too worn out to protest, but she felt shy about him spooning soup into her mouth. She couldn't remember ever being ministered to in such an intimate way, though she was sure it had happened when she was very young. But as she considered that she had been on the other end of the spoon from him only a couple months before, she allowed the shyness to melt away and let him serve her. It evidently gave him great pleasure, and she did eat more than she would have without his help. She realized that she really would not have taken the effort to eat if he hadn't come in. He knew her so well.

The soup was warm, soothing to her stomach, and delicious. The more she ate of it, the drowsier she became. Finally, with the bowl empty and her stomach full, he kissed her on the forehead and called for Hannah to return and help her into bed.

Before she drifted off to sleep, Samantha's thoughts were full of drowsy amazement. Sterling *did* love her after all! She should never have lost sight of that truth. And now that he was armed with the knowledge of what had transpired without his presence, he would be all the more vigilant in his efforts to protect her to the best of his ability. He was on her side and always would be. She was not alone after all! Slowly, confidence and faith seeped back into her being as she slept the long and dreamless sleep of one who has long been deprived of peace and finally found it again. Hope wrapped her in a cocoon of contentedness and she slept soundly.

Chapter 35

RELIEF

December 1902

Early the next morning, Hannah brought Samantha breakfast, which she fully enjoyed for the first time in days. Snug once more in the warm blanket, she sat by the fire, still trying to grasp her new reality. She kept looking at the ring on her finger and marveling that last night had not, in fact, been a dream. She thought about her former despair and grief at what seemed an inevitable separation from Sterling, then about the horrible confrontation with Cordelia. Had all that really happened only yesterday?! It felt like a week ago at least. And now, suddenly, she was engaged to the one man in the world she wanted to spend the rest of her life with, and she would be home this very day. She felt weak with relief—or was that persistent exhaustion?

She did feel rested, but fatigue still tugged at the corners of her consciousness. She knew she wouldn't feel completely herself until they left the house for good, but she thought she might be strong enough to face Sterling's mother again now, to say goodbye. At least, she told herself she was.

Fortunately, it didn't come to that. As they walked outside, Sterling told her with a wink that they were leaving before his mother arose. Under his breath, he added that he had learned as a youth that the early bird not only caught the worm but also avoided the hawk.

At that, a laugh escaped before Samantha could hold it back, and she clamped a hand to her mouth in surprise.

Sterling grinned at her. "I am so glad to hear that sound again."

Out on the sweeping drive in front of the mansion, she embraced James Sterling when he tentatively offered his open arms, and kissed his cheek, which made him blush and his mustache twitch. She didn't know what to say and he didn't speak either, but as she looked into his kind blue eyes and saw respect reflected back at her, she realized they didn't have to say anything. He was a good, humble man with a difficult burden to carry, and he did it with grace. She was grateful for his example of unselfish love and knew she would never forget it.

Just before Sterling handed her up into the sleigh, Lucas ran out to join them in his shirtsleeves, his straight brown hair bouncing, as if he had noticed them leaving from the window and dashed outside.

"Brother," he said, clasping hands with Sterling in a firm grip. "I am sorry your visit was cut short, but I don't blame you a bit. I only wish things had turned out differently."

He turned to Samantha with an apologetic smile, his features similar to Sterling's in that moment. She inclined her head to him and he bowed back, his gentlemanly manners as intact as Sterling's always were. "It was very nice to meet you," he said sincerely. "I enjoyed getting to know you better."

Sterling had, as yet, said nothing to his family about their engagement, and the diamond on Samantha's finger was hidden beneath the mittens she wore. Sterling would tell them in time, but for now, he just wanted Samantha safely away and settled back in Oberlin, and he still needed to speak with her father.

Suddenly, Lucas grasped Samantha's hand gently and, looking directly into her face said, "I hope when I own this estate that you will feel welcome to visit anytime. I am glad my brother chose you, and I hope someday to be equally as fortunate." He didn't even blush as he made this open confession.

Her eyes moistened as she thanked him, and he and Sterling embraced, slapping each other's backs in brotherly comradeship. Then Sterling helped her up into the sleigh and they sped off for the train station.

***

Now that they were engaged, a chaperone wasn't considered necessary, which was fortunate since they had left so hurriedly. Much to her surprise, Samantha slept much of the train journey back to Oberlin. The rhythmic motion of the train, combined with Sterling's reassuring presence beside her, and the relief of at last being out of the tense atmosphere of the Sterling household, lowered all her defenses. Before she knew it, she leaned against him and slept soundly.

With her tucked up beside him, content and well, though obviously lacking her usual energy and vitality, the stress and worry that had built up throughout their visit to Lexington began to dissipate and Sterling realized how tired he also was. God bless train travel!

About an hour before they pulled into the Oberlin station, both awoke, feeling rested from their long naps. Samantha stifled a yawn and stretched her neck to work out the kinks. She looked out the window at the snow-covered landscape speeding past and pulled the blanket more securely over her lap, glad they would soon be home inside, near the fire.

She turned back to Sterling and found him watching her. "What is it?" she asked, still blinking away the last of her sleep.

In answer, he reached for her hand, slowly removed the mitten, and smoothed his thumb over her new ring.

"I know!" she whispered, looking down at it. "I can scarcely believe it." Suddenly a new thought occurred to her and her eyes widened. "We haven't decided how all of this is going to work out!"

"All of what?" he asked.

"Well, I know you love teaching at the boys' school, and I would never want to make you quit what you love. And I love Worthington now too, because of all the people I love there. But," her brows furrowed, unsure of how to say what she felt. "Well, Oberlin is my home…and I feel like Father needs me still. Leaving him alone now, when he has just started to live again… I am not sure if he's strong enough to—"

Sterling's smile and shake of the head halted her mid-sentence. "I've learned much at the boys' school and will be forever grateful for my two years of experience there, but since the beginning of the year, I have known it would be my last. And Mr. Grover has too. I will be sorry to leave the Tomlinsons, but I imagine there will be much comings and goings between the two towns, with all the Lewises wanting to come visit you, and vice versa. Besides," he intertwined their fingers, "I love Oberlin as well. Where I live matters little to me, as long as you're there beside me. I agree that your father shouldn't be left to himself for long. That is a relationship you need to continue strengthening. And I seem to remember something else that is very important."

"What is that?" she asked seriously.

"You have a school to start," he grinned. "And that is going to take a lot of time and effort on behalf of many people. You can't do that in Worthington."

The brightness that suffused her face, then, was like the strongest rays of glorious morning sunlight. "Yes, I do—and no, I can't!" she agreed. "That is all true, but," she gave an incredulous, delighted laugh, "are you truly willing to throw your lot in with mine and see what we can make of my mother's dream?"

"I am," he replied, squeezing her hand with conviction. "I am ready to jump in with both feet, body and soul. It is just the sort of worthy venture I feel like I have been preparing for all my life."

"Really?" Her heart soared and her head swam with questions. "But what if it doesn't work out, Sterling?"

"Then we will try something else. That is the wonderful thing about living in America in this day and time: opportunity! And that is what our educational institution will be all about, giving children an education that will open up their opportunities for the future."

She clasped his arm with her free hand and laid her head against his shoulder in pure joy. "That is exactly right," she said. "That is precisely our goal." Her soul swelled just thinking about it, then she looked up at him again, eyes sparkling. "I love saying 'we' and 'our.'"

"Yes," he replied softly. "They are the most beautiful pronouns in the world."

***

When the horse pulled up to the Jennings mansion and the cab stopped, they alighted and stepped up the walkway, hand in hand. Samantha opened the big front door with her key and Sterling set their luggage inside. They both stood there, sighing at almost the same moment, happy to be back, then laughed together. "This place has definitely grown on me," Sterling said.

"Good." Samantha smiled up at him. "It feels like a real home more and more to me all the time. I must tell Father we're here. I'll be right back!" She hurried down the hall and he watched her lift her skirts and run up the main staircase.

Basil Jennings' face lit up when he opened his bedroom door and saw his daughter standing there. "You are home early!" His voice, always soft and a little gruff, sounded somehow stronger these days, richer and more modulated. His grizzled face beamed and the skin around his eyes crinkled happily. Samantha couldn't help noticing that he was aware of not only today's date, but also remembered when she was supposed to have returned—and that he genuinely rejoiced to have her home. He had made so much progress in so little time! She embraced him and he hugged her back tightly. "I missed you, daughter."

"I missed you too, Father. And I missed the Dolittles and Martin and Champion and this house and Oberlin..." She trailed off.

He chuckled at the long list but detected something else in her voice and sobered. He pulled back to look at her and asked, "It was not the trip you wished, then? You look thinner than usual, and pale. Are you all right?"

She couldn't think of the words to form a quick explanation and just shook her head. Her expression was pained, but she smiled again. "Sterling brought me back, of course, and I wondered if you would like to join us while we find something to eat."

"Of course. I have missed that young man of yours, as well."

As they walked down the staircase, Samantha asked briefly about her father's Christmas, about Mrs. Dolittle and Claire, and found that she had not missed much. It felt like a year since she left, that a great deal should have transpired in her absence! But she was glad to find that things were actually still the same and that she could pick life back up where she had left it. There was something stabilizing in that, somehow.

As they walked down the hallway toward the front door where Sterling stood, Professor Jennings called out a greeting and Sterling moved forward to meet him. They clasped hands and exchanged pleasantries. "Thank you for bringing my daughter home safely," Basil told him.

"It was my pleasure, of course," Sterling told him. "Christmas was not exactly a cheerful affair and I am sorry to say our goal was not achieved. These past days have been very difficult, particularly for Samantha." His eyes spoke of regret as he looked at her, but she gazed back steadily, unaccusing and open. Basil did not miss the exchange.

"I am determined to help her regain her former health and vitality before I head back to Worthington for the spring term," Sterling said.

Samantha drew close to his side and threaded her fingers through his. "It was not Sterling's fault," she hurried to explain. "There were issues outside his control, and as he and I have discussed, we did everything we could. Now, if anything is going to change, it is up to his mother. We just need to keep moving forward."

Her father nodded soberly. It sounded as if something serious had occurred and he wished to know the whole of it. "I am sorry to know it was so difficult, but you are right. Forward is the right direction to go, as I have only too recently been reminded in my own life."

After a moment of silence, Samantha said brightly, "Well, are you gentlemen hungry? Shall we go see what Mrs. Dolittle left us in the kitchen?" She felt an unexpected thrill of happiness at the realization that she could prepare the meal on her own and serve the men without anyone stopping her from being useful, and without fear of running into Cordelia in the process.

Sterling squeezed her hand. "Yes, a good meal would be wonderful after a long day's journey. But I need to talk to your father about something first. May we join you in the kitchen in a few minutes?"

"Yes, of course," Samantha responded, her heart clutching in anticipation of what their conversation would likely include. She let go of Sterling's hand and patted her father's. "I'll see what I can put together."

As she went through the door into the kitchen, she chanced a backward glance and saw her father and Sterling heading to the parlor. She sensed it might be several minutes.

***

Sterling's heart pounded as he and Basil took seats on the sofas opposite each other. He knew this man approved of him—liked him, even, as Samantha had reminded him. Already, they had been through quite a bit together. For heaven's sake, the man had helped him bathe and shave when he was ill and nearly as helpless as a babe! But the formality of the occasion and the importance of the question he was about to pose made his pulse quicken and his stomach tighten.

"Professor Jennings," he began.

"Basil," the older man corrected. "Please."

Sterling nodded and started again. "Basil, you know that I love your daughter very much and that we have gotten to know each other quite well over the past several months."

Basil's eyes brightened, knowing what must be coming next, and nodded slowly. "Yes."

"What with finding her family in Worthington last summer, her bringing me back from death's door last fall, and spending time with my family over Christmas—which included enduring the hostility and prejudice of my mother over this past interminable week—I think our devotion and loyalty have already been tested more than most couples'."

Basil nodded again, trying to look serious, but feeling a hint of laughter rising up in him over Sterling's loquaciousness. The poor boy must be nervous, in spite of his poise.

Sterling waved a hand, impatient with himself and determined to get to the point. "At any rate, what I would like to ask you is if I have your permission to marry Samantha."

A smile spread slowly across Basil's grizzled face and grew into a grin. "You do," he answered, without preamble. "I wondered how much longer you would take! A courtship does not usually last this long, but considering your months of separation during the school season, I suppose it could not be helped."

"Unfortunately, no," Sterling agreed. "Though the separation pained us both, I think we have grown and learned things we needed to, to be ready for the next stage of our lives."

"I agree completely," Basil said, "and I believe my daughter could not find a better, more faithful young man than you, Sterling. I am very happy to give my blessing—and to congratulate you." He stood and Sterling followed suit, surprised when, after another handshake, Basil put one arm around him and gave him a stiff embrace.

When they stepped back from each other, Basil asked, "When will you propose?"

Sterling shifted uncomfortably. "Well, actually, I already did last night."

Basil looked surprised, then began to chuckle.

"I planned to wait till we returned to Oberlin," Sterling hurried to explain, "but the timing and the situation felt right—demanded it, actually." He paused, trying to decide the best words to verbalize the terrible ordeal Samantha had endured. And reporting to her father made him feel more penitent than ever. His expression subdued, he explained, "You see, I hate to tell you this, but in only seven days, my mother's manipulation and cutting remarks managed to shake Samantha such that everything she *knew* about the strength of our relationship was severely undermined. In fact, even her own innate confidence in herself was eroded to such an extent that she came to believe we were completely unsuited for each other, that she was hopelessly flawed, and that by maintaining a connection with me, she was holding me back."

Basil made a noise that simultaneously expressed disbelief and sympathy, then said, "That does not sound like my self-assured and optimistic daughter." His gray brows drew together in concern.

Sterling shook his head. "No, by the end, she was not herself at all. My mother had squashed all her natural spirit and zest for life. Samantha stopped laughing and smiling, she slept poorly, and almost stopped eating. And what made it worse was that at the same time, Mother kept me so busy with unimportant things that I didn't realize the extent of what was happening. By some miracle, Samantha managed to retain some sense of self, refusing to give in to all my mother's demands to change who she is. But in the process, she came to believe that we were just too different to continue our relationship."

Sterling was vaguely aware that he was speaking faster than normal in his desperate attempt to fully explain the situation to this man whom he so respected. He also realized that, having not spoken about the ordeal to anyone but Samantha, he also felt a compelling need to express it all to someone older and wiser, to help him process the experience for himself.

"When your daughter needed me most, I wasn't there, Basil! I was the only person she had, and I failed her. I mean, I was *in* the house—it's huge, much larger than this one—but I had no idea what was really going on. Truth be told, I don't think Samantha did either, for a while. My mother is that calculated and devious." Sterling's face had grown pale and he looked at the old professor with sorrow. "I am so sorry, sir. I took her into that situation and thought I could protect her from any unpleasantness, but I failed miserably. I didn't expect... I wasn't aware..." He felt himself floundering for words.

Basil laid a hand on his shoulder and then indicated the sofas again. They sat and Basil leaned forward. "I can tell the experience was very difficult, not just for Samantha, but also for you. This is concerning and we should all no doubt discuss it, but for now: how is she, really? She looks paler and thinner, but her spirits seem surprisingly good for all you have described."

In his emotional weariness, Sterling brushed a hand down his face and realized for the first time that in all the events of the night before, he had forgotten to shave. "Yes, her good spirits do seem remarkably intact. I think she feels a great deal of relief and comfort in knowing I stand by her and love her more than ever, and that I care nothing for the things that matter to my mother. Simply leaving that house is a relief! But besides that, Samantha has a quiet strength and an amazing resilience that I recognize again and again. I keep thinking I know everything about her and then she shows another aspect of her character that I had not fully appreciated before. So...I do think she will be all right with time, though she deserves all the kindness and gentleness we can show her as she recovers."

Basil nodded in agreement, more impressed than ever at the depth in this young man and the breadth of his love for Samantha.

Sterling sighed. "But I feel terrible for putting her in that position." He clasped his hands together and leaned forward, matching Basil's posture. "When I finally realized what was going on and how bad things actually were for her, I proposed. It just felt like the right time. She needed that reassurance of my love and constancy, and my previous words did not seem enough to convince her. I had the engagement ring by then anyway and had wanted to ask her for months. Considering the circumstances, leaving a few days early was really the only decision to make. I had to take her out of there, and..."

Basil picked up his train of thought. "And such a spontaneous trip was made easier with an engagement."

"Exactly. But even though the proposal came slightly earlier than planned, in a setting different than I imagined, it was no less heartfelt. I have wanted to ask her to marry me since that day last summer when I returned to Oberlin." He paused in thought for a long moment and Basil waited patiently. Then, in a voice deep with emotion, he confessed, "Honestly, Basil, being with her always feels like coming home."

Basil smiled and his gaze shifted to a distant place, as if remembering something from long ago. After a few heartbeats, his eyes refocused on Sterling and he straightened. "I understand, son. I can see what a hard situation you were both in, and I don't blame you for what your mother did. You are not your mother. I can tell that Samantha does not blame you either. I know she loves you and that you make her very happy. May I ask just one thing of you?"

"Of course, sir!" Sterling straightened as well.

"I would like to ask that you never allow anything of this nature to happen again. Samantha is strong and resilient, but she has a tender spirit and a soft heart, and I would that neither be fully broken."

Sterling nodded emphatically. "I have already determined that must be my course, to never allow the experience to repeat itself. Even if it means never returning her to my home while my mother is alive."

"Good, then. I think we both understand that forgiving the perpetrator should not include allowing the injured to stay in harm's way. I believe you have learned something valuable from this ordeal and I trust you to take care of Samantha in future."

The tightness in Sterling's stomach eased and he found his gratitude for the man growing in leaps and bounds. He was kind and just, caring and loving as any good father should be, and he truly had Samantha's best interests at heart—though after what Basil had done in bringing her to him in Worthington when he was so sick, he hadn't doubted that.

"Thank you, sir. I appreciate your forgiveness and trust, and will strive to be worthy of both."

Basil smiled at him kindly. "Well, shall we head to the kitchen? Samantha will be wondering what became of us." He stood again and Sterling followed him out into the high-ceilinged foyer, then down the hall to the right.

Samantha raised her head as she heard them enter the kitchen and smiled at them. She set the last plate on the table and said, "I was beginning to wonder if everything was all right."

Sterling put an arm around her, drawing her close. "Everything is very all right," he affirmed. "Your father gives us his blessing."

"Oh, thank you, Father," she exclaimed, leaving Sterling to throw her arms around Basil. "That makes me very happy! Even though Sterling already proposed, I did very much want your blessing." She looked up at him, her expression earnest. "Thank you for not being upset with the order of things."

Basil returned his daughter's embrace and kissed the top of her head. "I can clearly see the love and devotion you two have for each other, and I want the best for you both."

"We appreciate that more than you know." Samantha gave him another hug and returned to Sterling's side at the table.

"You are good for each other," Basil mused, looking at them with a fond smile. "And your association has been good for me, as well." He paused and his eyes grew misty. He cleared his throat and said, with some difficulty, "Thank you for bringing me out of myself, Samantha. I..." he paused, unsure of the best way to express what was on his heart. "I needed it. All of it—including the scoldings."

When she started to apologize, he held up his hand and shook his head. "I *did* need a good scolding. I probably needed one for a good many years. I shudder to think what Lov—" he swallowed, "what Lovenia would say to me about how terribly I have neglected our daughter, and the community...and God."

Sorrow and remorse showed so strongly in his face that Samantha wanted to go to him again, but she sensed he was trying to collect himself, to find a way to tell her this difficult thing. At last, he straightened his shoulders and gave her a small smile. "Thank you for helping me feel needed again, and reminding me what a father should be. I...I do want to be a better father to you than I have been. Can you forgive me for all my faults? I know there are so many. And I am afraid you will still have to be patient with me as I work to merit the love and trust you have already given me."

Samantha held out a hand and he grasped it like a lifeline. She had never seen such contrition on anyone's face before, and it melted her already soft heart. "Of course, Father!" she exclaimed. "Of course. We are moving forward together and making great strides." It was a statement of conviction.

"We are." Basil's voice choked with emotion.

Sterling placed a strong hand over both of theirs and added his own feelings on the matter: "Onward and upward!"

For a crystalized instant in time, the words of her poem flashed into Samantha's mind and she saw a twinkling field of fireflies moving in just that way.

As they sat down to a pleasant, simple meal, Samantha felt wrapped in love and contentment. For the first time since they'd left Oberlin, she had her normal appetite and could eat with ease. The rock that had seemed permanently lodged in her stomach had dissolved.

Seeing her eating and smiling easily again in that sunny way of hers, Sterling was more relieved than he could articulate. This was where she belonged. He would watch over her for the next few days before returning to Worthington, to make sure she continued eating and that her color returned. And he intended to tell her over and over how much he loved her, to fill her chock-full of all the reassurances she needed, till he could return here for good. She seemed to be back to her old self, but he sensed there would still be internal healing and recovery, and he wanted to help however he could.

Before they finished their meal, Basil surprised them by suddenly asking, "Could you tell me more about this children's school you want to open? I think I am ready to hear your plans and ideas."

"Oh, Father!" Samantha's gray eyes shone with delight. "Really? We could very much use your expertise and insights."

Basil chuckled. "There you go again, making this old fellow feel needed. I am so out of practice in the educational world that I don't know if I will really be of much use to you, but I would be honored to try. And I know it would make your mother very happy."

Samantha did not miss the fact that her father had spoken about her mother twice in less than an hour—and had even mentioned her name for the first time! It was sweet progress, indeed.

Chapter 36

HEALING

Samantha retired early that night, wondering vaguely how she could still be so exhausted, and fell asleep quickly. She was disturbed by dreams of endlessly walking through the Sterling mansion, searching for Sterling while fearfully looking around each corner for Cordelia, always afraid the woman was trailing her or lying in wait. As a result, she had a rather restless night's sleep and slept in longer than usual.

When she did wake, she was disoriented for a moment and lay there, looking around, expecting to see the lavishly decorated rose room at the Sterling mansion. But as she recognized her own simple room with its wooden plank floor and rag rugs, and its familiar, unassuming furnishings, everything flooded back to her in a moment. The relief was immediate and immense. She smiled with the joy of it and stretched, reveling in the feeling of being home and comfortable in body and spirit, and that the bad dreams had all been a reflection of the past and not the present.

Then she felt the ring shift on her finger and remembered with a jolt what else had occurred, of even greater significance. She jumped out of bed and wrote a few lines in her journal, said her morning prayer, and readied herself for the day. Feeling truly herself in a simple, green flowered dress, with her hair brushed, braided, and coiled up in a large bun at the nape of her neck, she took her small Bible and headed to the guest room that the three of them had hastily prepared for Sterling after dinner last night. Outside the door, she placed the Bible on the small table and knocked quietly.

Sterling opened the door, his hair newly wet and combed, his clothing only slightly wrinkled from being packed in his suitcase. He smiled at her and drew her in for an embrace. "Good morning! How is my bride-to-be?"

With her head tucked against his shoulder, she smiled and breathed in the leather and spice scent of him. "That sounds so strange," she mused, "but also wonderful. I still can't quite believe you asked me to marry you."

"I can't believe I waited so long!" he answered back, laughing.

She thought what a lovely place this was to be, in his arms while he laughed.

But the doubt that had plagued her for a week and spread deeply into her heart like a festering cancer was still there. She kept thinking it was gone and then it raised its insidious head again. She drew back just enough to look up into his face and ask, "Are you...certain...you really want to go through with it? I mean, it was a good solution to the problems at your house, but I don't want you to feel obligated..."

"Obligated!" Sterling exclaimed in genuine consternation, his brow furrowed. He placed firm hands on her shoulders, pressing lightly, and his serious face looked intently at her. "My lady, I see I have more convincing to do, after all the eroding my mother did." He cupped her chin gently in his fingers and bent to kiss her. Slowly, their arms went around each other and the kiss deepened until Samantha couldn't breathe. She pulled away, gasping, and looked up at him in astonishment.

"Believe me now?" he asked, laughing again, his brow smooth and his eyes bright.

"I..." She swallowed, blinking, wondering at the constancy and loyalty of this good man she loved. He had shown her many times in many ways how much he cared for her. "I..." She didn't understand why she doubted him when he had never given her reason to. But then she reminded herself that it was only under Cordelia's recent influence that she had even thought to doubt. *I need to return to that place I was before, of trust and clarity, of light and truth.* Now that she was away from that stifling and damaging atmosphere, she felt she could, with time. She drew in a deep breath to steady herself.

Sterling traced a gentle finger down her cheek and caressed her chin with his thumb. "I am more certain of this than I have ever been of anything in my life! More sure than that I didn't want to be a professional gentleman, or inherit the family businesses. More sure than that I wanted to attend college and become a writing teacher. My love for you has not changed one jot, my dearest—it has only grown."

As he looked earnestly into her eyes, he yearned for her to feel what he felt, visualizing a string connecting their hearts, communicating directly. Such a thought reminded him of the quote from *Jane Eyre* that he had shared with her last summer in one of his letters. He willed himself to remember it now, to illustrate his point in a way she uniquely appreciated, and began slowly:

"I sometimes have a queer feeling with regard to you—especially when you are near me, as now: it is as if I had a string somewhere under my left ribs, tightly and inextricably knotted to a similar string situated in the corresponding quarter of your little frame. And if that boisterous channel, and two hundred miles or so of land come broad between us, I am afraid that cord of communion will be snapt..." [1]

She nodded meekly and exhaled, trying to let doubt flow out with her breath.

"I can't believe I remembered that whole thing," he said suddenly, with a chuckle of surprise and a little boy's look of pride in himself. "Forgive me for borrowing Mr. Rochester's words, but he said it so perfectly I could never improve upon it. That is exactly how I feel for you."

Samantha gave a small, contemplative smile in response and he thought he detected the disbelief dissipating.

"I expect it may take a while for you to regain your former confidence in us," he continued quietly, resting his hands softly again on her thin, strong shoulders. "But whenever the doubts return to your mind, please remind yourself they were planted there by a prejudiced, conniving woman and not by me. And pray that God will lift its weight and leave you only with the light of truth."

She nodded meekly, recognizing the rightness of his words and their similarity to her own thoughts. "The truth shall make you free." [2]

"Yes! And the truth is—now and forever—that I love you, Samantha. I want to be with you the rest of our lives, to keep learning and growing with you, to raise a family together."

"A family," she breathed in wonder. "A family of our own."

Sterling looked at her tenderly and his eyes danced. "Focus on our love and everything else will fall back into its proper place. And any time you need reassurance, I will tell you

---

1. Jane Eyre by Charlotte Bronte, Chapter 23

2. John 8:32

again," he kissed her on one cheek, "and again," he kissed her on the other cheek, "and again," he left a lingering kiss on her lips.

She was in his arms again, her heart lighter than she ever remembered it being before. "I love you, Sterling. I have never doubted my own love for you nor your goodness. The thought of being yours overwhelms me with happiness."

"Good." Sterling's smile was beautiful and tender. "I am always happiest when I am with you. I know your heart needs time to heal, so be patient with yourself. I am only sorry I won't be here every day to remind you of my love in person."

"Yes," Samantha sighed, "me too. But," she looked up at him again, "it will only be a few more short months. We have made it this long, we can endure a little longer."

"That's right," he agreed. "Somehow, we will survive another separation. And while I am away, you will have plenty to plan." Then, as an aside, "As if planning a new school weren't enough!"

"Oh my," she exclaimed. "You are right!" Her eyes widened as she thought about it all. "I will be so busy! And I know nothing about planning a wedding! I haven't thought much about those kinds of details! And I have no mother to help me." She felt a momentary panic.

"No," he acknowledged, "but you have many stand-in mothers now who would love to be of service. Mrs. Dolittle, Claire, and Katherine will all be quick to lend a hand. And Thora will want to help as much as she can. Besides," he held up an index finger for emphasis, "if I know the Lewis women at all—particularly your aunt Irene—they will want to take a great part in this event as well. You may have a house full of helpful women before long!"

She envisioned each of the wonderful women he had mentioned and how much they meant to her, and she knew he was right. Suddenly she began to laugh as she realized she would likely have more help than she could manage—but such dear and loving helpers they would be!

Hearing the lovely sound of her laughter, seeing the relief and joy in her face and the light returned to her eyes, Sterling grinned at her, his heart squeezing. He pointed at the Bible she had placed on the little hallway table and asked, "Shall we take this conversation to the library?" At her nod, he offered his arm and they walked down the long hallway. "I probably know less than you do about planning a wedding, but let's start with the basics. First of all, where should we have the ceremony itself?"

413

Their footsteps sounded down the hall as they walked toward the library, deep in conversation. Here in the Jennings mansion the echoing wood flooring was a great contrast to the opulence of the Sterling mansion's carpeting that muted all sound. But in the simplicity and function of a wood floor, Samantha recognized a symbol of openness and honesty and her mind felt clearer than it had in days.

Sterling looked at her affectionately as she walked closely beside him, her fair head bowed in thought. He remembered, with amazement, how reclusive she used to be, for now as they talked about who to invite, she obviously enjoyed the thought of filling the mansion with all sorts of people.

In the library, they seated themselves at the table and Samantha began writing down all the things they needed to decide for their wedding. Then, with the planning officially started, they took Samantha's Bible to the sofa and sat side by side for their morning devotional, made doubly enjoyable just be being together.

***

A few days later, Samantha stood in the library, looking out the window at the huge maple tree in the late afternoon light. It looked so forlorn with all its glorious leaves long gone, yet still its branches reached upward, though they were barren and lonely in winter's stark season. In this moment, the beloved tree seemed to her to represent never ending optimism, even hope. Sterling had officially left Oberlin and his departure had not been easier than any other. But this time was different, for it was the last time. She felt the heaviness of his absence, but also a new lightness for the future.

Yet her spirits were still weighed down. She reminded herself of all the happy thoughts she had to dwell on, so many precious times spent together and tender words exchanged. She didn't want to forget any of them! She knew that in the midst of all the busyness that would shortly come upon her, she would pull out each of these memories one by one and examine them, glistening in the light, for the jewels they were. Yet still, the melancholy clung to her.

She heard a soft clink from behind her and turned to see Mrs. Dolittle setting a tray of food down on the round table.

The beloved housekeeper, her confidante, smiled at her and her brown eyes smiled too. "I thought you could use an indoor winter picnic to lift your spirits, my dear. When Rupert provided one for you last year, I thought it was such a sweet idea. The only problem is that I am afraid we will have to enjoy this one at the table instead of the floor. If I get down there," she pointed downward, "I may never get back up again." She chuckled and the sound lifted Samantha's heart. When she joined Samantha at the window and held out her arms, Samantha leaned into them gratefully.

The older woman held her in her warm, soft love, saying nothing for a long moment. Samantha closed her eyes and soaked in her motherly affection. As she considered her feelings, she wasn't sure why she felt so melancholy and conflicted. She knew Sterling would be back. And when he did return, they would be married! There was so much to look forward to.

"So many goodbyes," Mrs. Dolittle said, low. "Even with the return of that young man into your life, things haven't been easy, have they? I doubt you expected that."

Samantha took a minute to reply, recognizing the truth of her words. "No," she said finally. "But there have been wonderful things too, joys to balance out the difficulties."

"Yes." Mrs. Dolittle continued to hold her comfortingly. "Like your dear mother, you always look on the bright side, and there is much good to see. But sometimes it is also important to give time to acknowledge what is hard and discouraging and confusing. Claire and I have been working through that a great deal since she and her husband separated. The human existence is made up of both good and bad experiences, and the good Lord made us to experience a wide range of emotions, so it is right to acknowledge each one."

Samantha swallowed a sudden lump in her throat and said nothing as images of her time at the Sterling estate flooded into her mind. These were mostly negative memories that she kept trying to push away, but maybe Mrs. Dolittle was right. None had lost their potency and all hurt her heart with a painful piercing. Leaving Cordelia's realm of influence had given Samantha great and immediate relief, but she was still left with an immense hurt inside that disturbed her almost as much during the day as it did in her night dreams. She stepped back and looked into the housekeeper's kind face, from whose eyes shone love and understanding, as they always had.

"Your father debriefed me this morning when I returned with Claire from Amherst. He felt I should know what you have been through, so I could be more sensitive to your needs."

"He...he did?" Samantha asked, surprised. And yet, he had surprised her so many times over the past several months, she *shouldn't* be surprised, she reflected.

Mrs. Dolittle nodded. "I am thoroughly sorry you did not have the happy Christmas holiday you anticipated." Concern and empathy had replaced the smile on her face and her eyes studied Samantha's. "Would you care to join me for a little picnic lunch here and tell me what you're feeling? You don't need to pretend anything with me, child. I don't mind hearing about the difficulties you went through. Sometimes talking about the hard things makes them easier to make sense of, somehow. If you feel up to it."

Samantha took a deep breath and held it, still trying to wrap her mind around all she was thinking and feeling. She exhaled slowly and nodded. "Thank you. I think I *would* like to tell you. I am still so confused trying to figure out what happened and why. And I have been pushing away negative feelings for a long time." She followed Mrs. Dolittle to the table and they set their places, then sat together. After saying grace, they began to eat a simple meal of bread, cheese, ham, applesauce from last autumn's harvest, and warm, sweetened herbal tea. It was nothing like the sumptuous meals provided at the Sterling mansion, but it was perfect.

"So," Mrs. Dolittle said, opening the discussion after a few minutes, "I hear Mrs. Sterling is quite the formidable character."

Samantha steeled herself against the wave of negativity she felt at the mention of Cordelia's name, involuntarily picturing her handsome face and form in her mind's eye, every white hair in place, no crease to mar the elegant dress she wore. "Yes," she answered quietly. "Formidable is a good word."

Mrs. Dolittle cut a small bite of ham and raised the fork to her lips. "And she was very unkind to you on multiple occasions." She placed the ham in her mouth and chewed thoughtfully. "That must have been quite difficult for you. I'm certain if Sterling had been aware of all that was going on, he would have put a stop to it. But from what I hear, his mother anticipated that."

Samantha chewed on her own bite and nodded slowly. Hesitatingly, she told Mrs. Dolittle about all that had transpired, all the cutting little jabs Cordelia had given, which eventually led to scathing outbursts and then that devastating confrontation, followed by Samantha's defense of herself and Sterling. When she finished, there was a pensive silence as Mrs. Dolittle digested all the information and Samantha's mind chewed on the ramifications.

After a few moments, Samantha spoke again. "I wonder now if I had told Sterling everything as it transpired, instead of keeping so much to myself, if he could have changed something, if maybe things would not have escalated as they did. But you see, I was trying not to complain, to give his mother the benefit of the doubt and be forgiving, to do the right thing. I hoped to fix the problem myself. But in the end, I am not sure I handled things in the best way. I would like to think that if I had to do things over, I would do them better. But then I realize that I am still me and she is still her, and it might have all still ended in a mess anyway." She spread her hands in defeat.

Mrs. Dolittle clucked regretfully. "I believe there is wisdom in that insight. But I feel certain you did the best you could at the time. I have no doubt of the purity of your intentions—and you shouldn't blame yourself, child. None of what happened was your fault."

Not until she heard her friend say those words did Samantha realize she had persisted in internally blaming herself for many aspects of the terrible experience. If only she were braver, if only she stood up for herself more quickly, if only she had the social standing to know how to thwart Cordelia's machinations.

Mrs. Dolittle watched her expression and leaned forward. "You do believe me, don't you, dear? Do you understand that you are not to be blamed for what occurred? You were a guest in that house, and as such should have been spared such treatment! And you entered it fully expecting to become acquainted with Sterling's family and have an amicable relationship—with all of them. Failing to do so with one member of that family does not make *you* a failure."

Samantha sipped her herbal tea in an attempt to distract herself from the tears that stung her eyes. With those words, Mrs. Dolittle had hit exactly on what Samantha had felt for days but been unable to identify or articulate to herself.

Perceptive as always, Mrs. Dolittle didn't miss the shimmer in those gray eyes, nor the heaviness of the silence that accompanied them. She grasped Samantha's free hand firmly between both of her rough, able ones. "Oh my, you actually believed you were a failure, didn't you?"

Samantha inhaled shakily, then cleared her throat, not wishing to cry anymore. She had done so much of that lately. She put down the cup and clasped Mrs. Dolittle's hands back. "I am trying not to feel that way, to recognize what actually happened. But when I was in the thick of it, I was acutely aware of all that I was not: well versed in all the social graces, equipped with the most fashionable gowns and beauty to go with them, comfortable in the Sterlings' set. Knowing that was the sort of woman Cordelia wants for her oldest son and that I am most definitely none of those things...yes, I felt the deficit."

She swallowed, feeling anew the intensity of all of the difficult emotions she had grappled with. "It quickly became glaringly obvious how different Sterling's and my backgrounds are and I was completely unsure of how to bridge the gap. In my mind, it daily became an ever-widening chasm. By that last day, I was convinced I had to figure out how to break things off before I ruined all Sterling's prospects." Her voice trembled despite her best efforts to control it, and she hiccupped.

Mrs. Dolittle squeezed her hands and her empathetic expression eased Samantha's heartache a little. "That was exactly what Cordelia wanted you to think. Do you realize now that Sterling truly cares for none of those things?"

Samantha nodded, looking perplexed. "He told me on several occasions how different his views on life are from his mother and that he wanted a completely different future for himself, but somehow, living in that oppressive atmosphere day after day warped my perception of what should be. I still don't understand how it happened and yet I find myself fighting against those doubts even now."

"She must be quite the skilled manipulator," Mrs. Dolittle said, her brown eyes blazing, reminding Samantha briefly of Claire. "Somehow she must control the whole atmosphere of that big place—and everyone who keeps it running."

"She does," Samantha acknowledged.

The women returned their attention to the food and proceeded to eat for a few quiet moments.

"Why do you think she is that way, Mrs. Dolittle? I have repeatedly asked myself that question and I don't have an answer. Perhaps it is not important, but I can't help wondering."

"I wonder the same," Mrs. Dolittle mused, "and I think it is a very valid question. If you understood what made her the way she is, it might be easier to understand the woman she is today, and that might lessen the sting of what happened."

Samantha finished her cheese and bread. "*Why* has always been my favorite question—as I am sure you are aware." She glanced at Mrs. Dolittle and her answering smile turned up the corners of Samantha's mouth in response. "So yes, I have postulated many reasons for her reaction to me, and her subsequent behavior. Was her mother also manipulative and controlling, so that is all she knew? Or does she simply believe that her parental role gives her the prerogative to choose her children's future?"

Mrs. Dolittle nodded, picking up the train of thought. "Or did something awful happen to her in her childhood that leads her now to hold tightly to things that she should not?"

"Was she always this way?" Samantha pondered aloud. "There is so much we don't know."

"But considering these possibilities gives us a better perspective on possible vulnerabilities and weaknesses Cordelia may have."

"Yes, it does. Perhaps I will never know the reasons."

Mrs. Dolittle nodded. "And perhaps, other than for purposes of compassion, it is unimportant. But I want you to know that Claire and I are here for you—as is your father—any time you want to talk about anything that happened."

"Thank you," Samantha said gratefully. "Where is Claire, anyway?"

"She agreed to finish the laundry while I made up the food and came to talk to you. She should be here soon."

A few minutes later, Claire walked in, much more collected and sure of herself than Samantha could have imagined on that day when she came pounding on the door in her pain and grief. Samantha greeted her with an embrace, glad to see her after what had seemed so long. Claire hugged her back and accepted the food passed to her. Before Claire could ask how her trip had gone, Samantha said, "Claire? How would you feel about staying on here permanently, to help with the new children's school we will be opening? I know we talked about it briefly once before, but what do you think?"

Startled, Claire looked at her in surprise. Then her mouth curved upward and she grinned that radiant, contagious smile. "Really?" she asked. "It's official? And you really want me here permanently?"

"I do, very much. And I am certain Father and Sterling will also agree about needing you for the school. We could use your strength and efficiency. This undertaking will require much planning and organization and I need many skillful people around me to make it happen."

"My," Claire said mildly, pointing her nose in the air and affecting a superior attitude. She brushed an imaginary spot of dust from the front of her blouse with dainty fingers and said, "I can see how you would need my expertise."

Mrs. Dolittle gave an involuntary snort as she tried to keep from laughing, and then all three women dissolved into peals of laughter. Everyone should have a Claire around to lighten the mood, Samantha decided.

"I also need help planning something else," Samantha continued, when their good-natured chuckling had subsided.

Claire looked at her shrewdly with raised brows. "Is this the announcement I think it is?"

Samantha held out her hand to show the woman her ring and Claire crowed, "I knew it! I knew that man couldn't wait much longer. It's a wonder he waited as long as he did. What kept him, anyway? I was about ready to see if he needed me to do it for him!"

Samantha laughed in delight. "As it turned out, he asked me at just the right time, but now I have a wedding and a school to plan simultaneously. Will you help?" She looked at both women hopefully.

"Of course, my dear," Mrs. Dolittle answered immediately. "It would give me the greatest pleasure."

"I would like nothing better," Claire replied, grinning.

And so the preparations began.

NOTE TO READERS

Thank you so much for reading this book! I hope you enjoyed the continuing journey with Sterling and Samantha. If you could take a couple of minutes to rate it on Amazon and/or Goodreads, it would mean the world to me! Ratings and reviews help indie books like mine become more visible to the general public, giving readers a better opportunity to know about them.

To review on Amazon, go to your account, find this book, and click on "Write a Review." Then select the number of stars you feel it deserves and write a sentence or two, if possible. Click submit and you're done!

Goodreads.com is a great place for book lovers to keep track of the books they've read, rate them, and give or receive book recommendations from friends. You can often find me there, too, keeping track of all the books I read.

You can sign up for my free newsletter at https://bit.ly/AuthorKatrinaJones, where you will receive monthly updates, news, book recommendations and freebies, including my free ebook, A *Diamond in the Rough,* about Katherine and Rupert.

I love to hear from my readers in all of the following places:

Facebook: Author Katrina Lyman Jones

Instagram: @authorkatrinajones

Email: katrinalymanjones@gmail.com

ADDITIONAL READING

A Girl of the Limberlost by Gene Stratton-Porter

Jane Eyre by Charlotte Bronte

Les Miserables by Victor Hugo

The Price of Freedom: How One Town Stood up to Slavery by Judith Bloom Fradin and Dennis Brindell Fradin

The Town That Started the Civil War by Nat Brandt

Up From Slavery by Booker T. Washington

Walden by Henry David Thoreau

AUTHOR'S NOTE

There's a saying, "Write what you know." As a reader who has always loved historical fiction and an author who has compelling ideas and characters that come at me from past eras, I have learned that a lot of research is required so that I *can* write what I know. However, the many facets of being human are similar regardless of the time period, and I have approached some of these from very personal experiences.

While I don't know, personally, what it's like to be neglected as a child, I have sometimes known, like Samantha, how it feels socially to be on the outside looking in. I also know the exquisite joy of connecting with a like-minded friend who understands what I cannot say. Like Sterling, I know the wrenching struggle of nearly dying of pneumonia and the bewilderment of a strong young body being so overpowered by illness that full recovery seems entirely impossible. All of these descriptions came from my own memory of that difficult time in my life. Without modern medicine and an inspired doctor, I probably would not have survived.

Now, a few housekeeping items that readers may be interested in:

I choose to include footnotes in the body of my books, rather than at the end of each chapter, because as a reader, I think that is smoother and easier to follow. Some readers expressed gratitude for them in the first book, so I decided to continue that practice in the second. Many of the links include pictures that help flesh out the history even further, along with additional facts to consider. It's such a fascinating time in history!

Initially, I planned to leave the missing letter an eternal enigma because in real life sometimes things are simply lost and we never find out what happened to them. (Think of all those socks seemingly eaten by the dryer!) But so many readers asked me, wanting to know, that I decided to search the recesses of my mind to discover where the letter ended up. And when I found it, I was surprised by what had happened and by whose hand. Discovering something while writing it is a unique and magical experience; there is nothing quite like it!

Another example of this magical discovery is the character, Claire, who was a delightful surprise for me. One day, when I was well into the writing of this second book in the series, I suddenly just knew that there needed to be an additional character and that I needed to figure out who she was *now*. After thinking about it all day, I awoke the next morning knowing that her name was Claire, that she was Mrs. Dolittle's daughter, and that she needed help—but also that she had much to give at the Jennings mansion. It was as if Claire herself knocked on my brain, waved a hand in front of my eyes, and said, "Hello! I have waited long enough. You can't leave me out of this story any longer." While she is not a main character, I hope you have enjoyed watching her unfold as much as I have.

I also hope you enjoyed getting to know the extended Lewis family, who introduced themselves to me in similar fashion, particularly Aunt Irene whose strong personality pushed herself into my thoughts and gave me her unequivocal opinions in her open way—sometimes blunt, but always loving and non-judgmental.

As for Cordelia Sterling, be assured that she is not based on anyone I know. As is often the case when a writer creates characters, Cordelia is a composite of various difficult people I have seen or imagined, then magnified. Fortunately, I have never had to live even a week with such a toxic personality, as Samantha did, but I could vividly imagine what it might be like for someone with as tender a nature as hers.

I would like to publicly thank Charlotte Bronte for her masterpiece *Jane Eyre*, which I fell in love with at the age of sixteen. When I re-read it in my forties, it captured my heart even more completely. Like Samantha, now that I know what it is to love and be loved, I can more fully appreciate Jane's experience and Mr. Rochester's perfect expressions of love for her. (While I would never wish to align myself to a temperament as brusque as his, I can appreciate Jane's lack of offense at his manner and her depth of understanding for him, despite his moments of callousness.) I also know what it is to sacrifice and hold to values that are ingrained upon my very character, and this is, perhaps what I most admire in Jane: Her strength and integrity, that she did not give in to what she most wanted because she knew what it would cost her in the end. And I love that her consistently holding to her self-respect and her God was what eventually brought her back to Mr. Rochester when the time was right, and in a circumstance that allowed her to grasp what she most desired—on her own terms.

It seems to me that men sometimes get a hard rap these days, that in all the push for equality of the sexes, they may often feel unnecessary and unappreciated. In creating the character of Sterling, I wanted to pay tribute to all the truly good men in the world with honor, integrity, self-control, selflessness, the humility to continually learn and grow, and the desire to help those around them and protect those they love. One day, while making yet another pass through my manuscript, I realized that all the main men in my story are good. Regardless of mistakes they have made or weaknesses they may have, they are all sincerely trying their best, and any girl could trust and feel safe with them. I asked myself if this was realistic. For many women, I know it is not! But while I ache for the loss, hurt, and betrayal many women endure, as I contemplated my own experience, I realized that I have been surrounded by good men all my life. I consider it a great blessing that I have a wonderful dad whom I knew, even as a young girl, valued me and would do his best to protect me. I knew two of my great-grandpas personally, both of whom were born in the early 1900s, and one of whom listened intently on our daily walks as I read him the manuscript of my first book (which is still unpublished). I still miss him, nearly twenty years later! I also grew up with two loving grandpas and several wonderful uncles who lived nearby and would sometimes take me on special outings in place of a spouse (I still remember a fancy dinner and a ballet). Likewise, I greatly admire each of my male cousins and brothers for the good men they are, and my husband gives me much to live up to with his kindness, generosity, gentleness, love, and loyalty. Just like Sterling, Basil, Samuel, James, and Lucas (oh, and let us not forget Rupert!), none of these men in my family claims perfection, but they are committed to their families and do all they can to protect, support, and be there for them. My hope is that good men everywhere will know how loved, appreciated, and *needed* they truly are.

Lastly, I hope that readers caught Samantha's progression from discovery of, love for, and desire to emulate her *mother* in the first book, to her discovery of, love for, and desire to emulate *Jesus* in the second book—a progression that Lovenia would have wanted for her daughter. *He* is the true source of light and hope in my life and I hope that each of us can recognize those "firefly moments" when we feel His love for us personally and the secret strength to just "hang on."

ACKNOWLEDGEMENTS

As always, I would like to thank my family for their encouragement and support in my writing efforts. Thank you to my beta readers for their helpful insights and questions, and to all the readers who asked, "Is there going to be a second book?" (In fact, much of it was already written!)

A huge thank you to my editor, Sarah Lamb, for her eagle eyes and expertise, and also her empathy and encouragement. Having her in my court makes a big difference in this sometimes-overwhelming endeavor!

And lastly, and most importantly, to God for those magical moments of inspiration when I found out—again—that this writing process works best when I involve Him.

ABOUT THE AUTHOR

Katrina Lyman Jones has always loved writing and considers it her first passion, after Jesus and her family. She reads constantly and, while she loves many different genres, her favorite is historical fiction because of all there is to learn about events through time, and how people throughout history dealt with difficulty. She holds a BA of English Teaching from Utah State University, and while raising her children over the past 20 years, has lived in Arizona, Ohio, and Utah. Currently, she resides in southern Utah with her wonderful husband and five children (who are rapidly flying the nest), where she loves her faith, gardening, and being a flutist in the Southwest Symphony.

www.ingramcontent.com/pod-product-compliance
Lightning Source LLC
Chambersburg PA
CBHW060807030726
47503CB00002B/377